abracadabra

abra

cadabra

✦

A NOVEL

✦

DAVID KRANES

UNIVERSITY OF NEVADA PRESS | *Reno & Las Vegas*

University of Nevada Press | Reno, Nevada 89557 USA
www.unpress.nevada.edu
Copyright © 2018 by University of Nevada Press
All rights reserved
Cover Design by Andrew Brozyna

LIBRARY OF CONGRESS CATALOGING-IN-PUBLICATION DATA
Names: Kranes, David, author.
Title: Abracadabra : a novel / by David Kranes.
Description: Reno & Las Vegas : University of Nevada Press, [2017]
Identifiers: LCCN 2017009453 (print) | LCCN 2017013219 (e-book) |
    ISBN 978-1-943859-44-3 (pbk. : alk. paper) | ISBN 978-0-87417-600-1 (e-book)
Subjects: LCSH: Las Vegas (Nev.)—Fiction. | GSAFD: Mystery fiction.
Classification: LCC PS3561.R26 A63 2017 (print) | LCC PS3561.R26 (e-book)
    DDC 813/.54—dc23
LC record available at https://lccn.loc.gov/2017009453

The paper used in this book meets the requirements of American National Standard
for Information Sciences—Permanence of Paper for Printed Library Materials,
ANSI/NISO Z39.48-1992 (R2002).

FIRST PRINTING

Manufactured in the United States of America

For Carol
Over fifty mostly playful
Years later

1 ♦ Lost and Found

Faye lifts Elko's hand, rubs it. It's midafternoon. They're in Ping, Pang, Pong at the Gold Coast, having dim sum and plum wine. "It's okay, sweetheart," she says. "You're a *finder*. Gifted *finder*. Famous. *Sought-after*. Business will pick up. People disappear. People disappear all the time. That guy who was two tables away? With the red beard? Where *is* he? Right? Who can say? People go. In one door, out another. You're just in a…I think it's called a *hiatus*. Between. Between doors. Usually you have two or three clients at the same time, desperate for you to find someone close—sister, father, wife. It's just a bad week."

"Two."

"Bad two weeks."

Elko slides his hand back. He's got his eye on the last chicken foot.

"Elko, my love, don't disconnect. Try to think *lost. Needing to be found.* Chant the word *vanish. Vanish, vanish, vanish!* Someone *will* disappear. Sure as rain. Well, this is Las Vegas, but you'll get called. Can you find my…uncle? grandfather? And you'll be in business again. Not that you *aren't* in business—I mean with the look-alike agency. But that's just paying bills, I know."

"You're a good person," Elko tells Faye. He changes his mind about the chicken foot and grabs a char siu bao.

"I'm your friend," Faye says.

"True. For which—given that I don't make friends—I'm grateful. Friend, advisor, and sometimes, even startlingly, psychic."

"I would prefer you not use that word."

"Which?"

"*Psychic.*"

"My lips 're sealed. Choose another."

"Besides, you know: we both see. We both hear…the voices."

"True."

"So, what are the best voices *you* hear?"

"The ones that say, 'The check's in the mail.'"

"Want to know my best voices?"

"Fire away."

"Mine are those I hear when I'm your lover."

"So, the *infrequent* voices."

"Sadly true."

"So, is tonight the night?"

"Tonight, I'm afraid, I've sold my soul again to Bally Beverages—their battalion of cocktail waitresses. Graveyard. But—"

"What?"

"There's time! And I have an idea! Are we through?"

"Well, I think. Almost." Elko drinks down his plum wine and snares the last chicken foot. "You going to finish yours? The wine?"

"Go for it."

Elko slams Faye's plum wine as well. "Okay. Say. Tell me your idea. I'm not depressed anymore. Not feeling incomplete because a client's not hanging around my neck pleading, *Oh, Mr. Wells, please, please find*— So, again, your idea."

"Good. My idea—"

"I'm poised. Ready! I just hope it's a *funny* idea."

"You and stand-up. My idea—sort of like noncontact practice—is for you to shut your eyes and count to a hundred. I go. I disappear. You have 'til, say, seven thirty to find me. Four hours. I won't be just walking around. That'd be cheating; you couldn't find *anyone* who was just walking around Las Vegas."

"Try me."

"So, what I'm going to do is either go to some familiar place, which is a pretty broad field, or go to some place about which you've heard me say, *Sometime, I'd really like to try out*...So, a usual or a fantasy destination. Shut your eyes. Start counting."

2 ✦ Monday Evening, September 16, 2007

"Just leave me alone! Disappear!" Lena Goodson says. She's backed against five pillows in their Treasure Island king bed, the top of her blue teddy sticks out above the pearly sateen sheet that she has bunched up. "I'm serious! Go! Out! To wherever you made dinner reservations that you didn't ask me about!"

Lena's husband, Mark, hauls in a breath. "I made our reservations at Picasso. At Bellagio. It seemed somewhere that we should—"

"*Seemed somewhere that we should*—but you didn't *tell* me."

"It doesn't matter."

"Picasso at the Bellagio!" Lena mocks.

"Lena, it's supposed to be—"

"Oh! I'm sure! *It's supposed to be!*" Lena snipes. "Did you go to *Zagat*? Did you ask if I wanted to go to Picasso at the Bellagio? No!"

"I thought—"

"Of course! *Thought*! Thought and thought! Besides, I hate Picasso. He's an axe murderer! He chops people up."

"Well, we wouldn't be eating his paintings, I don't think. Or him. I think they have—"

"You're such a pussy! You're such a Boy Scout!"

"What does that have to do with—?"

"I told you before we left Florida…What I wanted to do was go to a gentleman's club. Probably not a listing in Zagat, but there is on Yelp. Do you want some names? Here are some names: Rhino! Sapphire! Crazy Horse!"

"I'm hungry."

"I'm horny!"

"So, what's wrong with a little tastefulness every once in a—?"

"Hey, I've *done* tastefulness. I *do* tastefulness. I want to be in a room full of men with hard-ons!"

"Lena, Jesus. Please don't talk filthy. You know I hate it when you—"

"Then just go! Just disappear! Out into the clean world! Out of my life!" Lena pulls the sheet up over her head.

In the elevator, riding down, Mark inventories his feelings. Anger. Sadness. Regret. He feels bruised. Like a dog in a cage. Like an injured bird. Why does he endure Lena's cruelty? Why doesn't he do more to assure and help her?

Whence their silly, soft times? The bedtime stories? Miracle Whip fights? Oyster feasts? Backrubs? Taking the Bayliner over to Shell Island, hunting for shark teeth, sharing a sleeping bag under the full moon? Once upon a time, Lena was…Where? Did it just stop? Is it in a closet somewhere? Padlocked in some storage shed?

The elevator opens to the casino. Mark needs to find a place where he can call Picasso and cancel. He goes to the Breeze Bar, orders an Absolut and tonic, changes it to a double, dials Picasso's number and apologizes—says if they have to charge him for a late cancellation, do that. Picasso is gracious, says please consider us another night. Mark hangs up. His drink has arrived. He downs half of it.

"Careful, sailor." A blonde, sitting three stools away and drinking something the color of green tea, smiles at him. "The bar's here; the bar's not going away; it's a long night; ease into your dream slowly. You expecting company?"

"I'm needing to have a few moments to myself," Mark says.

"Well, have a few moments to yourself with *me*. My name's Candy."

"Mark."

"Hi, Mark."

"Hi, Candy."

"I like your blue blazer. It goes well with those gray pants. Nice tie, too. Conservative."

Look, ma'am—"

"Candy."

"Candy. I'm sorry, but I meant that...about needing to have some time. To myself. I don't mean to be rude, but..."

"No problem."

"Thanks."

"Except..."

"What? I'm sorry."

"Do you have a twenty? If you had a twenty, see, I could play Double Double Bonus on this poker machine. And it would absorb, you know, my attention. So's I wouldn't be bothering you."

Mark reaches into his pocket, pulls out a money clip, slips a twenty out, slides it over.

"Thank you," Candy says.

"You're welcome."

"You're a nice man."

"Possibly. The jury's still out, but...thanks."

"You're welcome." Candy smiles her best final smile. When Mark turns away, she glides his twenty into her machine's bill validator and begins to play.

Mark nurses the rest of his Absolut. He takes a small notebook from his blazer pocket, opens to a blank page, and makes two columns. On the top of the first, he puts a "+". On the top of the second, he puts a "−". Then he starts to jot notes.

With Mark's exit, Lena begins to sob. *What is wrong with her! Why does she do the things she does! Why does she treat this kind and careful man as if he were raw vermin! Why does she alienate him and send him away!*

Lena scrambles from the bed, trips on the billowing sheets, falls, claws her way up. *Why is everything about her so raw!* She gets to their room door, jerks it open, looks down the hall toward the bay of elevators. Mark is nowhere in sight.

She closes the door, leans against it, has trouble seeing the room. Her eyes are mud pools and mascara. "Fuck!" she says aloud. "Fuck, fuck, fuck!"

In the bathroom, she retrieves her stiff-bristled hairbrush, which she slams into the inner part of her upper arm and draws it forward, scoring the skin badly. She does it again. And then she does it to her other arm. Both arms are bleeding.

She finds her cell, calls Mark's. She'll be ready in ten minutes— all she needs is ten minutes. *Call Picasso and tell them we'll be late. Tell them I'm hungry. That was a wonderful idea of yours—Picasso. I'm going to have red meat.*

Mark doesn't answer his cell. Lena pulls her hair and punches her face. She sits on the bathroom tile floor not knowing what to do. *Why does she act like such a bitch? Such a whore? Why has she stopped taking her Seroquel?*

Twenty minutes later, Lena hears Mark's room card being inserted into their door. She crawls, then clambers to her feet.

Mark stands there—the door shutting behind him. "I'm sorry," he says.

"I'm sorry," Lena says. "I'm sorry. That's the truth. I'm a sorry person."

"Well…"

"Can we still go to Picasso?"

"I thought we could go to…what was it called? The Rhino."

"I want to go to Picasso."

"Even though he cuts people up?"

"That makes one of us an accomplice."

"You're quick. You're smart."

"I'm too smart. It's a problem."

"You mean well."

"Mark, I don't mean well. And we both know that. And it's a problem."

"You were good for a while."

"Possibly. But quite possibly I don't like being good. And that's a problem."

"Well, I guess we just keep on trying."

"Or not."

"Or not."

"Call Picasso. Tell them we changed our minds again and want to come."

"What did you do to your arm?"

"I did whatever I did. Don't look at it."

"Maybe you'd be better without me."

"Maybe I'd be better on another planet. Call Picasso."

Mark calls Picasso, talks to the same staff person. "Changing tides," he says.

"See you in an hour," the Picasso person says.

Lena cleans and arranges herself as best she can. She chooses a sleeveless dress with revealing cleavage. Mark suggests she change it.

"I thought you liked my boobs," Lena says.

"Baby, I love your boobs. Your boobs are world-class. Record-breaking. But the dress—speaking truthfully—isn't a confident dress. It says, *Look at my boobs* instead of, *Wouldn't you like to have these?*

Lena changes.

"Better," Mark says, then tells her that a hooker named Candy had come on to him downstairs.

"When we get back, I want to have rough sex," Lena says. "I'm craving really rough sex. I think a good night of rough sex will put me in my place for a while."

"And your place is?"

"Don't even start."

Lena attends to the final touches. Mark begins to pace, crossing the room randomly. "Baby, I don't get it," he says.

"What?"

"You tell me to disappear. You reward me for appearing again. You hurt yourself. You want me to hurt you. Why?"

"Why not?" Lena says, finishing readying with a stroke of aquamarine eye shadow.

3 ✦ Now or Sometime

Elko reaches a hundred and opens his eyes. Faye's gone. An old China-man at the next table has been studying him.

"You okay?" the old Chinaman asks.

"I'm good," Elko says. "Thank you. Fine."

"I thought maybe you…you know: *stop.* You understand *stop?*"

"I do."

"So sleep maybe. Dream."

"In a way."

"We dream, we travel." The older Chinaman smiles. His teeth look to have been purchased at different yard sales. He gestures toward the husks of lotus leaves on Elko's plate. "You like Lo mai gai?" he asks.

"Delicious," Elko says.

"Someday, maybe, you go to Chinese kitchen. Travel there. See how they make Lo mai gai. Secret is how you fold the leaves. I could show you."

"Then there'd be nothing to look forward to," Elko says, rising. He snares his bill. "Thank you for being concerned," he says. Then, when he sees the older Chinaman's eyes cloud, he adds, "About my being okay."

"Okay, good. Sleep. Dream. Travel."

"Sleep...dream...travel. Right. Have a good night."

"Have a good night," the older Chinaman says. He has a bowl of congee and returns to it.

Elko figures he's got three and a half hours to find Faye. How wide or narrow a net should he throw? Best to start narrow, then move wide, he thinks. Right here, at the Gold Coast, there's a bank of Deuces Wild machines she likes. She's also fond of a Danish beer they carry at The Red Zone. A hundred feet from the Deuces Wild machines, he thinks he spots her—an aging blonde in an emerald silk blouse. *Green?* What had Faye been wearing? The blonde's into her Deuces machine.

"Okay, you're busted!" Elko shouts, sixty feet away. Players' heads turn. But not the blonde's. Then Elko, closer, sees. The blonde is younger than Faye. Just her hair is older. And she's heavier. Now Elko feels silly. He's back playing in the NFL and has missed a tackle. He can hear the coach's voice, "Jesus, Wells! Open your eyes!"

Elko goes to The Red Zone. Faye isn't there. He asks a bartender if he's seen a blonde? Late forties, early fifties. She would have ordered a Mikkeller. Monk's Brew.

"I know who you're talking about. Name's Faye, right?"

"Right."

"Not tonight," the bartender says.

Elko orders a Tanqueray. Ten. Rocks. Sits and tries to draw a map in his head. Two seats away, a young African American's using his merlot as a microphone. "I'm tellin' you...She was so thin, her nipples touched," he says, and waits for presumed applause or laughter. Then applauds himself. "I mean she was so *fat,*" he rolls on, then points abruptly at Elko. "Ask: *How?* Ask: *How fat? How fat was she?*"

Elko takes a breath. Still, he's amused. He thinks the Black man looks a lot like the actor, Giancarlo Esposito. "So how fat was she?" he asks finally.

And Elko sees the Black man puffing himself like a cobra for the release. "Well, I'm not sayin' she was fat...but she had a green suit on the other day and looked like a pool table. I mean, man, when she dances, the record skips…at the *radio station*! Her cereal bowl comes with a *lifeguard*. She was standing on a corner the other day, cops came by, said 'Okay, break it up.' She got on a talking scale and it said, 'One at a time, please.' She has to shower in a *car wash*."

The guy finishes, whistles, stomps his feet, introduces himself—Willie Cooper. "Tomorrow, I'm auditioning," he says. "Comedy Club. Flamingo. How're my chances?"

"How is it you don't use any…I don't mean to be disrespectful, but…*Black* material," Elko says. "You know, who you are."

"Who I are?" Willie Cooper says. "And who's that?"

"Well, for starters, a person of color who looks like he could either be Black or Latino. Also, a person who's a dead ringer for Giancarlo Esposito. So, I would think it would be to your *advantage* to—"

"And who's he?"

"Who's who?"

"Your man, Esposito."

"In the right crowd, he's the ebony Robert De Niro."

"And I look like him?"

"More than a passing resemblance."

Elko talks Giancarlo Esposito to Willie Cooper. Tells him he's got Esposito clips at his office for when he gets a call for a famous Black actor—clips and the number of a guy who he's used on occasion. But Willie Cooper's more Esposito than his present Esposito, so, does Willie have a card? If not a card, can he give Willie his phone number?

Elko and Willie exchange cards.

"So, you didn't like my fat riff?"

"It was okay."

"Which joke was your favorite?"

"The joke about the swamp people."

- "That's a George Wallace joke."

Elko throws back the rest of his Tanqueray. "I love comedy!" he announces to Willie Cooper. "*Love* it! Because it's so confusing and clarifying."

"I don't understand," Willie Cooper says.

"Not to be rude, but I have a woman to find," Elko says. He sets his hand firmly on the bar. "Good luck tomorrow at the Flamingo. If they give you a spot, call me. I'll come over and see you."

Elko's got roughly three hours. He finds a remote seat in the Gold Coast Race and Sports Book. Clemson is smothering West Virginia.

In his blue-spiral notebook he maps a strategy. He writes, "Casinos." He writes "Lounges/Bars." He writes "Malls," but then crosses it out. Faye hates malls and only goes to one when there's a bookstore. So, Elko substitutes "Bookstores" and then jots a final heading, "Consignment Shops." Faye buys all her clothes at consignment shops. Again, he should remember this, *What was she wearing?*

He creates a ten-point scale—"Least Likely" to "Most Likely." He gives casinos a three. There are casinos which Faye would favor if she had to be in a casino, Bellagio for instance. But she would not opt for any casino as a destination. Bars and lounges he scores a two. Faye's a cocktail waitress. Coals to Newcastle! Sure, she enjoys a drink! Sure, she enjoys nice ambiance! But the frost is off the pumpkin; she's learned how the woman gets sawed in half, so sure, okay, it's fun, but "Bookstores" is tricky. Faye's a reader. She loves books. One time he came across her in Academy Books—sitting in a corner reading a used copy of *The Killer Angels*. Faye loves history. "What are you doing here?" she had asked. He'd been looking for a first edition of Roger Angell's *The Summer Game*. He gives bookstores a six. "Consignment Shops" gets a seven or eight. Faye loves clothes. She wears them spectacularly. Maybe it's the name *Faye*—some aura—but it's not uncommon for people to mistake her for Faye Dunaway. On an impulse, Elko thinks in a game of hide and seek, Faye would go and hang out in a consignment shop before she'd sort through shelves of a bookstore.

And then, he remembers, there's the whole open field of "Someday, I'd really like to..."

Except!

Except most of the places Faye's said, *someday, I'd really like to* about are way out of town—mountains, canyons, hiking trails. Someday, I'd like to ski at Brian Head. Someday, I'd like to drink with you... at midnight...at the top of Mt. Charleston. Someday, I'd like to see the Sonora in bloom by candlelight. Of course, there are more local *somedays,* but they tend to be nocturnal and sexual. Someday I'd like to go to the Green Room with you and start out by pretending we've never met each other.

Elko constructs a formula. Then revises it. When it's done, it reads:

$$x = \frac{1 + d + 70}{cd - ab/y}$$

He does the math. He does the math again and determines that

Faye is either at Ritzy Rags on Rainbow or Du Barry Fashions on Decatur. He checks his watch: five twenty. He's got time. He weaves his way back and out of the casino to valet parking. He offers his stub and crosses to the bench where his Z will be delivered. He checks the hours for the two consignment stores. Ritzy Rags closes at six, Du Barry's at seven.

Ritzy Rags is cozy. Vintage. Elko doesn't see Faye's Camaro but understands that she could have parked in the strip mall lot in back. He stands looking in through the window and recognizes one of the clerks—a fortysomething whose hair is a tousled bob with highlights. A woman he takes to be a second clerk is unfamiliar. He checks his watch again, amused he's come to measure critical disappearances or appearances by time. It's fourteen minutes before six.

He steps under the entrance overhang, pushes in and hears the recorded sound of bells. "Hello!" says the blonder clerk, who's without a customer. "Can I help you?"

"That's my hope," Elko says. "I'm looking for someone."

"Do you see her?" the blonder clerk asks.

"Altogether too infrequently," Elko grins.

"I meant *in the store*," the blonder clerk says.

"I know," Elko says. "She's a woman in her early fifties. Long blonde—her hair. Name's *Faye*. Last name, *Callister*. She loves this store. She's not trying on, is she, in a dressing room?"

"Was she going to meet you here?"

"She disappeared. I counted to a hundred and she disappeared. She wouldn't be in one of your dressing rooms would she?"

"No."

"Bummer."

"Sorry."

"I was hoping to find her."

"Does she have a cell?"

"Cell?"

"Phone?"

"Yes."

"Do you know the number?"

"I do...I do, but she wouldn't feel it fair...for me to call."

"I don't understand."

"It's a test."

"Of?"

"Of whether I need to be sent over to one of the Canadian teams."

Abruptly, nervously, the blonder clerk turns in the direction of the older, occupied clerk. "Carrie?" she calls. "Have we had a blonde customer named.... What was her name?"

"Faye."

"Faye?"

"Callister."

"Callister..."

"In here this afternoon? Early fifties?"

"Cocktail waitressy?"

"Exactly. Cocktail waitressy."

"Size eight? Size ten?"

"Size eight? Size ten...I don't think so," the clerk with the tousled bob says. "But I think I know who you're talking about. Nice lady."

"She is," Elko says.

"Sorry," the blonder clerk says.

There are two limos parked directly in front of Du Barry's. Silver stretch Lincoln Continentals. On the side of each, written in script, it says: Betty Blu's. Inside, Du Barry's is hopping. There are—Elko counts them—six black women of robust figure and weight, and, in an almost musical round, they are shrieking. What they are shrieking about are the boas and gowns they're wearing. Two blacks who look like they're ex-NFL sit in too-small chairs around a coffee table loaded with fashion magazines. There are any number of other customers, all of whom have become a backdrop of bustling *extras* in a seeming movie.

So, Elko snakes in and around the crowd, seeing if one of them might, perchance, be Faye. The store is big—heaped with bins of costume jewelry, segmented by racks and then more racks of vintage and theatrical clothes. The sense is some cross between a flower shop and a soup kitchen.

Elko hears someone humming and sometimes singing to herself in a changing room. She's humming Carole King—"You've Got A Friend"—and is into it.

"Winter, Springtime, Summer, or Fall," Elko croons from outside the change curtain. He loves the irony that his finding-moment with Faye is across a tapestry.

Faye pulls back the changing curtain slightly; she's in her underwear. She grins. "Somebody told you!" she says. "Somebody said you were the best disappeared-person finder in Las Vegas! How'd you do it?"

"Simple," Elko says.
"Simple?"
"Simple."
"How?"

Elko gives her the formula:

$$x = \frac{l + d + 70}{cd - ab/y}$$

Fay studies it. "Tomorrow morning, midmorning," she says looking up, "a woman's going to come into your office—a not entirely likable but complicated woman—and she's going to be beside herself. She's going to offer you, first, money, then real estate...and ultimately her own body to find her husband, who's disappeared during a magic show."

4 ◆ Lance Burton: Master Magician, Tuesday Evening, September 17, 2007

At 7:02 PM, Mark and Lena Goodson finish their dinner at The Mirage's Samba Grill. Still on their plates is a veritable game reserve of red meat, a carnivore's holiday. They pay their bill with an American Express Sky Miles card and visit the restrooms.

At 7:06, peeing, Mark rehashes yet again the argument he and Lena had dressing for dinner—the words she said and then said again when he'd challenged her: *You mean nothing to me! Nothing!* He'd called her a *tramp!* She'd called him a *child!* called him a *pussy!* He'd said she was *cruel.*

You mean nothing to me! Nothing!

At the same time, while adjusting her eye shadow, Lena thinks, *Why am I such an arsonist with words?*

At 7:19, the couple catches a cab to the Monte Carlo, where they have tickets for the Lance Burton "Evening of Magic" show. The cabdriver's name, as they hear it, is Vestra. He's originally from Belgrade and, from the rear seat, when he turns in profile, looks a little bit like a much younger Robert De Niro.

At 7:32, Mark and Lena Goodson's cab pulls in under the porte cochere at the Monte Carlo. The meter reads five dollars and thirty-five cents, and Mark gives the driver a ten, mumbling, "That's fine." The two climb out. In a far backroom of Mark's brain, he's still hearing, *You mean nothing to me!* And then the previous night's, *Just disappear!* The September evening is warm, though there seems to be a cool rippling of air from the Monte Carlo fountains.

At 7:43, the two enter the Lance Burton Theatre, a room specially constructed for this performer and his gifts. Lena thinks, *Maybe I should apologize for earlier,* but before she can, Mark tells her, "You look really good tonight." So, what happened to *tramp*? She thanks him. He adds, "Young." She thanks him again.

They find their seats.

"You look nervous," Lena says. "You only compliment me that way when you're nervous."

"No, I feel good," Mark says. "That was a good dinner. More than I could eat, but good."

"You don't think this dress shows too much?"

"It's fine."

"My boobs? You usually ask whether I don't want to wear something else when I wear a dress like this."

"It's fine."

"You think?"

"Sure. You're a beautiful woman."

"You seem...well, I said, before, *nervous*. Still, I'll say it again: *nervous*. And *preoccupied*."

"I'm fine."

There's music from somewhere—Norah Jones, "Come Away with Me." The lights dim.

At 8:07, Lance Burton appears on stage. He's all in black—black dinner jacket, black pants. Norah Jones is singing, "...in the night." Lance Burton stretches his right arm into the long tube of a spotlight and, at his fingertips, a dove appears. There's some applause. He raises his left arm above his head like a flamenco dancer and a multicolored silk blooms in the air above it. He covers the dove in his right hand with the silk. Now Emmylou Harris is singing "Wrecking Ball," and Lance Burton whips the multicolored silk away. The dove is gone. In its place is a huge, steely eyed falcon.

And so it goes. The world appears, the world disappears. Life in the small spotlit universe comes and goes. A woman and a horse trade places, then trade back again. A white sheep becomes a black sheep becomes a zebra.

Lance Burton asks a woman from the audience to throw a deck of cards into the air. The deck of cards swarms angrily and insanely like a hive of bees—darting, churning. "Do you know why the deck is doing that?" Lance Burton asks the woman. She doesn't. "It's because they have no queen," Lance Burton says. "Look in your purse!" The woman does. "Ohmygod!" she says, and proceeds to pull four suited queens out of her red Prada bag. "Throw them at the rest of the deck," Lance Burton says. She does. The queens zoom into the buzzing chaos of cards, at which point, suddenly, the deck composes itself, takes a deck-like shape in the air, then descends to land in Lance Burton's welcoming and expectant hand.

Lena leans in to Mark and says, "He's good."

At 9:27, Lance Burton requests a *male volunteer*. He moves to the footlights and puts his hand up to his brow like a sea captain and scans the audience. "You!" he says and points unequivocally at Mark.

Did Mark even raise his hand? Did he indicate in some way, which Lena didn't see, that he was a willing subject? Because *willing subject* is hardly in any profile of Mark. Still, he's up and out of his seat and moving along the row of knees and into the aisle. He seems to have lost weight—in just the time since dinner—to have become younger. Lena watches him bound the stairs to the stage. The audience applauds.

Lena regrets her earlier cruel words. Cruelty is often the mistake she makes. Cruelty is contempt for herself and her failure to accept.

"Thanks for helping here. What's your name? Never mind. Can I call you Mark?"

Does Mark look surprised? Lena wonders, that Lance Burton knows him? Are Mark and Lance Burton in cahoots?

"Or would you prefer that I call you *Mr. Goodson*? I'm sorry; I know you think I'm psychic. I'm not. It's just that I...picked your pocket." And Lance Burton produces Mark's wallet, hands it over to him. Mark checks his sports jacket, laughs appreciatively, takes the wallet and returns it to his coat. "Oh! And you'll probably be needing these," Lance Burton says, and produces a wad of credit cards. He hands them over. "Are they all there?" he asks.

Mark, looking—Lena is glad—chagrinned, checks them. "They are," he says.

"And your driver's license?"

Mark goes to check, but before he can, Lance Burton hands his license over.

"Never trust a magician," Lance Burton says, and the audience laughs.

"Never trust a volunteer," Mark returns, and the audience— appreciating the quickness—laughs louder.

Lena feels herself begin to sweat.

"You want to take over this show?" Lance Burton asks. "Be careful, or I'll send you to the time-out room."

A large metal box is wheeled out onto the stage.

"And here it is!" Lance Burton announces. "The time-out room! I warned you."

Mark moves stage left.

"Don't go away…yet," Lance Burton instructs Mark, then dramatically flings open doors on all four sides of the box, walking in and out of them to demonstrate unequivocally that the box is empty. An assistant then brings out a gold tuxedo on a hanger. Lance Burton holds it up. "Nice threads," he says. And then, as if in a fit of pique, he throws the gold tux hard onto the stage floor and jumps up and down on it.

He stops, looks out with sheepish glee into the audience. He has all the delight on his face of a bad child. He quickly gathers the sullied, rumpled tux, hooks its hanger onto a wire, and the tux is then hoisted above the stage where it hangs in a spotlight of its own.

"Now—!" Lance Burton says, and he summons Mark over to the box. "Ready for this?"

"Waiting all my life," Mark says.

What is this thing with Mark and repartee? Lena wonders.

"Still have your wallet?" Lance Burton asks.

Mark checks. He removes his wallet from his jacket pocket, waves it.

"All your money? Your identification? Your credit cards?"

Mark checks. He nods.

"Passport?"

Mark looks at Lance Burton quizzically.

"Where you're going—you can never tell—you may need it." And Lance Burton produces a passport, hands it over to Mark.

Mark checks it. He nods. It's his—or so, at least, the nod says.

Lena studies him. Oddly, inexplicably, he looks eager.

"Okay, then," Lance Burton says. "Step into my office." And he waves a hand indicating that Mark should enter the box. Mark does. And now Lucinda Williams is singing "Drunken Angel" as the four doors of the box are flipped shut. There's a drum roll, and then a flash of light where the gold tuxedo once hung. It's gone! *Thin air,* as the expression goes. And now Lance Burton, doing a kind of tango, throws open the four doors of the metal box and…

Empty! Nothing!

Well, not exactly *nothing.* The gold tuxedo is hanging in a transparent dry cleaner's bag from the top of the box.

In the dark, in the audience, Lena Goodson is thinking: *Okay, wait a minute. This is not the way it's supposed to go. Where's Mark?* But she knows: it's a trick; it's a magic show.

"One more time!" Lance Burton announces to the crowd, and he flips all of the metal box's doors shut. Again, there's Lucinda Williams singing "Drunken Angel." Again, there are flashes of fire in the air—here, there, everywhere. Again, Lance does his magician's tango. Again, he throws open all the box doors.

And?

This time, there's a large terra-cotta bull. The figure of the bull fills almost the entire box. Red beams of laser light arrow out of its eyes. And then the bull explodes, bursts open, flies off into terra-cotta shards. And inside the bull is . . . ?

A gold tuxedo in a dry-cleaning bag lying on the floor.

What? And although "what?" begins Lena's confused response, it's quite possible that the *what?* belongs to Lance, because Lance Burton looks *equally* confused. So confused that the collective audience can almost hear his brain spinning like unstudded tires on an icy road.

Everybody in the audience is thinking: *Where's the guy?*

Lance Burton looks to be scrambling, sucking for air. There's a sudden-blow-to-the-head, stop-action moment in the theater. And then, as though the nearly empty box is simply an intended bend in the ride along the Mysterious Magic trail, Lance Burton drapes a nine by twelve, black and crimson coverlet over the box, steps forward, and tells a joke.

"A magician walks into a bar, sits down, orders a Crown Royal—wishful thinking. The bartender delivers the drink and the magician gets up and crosses the bar to the juke box, intending to choose a song."

All Lena can think is: *this isn't funny.*

"'I've got something better,' the bartender calls over to him."

Lance Burton is improvising. Lena, herself, is an improviser, and she knows this.

"The magician returns to his seat and the bartender reaches under the bar and produces a tiny piano and piano bench.

"'What's that?' the magician asks.

"'You haven't seen the best part,'" the bartender says, and again he reaches under the bar and produces a miniature man in tails, sits him on the bench and the man begins to play—wonderful music!

"'Absolutely incredible,' the magician says."

Where's Mark?

"'Let me tell you a story,' the bartender says. And he recounts a walk on a beach, a bottle he found and rubbed, and a very old, old, old genie who appeared out of the bottle offering fulfillment of a single wish. The bartender says he made his wish and...He points to the miniature performance going on as the evidence of the wish's fulfillment.

"'What happened to the bottle?' the magician asks."

Mark's gone, Lena thinks. *Gone!*

"The bartender produces it. It's an old bottle—green, chipped; it looks like glass blown by a blower with hiccups. There's an ancient gray cork in it. The bartender hands the bottle over to the magician. The magician rolls the bottle between the palms of his hands.

"'Is it still...*active?*' the magician asks.

"'Give it a try,' the bartender says."

Lena begins to feel as though she's a sauce being prepared by re-duction—on constant, low heat, the heady brew of herself. Herself *without...*

Lance is unflappable. "The magician uncorks the bottle and—true to the bartender's word—a very old, old, old genie spirals out from the bottle. 'Your wish is my command, Master,' the old, old, old genie says.

"The bartender signals that the magician should make his wish.

"*What, what, what, what* should he wish for. 'I'd like a million bucks!' he says.

"'What?' the genie asks.

"'A million bucks,' the magician repeats."

Lena tries to just sit still and wait. Trust. Believe. But she feels ex-hausted. *Why did I say the things I said?* she asks inside her head... in a voice which is almost too tired now to be heard.

Lance doesn't stop. And although he's telling a joke, what it feels like is tap dancing. "'Yes, Master,' the genie says. 'It is done.' And he vaporizes back into the bottle, which the magician recorks and hands back to the bartender.

"The bartender smiles. The magician shrugs; nothing seems to have happened."

Lena's numb. She can't think, can't move.

"Except, outside, there's the sound of birds. Lots of birds. A skyful. What's going on? What's happening. There's an immense ruckus of quacking—*quack, quack, quack!*—raucous, deafening, abusive. The magician jumps up from his stool, runs to the bar door, flings it open, moves out into the street, looks up. The sky is almost black it's so filled with ducks. The magician staggers back into the bar. 'What is going on?' he asks the bartender. 'Must be a million ducks!'

"'Well, I'll tell you something,' the bartender leans forward and confides. 'One thing's for sure: when it was my turn, I certainly didn't ask for a twelve-inch pianist.'"

Rimshot. Flashes of light. Willie Nelson singing "Blue Moon."

At 9:47, Lance Burton strides over to the covered metal box, where he reaches up and unfurls the black and crimson coverlet, throws it up where it floats like a magic carpet. Again, he raises his hands into the air. Again, light flickers from his fingertips. Again, he flings open the four doors of the box. Again, he gestures toward its interior. Again, a terra-cotta bull glares at the audience. Again, the bull shatters dramatically. Again, the shattered bull is empty. Nothing. *Nada.* No audience volunteer in a gold tuxedo rematerializes out of the magic void. There is no Mark Goodson anywhere.

In the dark, Lena Goodson comes to life slightly and feels a premonitory panic sidewinding like a small snake in her bloodstream, beginning its flickering dance through the tall uncut grass of her brainstem.

She is a terrible person, and she's being punished!

Her spouse of nearly thirteen years has vanished, has disappeared, is no longer visible. From any appearance of the moment, he is no longer in the world. *Fuck, fuck, fuck! Why do I say the things I say?* her mind screams.

Watch and listen very closely. Magic is the art of misdirection. This is how the trick is done.

5 ◆ Reprise: "Tomorrow morning..."

"Tomorrow morning, midmorning," Faye says looking up, "a woman's going to come into your office—a not entirely likable but complicated woman—and she's going to be beside herself. She's going to offer you, first, money, then real estate...ultimately her own body to find her husband who's disappeared during a magic show."

"This a sure thing? A guarantee?" Elko asks.

"It's a thought," Faye smiles. And it's a sexy smile. "It's a thing that came to me. Kick the tires. See how it feels."

6 ◆ Again Magic, Looking More Closely

They pay their bill with American Express and visit the restrooms. In the men's room, Mark checks the zippered back pocket of his slacks for a Mirage room key. It's there, together with his and Lena's key for room 12008 at Treasure Island. He also checks the seventh stall to the right. Since Mark was in the same stall in the morning, someone—with a knife—has carved GIVE IT BACK OR DIE! into the beige paint inside the door. Mark feels a shiver—partly thrill, partly terror. He pees, splashes cold water on his face, takes a series of deep breaths.

In their taxi to the Monte Carlo, Lena wonders what it would be like to have sex with a cabdriver. She keeps the thought to herself.

Settled into his Lance Burton Theatre seat, Mark turns the pages forward and back in his program and Lena puts a hand over his hand to stop the turning.

"Do you not want to be here?" she asks.

"What are you asking?" he says.

"Never mind," she says.

"This is exactly where I want to be," he says. "I can't think of a more perfect place." Inside he laughs to himself. He remembers Lena's earlier words, *You mean nothing to me.*

"Do you not like my dress?" Lena asks.

The lights dim. Norah Jones voice, like sugar in warm water, permeates the room: "Come Away with Me."

Lance Burton materializes. He makes a dove appear, transmutes it into a falcon. And so it goes. The world appears; the world disappears.

A feeling much like lust churns inside Mark. It's like he's drunk. He remembers blocking a kick, picking up the ball and running for the winning touchdown in the Florida state class B finals. Magic! A magic moment! The randy sleight of hand transforming defeat into triumph.

Lena begins to sense a strange heat coming from the seat beside her, from her husband. Or is she just imagining? She's feeling strangely sexual, sluttish, hungry there in the transforming dark.

Lance Burton: "Please, a volunteer!" Mark bolts from his seat and, in seconds, it seems, is on the stage discovering that Lance Burton has, somehow, picked his pocket, gotten his wallet, his credit cards, his driver's license, his passport. We know this from before, but in the light of what's coming, it bears repeating. This is the second time around for Mark, too. He's watched the Lance Burton Show video, and, watching it, felt there might be an opportunity for him. An out. An exit.

On stage, Mark checks his back zippered pocket for the room keys—keys for rooms at both Treasure Island, where he's staying with Lena, and The Mirage, a room Lena knows nothing about.

Lance Burton has trampled a gold tuxedo and hung it aloft for all to watch. He's produced a large metal box from the wings and, opening its four doors, demonstrated that it is empty. "Step into my office," he instructs Mark.

Mark enters as Lucinda Williams sings "Drunken Angel." The four doors of the box slam shut with Mark inside.

Everyone—to spot the trick, find the magician's flaw, see how the effect is done—leans forward. There is a charge of hypervigilance now...in the replay.

Inside, in the dark, Mark thinks, "This box feels smaller than it looked when I measured it with my eyes before." Through the walls, he can hear a drumroll. He hears the audience's collective "ahh!" and then applause.

Suddenly he feels the floor of the box rotating. Hands are reaching for him. A man in a black skintight suit is whispering directions. There's a huge statue of...what?...it looks like a beast, a cow. Mark's being pulled and pushed. "Hurry!" the man in black says. Then Mark is sure he can see the whole backstage: lighting, wings, and—most importantly—a glowing red EXIT sign.

In her seat, Lena wonders why Mark volunteered. It isn't like him. Wherever he can, he avoids being the center of attention. She has to beg to get him to go to parties and, as often as not, he leaves the party without telling her he's going and she has to ask someone else at the party to drive her home. How many men from their Naples Yacht Club has she let kiss her wetly goodnight in their cars before saying, "I'm sorry! Stop! I can't. I can't do this" and bolting out the door?

Lena watches. Lance Burton has made the tuxedo disappear. Now he's throwing open the doors of the big metal box. And...Instead of Mark, there's a huge, studly plaster bull. Ohmygod! And then the bull cracks open and—is Mark going to be inside? No, he's not. There's just the tuxedo lying there, in a transparent garment bag.

Where's Mark? Okay, Lena thinks. It's all part of the act, the trick, the magic show.

Backstage, Mark is being pulled from the box, taking as much of backstage in as he can...especially, the glowing red EXIT sign.

But then Lena looks hard at Lance Burton's face and she realizes. Mark's gone. Mark's nowhere. Mark's disappeared.

"Retribution." She says the word out loud, to herself, in her seat. And then she says "retribution" again. Because she realizes that—however he did it—Lance Burton hasn't been the magician-of-the-hour here. Mark has.

7 ♦ The Space of Disappearance

Mark Goodson hears the Lance Burton stage hands intoning to just *go with the flow*. He can see a gold tuxedo hanging nearby on a rack. *Take your pants and jacket off*, he's being told. *Keep your valuables.* *Valuables?* Mark stifles a laugh. He has almost three million— chips and cash—crammed into a suite safe at The Mirage. Under the name...*what did he register under?* Valuables indeed!

Hands are on him, coaxing. He spins, swings. He hears some- one blurt "Hey!" He hears another say, "What the fuck?" And he's moving. *You mean nothing to me.* This is his opportunity! This is his chance!

And now he's at the stage door, wrenching it open—voices shout- ing behind him. Now outside. Now on the loading dock, from which he jumps, stumbles, rights himself and runs. Over his shoulder, he can see stagehands on the loading dock above and behind him. He hears "Wait!" He hears "Where...?" He's running along a delivery road. There are palms, leaves like wings, above him. It's a landscape of flight.

He turns left, then left again. The delivery road connects with Monte Carlo Drive and then with Las Vegas Boulevard. Mark stops to catch his breath, to orient. The Strip is not a good place to be if they send searchers out. So he breaks into a jog again, past Miss Liberty and the tugboats and the Stock Exchange, which is New York New York. Right onto Tropicana. Up and over Interstate 15 to Industrial Road, where he takes a right. Industrial is dark and iffy—shadowy, a kind of *anti*-Strip. Still, Mark knows, it runs parallel and can mask his approach to The Mirage.

Was the money he'd found even real? Was the person who'd scratched GIVE IT BACK OR DIE! a person who could ever *find* him? Who would do him harm? Well, Mark thinks, the die is cast; the choice is made. *You mean nothing to me*, Lena had said. Well, now, at least—three million—he might mean something to himself.

8 ♦ Elko Works Out

Seven years ago, Elko played defensive tackle for the Oakland Raid- ers. His career ended with a head injury. We hear "head injury" and cringe—the shoulders lift, the chin lowers. *Head injury* is, certainly, no laughing matter. Because, there's damage. Inevitably there is se- rious damage. But what are we, as organisms, if not compensators? So, *beyond damage*...What? *Beyond damage*, what do we find?

Elko—all the doctors agree—can no longer play. That's a given, which he accepts; and accepts with relish because he has learned that *beyond damage* there are other things. Like *voices. Voices* come in. For Elko, the voices come when he's near stand-up comedy. This is not a simple cause-and-effect—not like picking up a copy of *The Washington Post* from your driveway and turning to the editorial page. Stand-up comedy is a thing that Elko Wells has to buy admission to, search out.

Still, he's an athlete, with an athlete's body, who needs to exercise. Work out. This he does rigorously. Elko's friend, K. C. Chandra, works in the fitness area of the Palms and gives Elko a break; he calls it a *package*. The package is three days a week, Elko can do laps at the Palms Place Pool and use the Cybex lower-body elliptical in the fitness room.

Water supports dreaming, Elko read somewhere. And, for himself, it's true. On the most pedestrian level, he imagines himself crossing a channel—from a near shore to a distant one. He imagines a boat rowing past, oars close by. But then the water, the shores, the crossing becomes something else, something older. He's a sailor spilled from a Greek ship. An Argonaut. Someone in his crew has disappeared. The water of the world has swallowed a shipmate only moments ago, and Elko's leapt into the nothingness of water to find him. He analyzes the bubbles in the wake in front of him, reduces them to a formula, remembers a joke, remembers the teller of that joke, revises the formula, finds the spot of immersion, dives, finds the sunken sailor just in time: someone with air still in his lungs. They rise together to the surface.

Elko kicks and grabs the tile at the deep end of the pool. His lungs feel like tanks of propane. He has a smile on his face.

He kicks away from the tile, surges forward, does two laps of butterfly, then flips onto his back and does four additional laps of backstroke. In his mind, he keeps replaying Faye's forecast of a woman who will arrive and beg him to find her husband—*disappeared at a magic show.* Will that happen today? Is it on the docket for this afternoon? *A woman. Not entirely likable. Complicated. And she'll be distraught. Beside herself.*

Elko likes the Cybex. It's his favorite. He starts—and it's a confidence-builder, he confesses—with the resistance at four and the incline at three. After four minutes, he decreases the incline to one but raises the resistance to six. At about ten, he ups the incline to seven and bumps the resistance to eight. During the last fifteen minutes, he keeps the resistance at eight but goes all out on the incline, pushing it to ten.

He feels like he's back with the Raiders. But that's a joke. He was never *with* the Raiders, if he's honest; he just played *for* them. Also, if he's honest, he's almost never *with* anybody. Well, Faye. Faye, maybe. Faye's an exception. But he never *sees* Faye. Or rarely. Well... yesterday afternoon. That was fun. Their crazy schedules conspire and weave an almost sinister metropolis of distance.

In the shower, after his workout, Elko feels mean. Agile. Capable. *Bring it on!* he thinks. *Bring on the disappearing world! I'm ready for it.* He likes the way the water stings his skin. He likes the way his pores open, the way the soap glides over and into his pores. He can't wait to towel. He likes to whip himself with his towel, flog himself to full dryness. Which of his look-alikes—he tries to recall—are working tonight? Phyllis Diller is going to be hanging out at Harrah's. Liberace's going to be doing the Tempo Lounge at the Las Vegas Hilton. George Bush is going to be having dinner with Sara Palin at Bouchon at The Palazzo. It's a decent night for the look-alike world, and Elko's happy to be a facilitator.

After his workout, Elko feels pumped, thirsty, hungry, horny. All his life, he's been a person of contained urges, locked desires, cell doors straining against the jail of himself. He knows, as well, that there are jailbreak moments—moments speaking their own language and rampant in their own, odd, lifeform ways. So, pumped, thirsty, hungry, horny...which he slakes by driving his Z over to Taco Feliz on Flamingo near Decatur and ordering some carne asada and then, in the adjoining bar, Money Plays, sitting down with a Negra Modelo, letting its caramel and amber slide around in his mouth. He hears the clicking of the shuffleboard table, the banjo pings of the active poker machines. Tim McGraw is singing "Please Remember Me" on the juke.

Last night, someone *did* disappear, Elko feels assured. Faye's rarely wrong. This afternoon, a woman, a wife, will appear at his office and plead, *Please! Please, Mr. Wells: find him!* It's nice, Elko thinks, to find yourself necessary in another's life.

That Elko doesn't know the words to the Tim McGraw song doesn't bother him. He just sings along. It's not a matter of words—he's learned that—it's melody.

9 ✦ Billy Spence: Two Hours Before GIVE IT BACK OR DIE!

The applause in his head is like some high tide hitting the rocks in Monterey, like a hundred engines at the Indianapolis 500.

Billy Spence's whole life has been theater—sometimes crazy, sometimes mean. Sometimes, in theater, people get brutalized, even die. Tragedy! And some people think tragedy's the best theater. Billy, truth told, has had his share of tragedy. But there's comedy, too. For the balance. And romance. He's done those—when the time was right, when they worked, when there was an audience. Fact is, Billy Spence can become *any*body, play *any*thing—given the right circumstances and incentives.

Right now, for instance, he's a Texas high roller with a two-million-dollar credit line: J. Bob Marshall. J. Bob is a man who's maybe three inches taller than Billy. But, with the right shoes, that doesn't pose a problem. And J. Bob weighs easily fifty pounds more than Billy. But weight? You can lose and gain weight radically in just a month. Or you can wear really interestingly constructed padding and, if you know the craft, even construct it yourself. You can stuff foam into your cheek cavities to give your face more fleshiness. And there's always latex.

J. Bob has a kind of reddish mustache. And given his Mirage credit line, he's obviously rich; aswim in both reported and unreported income. There are the ranching interests in Texas and Australia. There's the offshore oil. And there are the "fees" J. Bob gets paid for enabling the routing of certain "substances" from Central America and Mexico to strategic US cities. How rich *is* J. Bob? J. Bob is *so* rich that...He's rich.

And though The Mirage player profile that Billy Spence has hacked into for his J. Bob Marshall act hedges the truth and calls J. Bob *temperamental,* truth is, J. Bob's just *mean.*

Still, Billy, called upon, can play mean. Could. Has. Any number of times. Or he could play J. Bob as charming. Play him as, say—pick a role!—Willy Loman or Hamlet! He's shrewd and crafty enough. Shabby as his own finances usually are, he can play the role of a man with a two-million-dollar credit line so convincingly—*look* the part, *be* the man—that even a close relative of J. Bob's would swear that Billy Spence *was* J. Bob Marshall.

So, here it is, just after five o'clock in the morning and the curtain music's about to be cued. Billy—now four full hours into his triumphant portrayal of J. Bob Marshall—is stalking The Mirage casino floor. King of the World, rich as any person with the name of Billy-Spence-as-J-Bob-Marshall could hope to be early on a Tuesday morning, and—still playing J. Bob—Billy's hunting for a woman.

Of course, transforming yourself into King-of-the-World-hunting-for-a-woman takes *work*—never mind incredible *talent*. You have to plan, prepare, have vision, be brilliant on the one hand, ruthless on the other. Learn your craft. *All great kings and great artists are ruthlessly crafty; they have to be.* Billy genuinely believes that and carries it like a mantra in his head, practices it at every turn.

And all the practice has paid off. Because, ladies and gentlemen, here he is! Forty-two and at the height of his powers, strolling the carpet of The Mirage, over three million dollars richer. Chips and bills are packed into a specially tailored body-form vest beneath his cowboy-chic leather jacket. Billy-as-J-Bob is over three million dollars richer. J. Bob as J. Bob is now the same three million plus *poorer.*

But that's America, right? Fortunes made, fortunes lost! Fortunes made again! Now you don't see it, now you do! Land of magic opportunity. But any fortune is never guaranteed. Fortune is a dog without loyalty; it shifts. That's a cliché! But clichés wouldn't be clichés without a core of truth. And Billy has just been brilliant and ruthless and lucky and crafty and visionary enough to have engineered a major shift of fortune toward himself.

What a stroke! What some might call a *legendary performance.* And he's up over—*count* it, peons!—three million!

Bravo, Billy! Bravo!

King of the World! J. Bob Marshall!

So, what now? Who now? He has a triple Tanqueray Ten in his hand, a couple of Cubans in his pocket. What does The King need? What is The King missing? A Queen! A woman!

There are two cheap whores at the Sports Bar, both nodding to him, one asking him to sit down. But a cheap whore isn't a Queen. Come on! These are two girls who'll ask four hundred, easily, for a lifeless fuck. They'll be drug-thin and basted with Elizabeth Taylor *Passion.* King and J-Bob-Marshall-enactor that he is, the queen/woman who deserves him—the one he'll crown—will be rowdy and Rubenesque, rich in her way, hungering for *him.*

Billy tries the Baccarat Bar. The lone woman there looks more Queenlike, more in the candidate class—better dressed, more flesh.

At the same time, she seems too focused on her video poker, not stationed for any kind of score. Billy wanders to the bar—within range but not crowding, which is one of his rules: never crowd. Always give yourself room to operate. Never crowd.

He asks the bartender to freshen his Tanqueray, glances toward the woman. The game has her. She's slapping buttons, running through hand after hand, looking for her royal.

"So, how're you doing?" Billy asks.

The video-poker-playing-woman doesn't acknowledge him. The Japanese bartender returns his drink. Billy tips him a twenty.

"How long's she been here?" Billy asks.

"Hour. Maybe hour and a half," the bartender says.

"Playing the whole time?"

"Whole time. She's a degenerate; comes in a lot."

"Hey, don't knock being a degenerate," Billy grins.

The bartender seems unsure how to respond.

"I'm a degenerate. Just not a gambling degenerate. Aren't you? Isn't everybody?...a degenerate?...of some kind?"

"I suppose," the bartender says and walks away.

Billy moves closer to the woman. He watches her play. The red J-Bob-Marshall-simulation-beard glued to his chin is beginning to itch.

"Shouldn't you have kept the king too?" Billy asks.

"No," the woman says. She doesn't look up.

"But—" Billy begins.

"*No*," the woman repeats. "Not the king when you've got the ace. This is Double Double Bonus. You don't keep the king in that situation."

Billy moves closer.

"I'm not available," the woman says.

"What makes you think—?"

"I can smell sex coming off you," the woman says, "like steam off garbage." But she doesn't look up.

Billy feels a rage, a sudden jolt. *Fuck you!* he wants to say. Christ, he's King of the World! Hidden on his body is over three million! Who did this woman think she was to not even—?

"A thousand," Billy proposes.

The woman turns her head from the video screen, looks at him for the first time. She sizes him up. "A thousand?" she asks.

"I don't have a room here. But we can go, say, to the men's room— into one of the stalls."

"Aren't you the sport!"

"You like it standing up?"

"No sale," the woman says, going back to her game.

Billy pushes himself from the bar, staggers a bit, begins to wander the floor. He's tired. And *tired* isn't right; it's wrong. A King of the World shouldn't be tired. He has too much adrenalin in him to be tired. It's the gin. He should stop drinking the gin—except he likes gin. *How much gin could you buy for three mil?* You could probably buy the Bombay Sapphire, if it was a stone. Certainly *get* stoned.

At a craps table, there's a woman rolling dice all by herself. Billy judges her to be in her midtwenties. She looks Italian... or Jewish. And a student... of something. Everybody's a student of something, Billy thinks. He wants to walk up to her and say, *Are you a student of something?* Instead he drifts over, puts his hands on the table rail and watches. The number's five. The girl rolls an eight, a ten and then a five. "Five: a winner!" the stickman announces.

The girl has a five-dollar chip with four others behind it for full odds. The near dealer pays her.

Billy reaches in his pocket, peels off five hundred and throws the bills down in front of the girl. "Play quarters," he says. "Play twenty-five-dollar chips. You've got the touch."

"This is for—?"

"You. Yeah. Give her quarters," Billy instructs the dealer.

The girl is racked—maybe a 40, even a 42D, Billy guesses. She's dressed in black toreador pants and a silver silk blouse with a low neckline.

"Why would you—?"

"I like to watch," Billy says. "I enjoy watching good fortune."

"Are you someone I should know?" the girl asks. She touches her tongue to her lips.

"Probably."

"Wow," the girl says.

"Wow," Billy says.

"So, then who, like, *are* you?" the girl asks.

"*King* of the World," Billy said. "A kind stranger. All your life—right?—you've depended on... blah blah blah. Someone said that line—know who it was? This is a quiz: I'm the teacher, you're the student. Can you tell me?"

"The King."

"The King! Excellent! Right."

"Thank you, King," the girl says. "I'm April."

"At least April," Billy says. "Me, I would have said *August*."

"Why *August?*"

"Why not? Full bloom, more heat."

"You're a smart King," the girl says. And when she says it, she makes her eyebrows jump.

"I'm a *brilliant* King," Billy says. "Fucking brilliant. Genius-bordering. Mensa's like...kindergarten for me."

The girl, April, plays with her new quarter chips and continues her streak. Billy urges her to place a couple of come bets in addition to the pass line and press her bets up when she wins. Twenty minutes later, she has nearly two thousand sitting in her tray and seems pleased that Billy's fingers are massaging her shoulders.

Within another ten minutes, when she sevens out, she's up over three thousand and is making sounds every time Billy squeezes the back of her neck. "Quit a winner," Billy whispers into her ear and licks it. He's feeling tired again. He's feeling the energy, the hunger, the spirit of the hunt for his Queen seeping out of him. If he's going to romp, he'd better romp now.

"What do I do with these?" April asks him.

"Set them on the table. Tell the man that you want to cash in."

April complies. Then, while the boxman stacks and counts her chips, Billy learns that April is from Atlanta, that she came to Vegas with her boyfriend and another couple, that her boyfriend and the other guy have gone off to a place called the Palomino Club. "Some lap-dancing place. Fuck him," April says. "He thinks he's going to find somebody hotter than me, but he's not!"

The dealer slides six purple chips, four blacks and three greens and a red across the table to April. "Thirty-four hundred and eighty dollars," he says.

"Jesus Christ!" April says.

"Give him the three greens and the red," Billy says. "Tip. Be generous."

April does. "I *feel* generous," she says.

"Good."

"Generous and frisky."

"Let's get a drink and talk about that."

"Let's get a drink and not talk."

"Better yet."

They take their drinks into the men's room near the Renoir restaurant. It's empty. They've kissed hard and deep twice before entering the mirrors and porcelain and tile. April seems to be wanting to prove a point, to make an irrefutable statement about the power of her sexuality. Before they're even inside, she's helping Billy off with his leather jacket.

They go into a stall. April, by turns, is all over him, then retreating, stepping teasingly away. "Are you up to this?" she keeps asking.

"Up to this, King?"

His jacket off, she sees the three-inch-thick vest.

"What's that?" April asks.

Billy shrugs and starts unzipping the vest.

"Are you, like... FBI or something? A cop? That a bulletproof... whatever? Vest?"

"It's a disguise," Billy says.

"For what?"

"It's a jaguar disguised as a goat. It's a bank account disguised as a straitjacket."

Billy slips his vest-stuffed-with-money off, hangs it up on another hook under his jacket. He grabs April's blouse on either side by its lapels and rips it open. She gasps, then laughs.

"Like those, huh?"

"I do... I do," Billy says.

She has a jade-colored bra on and slips it up over her head. She sets her tongue on her lips, rotates her neck, letting her hair fall.

Billy tries to put his mouth on her enormous tits. She pushes them into him, then pulls them back. "Your beard scratches," she says.

"I could take it off," Billy says.

"You mean shave?"

"Something like that."

"How much do you want me?" she says.

"Very much," Billy says.

"Have you ever wanted anybody that much?"

"I haven't," Billy says. "Not since... Never."

She grabs his jacket, unhitches the stall door and backs out, holding the jacket, wiggling it in front of her like a cape. "Toro! Toro!" she says.

Billy catches the game. He lowers his head and scrapes the ground with his feet. He's tired, but hard and juiced up as well. He can feel his blood streaming through his arteries.

"Toro! Toro!" April repeats, backing.

He charges her. She dodges him, passing his head under the leather-jacket cape.

"The Dance of Death," April announces.

Billy thought he'd heard that, heard that phrase. It was a title; it came from somewhere, but he couldn't remember.

"Toro! Toro!" April says. "Come and get what you want."

Again, Billy charges. Again, April passes him under the leather, where he stumbles and almost hits his head on a marble sink.

"Let's get *to* this," Billy says. He's feeling more than a little woozy. April starts backing, this time toward the men's room door, the exit.

Billy, no longer the bull, walks toward her. "Enough," he says. "King's a little dizzy. Enough. Let's just do it. Let's fuck."

"Toro! Toro!" April says, yet again. She disappears.

Billy follows. He follows her into the women's room, where she laughs, throws his coat at him, unzips her toreador pants, moves to him hard, kisses him. "My place," she says. "This is my place; not yours. I like it better at my place."

Not even taking the time to find a stall, they fuck on the floor. Fuck hard. Fuck brutally. Fuck orally and then with full penetration. Billy thinks that his blood is going to break through his skull. At one point, another woman enters the lavatory and screams. Then rushes out. Her presence, her scream makes the hunger in both of them that much more animal. When they're done, Billy has bloody scratch marks on his arm. April's breasts are soaked in his saliva and sweat.

April shakes her head, as if to get it back on straight again, as if to align it with her neck. "Fuck Jerod!" she says. "Fuck him and his lap dancing."

"You are something else," Billy says.

"Fit for a King."

"Fit for a King—right."

"Thanks for the craps lessons. Thanks for the encouragement. Thanks for staking me."

"That's what you have to do with vampires—stake them," Billy smiles.

"Did I suck all of the life out of you? Did I make you one of the living dead?"

"You get my vote."

April looks at her watch. She dresses quickly and silently. Billy sits on the floor and watches her until she's left. Then he pulls his pants up, buttons his shirt, slips his leather jacket on and leaves, too.

He goes back to the Baccarat Bar and orders another Tanqueray Ten on the rocks. It's nearly seven in the morning. And though there's still a tiredness, he can feel every capillary in his body buzzing like a power plant. The bite of the gin on his first sip is just perfect. It makes him smile. Everything in the world makes Billy smile—partly because he's King of it, partly because everything in the world seems to serve him, pay homage. If you're brilliant and crafty and ruthless and visionary enough, anything's possible!

The woman playing video poker is still there. She doesn't look well. She looks tapped out, desperate, angry. "I've reconsidered," she calls over. But Billy doesn't even look at her. She's a skank, a tramp. "Make it fifteen hundred, and you've got a deal," the woman calls. Her voice is coarse, ragged. She's been crying to herself; Billy can hear that. But, again, he doesn't even look at her. "Fuckface!" she calls over. "Creep!"

Billy laughs. He stands. It's so nice, having the distance of a King.

But then Billy remembers!

His vest! *Jesus fucking Christ!* His vest—left dangling on a hook in the men's room!

Fuck! And, No! All the blood drains from Billy. All his power... flushes away. *Please! Please! Don't let it be so!* he thinks. *I worked! I worked so hard! Let it still be there. Please! The King needs his...*

He stumble-rushes to the men's room. A man in baggy shorts and a Hawaiian shirt is exiting. And then another man in khaki slacks and an expensive sports coat.

Billy enters. He staggers to the stall where he and April had begun, where he'd hung his vest.

He flings open the door. *No!* his mind screams. *No!* The vest's gone. The stall is empty. Somehow what he'd carelessly hung there, his disguised jaguar, his disguised bank account, has disappeared, become thin air. One after the other, Billy flings open all the stall doors, hoping he's been confused in his remembering. But every coat hook on every stall door is vacant. Not a stitch of clothing hung from any hook.

All of us—at one time or another—can kill. Rage erupts, frustration fires. A person works for something, wins it...and then it's lost. Sometimes killing, at least drawing blood, seems like it should quiet that sense of loss or at least stuff a rag in its mouth. Billy feels that way.

So, forty-five minutes after Billy Spence discovers his vest missing from The Mirage men's room—the vest he'd removed only to free his body to have sex—he erupts.

Now, less than an hour later, a less-fleshy dead ringer for J. Bob Marshall, Billy—in a stew of rage and frustration—collars a young Hispanic who'd slapped a *Night Life* escorts directory at him.

"Wrong move," Billy says. "Terrible timing."

"Look, amigo—"

"You're fucking up all of your lines!" Billy spits. "And stepping on all of mine!"

And Billy drags the young man down an alley and behind the Imperial Palace, where he holds a knife to the man's throat and tells him not to scream.

The alley dead ends, and Billy pushes the man against the dead-end wall. "I've had a bad morning," Billy says. He's breathing through phlegm; he's breathing badly. "Bad morning, and I need to vent."

"Don't," the man says, and snakes his back and shoulders against the wall as though trying to climb it with his skin or in the hopes that, somehow, he can find a soft spot and the wall will magically open, give way.

"Bad, bad morning," Billy repeats. "And, hey, it's not your fault—but, you know, it's *somebody's* fault."

"Please, amigo!"

"You know what I'm saying? I've got to take this out on *somebody*."

"No!"

"And here you are. And there you were, getting too close. And here we are now."

"No…"

"And I'm very crazy in my head. Because something's gone that I worked very hard to get; very, very hard to get. So…"

"Please…"

"GET TOO CLOSE AT THE WRONG TIME! DO YOU KNOW WHAT I—?"

"No!"

And Billy slashes and slices. What else—losing what he'd lost—could he do?" And he leaves the young Hispanic ribboned but breathing on the ground.

"Hey, it's not you. It's nothing personal," Billy says over his shoulder as he moves back, between buildings, to Las Vegas Boulevard. "I *like* Spanish-speaking people. Chimichangas—all that shit. Don't take it personally. Huevos rancheros. It's not you. It'll all heal. You'll heal. I'll heal. I mean, it's Vegas, baby—you lose; you win. Beautiful women get their tits separated from their clits by magicians with huge buzz saws. Next minute: everything's cool! Everything that's yours—your shitty life—will be yours again. Everything that's mine will be mine again. It just takes time, brilliance, ruthlessness, vision, craft, dedication. And the Lord knows: I'm dedicated."

10 • Elko Wells—A New Day in The Life Of

He gets off the phone with George Bush and is about to call Willie Nelson with a complaint when, as forecast by Faye, a distraught Lena Goodson staggers—almost beside herself—into his office and tells him her that husband's disappeared.

"What exactly—what kind of *disappeared*?" he asks.

"Disappeared!" she says and mimes a *poof!* gesture.

Elko takes her in. Probably midthirties. Sloppy attractive. Panicked. Partly irritated.

"I'm sorry, disappeared from? Disappeared *how*? In what sense?" Elko asks. He has a bad habit going back to his double—prelaw and English—majors while playing football at Stanford: he parses words.

"Fuck! Are you an idiot? *Disappeared!*" Lena Goodson says. "Into… whatever, *thin air!*" And now she's talking like she's in maybe Portugal and is lost and needs directions. Finally, she adds a name: "Lance Burton."

Elko corkscrews his brow. "Now I'm the person confused," he says. "Your husband, I'm sorry, is Lance Burton?"

Lena looks to be on the edge; lost in a crowd. "No," she says. Then, she says, "Look, hey, I'm sorry I shouted and called you an *idiot*." Then, as if talking to a child, "Listen to me. Listen to what I'm saying: we were *at* Lance Burton."

Elko still feels off-balance. He tells her, "Sorry, but, I mean, given my business—my businesses—I have to ask you a question: We're talking about—I'm just going for clarity here—I mean, the *real* Lance Burton?"

"Mr. Wells," Lena tries to make peace, compose, explain herself. "Forgive me, but I'm very upset. And I need—"

"Mrs.—"

"Goodson. *Lena.*"

The phone rings, and because Elko's right hand, his assistant, Betina-Betina, is out on a late lunch, he tells Lena Goodson, "Just a minute. Sorry. Hold on. I need to get this. I think it may be Willie Nelson."

Elko answers, but it's a wrong number, a man with a barrel voice looking for Giaconda Seafood. Elko hangs up and tries to explain, in better detail, what his Lance Burton confusion is about. "I run two agencies. Different. One's a look-alike—celebrity look-alike—agency. The other's . . . so, you give me a name like *Lance Burton,* and—"

Lena waves her hands as though she's trying to stop traffic and cross a street. "Wait, you're saying—"

"I am. Or, at least, it's possible."

"—there are *other*—"

"Yes."

"—Lance Burtons?"

"Mrs. Goodson."

"Lena."

"Lena, there are always *other* Lance Burtons. Always. Or I'd be out of business. Any number. For me—" Elko's trying to see whether this woman here to see him is tracking, following his point.

She stands up, sits down, stands up again. Elko takes the initiative and rises; moves around his desk and puts a hand under an elbow that happens to be attached to Lena Goodson's arm. Then, without saying anything, Elko applies just a bit of pressure . . . lifts her, turns her, moves her, walks her to the door of what—if he can get away with it, he calls his office *suite*—into the *foyer,* or *anteroom,* or whatever.

He opens a door of pebbled, ash-colored glass. He indicates, in turn, each of the business signs painted in gold leaf: *Mirror Images* on the right, *Tracers, Inc.* on the left.

"What I'm concluding, what seems to be your intent is that who you're here to see given that you've a disappeared-husband is the guy who runs Tracers. Yes?" Elko then explains that his Mirror Images agency supplies celebrity look-alikes for all occasions. "This is why I had the confusion when you said *Lance Burton.*"

Lena leaves her chair again and drifts over to what Elko calls his Sardi's wall, where she starts reading the pictures like they were classifieds. "So, this woman with the big hair isn't really Dolly Parton?" she says.

"Well, to *me* . . . who else? Who *else* would she be? She's Dolly," Elko says. "I mean, when she's on a *job.* But to her fourteen year old, Meredith, she's a single mom named Sheri-Lu Childs. Where'd you get my name?"

"And this isn't Bill Clinton?"

"Which one? Oh, yeah. No. Well, when he's *working,* yeah. But his name—name his mother gave him—is Harvey Kendrick."

"That's amazing!"

"Actually, it's pretty much an everyday phenomenon."

"*Everyday?*"

"Well, statistics are..." And here, Elko pauses. Should he say? He'll say. "Chances are, probably a thousand people look like you," he says. "Exactly. Or me. Or like the woman due back at the front desk any minute, my...her contract says, *Administrative Assistant,* Betina-Betina. It's just that there isn't a cash value in someone looking like you or me, looking like someone not a celebrity."

Lena pulls a small compact from her purse, looks in its mirror.

Elko says he's read somewhere that there are only eight basic facial bone structures. He says, "It's like the six or eight or whatever basic plots for stories. I mean, you have to—once at least—have walked up to someone in a store, followed someone else in a mall, because whoever it was looked *exactly* like some person who one time you were close to. Right?"

Suddenly, Lena looks very sad, very confused, and ashamed. Elko thinks maybe she'll cry. Instead, seeming discouraged, she says, "Right," and lowers her eyes first, then head.

"So, where'd you get my name?" Elko asks again.

"A cocktail waitress," Lena says.

"I'm guessing it would have to be one of the Marys," Elko says. Then, "Finish the story. How you got my name. We'll come back to the Marys after. Then, after that, I'll need as much detail and information as possible about...what's his name? Your husband? Who disappeared?"

"Mark."

"Right. Mark. About Mark. About his having gone missing. And Lance Burton." Elko moves his Bang & Olufsen tape recorder to the center of his desk, holds a hand over it. "Ready?" he asks.

"I'm not sure I like you," Lena says.

"I'm not sure I like me either, but—" Elko raises his eyebrows.

Lena nods and begins. "Okay," she says.

"Thank you," Elko says, and he presses the RECORD button.

"Okay. So, I was sitting all alone in the Lance Burton Theatre after last night's show, thinking, *He has to reappear...*Mark, my husband *has to...*and crying. Crying because I wasn't sure I really believed it, his having to reappear. I mean, do *any* of us—if we don't want to—have to, finally, show up? And this cocktail waitress who was picking up glasses asked why I was crying. So, I told her. And she wrote down your name on a napkin—name and address—and said, 'If he doesn't materialize—your husband—call this man. He can help you.'"

Elko breaks in to explain that there's an Internet message board of Las Vegas cocktail waitresses, which started when one cocktail waitress—the first Mary—got murdered, hacked up pretty badly, and some of her other cocktail-waitress friends set the board up. "Thebloodymarys dot com," Elko says. He explains that in a crime like the first Mary's murder, "you always worry about serial" and underscores that it's a kind of support group.

Lena gets her cell out and is checking for text messages.

It annoys Elko, which makes his voice rise, his jaw tighten. "Very dedicated, very effective," he says, "these women," and, as proof, he confides that, in fact, "a couple at Union Plaza, where the first Mary worked, had some ideas, leads, or whatever. And they were actually the ones who cracked the original case. Because when they all started to talk—Plaza to Harrah's to Hard Rock to MGM to Arizona Charlie's—certain threads began to come together. And a profile emerged: this guy who'd been hitting on cocktail waitresses all over town, in a very particular and menacing way. So, they found the guy, tried him, convicted him. But the Bloody Mary message board kept on going, pledged allegiance, and stayed." Elko tells Lena, "I use them a lot in my own work."

She looks skeptical.

Elko tells her that one of the *great* cocktail servers, a woman named Faye, who retired to paint and sculpt, runs it. He tells Lena that if he takes her case, at some point—no question—he'll consult the Marys.

Betina-Betina, Elko's assistant, arrives back from lunch. He holds a hand up to Lena, indicating that he needs, briefly, to break, and tells Betina-Betina that Willie Nelson might call and, if he does, tell him—no nonsense—that he's in big trouble; they need to talk. He starts to introduce his possible client: "Betina-Betina, this is Mrs...."

Lena fills his pause. "Goodson," she says. "Lena Goodson."

"Mrs. Goodson."

"Lena." Lena smiles.

"She's here for *Tracers*. I'm getting her background. We may be a while."

"How do you do, Mrs. Goodson," Betina-Betina says, all white teeth, a broad smile. Betina-Betina's the charm in an office—a *double* office—which, if there was just Elko, wouldn't have any.

Elko's not charming. He's smart. Intuitive. Prone to what he calls *flash floods* of pain that shoot up his spine then along tributaries into his brain—igniting cortical light, which makes him wonder, sometimes, whether he's psychic. Elko also has a great affection for directionless ex-pro athletes and stand-up comics who tell jokes with a private vocabulary. He can be close to alcoholic, given the right places and times. He hates himself and, at the same time, is arrogant and unbelievably lonely. But he's not charming.

Elko stands, walks over to his inner-office door, starts to close it. "Thanks, Betina-Betina," he says. "You're my salvation. Take any messages."

Back at his desk and in his chair, Elko notices that Lena's staring and points it out.

"You look a little like Mel Gibson," she says.

"Right! *The Passion of*...whatever!" he quips. Then shakes his head. "Not enough though," he says, and slumps to show he's discouraged. "Traces of Mel Gibson, I agree, but not enough."

"Still, quite a bit."

"Yeah, but...quite-a-bit doesn't get you work."

"And a little bit like whatshisname, *Terminator*."

"Probably because I played football and spent too much time in the weight room," Elko says.

"Professionally?"

"Briefly."

"What happened?"

"Head injury."

"I'm sorry," she says.

"No need."

The office slips into silence, which is not Elko's favorite ambiance, so he picks the conversation up. "Actually," he says, "as it turned out, the injury made my head work...well, I suppose you could say *better* in certain ways. So, there's no need to—"

"Your secretary," Lena cuts him off. "Your assistant, is black."

"You noticed."

"I did."

"She's from Sierra Leone."

"I see."

"Quite a long time ago."

"And older."

"Than?"

"You."

"Right."

"Does she *mother* you?"

"Whoa!" Elko throws his hands up in surrender.

Elko feels Lena's hand—where did it come from?—covering his. He feels his hand squeezed and, reflexively, twists it, withdraws it. "It's all right," he says.

"I get confused about what's appropriate," Lena says. "I have boundary problems."

"Well, welcome to World Geography," Elko says

"I have to say something, tell you something." Suddenly Lena looks, at once, wily and penitent.

"Do it. Go for it. Tell away," Elko invites.

"I become your client—you're not going to like me."

"And...I'm sorry, but why's that?"

"Because I don't like myself."

"Again, sorry to repeat myself, but why's that?"

"Because my mother had me to keep my sister, Lynne, company. And my sister died. So, I was useless."

"You don't look useless."

"I know. And that's the problem."

Elko asks her to tell him everything about her husband's disappearance.

She takes a deep breath, stands, walks over to the Sardi's wall again, faces the pictures there—the look-alikes—for maybe twenty seconds, then turns back.

"I'm not saying it's a good thing, but...whatever comes into my head...I say."

"And?"

"*And*...sometimes I mean the words, sometimes I don't."

Elko wonders what he's being prepped for. "So's that good or bad?" he asks.

"It's what happens." She shrugs. "And sometimes it draws people *to* me; other times it drives them *away*."

"Yeah, well, welcome to language," Elko says. And he asks if she'd like a glass of water or a Starbucks Frappuccino.

"Anything stronger?" she asks

What Elko wants to say is, *Yeah, Liquid Plumber.* Instead he says, "I have some chilled Conundrum chardonnay."

Lena smiles. "So..."

"Yes?"

"If I take the...what-a-nice-name, *Conundrum*...will you join me?"

Elko checks his watch; it's just a little past three thirty.

Lena presses her shoulders back, hefts her breasts. "I don't know if I'm up to a Conundrum alone."

Elko stands, moves to his fridge, extracts the bottle, moves to a bookcase where he keeps his Quicksilver EZ-Grip corkscrew, opens the chardonnay and pours two glasses. He extends one. It gets taken.

"To *appearances*," Lena says.

"And, I guess, to *dis*appearances," Elko replies.

He takes a sip. She takes a slug.

Lena tells Elko everything she can about the previous night. Her husband, Mark's, volunteering. The trick working. The trick not working, then not working again. Lance Burton coming out after the show and talking to her, asking whether Mark was claustrophobic, because—even though the magic box looked bigger—inside the box was pretty tight. Lance Burton's saying that, at one point in the trick, Mark may have had the opportunity to escape. Lance Burton then walking her up and onto the stage, taking her into the wings, backstage where all of his equipment was stored. Her calling out in the dim work lights, "Mark?" but no one answering. The two police officers arriving and, after Lance Burton had excused himself, her telling the whole story again to them—the taller police officer entering it into a laptop as she talked. Then, finally, her going back to their room at Treasure Island, thinking that, for some reason, Mark had freaked out and would be there. But he wasn't—no sign—and how she hadn't slept all night waiting for the phone to ring. "Mark's an accountant," she ends. Her glass is empty and has been for five minutes. "He doesn't do this. He doesn't do things like this." She pushes her empty wine glass toward Elko. "Be a gentleman," she says.

He adds wine.

She gulps. "I mean, everything he does, Mark does...and I mean *everything,* has a reason," she says.

"Someone disappears, usually there's a reason. Someone's *husband* disappears, usually there's a *good* reason."

"Such as?"

"Well, is everything all right? Between you two?"

Lena draws a deep breath, spreads her left hand between her breasts. "I'm an impulsive person."

"Which means?"

"Which means I *do* things, sometimes before I think about them. Or the consequences."

"And?"

"I suspect you can guess."

"Yeah, but I'd hate to guess wrong."

"And it causes problems, my impulsive doing...occasionally."

"How bad?"

"Not irreconcilable."

"As far as you know."

"As far as I know, yes." Some kind of ghost crosses her almost ashen face. "Although..." She looks, momentarily, sad...confused.

The room draws into a small bead of silence.

Then Lena blurts it out—like a cork popping: "My husband and I have an open marriage," she says.

Again, she shoves her glass back across the desk to Elko. He ignores it. Instead, he stares hard and comments, "Really."

"Well," she says, "if not *really*, then certainly *after a fashion*...If not technically *open* it is certainly *ajar*. Push comes to shove: I'm open, and he's married."

When Elko tells her that it sounds like a good deal for her, she reddens and gives him a *don't be stupid* look and says, "Nobody's happy."

He checks her indefinite pronoun. "Nobody. You mean you and Mark?"

"Nobody-nobody," she says. "All inclusive. People who love each other attack each other, then they don't talk about it."

"Pretty sad thought."

"Well...I'm a sad person."

"Yeah. I noticed the tears."

She stands and crisscrosses the room without direction. Elko watches her.

"So, will you take my case?" Lena asks. "Help me?"

Elko tells her that he needs to ask just one more question, then he can measure whether the case seems a case he can, maybe, help with.

"What's the question?" she asks.

"Is it possible he ran off with another woman?"

Behind some kind of screen inside her head, Elko can see a video flicker. It's as though she's disappeared, momentarily, into some private viewing room.

"Hello?" Elko tries to get her attention back. "Anybody home? I asked, is it possible that—"

"*Everything's* possible," she says, maybe a little angry now. "This is the world, after all, so why not? It's possible—possible that Mark ran off with another woman...But unlikely."

"You never know," he says.

"I usually know," Lena says. "Most things."

"Such as?"

"Such as, you've been married twice, divorced twice. And you have a drinking problem."

"Not bad," he says. "Not bad. Three and a half stars out of five."

"And the head injury you got—when you were playing professional football—it reworked the lighting plot of your brain. Some things you can't see any more; they're totally dark. Other things are very bright, and you see what...very few others can, which is why you have a special gift for finding people, which you love to do. Though you're very wary of people finding *you*. Also, sometimes you imagine yourself, in another life, as a painter."

Elko clears his throat and manages, "I'm impressed."

"Hey," she says, "you asked a question."

"Still, maybe you got most of that shit from the Internet," Elko says. "Google. You looked me up."

"Oh, are you on Google?"

"I have no idea," he says.

Lena, feeling an advantage, presses.

"I get reception. I hear voices."

"So, if you hear voices, where's your husband?" Elko asks

Her eyes seep a little at the edges. "My voices..." She looks angry. "My voices tell me much more than I would like to know," she says. "But they don't tell me everything." She pushes her glass forward again.

Elko tops it. "Seems you drink a lot," he says.

"So, we're a pair then," she says. "I mean, *you* have a whole...*chat room* of cocktail waitresses keeping their eyes out, helping you...*find* people. 'The Marys!'" She raises her glass.

"The *Bloody* Marys, actually."

Now, Lena bites gloss from her lower lip. "Alcohol's a disease," she says. "My father had it. His father had it. I'm infected. I carry the gene. In a large Prada bag that's always with me. But the gene has nothing to do with the voices I hear. The *spirits*."

"I see."

"Will you take my case?"

"I will," Elko says, then adds, "assuming you meet conditions."

Lena brays, "Which are?" She throws her head back. "So, I do what, first? Get down on my knees?"

"Professional," Elko clarifies. "Please, *professional* conditions."

"And, if I do, will you drink with me if I need someone to drink with?"

Elko sucks a deep breath, holds it. He takes her in, measures her and says, "I think it's best we don't get ahead of ourselves. What's your room number at TI?"

"Excuse me? TI?"

"TI. Treasure Island. Used to be a nice place."

"And now?"

"And now, like you, it tries too hard to be sexy. What's your room number?"

"Room number," she says. "Twenty oh...seventy-eight."

Elko writes it down.

"Maybe we'll fool around while we're looking for my husband," she says. "Is that what you're thinking?"

"I think you're a spoiled woman who imagines danger's a board game."

"And I think electricity's an underrated phenomenon."

"So, okay, terms and conditions," Elko says. "Four hundred dollars a day and all, which means *all,* expenses."

She shrugs, smiles, slips her tongue out over her lower lip. "Whatever," she says.

"Okay, and one last question," he says. And stands.

She stands with a little sway. "You know in my experience, there's always a final question after the final question. But sure," she says. "Shoot."

"If your husband, Mark had...let's call it an 'escape fantasy.' If he had an *escape fantasy,* where is it, do you think, that—if he could escape there and not take any baggage with him—would be?"

She's really swaying now, swaying a lot, looking horny, predatory.

"I just want you to think about it. I don't need an answer today; I'll call you tomorrow," he says.

"An escape fantasy?"

"An escape fantasy."

"Mark."

"Your husband. Right. Mark."

"*An escape fantasy...*I like that."

"Imagine your husband as Houdini."

11 ◆ Early Tuesday Morning, April 17: Mark, Before Vanishing

What Mark Goodson likes to do when he's in Las Vegas is rise early—five o'clock usually—and head out by himself. This morning it's been made all the easier by Lena who is once again in a kind of lather of spit and tears, exiling him: *Go! Disappear!* Still, banished or not, he likes to walk the Strip, have coffee and play video poker at The Mirage's sports bar, play a little blackjack—always wonderful if he can find one-on-one with a dealer. And all these things he does, filled with rare pleasure and energy, on the morning of the night when he will disappear.

He descends alone in the Treasure Island elevator, studies himself in its mirror. For the most part, he's a stranger to himself, certainly a stranger to his own image. He is not, nor was he ever, his body: six foot three, two hundred and eight pounds, reddish hair and a pale complexion. Certainly he is not his body in his own mind, in his own eyes. And though he doesn't intimately *know* the person in the image he is now studying, and who is studying back, what stirs, and even surprises, Mark Goodson is that the reflected person studying back isn't uninteresting. Possibly because the person studying back has a *secret*. And this is what the mirror makes clear—the secret is that he's two people.

The elevator opens on the casino, and Mark steps out. It's just past five thirty, and the Treasure Island casino carpets are being shampooed, slot machine sound tracks are announcing *Wheel...of... Fortune* and erupting in Elvis vocals. Housekeeping staff are polishing brass.

There's an energy that zaps and crackles—a level of energy, and potential vigor, which Mark likes. He's not an imaginative person, by and large, but the energy of the room into which he steps makes him feel that he *might* be imaginative—that he might invent something, surprise people, on a day like today.

So, when Mark steps outside, he believes he can taste the distant mountains in the air. He ambles past the Treasure Island lagoon waters, pooled and glistening with spilled treasures—bowls, jewels, coins. So, in such a morning like this, he feels like a child.

He wanders next door to The Mirage, finds the sports book, where he's learned the name of the graveyard-shift bartender. Cindi. She says, "Hey there, stranger!" smiles, pours him the coffee that she knows he wants. "When'd you get into town?" she asks. He tells her: *yesterday*. "Wife with you?" Cindi asks.

"Always," he says.

"Always?"

Cindi says she can't remember: Does he have kids? And Mark, who had confessed once before, tells her a second and aching time: no, they don't. He and Lena don't. They tried. They tried in all sorts of ways, have been to all sorts of doctors. They remain hopeful, but no, not yet.

"You'll adopt, and then your wife will get pregnant," Cindi says. She smiles. "Happens all the time."

"If that happens, we'll be glad," Mark says.

"Trust me," she says, "it will."

Children! Mark thinks. *Children!* Lena has stopped being a believer. She's brushed it off, but if it happens in real time she'll be a good mother. She loves him most when he, himself, is most like a child: aching, hungry, helpless.

He slips his player's card into the bar-top video poker then feeds three successive twenties into the bill validator.

"Your morning for a royal!" Cindi says.

Mark chooses Deuces Wild, and it's one of those mornings when the deuces have decided to show up. He's ahead forty-five dollars when four of them line up for a thousand-coin payoff. On a quarter machine, that means two hundred and fifty dollars.

Mark hits the cash-out button, takes his ticket, and gives Cindi a twenty from his pocket. Cindi wishes him a good day.

He roams the near blackjack pit, finds a dealer standing alone beside her Shuffle Master at a five-dollar table. Thanks to the deuces, he's ahead almost three hundred for the morning. And though he's not a person who lives, day by day, with chance, with randomness, here—in Las Vegas, at The Mirage, this morning—he likes it. He slides two hundred-dollar bills across to the dealer, asks for half his chips in red. The dealer calls out *two hundred!* to the pit boss, who okays the transaction, and she begins to deal.

And here, again, it's Mark's morning. The dealer breaks hand after hand. He gets dealt twenties, nineteens against her eighteens. He has a streak of double-down hands, which he almost always seems to win. He presses his five-dollar bets to fifteen-dollar bets to twenty-five dollar bets, and almost an hour into the game he's up just a bit over four hundred.

"Start betting green," the dealer urges.

"If I start betting green, all my luck will change," Mark says.

"You believe shit like that you shouldn't be playing," the dealer says.

"Well, I don't believe it...obviously, of course, as a reasonable person. But I do as a player who doesn't *win* very often."

The dealer's flat cynicism makes Mark uneasy. He plays the next three hands and loses them all. Mark cashes out, gives the dealer two fives as a tip, then takes his chips to the cage and cashes in three hundred and thirty dollars, plus his slot ticket.

He feels almost giddy. It isn't even seven thirty, and he's up over five hundred. Lena wouldn't believe it! She liked to call him "Mr. Conservative" and wasn't shy about bearing down—usually too hard and too often—with the name. So, what would she think when *Mr. Conservative* ambled back into the room with over five hundred dollars that he'd won? What would her name be for him then?

He goes to the Baccarat Bar, where there is a woman who looks a little like Lena and who is totally absorbed in her own video-poker game. He orders a Bloody Mary, feels even giddier and suddenly needs to find a rest room.

He finds one across the casino, between the Italian restaurant, Onda Ristorante, and the stylish new buffet called Cravings. Mark has never eaten at either place. Onda looks beautiful and moody. Cravings looks a bit glass-wood-and-chrome top-heavy. Still, he makes a note— maybe this trip they should try one, or even both, of them. He enters the men's room and finds a stall, and it isn't until he's seated that he glances up and sees the strange vest hanging from the stall hook.

The curious vest appears to be made of a canvas material and bulges like an insulated ski jacket. It's lined with zippers—in rows, about five inches apart. What kind of vest is it? It looks like winter, a vest insulated for cold weather. Certainly, it's not the sort of suit or casual vest a traveler would be wearing in Las Vegas.

He finishes, takes a deep breath, remembers the over-five-hundred he's ahead, laughs to himself in imagining Lena's reaction: *Mark! Mark! You're serious?...Baby!* She'll be buoyed and will snap out of the shadowed, sulky mood she's been in. And she'll probably want him.

Mark smiles. He stands, raises his pants, tucks his shirt in, buckles the belt. The automatic-flush toilet whooshes its cascade behind him, and he steps forward to examine the vest.

Everything that it has appeared to be, it is: canvas, padded, zippered, unseasonable. Then Mark touches it, takes the padding in his hands, squeezes it. It's hard, bulging, pulpy. Whatever the padding, whatever the fill, the insulation, it isn't something like Koala Foam—the stuff they used everywhere these days for ski jackets, sleeping bags, and the like.

When he tries to heft the vest, it feels like lead—beyond heavy; it's a vest weighing as much as fifty pounds. Maybe more. Wouldn't that much weight be uncomfortable to wear? And why the zippers? Zippers everywhere. Front and back.

Mark feels a strain on his shoulders. His arms ache, so he re-hangs the vest so he can unburden and free his hands. He pulls the vest taut, takes the tongue of a zipper and moves it right. At first it resists, but then it slides. A pocket opens. And what Mark sees inside takes his breath away. Bills! Jesus! Hundreds! Packets with paper sleeves. And then... More staggering than the bills—fastidiously lined in long ruler-like plastic bags are butter-colored chips! Mark squints to see their denomination. Jesus again! Thousands!

Who? What?

Mark does some quick Kentucky-windage math. Accountant that he is, he can do the bills. All the butter-colored chips... He can't!

He needs to find a Mirage security guard... probably... maybe.

God in heaven! Holy! It's possible that what's in the vest is close, maybe even more than—is that possible?—to a *million* dollars!

He should inquire, right? Of course! Find out if somebody's reported the vest missing. Or?

Suddenly he's removing his own Eddie Bauer blazer and slipping the vest on.

He has to think.

In a way, the vest fits. When his blue blazer is back on and buttoned, none of the vest shows. Mark wears a forty-four tall, and this one clears the vest by maybe a half-inch.

Three hundred and fifty thousand dollars—maybe as much as...!

Lena will freak out. She'll go crazy. She'll do all sorts of things which are totally unpredictable. Say things. Scream. Make demands. It will be a mistake—clearly, clearly a mistake—to go back to their room and tell her. It would be the worst thing he could do... probably.

So then... what? If not back to the room, if not telling Mirage security, if not reporting it to The Mirage lost and found, what?

What he needed to do was stop, calm himself, clear his mind. What he needed to do was: *count the money.*

But where? Count where? Not here. Not in the stall, not in the men's room. Someone could come in. Maybe even the person who'd left the vest could come in. And maybe that person was a... who could say? *Anything!* A crazy person...a criminal. Mark could end up dead and some fiendish sociopath would walk off with the money. That was not what should happen. That would be wrong. There was a kind of logic to this—ethics, morality, something. And Mark was struggling with it.

But if he could calm down. And count the money. Then he would have a better idea, could form a plan. A strategy.

He just needs to be by himself. Safe. Secure. In a private place. Like where? Well, like here.

He was, after all, in a *hotel.* He could get a *room!* Why not? He could get a room here at The Mirage and use what had strangely and darkly fallen into his hands the month before. His secret and guilt—a second set of credit cards and identification—driver's license, social security, two Visas and a Discover. He could get a room, and nobody would be able to find him or trace him. Because, if they tried, he'd be invisible, he'd be...*the other person,* the *not*-Mark—a man no one who knew him knew: *Anthony Francis.*

Briefly, Mark relives the bizarre, phantom story: the contact, the e-mails, the pleas and challenges, the journey west he had taken, the dark, the river, the death. Lena has no idea! Lena can't even imagine...her Boy Scout! Why has he kept all the identification? What did he think he would ever use it for?

Mark moves the slide-lock on the stall door to the right. He swings the door open and advances. For the second time in less than three hours, he studies himself in a mirror. A paunchier self. A jumpier self. A more feral self. This man—same height, same reddish hair, though it seems now he's forgotten to comb it—this man looks, he has to confess, savage in some ways. Primal. Is this him? Mark Goodson. Adopted son of Richard and Ramona Goodson? Husband of...for an instant, Mark finds himself searching for Lena's name.

Okay, he has decided something—the man in the mirror, the stocky man wearing the too-tight Eddie Bauer blazer will go to the lobby, stand there in front of the shark aquarium. Ask for a room.

There's no line at the registration counter, so Mark approaches and asks whether there might be a room available.

"How many nights, sir?" the clerk in a coral-colored blazer asks. She wears a nametag: JANICE.

"One," Mark says and then revises it immediately: "No. Two."

"Starting tonight?"

"Yes. And I'd like to get into it as soon as possible."

"I'm sorry but rooms aren't usually available until, at the earliest, noon."

Noon is over four hours away. "Okay, but if I pay for *last* night," Mark asks, "can I get into a room now?"

"I'll check. Just a minute." The clerk moves off and confers briefly with a supervisor. She returns. "Yes. That's possible. We can do that. But the only room that we have available, one I could check you into right away, would be three hundred fifty-nine a night. It's a suite."

"That's fine; a suite is fine," Mark says. He can feel his back, under the vest, sweating.

"If I could have a driver's license and a credit card, then, please," Janice asks.

Mark pulls his billfold from his blazer. He lifts a leather flap behind a leather flap and takes out a cached elastic-banded packet of credit cards and identification. Less-than-month-old images of the Salmon River swirl in an eddy of hallucination, making Mark feel momentarily drunk and dizzy.

"Sir?" Janice casts gently for his attention.

"Sorry," Mark says. "My mind..." For an instant, he can't find an end to his sentence. "My mind was wandering," he manages. And riffling the pack of not-Mark cards he removes a Visa and slides it across the counter.

"And a driver's license, please?"

Mark finds and offers it. He watches Janice check the picture, check his face, check the picture again, then move on.

Wearing the money vest and being another person makes Mark feel momentarily and preternaturally powerful. Lena should see him! Or maybe not. Maybe it would be giving something away to her that he should keep to himself. He watches Janice processing the Visa card that is only *relatively* his, and it makes him all the dizzier.

"Do you want some luggage help?" Janice asks.

"No, I'm fine," Mark says.

"You sure?"

"I'm sure."

"You look, I'm sorry, but...a little—"

"I can imagine. I've been driving all night. I'm exhausted," Mark says.

"Well, it's a nice room," Janice says.

"Thanks for being...*accommodating*." Mark spreads a tentatively playful smile.

The twenty-eighth floor suite is right off the elevator foyer and has two doors at its entry. Mark uses his key, enters and double locks the doors behind him before he even takes in the room. When he does, it's impressive—in a to-be-expected, overdone Vegas sort of way. There's a large living area with a bar, a couch, comfortable chairs; beyond that there's a sizable bedroom. The floor-to-ceiling windows look out over The Mirage's pool complex.

God, he's hungry! Should he order room service? No, he'd better wait and have breakfast with Lena. She'll be pissed if he gets back to their room and he says he's eaten. But, is he even going *back* to their room? Jesus, what is he thinking? Of course. Why wouldn't he?

He hangs his blazer in the entry closet then looks for the minibar. He takes two Absolut vodkas and a can of Mr. & Mrs. T's spicy tomato juice, mixes himself a Bloody Mary and takes a healthy slug. It feels good.

Mark unzips the vest, shrugs his shoulders and it slides off. He lifts it from the carpet's deep pile and carries it with him into the bedroom, where he lays it on the bedspread, takes a breath and begins unzipping, taking out all the money packets and chip ziplocks, arranging them in even parallel lines like some crazy abacus. Removing a Sanyo pocket calculator, his intent is: *begin counting.*

Each money packet holds ten thousand. That's easy. Mark's seen money, seen cash. Money's, in fact, what he *does.* Money's what he drives to and from work to count and manage for others. Money's his job.

But the chips! At first, he thinks, where are the blacks? They seem chips in curiously-low denominations: twenty-fives and fives. But the colors? Mark's never seen these odd, pastel colors.

But then he sees! Emptying a ziplock, he *sees.* The twenty-fives aren't in *dollars.* Each one, each fruit-pastel-colored one is worth twenty-five *thousand.* And what he'd thought were five dollars are five *thousand.* Mark sits on his king bed, stands, sits again, stands, crosses to the bath, washes his face, slaps his face, washes it again, wraps his head in a towel. All the while, his breath sounds like someone hitting a punching bag.

"Okay, *slow,*" he instructs himself. "Calm down. Slow."

And he begins counting.

Most of the pastel-colored chips are twenty-five thousand. Other than on a stock portfolio statement, Mark has never seen so much value take up so little space. Twenty minutes later—the king-sized bed strewn—Mark Goodson sees that the exact contents of the vest total three million, two hundred thousand dollars. He mixes himself a second double Bloody Mary and recalculates the money. Mark—Boy Scout, CPA—is not a person-of-error. It's three point two million. Exactly.

He drifts out to the couch, sits, rubs his head, his eyes, takes deep breaths. Three point two million dollars! Nearly ten times what he had originally estimated. If he lived off one-hundred thousand a year for the next thirty years, never having to pay taxes, he'd have lived a life; he'd be seventy-four.

He's thinking, of course, himself—himself only, living such a life until seventy-four. He's thinking a new Mark. He's thinking: the person who just took this room. He's thinking he could live the life of the other Mark—the person who died, months before, in Idaho and who has just come to life again here in Las Vegas. *I am my brother's keeper*, Mark thinks. Why not? *I am my brother's keeper.*

Lena can manage. Lena'll be fine. Happier. They probably have half a million now in assets. And certainly, she's resourceful. She'll find another man…or two, or three. Or she'll burn a bar down, and there'll be a couple dozen. Mark feels he isn't a man who pleases her anyway, most of the time. People say, if they hadn't been high-school sweethearts, they probably never would have married. No children. Oh, there's occasionally talk. But, no. Just a business, a house, a boat.

So, where would he live? He could live abroad—some place like Croatia or Portugal, where the money might go twice as far. He could fish. Start carving wood animals—a fantasy he'd always had about what he'd do if he had a lot of time.

Jesus! What was he thinking? That he'd just disappear? Poof? What kind of galloping insanity was that?

On the other hand…

Obviously, he needs to think. He'll keep the room but go back, get Lena, go out and get some breakfast. He won't tell her. Yet. Maybe, after they've had breakfast. He'll tell her about what he won at video poker and blackjack. But not the vest. He'll wait; certainly until after breakfast. Maybe, then, he'll bring her up to this room. Surprise her. Show her. Maybe.

The closet in the bedroom has a large safe. It operates by punching in a code. To assure himself, Mark works the opening and locking of the safe three times. When he's comfortable, he stacks the bill packets and the chips inside—neatly and orderly, almost filling the space, and locks it. When a flash of panic hits, he opens the safe again and stares in.

It's like a movie. Like some scene where the bank robbers use an acetylene torch and dynamite caps and blow open the vault and then stare in at all the money. It takes your breath away. Makes you giddy. Mark feels like he's watching some person he doesn't know yet, but is discovering suddenly in the possession of a lot of money. The whole event makes him feel dizzy. And horny.

And hungry. He has to get back to Lena for breakfast; it's almost nine o'clock. And even though she still might be sleeping, if he doesn't get back at the time he almost always gets back it will register—even in her sleeping brain. She has proved herself to be a woman of uncanny senses and intuition.

So, he closes the safe one last time, locks it, tests its tightness, slides the closet doors shut and begins to leave.

A last impulse catches him, and he withdraws his wallet and, from it, the banded packet of credit and identification cards. He pulls the elastic off, spreads the cards out on the bar.

Less than a month ago, he'd discovered a person who could almost have been him. Or who he could have almost been.

None of it had seemed real. One day an e-mail: *We may know each other.* Signed, Anthony Francis.

And though he wasn't precisely sure why, Mark hadn't told Lena. Perhaps she'd demand that he—that he…what? *Something.* So, Anthony Francis became the first genuinely kept secret of his life.

Then came the suggestion to meet. His doppelgänger, his lookalike, his twin. Then his own agreement. The plans. The subterfuge. It had been the first time Mark had lied to Lena, had known the sweetly fermented taste of duplicity.

And now, standing in his Mirage suite, that taste reasserts itself—under his tongue, along his gums. He could feel deception's charge—a current strange and distant from the daily world of tax codes and actuarial charts.

And then…And then…And then…! He'd never been so drunk ever. He'd never before landed a rainbow. He'd never been in water in the dark and fought a current. He'd never shoveled earth onto the body of another person.

Mark looks down at the half dozen credit cards and picture IDs—with his face…or certainly *almost* his face…on them.

What might it be like, Mark thinks, to return someone from the dead, bring them back to life, slip under that *other* person's skin and do it with three point two million dollars in your pocket?

12 ◆ Elko in the Morning

Elko meets Shaquille O'Neal for coffee at Seattle's Finest a half hour before their morning program meeting at nine o'clock. They do this at least twice a week. Obviously, when they first met, the man Elko calls Shaq wasn't *Shaq*; he was LeRon Wesson, but clearly a keeper, a ringer for the real O'Neal. So Elko cornered him. And he was cool, he bought in. LeRon's always cool. He played ball at Texas Tech, then in Spain for about four years. Now, he does something with the culinary union.

Elko uses Shaq a lot. Certain casinos—Arizona Charlie's, Boulder Station, El Cortez—love to have him on property and get excited that their VIPs think the resort draws athletes. Most weeks, he gets about twenty hours and loves it when people point over and say, *Look! It's him!* He feels, just as easily, it *might* be, *could* have been, *him*. With the right breaks—if he hadn't been injured. And he's developed a way of signing *LeRon Wesson* with a whole bunch of swings and swirls that look, easily, like they could add up to *Shaquille O'Neal*.

They get their mocha lattes and sit. "Wassup?" Shaq asks.

Elko explains that he's got a disappearing husband and shakes his head. Shaq laughs. Shaq appreciates ambiguity; he was a Rhodes scholar at Oxford for two years.

"So, you're doing, like, a classical motif—classic disappearing husband?" he asks, and laughs again.

"I'm doing, like: guy goes to see Lance Burton at Monte Carlo, volunteers, steps into a metal box and—okay?—*disappears*. The trick doesn't end. The trick doesn't get completed. He steps in. *Abracadabra*—he's gone. And that's it! *Poof! Vanishito!* He doesn't come back. Show ends, he doesn't reappear."

"So, you ask Lance?"

"Not yet. But the guy's wife, my client, did."

"And?"

"And Lance's best explanation is: he freaked. Lance thinks the guy panicked and took off."

"*Will* you talk to Lance?"

"I will. It's on. Today. Later this morning."

"Abracadabra," Shaq says, and he makes a *poof!* gesture with his hands.

"Abracadabra," Elko says.

"So, how's the wife?"

"I'm not married," Elko grins. "You know that."

"The *disappeared-guy's* wife. Would *you* disappear from her if you could?"

"Yes and no. Hard to tell yet. She's a pain in the ass, no question. But she's also half sexy."

"Which half?"

Right then, their friend, Amana walks in. Before his injury, Amana played most of his years for the Chicago Bears. Shaq's big—a monster in his own right—but Amana's bigger. He's not a person you'd ever want to try to move, or to have moving you. Amana spots his friends, gives them a *Yo!* and orders an espresso grande before sitting down.

They begin instant-replaying the week's NBA games, wondering where all the Croats and Russians are coming from. And almost cued by Amana's uttering the name *Juventus,* some sort of mobile commotion, dysfunctional-small-three-character-mob-scene feud slams in through the Seattle's Finest front doors. These are three people who have hated each other for forty years and want company in their hatred.

Pretty much everybody, except Elko and his two buddies, take breaths, lower their heads and turn away.

Even the staff, who are squealing, scramble, like small barnyard animals in uniforms.

Elko sees Shaq and Amana give each other a nod. Then even before the nod is done Shaq has lifted one of the mob and Amana's lifted the two others. They push the three elevated bodies into each other, so that there can be a serious conference. Then they lower the mob, walk them to the door and, opening it for them, tell them, "Have a good day."

"So! As you were!" Amana barks out, like a Marine sergeant, to the crowd. People take their seats, resume their caffè Americanos and caramel macchiatos.

Amana and Shaq wander back to where Elko sits.

"The guy I like," Shaq says, "is that Russian guy, Andrei Kirilenko, played with the Utah Jazz. Retired to Russia. Came back with Minnesota."

"Long arms," Amana agrees.

"Great hands," Elko observes.

They're all recovering athletes. Professional athletes. *Athletes Anonymous.* Ex-pro ball players whose careers were cut short by injuries. Elko can call on either of these guys. For back-up. For assistance.

If he got leaned on heavily, he could assemble an imposing A-Team. Or, more accurately, an AA-Team.

So, they dump their cardboard containers and walk the half a block on Charleston to the community center where they always have their meetings. And ten minutes later an ex-World-Cup soccer player is standing in front of an assembled dozen saying, "Good Morning. My name is Carlo and I'm an Athlete" after which, he starts in on a familiar story about his three-times-repaired knee and then moves on, as these stories always do, to his abuse of injected steroids.

Elko doesn't often take the podium, but, for some reason, today he does. "Good morning," he says. "My name is Elko and I'm an Athlete." *Good morning, Elko,* the group intones back. Elko rambles on, and it feels good. To be in a shitty little room with bad coffee but with a dozen banged-up guys who all happily give each other the gift of listening feels outside any world of greed or expectation and feels nice. Words don't need to be in a sequence or make sense. Elko hears himself throwing out insanely meaningless phrases like *a grab bag of concussions* and *chrysanthemum starbursts of pain.* Before he knows it, someone from the group is standing behind him, his huge black hands on Elko's shoulders, massaging them. "Go for it," he's saying.

Elko leaves the meeting ten minutes early because he and Lena Goodson have a ten thirty appointment with Lance Burton and his stage manager at the Monte Carlo. When he arrives, he hands the car over to the valet. Elko tells him, "Don't touch any of the money in the trunk." The lanky valet does this thing with his lips and his nose— a kind of *ha, ha, fuck you.*

Lena's standing in front of the double doors outside the Lance Burton Theatre. Lena's wearing a summer dress and large sunglasses— lenses the color of apricots. When she sees him, she almost runs to him. "I've been a wreck!" she says.

He asks whether Lance or his manager have shown their faces.

"Not yet," she says. Then: "What have you found out? Just tell me he's still alive. How long does it take you, usually, to find someone? Do you need to swab parts of my body for his DNA?"

"You can just stick out your tongue."

Elko rattles off a half-dozen questions. Has she had any phone calls? Does she have an e-mail account, and has she thought to check it? Has she thought about where—in some fantasy her husband—her husband might have *chosen* to disappear *to?* In Mark's CPA work, did he deal with any individuals, or businesses, which might have been involved in illicit activities? Asked another way: Had Mark ever blown the whistle on anyone? Is she sure there's no possibility of another woman?

Lena takes the last question first. Every once in a while, she says, after she's provoked him, Mark threatens to find a very tall, caramel-colored woman from someplace like Trinidad or Tobago and run away with her.

"So, you're saying—"

"I'm saying tall, elegant black women arouse him."

"So, we shouldn't rule it out," Elko says.

"Although I think he's just trying to tell me that he could *do* something like that...if he wanted to."

"Would he want to?"

"Listen, can we leave this alone? I told you, he's my whole life. I can't live without him."

Lena moves on to the question about clients or someone he might have angered by not cooperating with? "Also very unlikely," Lena says. She says that back in high school Mark was always the Eagle Scout—doing more homework than was ever asked, helping old teachers across the street. "True story: he earned the Good Citizenship badge seven times, because he liked doing the work *so much.*" She sees the skepticism on Elko's brow and adds, "He still has the...what do they call it, the merit badge sash? His *bandolier,* with the seven identical badges, all sewn on with red thread, because he was earning his Bookbinding badge at the same time. When you come to the house, I'll show it to you."

"When I—?"

"Come to the house. Don't you think you'll have to come to the house, possibly?"

"Your house?"

"Well—"

"In Naples? Florida?"

"Yes."

"Why?"

"I don't know. To *investigate.*"

A man in an olive jump suit approaches them and introduces himself as Jeffrey Kane. He says Lance will meet them back stage, then pulls out a ring of keys and opens the doors to the theater. He holds the door and Elko and Lena slip past him and walk into the dark.

The theater door closes behind them. They squint.

"Where were you sitting?" Elko asks Lena.

"I have the ticket stubs," Lena says.

"Could we please turn on some lights?" Elko asks Jeffrey Kane—his voice bristling a bit with impatience.

Jeffrey Kane tells them, "Just stay where you are."

The lights pulse on. Lena produces her stubs and they find the seats. Jeffrey Kane is back. "I don't think you're going to find anything in the auditorium," he says.

Elko, grinning, tells him, "No tern unstoned."

Elko turns to Lena. "So, who was in which seat?" he asks. She tells him.

"They clean the entire theater every day," Jeffrey says.

He's right; we're not going to find anything, Elko thinks. Still he goes on, interrogating. "When Mark volunteered—when he stood up—did you try to stop him?" he asks Lena.

Lena looks uncertain, unsure. "He was gone. He was up, down the aisle and out before I could stop him," she says. "I was, mostly—I don't know—just surprised. He was a little pissed at me, but— Mark's not a public person."

They follow Jeffrey Kane up the stairs that lead onto the stage and then across the stage and into the wings, where Lance is standing next to a large metal box. He's a good-looking, well-toned guy wearing Army fatigue shorts and a University of Kentucky tee shirt.

"Go Wildcats!" Elko says.

Lance smiles. "Any clues?" he asks.

"Any clues?" Elko checks with Lena.

She shakes her head.

"Okay, now I'm going to show you the trick," Lance Burton says. "The mechanics. Which I would never normally do, except these are extraordinary circumstances. Who wants to go first?"

Lena and Elko look at one another.

"I thought I'd walk each of you through the illusion," Lance tries to explain. "So you have the experience."

"You go," Lena says. "You first."

Elko, on-deck hitter that he always tries to be, steps up to the plate. He likes the stage. He likes the lights. He likes imagining five thousand people out front in the dark, all of them leaning forward in their chairs. *Magic time!* he thinks. He has an entertainer's heart, he thinks. It's not a world unlike professional sports.

"Okay!" Lance says. He does a flourish with his hands. "Okay, imagine music. Music: blah blah blah blah! I throw open the doors—voila!—walk in and out, demonstrating it to be what it is: a box! An assistant brings me this gold tux—" He picks the tux-on-a-hanger from the top of another piece of equipment. "I throw the tux on the floor, stomp around on it in a petulant fit. Blah blah blah! I fly the tux." Lance hooks the tux hanger to a wire. It's hoisted. "I ask you a bunch of questions about the items in your wallet. Then I produce a passport, hand it to you, say you might need it." A passport appears at Lance's fingertips. He hands it to Elko. It has Elko's name on it. "I tell you step into my office." He gestures into the box, so Elko enters it. The doors are shut. It's dark as shit and Elko's feeling a little claustrophobic. He hears Lance's voice outside. Then feels something under his feet—like a turntable—rotating. He feels a bunch of hands on him; black-sleeved hands with black gloves, reaching in from the sides; moving him around; pulling him backwards. He turns and makes out a stagehand's index finger to his lips. He hears Lance's voice—somewhere ahead...or behind—going on: blah blah blah, but he can't make out the words.

Elko can see, beyond the darkness, flashes of light. A stagehand whispers, *Take your jacket off. Keep your valuables.* Elko feels the same stagehand helping, slipping his jacket off, then handing him things from his pockets. Finally, some other kind of jacket which feels silky is slipped on over his shoulders. It's a one-minute costume change.

What happens next is a kind of commotion that seems like it wasn't intended. Backstage-assistant-gloves push Elko forward. He's on a turntable which is rotating. Suddenly he hears all four doors of the box being thrown open. But he's still in the dark! Why, he wonders, would he still be—? Then, suddenly, something around him shatters and he's standing inside the open box with, like, pottery shards, scattered all over the stage.

Then Elko sees Lena lying, crumpled, by Lance's feet.

"She passed out," Jeffery Kane fills in. "When the doors opened the first time, and you were gone, she passed out. Someone's getting ammonia."

Another stagehand runs on with a first-aid kit, opens it, pulls a tab out and breaks it under Lena's nose. She startles. "Get away! Get away!" she screams.

"It's okay; it's okay," Lance is saying.

"Lena, I'm here. I'm back!" Elko tells her.

Lena stares, looking like he'd been the abuser of her child. Then she growls, "Where were you?"

"I—" Elko starts. But he barely gets the syllable out.

"*Where were you?*"

"Mrs. Goodson—" Lance begins.

"I'm sorry," Lena says. "I'm sorry. I'm sorry."

"Do you want an inhaler?" the stage hand who brought the first-aid kit asks.

She shakes her head.

When she's calm and breathing regularly, Lance crouches beside her. "It's up to you," he begins.

"No," Lena says. "I can't. I can't do it."

"You don't want to walk through the illusion from the inside the way Mr. Wells did?"

"No. I'm sorry... No, thank you." And she reaches a hand above, so that someone will take it and lift her to her feet. Elko does the honors. "Thank you, Elko," she says.

Elko looks straight at Lena. "If you trust my experience," he begins, "Just now—going through the trick. My estimation is, Mark had about two minutes—in the dark there—" Elko points. "—behind the box... to just cut and run."

He pauses, to see that Lena's following him. It seems she is.

He confesses: "I didn't see exactly how it worked, but I was out of the box for about that length of time. One or two people were moving me around—undressing me, dressing me." Elko looks down at the silly gold tuxedo jacket he's wearing.

Lance takes over. "Cody says—" One of the nearby stagehands—obviously Cody—raises his hand in the shadows. "—that your husband must have run for the wings at the last minute. Because the last time he saw him, he was in the box. So—"

"You're saying—?"

"We think he ran."

"But—" Lena starts, then stops.

Lance raises his voice. "*If* he ran, no one saw him."

"But he had the opportunity," Elko says. "He *might* have; he had the opportunity."

"Exactly. That's the point."

"But why would Mark run?" Lena asks.

"That's a good question, a very good question," Elko says. "And when we leave here, we'll get back to it." Then Elko asks Lance questions: "Who gets to be back stage? How secure is it? Say there's someone who—some way—knows Mark Goodson is going to volunteer... and somehow knows things about your show—how it works. Say this same person wants to grab Mark...for whatever reason...and has the idea that what he'll do is just wait back stage and, when the moment comes, grab him. Could—?"

"Back stage is a totally secure area," Jeffrey Kane interrupts—" fully controlled."

"So, then, nobody—" Elko starts to press.

"Totally secure. Airtight." Jeffrey Kane is having none of it.

But Elko's not a person to be put off. "What you're saying is that nobody—no person not with the show—could gain access?"

"Exactly. Nobody. Impossible," Jeffrey Kane says.

Elko tries another tack. "But that's the show, right? *Impossible.* Am I right? Maybe I'm wrong. But isn't the show about—isn't Lance about—doing the impossible?"

Jeffrey's eyes first, and then Lance's, shift. Their jaws tilt.

Elko senses an opening; he goes on. "I'm being serious," he says. "Okay, I'm playing with words, but I'm being serious. That's the show: impossible stuff happening."

"We call it *Illusion,*" Jeffrey Kane says.

"Actually, *misdirection,*" Lance says.

On the small spiral notepad in his head, Elko makes a check-mark and writes a note: *Did somebody get to Lance Burton before the show?*

There's a waiting silence. Elko has his head down. He's calculating. "We appreciate it," he finally tells the assembled group. He lifts his head, smiles. "Thanks for your time," he says. "Thanks for helping us."

Lance smiles and nods and peels off left into the wings. Jeffrey Kane has descended the stage stairs and is waiting for them.

"Are you okay?" Elko asks Lena.

"I'd like a drink," Lena says.

When Elko, for the sake of convenience and proximity, suggests the Monte Carlo sports bar, Lena shudders and says Monte Carlo has too much negative energy. He asks if he should call Las Vegas information for positive energy bars, and sees Lena's fists clench tight. Maybe she'll hit him. Instead she says, "I'd like to go to Paris."

So, they walk down to Paris. The air's nice—high seventies, low eighties. Perfect Vegas weather. When Elko tries to readdress his previous questions, Lena says, "Let's sit first. And order. I think better with a drink in my hand."

"And twice as well with a drink in each."

They walk without talking. Every once in a while, she falls into Elko. "Sorry," she says, "balance."

"Not enough or too much?" Elko asks.

"If you wouldn't try to be funny, I'd like you better," she says.

"Liking me isn't necessary," he tells her. "I'm not like you. I don't need skin on my skin."

At Paris, they decide to sit outside at Le Café Ile St. Louis. It's warm; there's a breeze. Elko orders a double Tanqueray Ten on the rocks. Lena orders a Long Island Iced Tea. They each order a salad.

"I think we need to talk money again," Elko announces. "When I used the word *fee* yesterday, it seemed to go over your head. I'm not cheap."

"I never thought you were," Lena says.

"Four hundred a day, plus expenses," Elko says.

"Sounds reasonable. Sounds fair."

They clink glasses. "The question I want to hear you answer," is this: If Mark were to *choose* to disappear—some fantasy—where would it be? Where's his Fantasy Island? And why would he want to get away from *you*?"

13 ♦ Billy Spence: Headshot, Resume, in Action

Billy Spence got his training at Yale Drama School, where he was an actor fascinated with the art of theatrical makeup. When people ask him: *Were you at Yale with Meryl Streep?* what Billy wants to say is, *How old do you think I am?* Instead, he says, *Since you asked, and for the record: yeah, I've worked with Meryl,* which is true because he did some of her makeup on the set of *The Hours.*

Like a million other actors, Billy went to New York after Yale. And he'd actually done fairly steady work for almost four years. He'd done a very strange version of August Strindberg's very strange play, *The Dance of Death.* He'd done a workshop of an Edward Albee play, *The Goat,* that didn't get produced until much, much later, then won the Pulitzer Prize. Billy played the goat. That's, at least, what he told people. He'd done six weeks on *Days of Our Lives,* from which he made enough money to stay in New York nearly two more years. He'd done the O'Neill Playwriting Conference. He'd done Sundance, where he'd had a role in a reading of Tony Kushner's (unfinished yet) *Angels in America.*

But more than acting, Billy's real passion is for transforming people's faces—making old people young, young people old; making thin people fat, fat people thinner. He can erase gender, given the time. He can make timid people monstrous. Messiahs and magicians transform water to wine, loaves to fishes; Billy Spence transforms Beauty to the Beast, the Beast to Beauty.

At times of loss and crisis, any of us, if we're wise, return to strengths, which is what Billy did an hour after he left the Latino slashed and bleeding in the alley behind the Imperial Palace. He's come to Vegas with three roles to play, and he still has one. With the right performance and ideal circumstances, he might still leave the city with at least a couple million.

He's taken a six-month lease on a studio apartment at the Vegas Towers on East Flamingo. It's come with its own minimal furniture—a serviceable bed, cookware, dishes, a couple chairs, a couch, some lamps. What he's added is an elaborate computer workstation. Billy learned computers when he was very young. By the time he was ten, he was having Internet conversations with others all over the country. He has a dozen different imagined names: *Karl Bennett* is an astronomer. *Willie Clare* is an inmate at Folsom Prison. *April Zephyr* came later. *April* is an expensive call girl with a serious cocaine habit. And almost as soon as Billy found *April,* her alter-ego older sister, *Sister Loraine* followed. *Sister Loraine* is a penitent in a religious order. She chats with CEOs of Fortune 500 corporations—at first humble and shy in her words; minimal, pious, but quickly evolving into statements like: *What I want is to fuck you. I want to fuck a man as powerful as God.*

Actually, it was through *Sister Loraine* that Billy Spence's first Internet crime had occurred. A pharmaceutical CEO became so enamored with *Sister Loraine* that he became willing to unsecure certain secured corporate secrets—opening certain informational doors just a crack; still, a wide enough crack for Billy to slip into and gain access. There were a half-dozen hits over a two-week period for a total of just under eighty thousand—money that didn't get zipped into a vest but got zip-disked through two phantom accounts.

This was how Billy began to work his game in Las Vegas. His second phantom account was in the name of *Harley Hanson*. In Billy's mind, *Harley Hanson* is a Minnesota ski-mobile manufacturer. What Billy did to get his eighty thousand in hand was first to make himself up to fit his mental image of *Harley Hanson*—jowly, red-faced, blond-going-to-gray hair, leisure suit. Then he went to the Tropicana in Las Vegas and inquired about setting up an account. When he was able to give the account numbers and routing numbers that would allow the transfer of all but five of the eighty thousand to a casino account, management gave him the account and credit line willingly.

Through the arrangement, Billy learned all the details and facets of those who have casino accounts. He hacked into his own account and saw what was on file:

> personal signature
> photo images
> credit card companies and numbers
> date of birth
> marital status
> contact information (phones, e-mail, FAX)
> how client would like to be addressed while visiting
> playing patterns
> drink preferences
> food preferences
> sexual preferences

Over the last four years and with the help of algorithms, Billy has set up casino accounts for: *Thomas D. Claverly* at Harrah's, *E. Wilson McFarland* at the Venetian, *Chas Benake* at Wynn and *Wendy Lowenstein* at New York New York. In the process, he's grown intimately familiar with the format of high-roller "whale" accounts. Billy knows that when a casino executive or pit boss pulls up account information—together with an account history—it's all pretty much boilerplate.

So, Billy has come to Las Vegas casinos and played the entire fictional cast of his characters. *Wendy Lowenstein* was fun. Drag amuses Billy. Wendy ended up a redhead with big boobs who chain-smokes. She wears Donna Karan culottes and a Hawaiian shirt. She hums show tunes—especially from *Mame* and *Gypsy*—to herself at the blackjack table and drives the other players crazy. And, best of all, on her first outing, *Wendy Lowenstein*—when she played only a half hour, after taking the first thirty thousand out of her account—*won!* She'd walked off with all her rerouted money plus seven thousand. Usually, Billy will have to forfeit a thousand, two thousand, in play for a half hour before he cashes in. But *Wendy* had a great opening night.

This afternoon—in hopes of recouping even a third of his vest money—Billy is doing drag again. And not only is he doing a woman, he's doing a Chinese woman, *Yung Hi Chow*. If you're an actor at Billy's level, challenge is critical.

Yung Hi Chow is *real*. She's from Macau and the recent widow of *Elgin Chow*, a commercial real-estate developer and construction company magnate, who's left her well over a billion in assets. She loves blackjack—especially in Las Vegas—and Billy has hacked his way into her MGM/Mirage whale account—as he has with *J. Bob Marshall* and—in the Caesars files—*Tony Campisi*. Billy's studied Yung Hi's signature. He's blown up her photographs life size—one of them is taped up in his makeup room.

That has been the game plan of Billy's hit-and-run mission. First, he's cracked the whale files of two of the world's largest casino corporations—MGM/Mirage and Caesars. Next, he's studied the individual profiles—looking for a part, looking for a challenge. Who will be amusing to play? Who will allow him to be the most theatrical? Who will pose the most intriguing challenges and obstacles? What roles would qualify him for the Scam-Artist Tony awards? The Embezzlement Oscars?

It's also important that he select high rollers whose profiles reflect no planned September visits. If he can find players with large enough accounts whose last visit has been in March, then there will probably be just enough recognition that he'll be treated well. Also, it's important to find players whose standard markers are three hundred thousand and above. That way he can accumulate a million or more in only two or three acts before he leaves the audience, wanting more, in their seats.

J. Bob Marshall, for instance, always writes half-million markers. He plays dice—placing the four inside numbers with occasional huge bets on the hardways. He presses all of his bets aggressively and always orders dealers around as though they were ranch hands. He's vicious to black men but likes to sleep with black women. He drinks Maker's Mark—sometimes on the rocks, sometimes in orange juice. He once hit a million-dollar bet on a fourteen-to-one horse. His bet affected the pari-mutuel odds so much, he only won three hundred thousand, but he had no complaints. His credit line with MGM/Mirage was twenty million.

To fill his vest—the vest that Mark Goodson will later empty into the room safe in his Mirage suite—Billy has first played Tony Campisi at the Hilton for a million-four then J. Bob Marshall at The Mirage for just over two million. Yung Hi Chow has a MGM/Mirage credit line of *fifty* million. Her usual marker is for seven hundred thousand. If Billy plays her for only three scenes, three sessions—once this afternoon, twice during the graveyard shift—he can recoup almost two million.

Of course, two million isn't three, and it certainly isn't five—but it will keep him in dance shoes for the Rainbow Room. Yung Hi Chow has a reputation—notorious—for playing through the night, so the late graveyard sessions wouldn't seem out of the ordinary. Casino Services always comps Yung Hi Chow a suite—two elegant rooms with a full bar, a small forest of ficus trees and an enormous dressing room. Billy has the name of Yung Hi's casino host, Jason Gwynn. For eighteen hours, he can use the room as a base of operations. Then split.

In his condo dressing room, Billy studies his mirror, *Yung Hi's* mirror, *whoever's*—all the world's a stage! He's getting there. Except he needs to corset himself, pull his waist in more, make it more waspish. At five nine, he's probably three inches taller than Yung Hi, but for the most part he'll be sitting, so that should work. What next? He's changed the color of his eyes, blackened his hair. Just a little more cotton stuffed up over the gums should get the cheeks right. Some adhesive strips should pull the eyes back and up; he can pancake over them. And some latex should do the right re-shape of the mouth.

He touches his face. He puts the tips of two of his fingers on his tongue. Billy loves his body—the plasticity of it: how it can be tucked and padded and reshaped. Most actors hate latex, but he loves it—what it can do, the transformations it's capable of. And, most of all, Billy loves having sex as another person, in another person's skin and body. He has never had sex, yet, as a woman—although Wendy Lowenstein got her share of offers and had, riding up in an elevator, kissed a black man and allowed herself to be felt up. Becoming another person is like having sex with that person. Billy loves that his skin—through the magic of makeup—belongs to so many people.

But he hates whoever it was who walked off with his vest. He had sewn in the lining and the zippered pockets himself! And if he can find that person—it's not even a question—he'll kill him. Kill *her*? Not likely with the vest stolen from a men's room, but it doesn't matter. It's a sin and a mortal sin—like somebody in an audience yelling something over the footlights at an actor during a performance. It's intolerable. Someone doing that should simply die.

Too much goes into any major performance. And Billy has been brilliant as J. Bob Marshall. Standing ovation, King of the World material! Breaking the concentration, breaking the flow of things bound to a performance like that, is unthinkable. Anyone guilty of such a breach has to die. Billy believes that. And die violently!

Almost ready! A little cadmium yellow tinged with just a touch of burnt umber worked into the skin—face and neck, back of the hands. How are the eyebrows? Billy checks Yung Hi's picture. He can get just a little more point. Good. Almost time to call a cab to McCarran, where he knows a fully stocked—plum wine and dim sum—Mirage limo will be waiting for him...because he's set it up, written the script.

Billy walks to his closet. There are three silk dresses, two of which he found back in New York in a consignment shop above a Chinese bakery on Pell Street. He lifts the sky blue one on its hanger, holds it up to himself. He wrinkles his nose. Blue isn't his color. He tries the emerald green dress and likes it. He can wear it with the black velvet jacket and the black pearls. And the lipstick that he has renamed *Dried Blood*.

By one thirty, Billy-as-Yung-Hi has a Mirage room key in his purse and is sitting in the high-stakes room with seven hundred thousand in chips sitting in front of him—betting a thousand a hand and sipping a Chopin vodka martini. The six-deck shoe is being kind. Yung Hi has pressed a thousand to three thousand to five thousand, split eights, gotten a three on one of eights, doubled down and won all three bets. She keeps the next three bets at five thousand and wins all three. If Billy walks away now, he'll have a bonus thirty-four thousand.

"Nice start, Mrs. C.," the pit boss named Jack smiles.

The file on Yung Hi says her English is minimal. "Sank-ku," Billy half bows, half nods.

"Don't you usually play on the floor?" the pit boss, Jack, asks.

"Too crowd," Billy-as-Yung-Hi says. "Tonight...late."

"Right," Jack says. He seems not to question her.

"Do you want to hit that?" the dealer—Kandace from Kansas City—asks.

Billy scratches and Kandace gives him a breaking card. He pulls his next bet back to two thousand, loses that, cuts back to one. Maybe it's time to cash out. If he loses the next two hands, he'll do that. Yung Hi Chow is famous at The Mirage for changing tables.

"Table-shifter!" has been logged at least a half-dozen times under "Playing Habits."

Billy-as-Yung-Hi loses the next two hands, pushes his chips out into the middle of the table. Jack, the pit boss, is immediately present—as is a hovering and scrutinizing Mirage security guard.

Kandace stacks the chips procedurally—by color and in rows. She does a second count. "Seven-hundred and twenty-four thousand," she says.

The pit boss, Jack, does a count. "Seven hundred and twenty-four thousand," he echoes. He nods to the security guard; the security guard nods back. "Should we put it back into your account, Mrs. C?" Jack asks Billy.

Billy shakes his head. "Safe-deposit box," Billy-as-Yung-Hi says.

It's like the table loses its audio. Jack and Kandace and the security guard triangulate confused glances at each other.

Jack looks unsure—as though he should probably say something in Chinese. "Ma'am?" he tries.

"Safe-deposit box," Billy repeats in his best Yung Hi voice. "Lucky chips," he says. "Keep. Play again." *God, he is giving a great performance!* By three this morning, he'll be *Queen* of the world!

The pit boss, Jack, has his cell phone out and is dialing. "Just a sec. Just a moment, Mrs. C.," he says, then, getting his connection, turns away from the table and has a brief, muted conversation, after which he lowers his phone, pockets it and turns back.

He tells Billy that Yung Hi's chips will be placed in trays, after which, the security guard carrying them, they will walk over and deposit them in a safe-deposit in the cage. "Do you have a safe-deposit box there?" Jack, the pit boss asks.

"Need to get," Billy says.

"We can do that," Jack says.

A second security guard, carrying chip trays arrives. The four gathered employees exchange *these-Chinese-are-weird* glances, but the trays get filled.

Billy plucks a lilac-colored five-hundred chip from one of the trays and slides it across the table to Kandace.

"Thank you, Ma'am," Kandace says.

Twenty minutes later, Billy has seven hundred thousand in chips and twenty-four thousand in cash in a Mirage safe-deposit box. And he has the key to the box in his pocket. Everyone has been so nice!

Billy-as-Yung-Hi baby-steps around the casino. After all, when he'd been a tiny girl, hadn't his feet been bound? He orders another

Chopin martini and is drinking it and watching a game of pai gow when his attention jumps to a man approaching down the carpet. Something clicks; there's a shock of recognition. Because he's a master of disguises, Billy's a master of faces, postures, gestures, body shapes. And this is a familiar shape, a remembered face. *That guy! That navy blazer! When had Billy seen—?*

What flashes into his head are two words: *men's room.* This morning, when Billy had returned to The Mirage men's room...hadn't this been the man coming out? Except—? Except in Billy's memory...the man in the blue blazer coming out had been...*heavier?*

Bingo! Jesus Christ! The vest! That had to have been the man who found the—!

The man has passed him and is taking long strides. Billy tries to follow, but his tight silk dress binds him. He tries shuffling faster, but he understands how absurd it is, how much it makes him look like a cartoon, so he stops. The blue blazer has stopped just a bit ahead to watch the play at a blackjack table, so Billy-as-Yung-Hi moves again, closes the distance at a pace which he hopes doesn't make him appear foolish.

Then—*shit!*—the man is off again. And heading toward the elevators!

Once again, Billy hurries. He sees the man hook a left into the bay of elevators for the top floors and moves as swiftly as he can. But just as Billy arrives at the bay, an elevator closes, and Billy watches its numbers ascend—stopping at the twenty-seventh floor—where it pauses for no more than ten seconds before descending. Which means the blue blazer had been the only passenger...which means the man who stole Billy's vest has a room on the twenty-seventh floor.

Billy-as-Yung-Hi takes an elevator up. Beyond the marble lobby of the twenty-seventh floor, three corridors lead away, each housing at least fifty rooms. Guests come and go in the corridors, but none are the blue blazer. A couple in shorts arriving at the elevators and seeing Billy asks, "Ma'am? You look upset. You all right?"

"Sank-ku," Billy bows.

"Are...you...lost?" the man asks, speaking the slow speech natives sometimes speak to a foreigner.

"I fine," Billy says.

"Would...you...like...us...to...send...someone...from... security...up?"

"No sank-ku," Billy shakes his head. He wants these people the-fuck-away.

The couple wishes him a good night, take their elevator. What can Billy do? If he can get his vest back, he won't have to play *Yung-Hi* any more. But finding blue-blazer's room...!

He can walk the green-on-black carpeted corridors, knock on every door and say, "Housekeeping—" But come on! In this outfit? He's a fine actor, brilliant often, but the script won't hold up. And trying to keep a watch on three corridors, hoping that the man in the blue blazer will emerge and Billy will have an accurate spot on his room is unreasonable. He can go back to Vegas Towers and hack into the current registrations on Mirage's twenty-seventh floor, but it won't tell him what he needs to know.

Jesus, *the man is staying here!* The vest—the three-million-dollar vest, Billy's beautiful vest—is down one of these corridors! Waiting for him! Asshole! Blue-blazered fuck!

Billy goes to his Yung Hi Chow's suite, a floor above Mr. Blue Blazer. All his pistons are firing adrenalin. His skull feels clamped. He paces, drinks some scotch. In a kind of mantra, he tells and retells himself: *focus on what's possible!*

Focus on what's possible! Point of fact: he might be *wrong* about the man in the blue blazer. He's seen the man only twice and for a total of about four minutes. The first time—in the men's room door—had been five seconds at best.

Probably—because he needs to find *some*one, blame *some*one— he's leaping to a conclusion. What he needs to do—for the moment at least—is let it go.

Focus on what's possible! Two more Yung Hi playing sessions after midnight and he'll leave The Mirage with at least a couple million. That will last him a while. He's been brilliant tonight as Yung Hi! Radiant! Enigmatic! Billy writes the headlines of his own review. *Run Don't Walk to Your Nearest Mirage Casino and See...!!!* She's been fun to play. *Focus on what's possible!*

Billy sleeps fitfully until well after midnight. When he wakes, his mouth tastes like raw scotch; his head still feels pinched. He drinks water, gargles, studies himself. The image of Mr. Blue Blazer floats into his head and floats out. *Focus on what's possible!*

In the small suitcase he's carried into The Mirage as Yung Hi, there's makeup, makeup brushes, creams, hair pieces, latex, flesh-colored tape, pancake, powders. He sets everything he will need to revive himself as Yung Hi Chow out on the vanity, sits, and studies his face.

Should he just strip everything off and start again, build Yung Hi from the ground up? That will take a couple hours, maybe even three, which means he'll probably not be able to begin to play until after four. Assuming two play sessions with at least a two-hour break between, it might be at least six in the morning before he has his chips and cash from the safe-deposit box and is gone.

He opts for *repair* rather than *rebuilding,* still it isn't until well after four in the morning that he's signing his second marker for seven-hundred thousand—this time at a hundred-dollar minimum table on the main floor. This time, the pit boss is named Rebecca. "I'm showing that you have at least this much here in a safe-deposit box. Do you want to play with that?" Rebecca asks.

"No sank-ku," Billy-as-Yung-Hi says, his voice catching, like a slightly serrated edge, on the delivery.

"You don't think it would be easier to—?"

Billy-as-Yung-Hi shakes his head...*her* head. Bad luck," she says.

"Your choice," Rebecca says, and turns back to her pit computer, where she does a player search: Yung Hi Chow. She studies the profile, quick-scanning the recent visits. Reviewing the current one, she finds a surprising detail. Yung Hi shows up being hosted in two different twelfth-floor suites. It's atypical data, but Rebecca's savvy; this is not her first rodeo; she knows Asians often come with...what's management's word? *Entourages.* Extended family. So, two suites...credit line of two million. An entourage would be accommodated; she's seen it.

Moments later, she crosses back to Yung Hi's table. No harm in a double-check. "Do you have two rooms, Mrs. C? I'm showing that you have two suites on the twenty-eighth floor."

Billy's head goes white. *Ohshitohfuck, she's here! The lead's walked on stage with the understudy! Nevermind: Play through! Play through! Stay in the moment!*

Billy swift-processes. *Okay, could be either a data-entry error... or...*He takes a stab. "Friend," Billy-as-Yung-Hi says.

"Well, given who you are, you could probably have *twenty* rooms." Rebecca laughs.

"Twenty room—Sank-ku—good idea! Next time! Twenty room!" Billy-as-Yung-Hi laughs.

Rebecca laughs. "Good luck, Mrs. C," she says and walks away.

Billy-as-Yung-Hi has seven-hundred thousand in chips stacked in front of him. The dealer is a huge black man with a name tag that reads: BOSS. Boss is stone silent and without affect. Billy-as-Yung-Hi pushes a lilac five-hundred chip out and loses. Boss says nothing.

Rebecca's now obliquely behind Boss, watching.

"Cash in," Billy-as-Yung-Hi says. Something has begun to feel very wrong to Billy. Something has begun to feel fucked. Two *Antigones* on stage at the same time—he can see—is just asking for trouble. Big trouble. He pushes his chips forward.

Rebecca crosses to the table.

"She says she wants to cash in," Boss reports.

"Mrs. C! You've barely sat down!"

"Cash in," Billy-as-Yung-Hi says emphatically.

"I tell you what—" Rebecca begins.

"What we'll do is: count these, credit them to your account. That way—"

Billy, opening Yung Hi's purse, begins sweeping handfuls into it. Chips are money. Maybe he'll move to Las Vegas and simply redeem five or ten thousand when he needs it.

Rebecca motions for security. A tall, black pit supervisor—cell phone to his ear—moves in. He bends down, speaking in confidence to Rebecca, but Billy's ear for cues is acute, and he hears. "She wants to keep her checks in her safe-deposit," the supervisor says. "For luck."

Billy finishes his chip-sweeping, closes the black purse and slides from his chair.

"Mrs. C—" the pit supervisor says. "Please, security needs to walk you over to the—"

Before any security arrives, Billy's off—the supervisor's voice fading behind—off and into the traffic. *Jesus, walking's a bitch*, he thinks. *And walking Chinese is even bitchier!* The problem with tight silk dresses and designer shoes is you have to move like an insect.

Christ, he's hungry and needs a drink but is bound up in constricting clothes. It's four thirty in the morning, and life in the theater isn't all glamour. And, right now, it sucks. Billy thinks he best go to his suite and order room service.

Or—! An on-stage and an off-stage Billy scramble in the pleasure-center of his brain. Why not simply push ahead? Test the limits? Find another blackjack table, make his last seven-hundred thousand withdrawal from Yung Hi Chow's account before she comes down later?

Billy tries to take his own pulse. Which is he feeling more of, greed or simple satisfaction?

It's an uncharacteristic moment, but greed somehow steps aside.

And Billy plays what he knows are his best trump cards: satisfaction and reason.

Too many red flags have already been tripped; they flap in The Mirage's posh, ventilated air. You can only have two Hamlets on stage for so long before something's rotten in Denmark. Billy tries, briefly, to believe that the host arranging the real Yung Hi's suite simply thought that Billy-as-Yung-Hi wanted another room. But the script won't fly—even with some quick Billy-adrenalin-high rewrites. No. Curtain down. Forget the epilogue.

Back in his suite, Billy changes to Billy, chugs from a Maker's Mark bottle, finishes the sashimi he'd room-serviced for dinner, isn't satisfied. Some invisible prompter keeps stage-whispering that he should go down again, walk the floor. *Why?* Billy thinks. *It's in the script. Just do it,* the invisible prompter says.

So Billy does. Listens to the voice. Descends. Wanders. Here. There. Casino floor. High-stakes room. Baccarat. And it's all...*nothing.* Bullshit ambiance. College kids. Middle-of-the-night degenerates. *In the script? Fuck you, prompter; I'm going to bed.*

But before ascending, yet again, to his suite, Billy swings by the lobby, where he glances down at the empty line of reception positions— empty except for one man finishing his check out.

And a flashbulb goes off in Billy's brain. Then another! It's a familiar shape, familiar headshot. Billy blinks; his vision blurs. The man finishing his checkout is wearing a tan summer suit. The reddish hair...No blue blazer obviously, still—!

The man completes his check out and begins walking toward Billy. The outline of his body is right! Billy moves in front of the man, blocks his path. "Excuse me," Billy says. He stares into the man's eyes, replays the man's cheekbones, eyebrows. They seem the same eyes he had stared into early the previous morning at the entrance to the men's room. This man looks thinner...except his face.

"I'm sorry," the man says and tries to move around Billy.

The curtain is up; the overture's playing, and Billy's into a new role. "Don't I—? I swear I know you!" Billy says. "Charlie?"

"No. I'm sorry."

"You're not from Scottsdale? Wait! Jack!"

The man shakes his head, holds a hand up in denial, tries to move past.

"Help me! C'mon, I know you," Billy says.

"I don't think so," the man says. He looks momentarily dazed and uneasy.

"Okay, not to be rude but just to satisfy myself that I'm mistaken: tell me your name. Mine's Billy; Billy Spence. You'd be?"

"Anthony."

"Anthony."

"Anthony Francis," the man says.

"From?"

The man looks—Billy believes—either angry or…it's possible, panicked. Blood is swelling the size of his neck. "Boise, Idaho," the man-calling-himself-Anthony-Francis finally says.

"Tony Francis…Tony Francis…" Billy chanted. "Boise, Idaho. But not always, right? Before that?"

"Naples, Florida."

"Wait a minute! You're married to a woman named?"

"I'm not married."

"But you *were.*"

The man draws a breath and, when he draws it, looks vaguely gilled and desperate—fishlike.

"You *were.*"

"Once. Yes."

"To a woman named?"

"Look, I'm sorry. I need to get to the airport," the man says.

"Share a cab?" Billy suggests. "Same destination. I'm going to the airport, too."

"Well, I'm meeting some people outside," the man says.

"Sure," Billy says. "Tony Francis. It's very familiar." *Mr. Blue Blazer,* Billy's brain is drumming. *Mr. Blue Blazer…Mr. Blue Blazer.*

"People look like other people," the man-calling-himself-Anthony-Francis says.

"All the time," Billy says. "I know. They do. I believe that. Take care."

"Take care," the man says and begins walking.

But Billy, fierce as a little fox terrier, pulls alongside him. They cross through the entrance doors together and out under the porte cochere—both moving into the taxi line.

"How was your luck?" Billy asks.

"I had one good morning. The rest of the time, not so good," the man says.

"*One good morning.* So, how good is good?" Billy asks. Then, in his best annoying-character role, pushes ahead. "Look, I'm nosey; I'm a nosey stranger; indulge me; we're in Las Vegas; the sun is out. How good is good? Your one morning."

"Not bad."

"Where to, sir?" the doorman asks, opening the cab for the man. The man hesitates. "The airport," he mumbles.

The cab door shuts, the cab rolls out. The next cab slides into place. "Where to?" the doorman asks Billy.

"I'm with my friend," Billy says, sliding in, nodding to the cab ahead. The cab door shuts. "I'm with my friend in the cab ahead," Billy tells the driver. "I don't know where the hell I'm going, but he does."

14 ♦ Elko Sniffs Around

"Because, too often I try to punish *myself* by punishing someone I love," Lena answers to Elko's: *Why would Mark want to get away from you?*

"Well, yeah, that'd do it," he agrees.

"No question. Except, of course, that Mark loves me and needs me," Lena says.

Elko switches the subject back to his fees. "Okay, I'll need three thousand up front," he says. "If I find your husband in the next hour, I'll give you twenty-eight hundred back."

Lena does a slow drain of her first glass of red. "That's fine," she says.

"So, agreed?"

"Sure. Why not? Given that you're so agreeable. Except—"

"Except?"

"Except I don't have any money. I mean, any of *that* kind of money. That is…*with* me," she says.

Elko says, no problem; he's easy. He'll take a check. A credit card.

"Mark handles our money," Lena says. "That's his job."

Elko nods.

"That's his profession. He keeps track. When I need money, I just ask and he gives it."

Now it's Elko's turn for glass-draining. "Whoa. Back up, wait a minute," he says.

"You'll get paid," Lena says. "Please. I wouldn't hire you, if I wasn't paying you. Can I have another cabernet?"

Elko waves the waiter over, touches the rim of Lena's glass.

"So, let's just say—argument for the sake of argument—that your husband's gone, that I can't work the magic that I work. Given that he's the dude holding all the purse strings, how then—in that event— do I get paid?" Elko asks.

"Easy. Once I'm home, I write a check on his account," Lena says.

"*His* account. I see. How do you do that?"

"Forge it."

"Right. Or course."

"I do it all the time."

Elko takes into his lungs half of the ozone in the air from the lake at Bellagio, holds it.

"Don't back out. Don't cancel this. Really," Lena pleads. "Don't. Please; please don't. Mr. Wells, I need you. Mark's my whole life. I can't live without him. You can have my car."

"I can—?"

"Have my car."

"Do you have it with you?"

"No, it's in Naples."

"Make and year?"

"Mercedes. Not even two years old. Or—"

It seems she has a bright idea. She tears open her purse.

Her second cabernet arrives. Elko asks for more gin.

"Just a minute…just a minute…just a minute!" She pulls a small leather album of photos from some pit near the bottom of her purse. "How about a condo?" she says. "On Boca Grande. It's in my name."

"What if I never find him? What if I find him and he's dead?" Elko asks.

"If you just stick with me, let me be your client," she says. "Everything will be fine."

She pushes her photos at him, open to a snapshot of a condo complex on the water somewhere. She turns the page to a second snap of a cathedral-ceilinged interior, which leads out onto a balcony, overlooking water.

"It's very nice," she says. "Here. This place. Two bedrooms. Big kitchen. I would give it to you furnished."

Elko studies what's-been-presented. "Pardon my bluntness, but this is crazy," he says. "Capital-C crazy."

"Possibly. But that's fine. Because *I'm* crazy," she says. She studies Elko, her eyes like a refugee's. "Please," she says and reaches, yet another time, for his hand.

Elko withdraws his hand. "Someone should buy you a chain of worry beads," he says. "So, do you carry the title and registration to your Mercedes in your purse? You ready to sign it over to me? What's the year?"

"It's a year old. But I don't—"

"Never mind. And it's only because I don't like myself when I'm distrustful, so okay. I'm going to need some things," Elko says.

He tells her that he'd like the URLS on any of Mark's e-mail accounts—business and personal—plus the passwords. Also, he says, he needs Mark's client lists for the past three years. Phone bills. All their credit-card statements. Access to any of Mark's business records. Finally—and given that she has the mini photo-album out—he asks her if she's got a picture.

"You want—?" she starts. Behind her eyes, her head looks like it might be a smoke-filled room.

"Here, I'll write my list down," Elko says, and lifts a small spiral out of his jacket. He writes out what he's enumerated, tearing the pages out and handing them across the table to Lena.

"You're asking for a lot of private information," Lena says.

"Disappearing is a private act," Elko reminds her.

She studies the list. I've never even *seen* some of this information," she says. "Mark's the bookkeeper. He keeps the records."

"Well, in his absence—"

"I'll try; I'll do my best," Lena says

Elko learns that Mark has a secretary at his office who might provide the files and access. Lena agrees to call and okay her cooperating.

Elko reminds her again that he needs a picture.

"Mark's camera-shy," she says.

"So, nothing in there?" He points at the mini photo-album.

She riffles the collection all housed in soft, milky Lucite then stops at one photo, studies it, wrinkles her nose. "He hates this picture," she says. Then she points to a photo of two men standing on a dock with a boat behind them. The two are holding a large fish over their heads. "Tuna," she says, and points to the older of the two men. "That's my father," she says. "He's a monster. He was a spy. We were living in Saudi Arabia when I turned sixteen. For a birthday present, he sold me for the night to a Saudi...*whatever*...for ten thousand dollars."

"For *your* birthday present?"

"He figured, kill two birds. Initiate me sexually and make a buck. That was the way he was."

"And he and Mark are...excuse me, *buddies?*"

"They're like father and son. They adore each other."

"So, then, this is Mark?" Elko points. "Here? On the left?"

"Yes. But, like I said, he hates this picture."

Elko slips the album gently from her, studies the shot. Lena's father looks groomed and calculating. Mark, looks overgrown and like a nine-year-old who's just awakened. His hair's uncombed. The back of his hand's pressed against his forehead—fingers spread wide—in an attempt to shade the sun. "Is this a reasonable likeness?" Elko asks.

"Well—"

"*Reasonable*. All I'm asking is if it's *reasonable*. In *likeness*. If you tell me that Mark's actually short and blond, I'm dropping the case."

Lena retrieves the album and photo from Elko, studies it. "Okay, yeah; sure: *reasonable*."

Elko stretches his hand back toward the snap. "Can I have it?"

"He won't be dressed like that," Lena says. "He'll be wearing a pair of khaki slacks, a blue shirt and a blue blazer. That's his uniform."

Elko slips the photo out of its sleeve and notices that Lena's about to order her third glass of wine. He holds a hand up like a traffic cop to stop her then tells her he needs to have something checked out at TI. He says he wants the management there to check the room lock to see whether anyone used a key between the time she and Mark went out to dinner and the time she got back well after midnight.

"And? I'm sorry, what will that tell you?" she asks.

"Maybe Mark made a quick stop at the room. You know, before his final vanishing."

"Why?"

"To pick up something."

"What?"

"*I* don't know. *Something*." Elko's beginning to feel agitated. "Something he left there. It would be an indication of whether Mark's thin-air act is of his own devising. Or whether someone else intercepted him and might have him. *Don't ask who!*"

Lena stares at him wide-eyed.

On their way down to Treasure Island, Lena turns to Elko out of the blue and says a single word. She says, "Eagle." When he doesn't respond immediately, she says, "Eagle's probably the password. For his e-mails. I mean, I can't be sure, but *Eagle* is what he uses everywhere else when he needs a password. The Boy Scout thing again."

Elko makes a note.

"You're not married," she says. It's less a question; more an announcement. "Unmarried—and my guess is: unavailable."

Elko says, yes, she's right.

"You *wanted* to be though. Once. Right?" She's staring at him.

Again, he tells her she's right.

"Her name was…Don't tell me; it's coming…it's coming; I'm seeing it. Her name was—what a pretty name, so unusual—*Clea*."

Elko stops, stunned. Stares.

"Information comes to me," she says. "I told you that. Under the right conditions and at certain times, it comes. I'm a receiver."

"Okay, so what happened?" he asks, finding what's just happened both exciting and disturbing. "Between Clea and me—why didn't we marry?"

"Do *you* know?" he hears Lena ask.

"I wish I did," Elko confesses, and it's honest.

"You still might."

"Unlikely. I have no idea where she is."

"She's in Taos, New Mexico," Lena reveals.

"I see. Taos, New Mexico. Really."

"Really."

"Okay, so what's her phone number?" Elko asks.

"I have no idea." Lena says. "I'm a kind of abstract impressionist… with my voices. With my information. I mean, it's fierce; it comes… but it's piecemeal. And I probably wouldn't give it to you anyway. I have some ethics."

Elko feels the way he did in the crucial Detroit Lion's game when he made the tackle head-on and got the concussion.

"Are you all right?" Lena asks.

"Yeah, sure. I'm fine," Elko says. He takes a deep breath, stretches his neck muscles. "Should I not say anything to you?" she asks. "When the voices speak? When I receive things about you? When they come into my head?"

"Let's both just try to keep our eyes on the ball here," he suggests. "On the task at hand. Finding Mark."

At Treasure Island, the management agrees to check the room's lock for entry times. Lena asks a security guard whether he might get her some Treasure Island stationery and—while he's out getting it— maybe bring along a notary public who's on staff. "I want to write a document for my friend and have it notarized," she says. "It's an important document."

He points her to the Guest Services desk in the lobby. "They'll help you," he says.

Twenty minutes later—with the help of a pseudo-lawyer on the

T.I. Guest Services staff—Lena hands Elko a notarized document conveying transference of her Boca Grande condo from herself to him. Elko thanks her and says he'd be perfectly happy to settle for the Mercedes.

"My car's in Mark's name," she says.

Elko starts to protest this arrangement, then thinks better of it and agrees to stay with the case until Mark is found "*in whatever condition*" the document reads, "*or for a period of time not exceeding three years.*" He folds the document lengthwise and slips it into his jacket pocket.

They agree to check in with each other later in the day. Lena wraps her arms around Elko. "I'm glad you're in this," she says. "We're going to be a good team."

He eases her away. "Most of the work I do, I do alone," he advises her.

When Elko gets back to the office, Betina-Betina tells him that George Bush and Dolly Parton are having an affair.

"As long as it doesn't interfere with their work," he says.

"Dolly called me an hour ago. She's pretty excited," Betina-Betina says.

"Well, it couldn't be happening to two nicer people."

"Oh!" Betina-Betina says, remembering. "The Orleans called. They'd like Kobe Bryant and Brittany Spears at Brendan's Irish Pub tonight. And somebody who could act as Kobe's bodyguard."

"Did you make the calls?"

"I did. Everyone, but the bodyguard."

Elko rolls over a half-dozen possibilities, then decides. "Use Steven Seagal," he says. "He'll appreciate the work."

Betina-Betina asks how things went with Lance Burton, and Elko confesses that he still has a lot of questions. "They were almost too cooperative," he says. "It was as though—like the missing husband—I had volunteered for a trick. Like both of us, but especially me, were just the props in an illusion." Elko tells her about his taking the disappearance/ reappearance journey, and that—when he'd gotten back—Lena Goodson had freaked out. "There are more stable women," he says.

"You want to know what my advice is?" she asks.

He takes a stab: "Watch out," he offers.

"*Double* watch-out," she says.

Elko tells Betina-Betina that his current and best read is that Mark Goodson's gone because the trick gave him the opportunity of a lifetime, and he took it. But he may have given Lance Burton, or someone in Lance Burton's crew, a payoff for help.

"So, you don't believe in magic?" Betina-Betina says.

Elko doesn't even swing at her pitch; it's such a slider. "Hey, listen, *magic's* not even magic." And he explains all the behind the scenes, boxes-within-boxes, and black curtains.

"Disillusioning," Betina-Betina grins. "Did she write a check?"

Elko announces himself as the proud owner of a two-bedroom condo on Boca Grande.

Betina-Betina takes her red Ferragamo shoe off and, holding it by the heel, points it at him like a .38. "Pow!" she says.

"Pow," he acknowledges.

"So, where do you start?" Betina-Betina asks.

Elko informs her that he's having TI check the Goodson's room-lock activation times. "My hunch is: he had something stashed there, came back and picked it up." He pulls out and shows her Mark Goodson's picture.

"He looks like a teddy bear on a bad hair day," Betina-Betina says.

"Raggedy Andy."

"Who's the other guy? Looks like a paid assassin."

"Lena says he is. He's her father."

"Maybe Daddy killed Hubby."

"Anything's possible." Elko starts into his office.

"I'll call Steven Seagal," Betina-Betina says. "If he's not available, who should I try next?"

"Your call." Elko shrugs. "Stallone or Hulk Hogan," he says, and he closes his door.

Inside his office, Elko scans the husband photo, then using Photoshop, he plays with it. He does a blow-up of the face and sends it over to Faye and the Bloody Marys. He attaches it to an e-mail, where he tries to give Faye and whoever-else-might-be-interested the background. He tells Faye that his radar hasn't found anything on the screen yet, so it would be nice if hers could.

She pops him back a reply calling him *Lover,* saying that she misses their white-zinfandel encounters and that she'll post the photo on the Marys message board. She adds a: *Where have you been? Is there a reason that you've become the Invisible Man?*

Elko replies and promises to drop by Bally's during her swing shift tomorrow. She replies saying: *hey, come on,* she doesn't miss him during *work.* Forget dropping in on her at *work;* it's the *after*-work stuff between them that she misses.

Every couple of months or so, Elko and Faye hang out in bed together, just the two of them...and some ice and some white zin. If they're feeling especially frisky, some Crown Royal. And they talk and they don't talk. They laugh a lot. And then there are all the sounds that they're not responsible for.

Elko plays a little more with the picture. First, he tries to make the face into the face of a man who works with money—a financial advisor, a CPA. He can't. Whatever he does, the face and large sums of money don't line up. Mark Goodson's face stays the face of a kid who has to do chores for his allowance.

Elko gets a call from the manager of housekeeping at TI. Nothing activated the room lock Tuesday night between 5:58 PM and 1:13 AM, which means that wherever Mark Goodson went or was taken after his disappearance, nothing was retrieved from the room. He had what he needed, or—if he'd been abducted—the people who had him had what *they* needed. Elko thanks the manager and asks him for an e-mail address in security where he can send a photo. The manager gives Elko the name and e-mail of a Darryl Hanks. Elko thanks him, hangs up and sends a Mark Goodson image to Darryl.

A message pops onto the screen from Faye. One of the Marys—a Mary named Lynn working on graveyard at Mandalay Bay—thinks she spotted Mark Goodson at around five in the morning. He was playing blackjack alone at a twenty-five-minimum table. She said he looked very drunk—but she described it as *lonely-college-kid kind of drunk*. She brought him a couple of mai tais. He tipped her five dollars the first time and twenty-five the second.

Elko e-mails Faye right back, asking: please could she describe Lynn so that he could pick her out; could she send an e-mail to Lynn saying that he'd be dropping by sometime during her next shift; would she please just move in a little closer to her e-mail keyboard so he could smell her skin.

Then he calls Lena at TI, but she doesn't answer. He leaves a question or two in her voice mail: what does Mark usually drink? Are there ever occasions when he orders mai tais? If so, when?

Betina-Betina knocks on Elko's door. When she comes in she says there's a possible Dennis Rodman who would like to talk with him.

"How is he dressed?" Elko asks.

"Ripped shirt, baggy pants—lots of tattoos."

Elko asks Betina-Betina to explain to the possible Dennis Rodman that he's extremely busy. "Tell him that the *real* Dennis Rodman's in town a lot on his own. There really isn't a market."

Betina-Betina looks reluctant but leaves. A minute and a half later, she's back. "He won't leave," she says. "I think you need to see him. He scares me."

Elko marches out, and the possible Dennis Rodman is sprawled out in an office chair. "This isn't a good time," Elko explains.

Dennis Rodman looks brain-dead and dangerous. He has a look that says, maybe he'll kill Elko for the novelty, for his own amusement. "I jus' got thrown outta the Hard Rock," he informs Elko and starts nodding his head. When neither Elko nor Betina-Betina comments, he goes on. "Pit boss say to me: *Mr. Rodman...nobody's more of a fan than me, but I has to ask you to leave.*"

"So, can you tell us...what you were doing?" Elko asks.

"Talkin'. Tha's all. All I was doin' was talkin'."

"And what were you saying?"

"*Listen here, you muthafuck*—I had this dude by the shirt. Lifted up. They was a crowd. People gather roun' to see me." He stands up, all six foot ten of him, and towers in the office anteroom. "I'm an attraction," he says. "I'm a crowd-maker."

The last thing Elko wants is a scene, so he tells the possible Dennis Rodman that he'll have Betina-Betina fill out a client card for him. And if any of the resorts call for a really colorful NBA legend, they'll ring him up. Elko explains that his start-up look-alikes get paid a hundred-twenty an hour; fifteen percent to the agency.

"I don' work by the hour," the possible Rodman says.

"Well—"

"By the hour's not my style."

"I see. So how *do* you work?"

"On commission." The possible Rodman bobs his head. Smugly. As if he's just made a three-point shot from forty feet out. "On commission," he repeats. "I go in. I be Dennis Rodman. People gather. Word goes out. *Dennis Rodman's over at...wherever—The Hard Rock.* People get into cabs, come over to see me. They play."

Elko tells him he may not be following.

Rodman points an accusing finger and explains that he should get a commission—for attracting the crowd. A percentage of the casino drop. All Mirror Images has to do is set it up. He'll give them their fifteen percent.

Elko says something about the cart and the horse. He says that Betina-Betina will take all his information. They'll do their best to promote him.

"Hey! Promote me?" For some reason, now, he's getting angry.

"Chu jus' say: *Promote me?* I don't need no dudes *promote me*—
I promote *myself!* People *know* me already. People *recognize* me."

An eerie realization creeps over Elko. This is not a *possible* Dennis
Rodman. Betina-Betina's gotten it wrong. This *is* Dennis Rodman—
looking for a job as a Dennis Rodman look-alike. "Might I see your
driver's license, please?" Elko asks.

He fishes in a pocket, produces a billfold, flips it open to his
license.

"Great. Terrific. Thanks, Mr. Rodman," Elko says and smiles.
"Betina-Betina—? Would you take down Mr. Rodman's information?
Set him up on our client list?" Elko salutes Dennis Rodman. Dennis
Rodman salutes back.

"I saw your ad—*Hire a Legend!*—and I thought: *hey, this be me!*"

Back inside his office, Elko's filled with undirected energy. He
pulls the notepad from his pocket where he's written down both of
Mark Goodson's e-mail addresses plus the possible MSN password
Eagle. Sitting at his computer, he gets himself into MSN, types in
mgood2son@msn.com and tries *Eagle.* It doesn't work. He tries *Scout,*
but it denies access as well.

Elko gets up, moves. He considers putting on his CD, *Great Stand-
Up Comedy Routines from the '90s,* to kick-start his brain. He roams
over to the keyboard again, tries *Boy Scout* and then *Citizenship.*
Then he tries *Citizen.* It gets him in.

Mark has 347 messages in junk mail, three new *Inbox* messages.
Elko goes through all the possible files, including *Drafts* and *Sent
Messages.* No red flags get raised, and the profile that emerges is of
a cautious man who maximizes the element of safety in his life. His
approved list for his mailbox is only seventeen; any other sender
goes to *Junk.* Little that's playful or chatty occurs in his e-mail; most
messages are a single sentence: *Meet at the Bay Marina at 2:30. I'll
bring the bait.* He's not social: *Thanks for the invite, but Lena and
I aren't really cocktail party people. Maybe the four of us could go
out to the Crab Shack some night.* There are a considerable number
of messages related to the First Baptist Church. It seems that Mark
holds some sort of fiscal lay position: *Sunday's collection of $324.00
brings the stove fund up to $1278.50. I'd suggest that we order the
top-rated Amana as soon as possible.*

But there are no flirtations, no secrets, no toying with transgres-
sion to be found. Everything is clear and factual. Almost every *sent*
or *received* message reflects a life of work, church affiliation, personal

containment and privacy. Any message in any file only leads Elko to Mark's home, his office, his church, his boat marina.

So, it seems to Elko that he's on the trail of a man whose life is almost entirely void of either passion or adventure.

As a final stab in the dark, Elko tries Mark's *office* e-mail. Lena's provided her husband's CPA e-mail address: *markgoodcpason@msn.com*. When Elko types it in and enters *Citizen* again, *access denied* is the message. He goes through his scribbled list of other possible passwords. This time *Eagle* gets him in.

15 ✦ An Orphan's Heart

At McCarran Airport, Mark Goodson—using his double's driver's license and Visa card—buys three one-way tickets to different destinations: New Orleans, Honolulu, and Mexico City. Each destination, in its way, sounds vaguely appealing. With each, there's a sense of the remote and exotic. Each sounded like a place where he could reinvent himself, become whomever he wished. For a while, at least he would have to be *Anthony Francis*, since it was *Anthony Francis'* documentation that he carried. But he could reinvent his dead twin as *anyone*. The two brothers—before the still-nightmarish drowning incident— had spent only two days together. They'd not shared that much. Mark had little or no sense of *who* his twin brother, in fact, was.

Mark crisscrosses the McCarran check-in area. He tries to sell himself on what he's doing. *This is all...Now*, he tells himself. *He is a person...Becoming.* Anybody—*all people*, he tells himself—move away and toward at the same time. So whoever he is, he is moving *away* from and *toward* something. Mark laughs crazily to himself. The voice in his head has a vocabulary like Lena's.

He's a person liberated! He's a person going away, lifting off, sailing to freedom!

Except that...except that...well, in this open and crowded public space, with over three million dollars in his attaché case—neither the idea of freedom nor flight—swaddle him.

He feels frozen in place and anxious. When, for instance, he goes through security, will he have to let the money go? Set the case loose on the belt? Could the TSA staff recognize—with their enhanced x-rays— that the case held all that money? Or would it just show up as paper? Bundles?

Besides that, Mark keeps seeing the strange man who'd come up to him and then wouldn't stop talking when he left The Mirage.

He'd never been to any of these places—New Orleans, Honolulu or Mexico City. Which to choose? And then, of course, when he *did* choose, what would he do in any of them?

Of course, the answer was: *anything!* He would do, could do, *anything!* Because, as of the previous day's morning, the world was his...what was it they said? *Oyster?* But what? Do what? In his totally freed state—his *oysterdom*...do *what?* Live in a hotel? Buy a house with a pool? Drink a lot? Eat food that he'd never tasted? Maybe he should go to China—he liked Chinese food. Would he telephone escorts? Have them come over and—what was the word he'd heard some men use? *Service* him?

So, what is Lena doing right now? Mark wonders. Does she miss him? *You mean nothing to me!* That had hurt. Lena knew how to hurt, how to do damage. But she knows love as well. Sometimes lavishly. In her way. In her own Lena-like way. Will she know to check their retirement fund and find that they have plenty? He can, periodically, send her money from...*wherever!*

Servicing. For some reason, Mark's mind circles back to the word, servicing. Lena's wildness in bed—was that what was meant by *servicing?* Was that the sort of thing that would happen if he got drunk on mai tais and called a *night companion?*

Why did he have to go anywhere? He could do any of that, *all* of that *here*—couldn't he?—here in Las Vegas: indulge, go over the edge, gorge himself on walnut duck, Peking chicken, swim in a pool, phone up escorts, drink drinks he'd never had before! Bloody Russians! Long Island Nesteas! Or just more mai tais!

Mark thinks he spots that man from The Mirage again, but the guy, whoever he is, disappears around a corner, perhaps into a men's room.

Then, suddenly, a kind of emotional *subfloor*—something below his heart or mind—drops out. His chest feels like rinse-water. His knees feel like sockets of air; his ankles, like syrup. And with this, all of Mark's eagerness and anticipation—for new places, new things, a new life—wash away.

And instead of feeling *new* and *possible,* what Mark feels small and unnecessary, like a single and torn canvas sneaker found by the edge of the road, like a discard. In a sad and blindsiding moment, he is flooded by all the feelings he'd had when—at the age of twelve—his Goodson parents had announced on an evening at dinner: *Mark, there's something that we think you need to know—we think you're old enough—something important.*

And that *something, something important,* which he'd grown old enough to hear had been, of course, that he'd been adopted.

Then his soft-spoken Goodson parents—each with a hand touching him—had revealed that he'd been a twin, that he'd had a brother. As far as his Goodson parents knew, they said, the two brothers had been born identical—*though we don't know for sure; there's no photograph.*

After the bombshell revelation, they'd gone on to say that his birth mother—*What had been her name?...Carter?...Cartwright?... Something like...*they had it written down somewhere. There was a document. Anyway, they'd said—whatever the name—the woman had given up both boys for adoption. To different sets of parents.

Who?

Honey, please; don't be upset. Please, don't be upset, Marko. They didn't *know* who his twin brother was, where his twin brother might be. That was an entirely different—what was the right word?— *arrangement.*

Every other word out his parents' mouths was *love* or *our*—*We love you. You're our son. This is our family, your family. We all love each other just as much as if you'd been here from the start, as if we'd had you ourselves.*

It hadn't been that Mark hadn't believed them—his Goodson parents—or felt at all that they hadn't loved or deeply felt that he belonged to them and was their son. It was more that he felt himself— like a balloon suddenly let go in the hand of a careless child, impulsively detached and floating, drifting, being blown away. Suddenly there'd been no *closeness* for him anywhere in the world. Everything had felt almost violently distant, unconnected, unbound. All of his senses of safety and protection had simply evaporated.

And only age twelve. In a blink, in a holding of breath, he'd stopped being a *son* and had become an *orphan.* He'd become one of those cats or dogs he'd seen—hungry and sad—behind the mesh of cages at the Humane Society. He'd become a stray, a mongrel, a pack dog. *Love...love...love. Our...our...our.* The not-really-parent assurances had sounded and resounded, echoed and ricocheted. He'd known that his Goodson parents had meant everything they'd said, but he'd also known: nothing would ever be the same.

And then, when he was nineteen, his Goodson father died. Rain. A stupid car accident—Jeep Cherokee through the guardrail of the Cape Coral Beach bridge. Mark had been away—not far—at Florida State. It had been early October. He'd come home to comfort his mother and to attend the funeral. And again, she'd said all of the right things, but, at the same time, she'd seemed so very, very far away. And he'd heard all the questions whispered at the funeral—*had it, for certain, been an accident?*

And it had seemed that, after that point, whenever he'd tried to step in and assume his father's role, she'd pushed him away, told him *live your own life. I'm a strong person. I have friends...and resources. I'm fine.*

So, he had an orphan's heart! That's the only way to explain it. Forever and always. He has an orphan's heart.

Then he married Lena, thinking that marriage might stop it all and end his profound sense of disattachment. Because he and Lena—at least that was the hope—had a deep and present connection. After all: *husband and wife! Promise* bound to *promise.* My God! The hope! That they'd be inseparable! Inextricable!

Then, of course—in the original game plan—they'd have children. And all the scar tissue would go away! And all the orphan feelings would drift off like their own balloon. And for a while, it *had* felt that way, that good: so sweet, so interlocked—the marriage. It had seemed like it might give him legitimate connection and closeness.

But Lena—though always quick and easy to be pressed *against*—wasn't always easy to be close *to.* She was easy to be *entangled* with—and that felt sometimes deliciously, even *wickedly,* connected. He *belonged,* during those moments. He had true *family...*for a while.

But then—within even the first year—their closeness began to feel more like sumo wrestling. There had been moments when Mark had felt aware of every corpuscle in his body. But there had also been moments when it had seemed possible he was losing consciousness or might even be dead.

Still, and he thinks this now at the same moment when, for the third time, he believes he's spotted the boorish man from The Mirage: Lena is all he has. She's *it.* His Milky Way, his Andromeda. *I'm your only hope, Sugar,* is something she sometimes says. And there's a truth in that! With children not yet entirely out of the question, she's his lifeline; she's his one connection in life's far-flung and remote space, so if he boards a plane, now, to New Orleans or Honolulu or Mexico City, then that admittedly frayed connection will be broken. And he'll be—irrevocably and irreversibly—an orphan for the rest of his days. Okay, an orphan with over three million dollars, but an orphan nevertheless.

Mark finds a phone and places a call to Treasure Island. At a far bend in the concourse, he thinks he sees The Mirage Man yet another time. It's a phantom image, a phantom thought—he's in the middle of being haunted, after all—but it's possible. Hadn't the man said that the airport is where he's headed? Still, it unsettles Mark.

When the TI operator answers, Mark asks for Mr. Goodson's room and gives the room number. The phone begins to ring.

Lena's still there, he thinks. *She's still checked in!*

He starts to hang up, until something akin to liquid nitrogen freezes his hand in place.

He hears a *Hello?* Then another *Hello?* It's Lena. Something starts to form in Mark's brain—a clump, a tangle of words. *The other night, did you really mean what you said: that I meant nothing to you?* And he's about to voice something when Lena says, "Mr. Wells?" Then again, "Mr. Wells?" Then, "Elko?" Who does she think she's talking to? Who, besides Mark, would be calling her? Is he, then, really so *nothing* to her that she has already?

Mark hangs up. He stands, gripping his attaché case, staring at the phone. He feels an unexpected grief. He feels bruised. The whole world—the whole universe and cosmos—is distance. And then distance beyond distance. His heart—his orphan's heart—will be a million miles away if he boards a plane for New Orleans or Honolulu or Mexico City. He'll be light years from the only person alive who can bring him to his knees with love.

His sole chance for attachment—as he reevaluates—is to at least stay in the same city as Lena. He can still reinvent himself—can't he?—here. Become another person, experience another life? Be reckless? Extravagant? Break the rules?

He loops his hand through the grip of his attaché so that his fingers can be free to flip the yellow pages. Certainly, he can't go back to Treasure Island, that would be too close. A return to The Mirage would also be a mistake. What Vegas resort, when Mark says its name in his brain, sounds faraway yet close at the same time? Real, yet fantastic, elegant yet wicked, pristine yet pornographic? He shuts his eyes; he concentrates... *Mandalay Bay!* Mandalay Bay—in his orphan's heart, tripped from his brain's tongue—sounds like all those things. He calls, and using his dead twin's Visa card, reserves a suite. At only $649.00 a night, it seems a gift!

As Mark's writing down the Mandalay Bay confirmation number, he begins to hear—somewhere behind him—screams. The screams grow louder and the sense of their chorus, more dense. Fear vocalized has always made Mark nervous. He thanks the Mandalay Bay registration person and hangs up. When he turns around, he can see that perhaps fifty feet away a crowd is gathering. He can see airport security staff converging from at least three separate directions on the scene.

When Mark gets to the rim of the circle that's formed, his vision drops to see a man facedown on the tiled mosaic floor. The man is wearing a blue blazer and khaki pants. And there's blood flooding out of a gap in the blue blazer's back—chest level, between the shoulder blades.

And then Mark hears someone in the crowd shouting *Hawaiian shirt!* to one of the security officers: "I was this close! I saw him! A man! A man wearing a Hawaiian shirt! Stabbed him! Then ran away with his briefcase!"

Dust devils swirl in Mark's head; under him, the level ground buckles. He feels scrambled and shocked. Dislodged. Were his emotions to have been recorded on some sort of *reaction meter,* wired to his skin, they would have registered somewhere between *Holy-Mary-Mother-of-God!* and *I-need-to-get-out-of-here!* Because Mark—seeing the dead man pooled in blood on the terminal floor—realizes who the intended victim was to have been. *Jesus, it's me!* His mind shouts and then re-shouts...*Man in a Hawaiian shirt! It was supposed to have been me!*

And he's right! Absolutely! No question! From the back and facedown, the man could, just as well, be him, Mark Goodson, out in public on a typical day. In general stature and style: almost identical. Except that the man on the airport tile has a lethal wound. Except that that man appears not to have a future.

16 ✦ Elko Catches the Scent

With only one possible exception, Elko discovers, Mark Goodson's office e-mail files—*Saved, Sent, Draft, Trash, New, Junk*—are Boy-Scout clean, beyond suspicion or reproach, business and strictly business. There are no website visits that suggest he's not boring. No *Anal Grandmas* or *Facials.* No online gambling or, even, solitaire. No eBay, Amazon, Expedia or Orbitz.

With *one* possible exception.

And that one exception is a brief nearly year-old correspondence with a man named *Brother Anthony*.

Out of the blue, it would seem, on a June third, Mark receives an e-mail at 5:47 AM saying, *You were born at Naples General Hospital at exactly the moment I am writing this e-mail. How do I know that?* And it's signed: *Brother Anthony*.

Brother Anthony... Elko's guess is that the e-mail threw Mark seriously off balance. What's reconstructable is: after an initial gap of time, Mark began a reply—*I don't know what you're...* but then abandoned it. The aborted reply got saved. Elko follows the trail. A day goes by, a second day. At exactly 5:47 AM on the third day, the original e-mail from Brother Anthony was resent with additional comments: *Are you afraid? Fear is the ultimate loneliness. Never embrace it.* Again, the e-mail is signed: *Brother Anthony*.

Again, Elko uncovers that Mark started, but didn't finish, a response. But *with* this second e-mail, Mark creates a separate file: *Brother Anthony*.

The very next morning—written again at exactly the same time of day—*Brother Anthony* writes a third time. This e-mail's a bit longer, though whether it could be called "detailed" is another matter. *Brother Anthony's* third e-mail is less a series of connected sentences, more a scattershot of physical details: a crude portraiture, a sketch of medical history. It reads: *Green eyes. Too-large hands. Red hair until early thirties; gradual color change; black now. Weak chin. Six foot two. Size eleven shoe—wide. Periodontal problems. Right eye— 20/30. Allergies to walnuts, chickpeas.* It's signed, *Identically yours, Brother Anthony*.

This is the first message Mark answers—all continuation of the first document. His reply is more correction than response. He writes: *Six foot three. Left eye—20/30.* To this Brother Anthony immediately responds, *Yes! Excellent! Good, I have your attention!*

Elko rereads all of the documents two more times and then pushes back, gets up from his chair before going on. He needs to move. There's something he can't quite name rolling around in his head— an instinct, an intuition, something that feels obvious, but won't slip into alignment. Pacing his limited office space, he keeps repeating the words, *Brother Anthony, Brother Anthony*.

Elko sits again at his computer, sniffs the air, picks up the scent.

What follows, until the document ends, nearly two weeks from Brother Anthony's originally posted e-mail, is a kind of minimal, clipped, oblique, staccato dialogue, which goes like this:

Okay, what do you want?
Reunion.
With?
With my Better Half.
And if I call someone in? Police? FBI? *Authorities?*
I won't exist. I'll disappear.
But what do you want?
Want? What do I want? Such a burning question! Oh, I don't know. Want? Talk to me, speak to me. What have you got? What are you offering?
I need to know. Otherwise, this is it; no more. Three strikes and you're out. What do you want?
I want to discover the difference between an apple and a pear.
Shape.
Why, inside one shell is there just irritating sand but inside another, a pearl?
Partly environment. Partly chemistry.
Why is it that two drops can cure you, but four drops kill?
Okay, You need to tell me that you understand one important thing if I'm to continue. My family is out of bounds.
Family? You must mean your wife.
My wife. Her family. Our friends. If we go on, it's just me.
You mean, no "Mi casa es su casa?"
Exactly.
Fine. No problem. Agreed.

In the document's next-to-last reply, Mark tells Brother Anthony that he wants to stop communicating by e-mail. His office, he says, is meant to be only a professional office—simple and pure. Mark asks for a phone number. In the final entry, Brother Anthony gives Mark a thirteen-digit number beginning with zero one one. When Elko checks the prefix, he discovers it to be the prefix for Aruba. Brother Anthony writes that Mark should feel free to call...*any morning at 5:47 AM.* Any other time—within a five-minute window—and Brother Anthony won't be available.

And that's that. That's the end of the file.

Again, some kind of hunch—some investigator's greater truth— teases Elko. It's no more than flickering candlelight at the back of his brain. But, again, it diffuses like smoke. Elko stands and moves without direction, crisscrosses his office. He wishes he had a Seinfeld tape that he could play, unroll in the background. *Any* comic would do; doesn't have to be funny—Drew Carey!—or even good. It's just that Elko thinks better with the white noise of stand-up comedy out there in the background.

He calls Betina-Betina in and has her scroll the entire file of e-mails. "So, what comes into your head? What do you think?" Elko asks.

"Mark Goodson has a brother," she says.

"Ergo, *Brother Anthony*."

"Ergo."

The idea rustles vaguely, but it doesn't click. It's not precisely the shadow on the cave wall of Elko's brain. Elko gives credit where credit—

"Makes sense," he acknowledges.

"Which is why you hired me," Betina-Betina grins. "I make sense."

"I hired you because you're an exotic," Elko says.

"Mark Goodson has a brother—trust me."

"Why would he be so mystified by his own brother? Even an alienated brother."

"That's what it seems—good twin, bad twin. Good brother, evil brother. Brother Frances."

"You've, possibly, read too many bad gothic novels."

"You, possibly, haven't read enough."

"Twenty dollars says Mark Goodson's an only child," he says. "Or is the only boy in a family with older sisters."

Betina-Betina takes Elko's bet. "Call his lunatic wife," she says. "I need the money for lunch."

Elko calls the TI front desk, gets switched to Lena Goodson's room. The phone rings. And rings. An automatic message intrudes saying that the guest being called isn't available and that if the person calling wants to leave a message...

On the word, *message,* Lena answers. She sounds drugged. When Elko says as much, she snaps back that he doesn't know her sleeping habits. He tells her that if she writes them down, he'll read them. She says, they'll become apparent soon enough.

"I have one question," he says. Betina-Betina is making faces in the background.

Lena purrs—her voice half sleepy, half something else. "I'm all yours," she says.

"It may be two questions," he says.

"Then I'm all yours, twice."

"Best keep something in reserve," Elko says. Somehow, he thinks, he's having phone sex, but he barges ahead anyway. After all, twenty dollars is on the line. "Your husband...Mark," he begins.

"Did you find him?"

"Your husband, Mark," he repeats. "Does he have a brother?"

"Mark's an orphan," Lena says. It's the first time during the call that her voice has sounded awake and serious.

"So, no brother?"

"You just asked that."

"I did." And Elko grins. He does a little victory dance where he's standing and rubs his thumb greedily against his first two fingers. He sticks his tongue out at Betina-Betina. She says, "I need a recording of this conversation. I'm not paying until I have documentation." Elko extends the phone to her, but she waves it away.

"And your second question?" Lena asks.

"My second question—"

Betina-Betina drifts out of the office.

"Mmmm."

"Does the name *Brother Anthony* mean anything to you?"

"Again?"

"*Brother Anthony.* When you hear the name, *Brother Anthony,* does a bell go off?"

"One more time."

"*Brother Anthony.* Do you know who Brother Anthony is?"

"Oh, no. *Brother Anthony?* No, I don't."

Elko tells her that he's sorry to bother her; go back to bed; he'll call her again in a couple of hours; maybe they can have dinner that evening; he can't say for certain, but maybe he'll have a lead. He's uncovered some *possible* leads but he has to check them out.

With the word *lead,* suddenly she's a different person. Her voice changes. What does Elko mean, *lead*? Has he been hiding something? Has he been keeping something from her? "Don't try to deny me!"

Elko tells her to calm down. He explains that if he shares every hunch and possibility with her, it will make her crazy, then she'll make *him* crazy. "Look," he says, "I told myself years ago that I would only *work* with crazy people—not become crazy myself." He promises her that when he knows—not just senses something—he'll tell her. He emphasizes that a *lead's* a *lead,* no more. It's the scent of baking bread in the air when a person's looking for a slice of pastrami. It's a possible trail, something to whet the appetite, nothing more. Finally, he says, "Listen, I'll tell you what: If I'm still alive, still fresh, eight hours from now, we'll have dinner at Ellis Island. Seven o'clock."

"I told you I can't live without him. Don't lead me on."

Elko tells her that he'll swing by at seven o'clock; be out front.

He scrolls through Mark Goodson's *Brother Anthony* file one more time, hoping for lightning. There's a faint rumble, and, behind the rumble, a flicker, but nothing strikes.

He can hear Betina-Betina in the outer office. She's on the phone with Bill Clinton. She's going to be a while, Elko figures, because that's the way Bill Clinton is. He's a good guy; Elko likes him and gets him work, but when the work's slow, when the work's not there, Bill Clinton has trouble taking a *no*.

Elko makes sure he's got his mobile and his single picture of Mark Goodson and heads south to Mandalay. Faye's Bloody-Mary friend, Lynn, will have started her swing shift. If it's really Mark she's seen, Elko's anxious to hear what she has to say.

17 ✦ Rage Is Confusing

Rage is confusing. When the dam breaks and the full force of fury floods in, it's hard to see straight. It's hard to think. It's hard to measure the action to the moment. The wrong words tumble in the mouth. Distorted images replace the real world on the retinal screen. The brain shouts the wrong commands and the hands follow them.

In his reflective and reasonable mind, Billy Spence knew—absolutely knew—that the man he'd followed to McCarran Airport had been wearing a light summer suit and not khaki pants and a blue blazer. But for two obsessive days, he had thought about the probable thief of his money vest as The Blue Blazer Man. And the attaché case was similar. And if the man went through security to board, Billy's money might be lost forever.

So, he'd felt under pressure. Only so much time in which to move, to act. Then, suddenly, there he was! The Blue Blazer Man! Only twenty feet ahead! Within striking distance and carrying his attaché! The man who'd walked off with his money and made a fool of him, turned him into a drag-queen-Chinese-understudy.

And so, the rage had erupted. The flood gates burst. And he'd done what he had to do. A man of genius has to retrieve his pride, his sanity, his fortune. Okay! Sure, okay! It had been the wrong person! Wrong attaché. But…c'mon! People look like each other! People resemble one another! Billy had done what he had to do!

But, if rage is confusing, rage is also airborne and communicable. Someone writes an angry letter in Detroit and ten people in Tunica, Mississippi start coughing blood. Someone in Waco, Texas shouts,

"Fucking slime! I wish you were dead!" and a fire breaks out in Walla Walla, trapping a hundred women and children—screams traveling up to five miles, until they are ashes. Someone stabs the wrong man in McCarran Airport, and the arc of the confused and mistaken blade becomes the arc of as many as ten thousand deluded scimitars in Saudi Arabia, Syria, Pakistan.

And so, at the exact time Billy Spence followed the wrong scent and killed the wrong man in McCarran Airport, there were two others—J. Bob Marshall in Houston, Texas, and Darrin Folger in Norwalk, Connecticut—also feeling rage's communicable power and confusion. Two other men aroil with vengeance and feeling that killing a particular person would relieve the headaches and sweats and blurred vision.

So, in this far-flung and triangulated way, J. Bob Marshall and Darrin Folger formed a kind of wild and contaminated trio with Billy Spence. A wild, savage pack. Each felt their gums recede and teeth grow ready. Each sniffed the tainted scent of trespass in the air—contact gone bad. With each, the hackles of their hair began to rise and stiffen. They were feral dogs—each one and collectively—rabid with dispossession and rage. Another animal had invaded; another had taken their store; there was the need to taste blood, tear open the presumptive other's throat.

Justice: a throat for a throat! The only path to satisfaction was to *strike*.

On Thursday, September 19, J. Bob Marshall gets a call from his host, Michael Vincentes, at The Mirage, thanking him for his visit, inviting him to return whenever he'd like, reminding him that he still has not wired the funds to pay off his two-million-dollar marker, and saying that on his next visit, Mirage would even be happy to give him twenty thousand to start off with and, if he loses, forgive fifteen percent of his debt.

Somewhere in J. Bob's chest cavity a sound begins, a rumble on its way to words living in the landscape between denial and disbelief.

But Michael Vincentes' upbeat voice overrides the subterranean rumble. *Had he enjoyed his stay? Had The Mirage service been satisfactory?* Michael Vincentes apologizes that he had been out of the country and missed the opportunity to see J. Bob. *Had he had the chance to play any golf?* By the way, The Mirage is sending him a case of the Far Niente cabernet that he'd liked so much when he'd had his dinner with the young lady at Renoir. It should be arriving—probably—the first of the week. But, and Mirage understands that he's a busy man, please don't forget to wire those funds.

There's a pause.

"Hello? Mr. M—?"

"Whoa. Back up," J. Bob Marshall begins. "I'm sorry. Michael, we on the same page here?"

"*Same page?* I'm not sure—"

"What *recent visit*, exactly, are we talking about?"

"Well—"

"*How* recent? How recent is *recent*? I could swear you said—but you couldn't have—*this week*."

"Well—"

"I misheard, right?"

"Right. I mean, no…right…yes, this week. Yesterday."

And this is when J. Bob Marshall learns that another person—*looking exactly like him,* Michael Vincentes says—has just spent three days at The Mirage and lost over forty thousand dollars, using J. Bob's credit line—after which he departed without cashing in the two million or so in Mirage chips he'd taken out on a marker.

When there's a murderous silence at the other end of the line, Michael Vincentes clears his throat. "So…you're saying—you mean, it wasn't you?" Michael Vincentes asks.

Sometimes it's hard to talk; sometimes it's hard to see. For J. Bob, piecing the impersonation together, it's like being submerged in a swimming pool filled with blood.

"Mr. M?…Mr. M? Are you saying you weren't here?"

"Exactly. Exactly, Michael. It wasn't me."

"Well—of course we'll need to check the surveillance tapes. But—"

"HEY! I DON'T GIVE A FLYING FUCK ABOUT YOUR SURVEILLANCE TAPES!" J. Bob Marshall shouts. "I want every penny of that money, the minute you hang up, restored—EVERY PENNY!—back in my credit line. Do we understand each other?"

"Well, certainly, if there's been some kind of deception—"

J. Bob Marshall tells Michael Vincentes that he will be on a private plane from Houston to Las Vegas that night and to have a room ready, to get the books straight. He wants to sit down and watch every minute of the J. Bob Marshall wannabe-snake on tape.

When he hangs up, J. Bob walks over to his collector gun case, stares at it for a while, feeling the heat coil forming at his forehead, aware of the venting from his nostrils. Light plays like a kind of music against the gun–case glass. At the same time, there are frag-mentary dim reflections of J. Bob's own image—a ridge of teeth, a small thicket of red hair.

He opens the case, takes out a hand-tooled, ivory-handled pistol—antique, beautifully restored, used in the Spanish-American War. He feels the weight of it, runs two fingers along its barrel.

Some scorpion-in-the-dark had crept into The Mirage and pre-tended to be him!

Some three-legged coyote had just decided to dress up like J. Bob and trick-or-treat for two million dollars!

Hadn't whoever-it-was done his homework? Hadn't he consulted the worm in the bottle of Jose Cuervo? Wasn't he aware that when the Lady-in-Red wore a veil and danced...it wasn't a festival day, it was a funeral?

J. Bob slips a silvery shell into the barrel chamber of his collector pistol and walks outside to where the early afternoon light was the color of fresh-sliced peaches. He walks across to his barn. At the back of his barn, are a half-dozen goats. He herds one of them aside, and, when it's far enough apart from the others, shoots it.

The goat stumbles to the ground. With both hands, J. Bob, hunch-ing over, reaches into the goat's wound and tears open its belly, for-aging in, and in further, and then pulling out and scattering entrails across the ground.

"READ THE SIGNS!" he yells up at the sky. "READ THE SIGNS! YOU'RE A DEAD MAN!"

♦ ♦ ♦

Darrin Folger—who now enters this story, from Connecticut—is a good man. He is generous, loving and kind. Like J. Bob Marshall, though, he becomes confused by rage. Growing up, Darrin Folger had, first, become confused about his hands. It was a confusion that ran in his blood, gathered in his moss-colored eyes and spoke to him in the ancient code of legacy. It was unsettling and it had been Darrin's *father's* confusion and Darrin's father's *father's* before that. *What is the power of a hand? Two hands? Is it to shape something beautiful in the world? Or is it to take the inspiration out of all breath?*

Darrin's father had been a cabinetmaker and had worked out of their home—a workshop where, on every available wall inch, hung magical tools. There were clamps and planes and woodcarving knives and one long metal spike that his father called an *adz*. There were band- and table- and circular-saws. There was a file drawer filled with various gradations of sandpaper. Sometimes Darrin would see his father prowl his shop, saying things like, *There's the perfect tool for this. I know. The perfect tool. There has to be. C'mon! C'mon, where are you?* Then he would pluck something out of a drawer or from a shelf or off a hook and turn back to his work and begin to hum. He loved opera!

But Darrin's father's work wasn't always an aria. It was because of his hands, he told Darrin. It was because sometimes his hands took on a wild life of their own. "It's like weather," Darrin's father apologized once. "My hands. It's not me. Sometimes there are storms— bad storms, hurricanes. You can't stop them." Darrin had seen his father tear a nearly-finished cherry-wood cabinet apart, smash its glass, have to wrap one of his slashed hands in a staining rag. "Son, it's...not me," he'd said, near tears. "It's just a bad storm. It's only weather. You know, you can't control the weather."

So, as Darrin had grown—as he'd lived and begun to move out into the world—he'd become aware of the same destructive meteorology in himself. Sometimes he would sketch something delicate only to, abruptly and violently, scribble over or tear up his own drawing. And though his heart was reflexively tender, his hands could be genetically mean. Darrin's wife, Annabella, called him a *saint,* but he knew it was only by the grace of God because—given any stretch of bad weather—he could have the evil and dismembering hands of a butcher.

However he could, and whenever he could, he fought the evil use of his hands.

But then!

Present moment...or the lead up *to* the present moment.

Darrin works as a magazine layout assistant editor and lives in the north side of a duplex in Norwalk, Connecticut with his gentle wife, Annabella, and their three children. The oldest child, a daughter, seventeen, Mary Beth, is the victim of a reckless driver—struck crossing a street on Halloween when she was twelve. She walks with braces. Whether she'll walk free of those braces gain is an open question. She'd been dressed as an angel and both her wings had been broken.

Darrin's son, Marko, as starting point guard for his middle school's basketball team, is a source of boundless pride. He keeps breaking his own, and the school's, assist record. Every so often, though, during a close and physical game, Marko will have anger-management problems and a fight breaks out. After such games, Darrin pulls Marko aside and they talk. "Just tell your hands, *No,*" Darrin urges.

And Marko looks at him.

"Tell them *No,* Darrin repeats.

And, each time, Marko asks, *How?*

Darrin demonstrates. "Hold them in front of you—look at them, *stare* at them—and tell them *No,*" Darrin says.

Darrin's younger daughter, Lisette—an angel in her own way—dreams of being a dancer in a ballet company, and Darrin, thrilled, has arranged for her to have studio lessons, and has financed them gladly.

All of this—cherished life with wife and children—is the life that Darrin Folger has chosen. And is grateful for.

Until...! Until Darrin goes to an "Opportunity Seminar," where a tall, square-jawed man named Frank Anthony convinces him that a property scheme he's managing—and that he can, for a price, cut Darrin into—is a financial "home run."

"You get in on this," Frank Anthony predicts, "and it's fast-and-high, bat-on-the-soft-spot, smacko, totally out of the park!"

It sounds good! As his kids say: *awesome!* And the square-jawed Frank Anthony appears sure as he looks deep-deep-deep into Darrin's eyes.

Frank Anthony. A man with the name of a saint!

"Brother!" he begins his sure-thing project description. *Brother Darrin: Look at me! Listen to me!*

And Darrin does.

"Brother Darrin, I look at you and it's unmistakable. Okay, I know, you ask. *Oh? Really? What's unmistakable?* And certainly, you should. I understand. But I see you, and I see a person with, I have to say, obvious powers. I see a man haunted by visions of a life greater...a life *more possible.* You do *not* want to coast; you do *not* want to settle. Brother Darrin, destiny stalks you in your dreams as it stalks only a few. And I recognize that, because—who better to say?—destiny stalks me. Destiny's a monster—but we, you and I, are monster-slayers. You are me; I am you; we are brothers."

It's an *event*—Darrin Folger's face-to-face with Frank Anthony there in the Days Inn conference room. Electrifying! A performance!

Still, one has to grant that the kind, loving, generous Darrin is also shrewd and that what he's being told—on another day, in another room, at another seminar—would only make the rustle of trash bags heaved into a landfill. But, as it transpires, on *this* particular day, sadly, *something*—who can say?—in the tall, square-jawed man's voice wins Darrin over, shuts down his instinct for wariness, creates a trust. Perhaps it's the light heft of Frank Anthony's arm around Darrin's shoulder. Perhaps it's some strange instrumental sense in the weather of Darrin's own hands. Maybe it's the low-watt ambiance in the Days Inn conference room. But *some*thing.

So, Darrin yields. He yields his trust and—for no reason at all, really, except that he's a man prone to unusual hope and unselfish dreaming—he withdraws seventy-five thousand dollars from a combined savings and inheritance account and hands it over. Of course, there are papers—all of which look legal and are in triplicate. There are notary seals and assurances and guarantees and promissory notes.

Trust dresses up. Trust masquerades. For any person running a scheme, every day is Carnival; it's Halloween. And trust—given at the wrong moment and in the wrong place—can be brutal, even murderous.

Within two days, of course, all the money and the tall, square-jawed man disappear. Mary Beth's medical expenses mount. Darrin tries to convince Marko that he doesn't really need the next summer's UConn Jim Calhoun Basketball Camp. Lisette's dance studio lessons have to come to a halt. In his own thought process—in almost every way that Darrin can imagine—he has failed his marriage, failed his family. And, of course, the tall square-jawed man—Frank Anthony— to whom he's given the money is nowhere in sight.

But, to underscore an earlier point, Darrin Folger—kind and loving and ordinarily gentle as he might be—is not stupid. Though, back then, he'd not been brave enough to take it, he'd once been offered a full scholarship to MIT. So, though he's a person always trying to be good—at war, yes, with his hands—he's also a person who can be ingenious.

At one point in his exchanges with Frank Anthony, Darrin has acquired one of the square-jawed man's Visa-card receipts. It's fallen from his money clip and, for whatever instinct or reason, though Darrin *thinks* about giving it back, he doesn't. The receipt's signature name is blurred and badly inked—a first initial—an *A* possibly or an *M*. And there's a last name that looks to begin with an *F* or *E*—maybe a *B* or *G*. Six letters it seems. An *O*, an *S*. But the fifteen-digit card number is clear.

And so, the *smart* Darrin harnesses the ingenuity which might have seen him through MIT and hacks into the MBNA banking system and creates an "alert" surveillance for the card's account and use. In the program that he sets up, whenever the tall and square-jawed man's card is used, the card's use will be flagged and the information forwarded to Darrin. Each card-use will be a dot on a map. Darrin will connect the dots. When the connections—dot-to-dot—make a line, that will mean motion. But when the dots create a cluster—that will mean settlement. And as soon as Darrin gets a cluster, he will act. He will go immediately to the cluster—fly if necessary—and find the man. First, he will speak to the square-jawed Frank Anthony (or whatever his name), confront him, demand the return of his seventy-five thousand. If the man refuses or tries to escape, Darrin, for once in his life, will not be able to say *No* to his hands. He will, simply, kill the man.

For the first month and a half, the dots are random. The line is zigzag and without direction: a gas station on the New Jersey Turnpike, a Sharper Image in Chester, Pennsylvania, a Days Inn in Claymont, Delaware. Reading the Days Inn card-use, Darrin feels a tangled hot-and-cold electrical surge. He imagines others, like himself, handing over money. He calls the Days Inn. "Is there an Opportunity Seminar happening there for the next few days?" he asks.

"There was, but it's over," the desk clerk says.

Darrin hangs up and feels like some cyclotron for rage. He stares at his hands. Were the square-jawed man to appear within range, he could not tell his usually gentle hands *No.*"

Then there are a half dozen other card-use flags over the next weeks—all random, nothing close to a cluster. And then, in August, with a United Airlines ticket—one-way, JFK to Boise, Idaho—all card-use stops. Darrin waits for the next record. And waits. But none comes. And none comes and none comes and none comes. The card seems to go dead. And his hope of retribution with it.

Darrin has inherited his father's tools. Among them is that particularly long and fine-honed adz. Once—during one of his father's worst storms—he had watched him put thirty-seven punctures into the workshop's oak-paneled walls with that adz. "What makes wind?" his father had stammered, ashamed, afterwards. "What makes lightning and thunder?" He'd cried. "It wasn't me," he'd said, hugging Darrin. "I'm sorry. It wasn't me. It was the weather." If Darrin kills Frank Anthony—if that happens—it won't be him. It will be his hands. It will be the weather.

His father's adz is buried in one of his own tool boxes. He's placed it out of sight, but he knows where it is. So, when the tall, square-jawed man's card alert flashes on Darrin's PC screen, announcing that the card, finally, is in use again—Merchant: Mandalay Bay Resort and Casino; Location: Las Vegas, Nevada—and repeats various uses in that location over three days, Darrin goes to his garage and to his tool box, where he stands frozen at first, his breath coming in drafts and backdrafts, his hands shaking.

Rage is confusing.

The following morning, Darrin tells his family he will see them soon. He is taking a trip. A vacation? No, not exactly. He'll be gone maybe a week. He's not sure. Maybe he'll be home sooner. He has business to transact. He wishes he didn't; it's difficult business. But when he comes back, he promises his younger daughter, Lisette, she will finally begin her ballet lessons.

18 ◆ Elko Follows the Scent—Does He Lose It?

Elko valet parks at the Mandalay and finds Lynn, the Bloody Marys cocktail waitress who may have seen Mark Goodson. She's blonde, early thirties, a bit hefty, but she smiles everywhere. Elko likes people who smile. He watches them, studies them, every opportunity he gets, because it seems they have a secret, one he'd like to know and wishes he was able to use. Sometimes he stands in front of the mirror for hours, trying to get his face to do what faces like Lynn's do just naturally. He's still working on it.

"Faye says that I should trust you one-hundred percent," Lynn says, "But also that I keep my hands off of you." Lynn says she's on the run until her break, which should be at about three thirty or so. She says, "I'm sure it's him. The guy I saw. The guy you're looking for. It's a crazy story." They agree to meet by the casino cage in an hour.

Elko walks around the floor as if he's a supervisor without a nametag. He plays at being a *suit*. A young couple stops him and asks directions to the China Grill. He points the way; they say *thanks* then ask where the hot quarter Wheel-of-Fortunes are on the floor, and Elko walks them over to a row, pats one, nods his head. The two grin at each other; one pulls a stool out.

He continues to roam—nowhere special, no direction. A man who could just as easily be Martin Sheen passes by, and Elko wonders if he's local. He lost his Martin Sheen, in February, to a flash fire. After the reconstructive surgery, he doesn't look presidential any more. So Elko begins to follow the possible Martin Sheen, who doesn't seem to be going anywhere in particular until he ends up at the Eyecandy Lounge.

Martin Sheen sits down and Elko does the same thing, a stool away. The possible Sheen orders a Dewar's and water, slips in his club card, glides a hundred into a multigame validator and starts playing Double Double Bonus.

"That's a hard game to stay alive in," Elko says across to him.

"It is. But when you hit, you hit," he says. "I like that."

"Good luck," Elko says, then takes a breath and initiates his agenda: "You need to pardon me," he begins. "But you look a lot like someone who's famous."

"I know. I get that," the possible says to Elko, but his eye's on his game.

"*West Wing*, right?"

"Right."

"So, you local?"

"Dearborn, Michigan," he says.

Out of town. Not a candidate. "Nice to talk with you," Elko says. "Good luck. Hope you hit four aces and a two." And Elko pushes off his barstool.

"Me too," the no-longer-possible-Martin-Sheen says.

Elko watches some dice being rolled—only two guys at a ten-dollar table. One's very thin, a black guy with a crazy hat, who bounces around; can't stop moving. And he's playing the field—doubling, tripling up. The dice are being deceptive, and he's winning. The other guy is buying the four and ten for fifty each. He's got a lot of black chips in his rack, but right now he's losing.

Elko checks his watch. It's moving up on three thirty, so he wanders over toward the cage but not before a trio of what look like college kids—they're all carrying bottles of Dos Equis—stop him. They ask where the nearest restrooms are. Elko points off, takes a guess, makes up a place where some Mandalay restrooms might be. "Thanks, dude," the three Dos Equis say.

Faye's Bloody-Mary buddy, Lynn, is extremely prompt and cheery. Again, the smile. She walks Elko across the floor to a dollar Double Diamond machine—stands there with her hands out in *voila!* gesture and says, "I was just walking away from serving him his second mai tai last night, when he hit this for over three-hundred-thousand."

Elko's brain does a kind of shift and adjustment. His response—inside his head as he says it—feels like brain damage: "Whoa. Wait a minute. Three—?"

Lynn fills the gap, gladly repeats: "Three hundred thousand. Seriously! Three hundred and thirty-something."

Elko produces Mark Goodson's picture—the only one he has—Goodson holding fishing gear on a dock with his father-in-law. He points: "This guy? Him?"

"Same guy. No question."

"Here? Right here?"

"That's what I'm saying. Here. Him. Three hundred and thirty-something thousand. It was pretty crazy. Pretty out of control."

Elko asks what she means—*out-of-control?*

"He sort of freaked. You know: like...*freaked*. Went over the edge," she says. "Broke a camera."

Elko asks whether there might be surveillance tape.

Lynn looks dubious. She says that when the possibility of him being photographed came up, he pulled his suit jacket up over his head. And started screaming.

She says he'd been a really nice guy, when she'd brought him drinks—joked with her; each time, tipped her twenty dollars. "He seemed really nice, really happy," she says. "Really to be having fun. Oh, possibly, maybe a little goofy—a little shy. But nice."

He lined up three double diamonds, she says. But the whole bank was progressive, so the jackpot was high.

"He seemed kind of confused at first," Lynn says. "It seemed to be the attention. People around him were yelling. They were congratulating him, slapping him on the back. But then, suddenly, he got really happy—laughing. A little bit like a crazy man. But when what's-her-face, *Karla,* from the players' club approached him with her camera, he went crazy. Karla said, *How about a picture?* And he went, like, really angry—kind of barked—*No! No!* He grabbed her camera and smashed it against the machines. Karla screamed. Then he started yelling, *I'm sorry! I'm sorry!*"

Elko asks, *what happened then?*

She says, *He got quiet.* She says he asked her if she would get him another mai tai, and she'd gone off to do that, so she hadn't really seen everything, but when she'd gotten back with his drink, he was filling out IRS forms at the cage. The crowd around him had sort of drifted away.

"So he would have to have produced an ID," Elko says.

"I suppose so. Yeah, sure," Lynn says. "And he said he had to have cash, because he was traveling."

Elko asks Lynn who might be the best person in surveillance to talk with, in case there are any good face shots of Mark Goodson on the surveillance photos. She tells him to talk to the slots manager.

"So, are you and Faye...what?" Lynn asks.

"We're friends. We're very good friends," Elko says.

"Faye's the best," Lynn says.

Elko nods. "That's a fair statement."

"So, I don't mean to be nosey, but who *is* this guy?" she asks.

He says, "A guy who disappeared two days ago."

"Disappeared?"

Elko tells her the condensed version of the Lance Burton caper.

"That's a wild and crazy story!" she says.

"Crazy and getting crazier," Elko says, and they go their ways.

Elko feels buoyed. He feels he's not in a black box with no light anymore. He has some sense that he's on a trail and that there are bread crumbs. In fact, there are so many bread crumbs that with what Faye's friend, Lynn, has given him it seems like he might be—luck willing—face-to-face with Lena Goodson's husband, Mark, before evening. Still, while he feels hope, he also wonders whether there might not be a third party on the trail, someone up there ahead—closer to Mark Goodson, maybe even chasing him—with a sack of bread.

Elko starts his tracking with the shift manager for surveillance. The surveillance director knows a guy who knows a guy who Elko knows, so he's heard Elko's name. The director's name is Lon. Last name sounds Greek—five or six syllables.

"They say that you're like a GPS," Lon tells Elko. "Like a heat missile."

Elko thanks him but shrugs the compliment away. "Sometimes I get lucky," Elko says.

Lon asks how he can help. Elko recites his wish list, and Lon takes him up an elevator to the surveillance room and finds the tapes Elko needs from the previous night. Lon runs them three times, with Elko watching—the third time almost frame by frame, but there's not much there. All they see is a man-in-a-suit's body, from the back. There's a sense of size and shape, but there's not a single face shot. Lon pulls up the photos from the cage when the slot win was paid. The face shots at the cage window are excellent. Elko gets Lon to print up a half dozen.

Next, Elko tracks down Karla, in the Mandalay Player's Club, and when he finds her at her desk, the trail that had gotten overgrown with stinkweeds and thistle suddenly opens up and has direction again.

"Oh, definitely yes!" Karla tells Elko. The Double Diamond guy from the night before had broken her camera. *But* it was a *digital* camera, and the chip was fine. She'd transferred all the photos she'd taken that day to the computer. She had a good shot of the slot winner.

She brings it up on the screen. It's a head and shoulders shot. The expression on the guy's face is pretty zoned. He looks like some guy from Missouri who's just suddenly found himself in an opium basement in Kuala Lumpur where he's been slammed by a two-by-four alongside his head.

"How tall was the guy?" Elko asks.

"Hey, any guy breaking your camera, you know, seems really big. But I can't say."

Elko thanks Karla and asks her to print up three copies of the photo. He wants to show them to Lena. He also gets Karla to send the digital photo to him in an e-mail. His intuition tells him he's got something significant, but he hasn't heard enough good jokes recently to trust it. Jokes clear his mind. He needs the voices of stand-up comics in his brain.

"I have a big favor," Elko announces. He breathes deep, and again recites the Lance-Burton-Mark-Goodson-disappearance story, then asks whether there's any way he might check Karla's departmental documentation for the previous night's Double Diamond payout. "The man had to produce a driver's license and Social, right?" Elko says.

"Yes."

"So, is there any way?"

"I'm not the one to ask," she says.

"Who should I ask?"

She tells him, "Just a minute," and walks out of the small office, calling something Elko can't quite hear to someone Elko can't quite see.

He studies the possible-Mark-Goodson-face again. Being in the look-alike business has made him a skeptic. Ninety percent of what he's looking at tells him it's Lena Goodson's husband, the same guy who goes fishing with Lena's father. But then there's the other ten percent of what Elko sees which could be a grain salesman from Washington, Iowa.

Karla returns with a short, very muscular man whose shirt's too tight at the neck. His skin is the color of extra-extra-lean sirloin. "This is Mr. Richards—Robert Richards."

"Richards, Robert," the meaty man says, and he sticks his hand out.

Elko takes it. *Was his name Robert Richards, or Richard Roberts?*

"Pleased to meet you," Elko says; "Wells...Elko."

"Karla tells me you'd like to document something from our records," Robert-Richards-or-Richard-Roberts—Elko's renamed him *Meat Neck*—says.

Elko tells him, *Yes.*

He asks for Elko's identification. Elko produces his license.

Meat Neck studies it, turns it over, spends more time looking at the embossed leather on the back of the case than at the license itself. He hands it back. "If you were with the IRS, or Gaming, I wouldn't hesitate," he says.

Elko nods and tells him he understands.

"As much as possible, the gentleman you're inquiring about wanted to remain anonymous."

"I realize that," Elko says.

"And it's important—and I'm sure you know and understand this— it's important that we protect our players."

"Of course," Elko says. "I understand—hundred percent." But as Elko's saying what he's saying, what he's thinking is: *Jesus Christ! I'm back in Luther Burbank Grade School being instructed by Mr. Tripp!*

"Has any crime been committed?" Meat Neck asks.

Elko thinks he should, maybe, just walk away. "Not to my knowledge," he says.

"Has anyone been killed, or assaulted? Have any funds been misappropriated? Has there been any evidence of a conspiracy to the best of your or anyone else's knowledge?"

Elko takes a deep breath. He says, "Listen, sorry to have bothered you. I have a client whose husband has disappeared. She's beside herself in emotional pain. Her husband has a diabetic condition—a severe one with neural-synapse complications. He left all his medication behind. It appears as if your Double Diamond winner is our man. But I know that you're under stringent governance. You can't be too careful. So, no argument about it, I'm sorry to have complicated your day."

Meat Neck's eyes cloud. Elko can see that he's trying to stack Elko's

words in columns, make a graph out of them, fit them into his manual.
"I wasn't—" He starts to say something then seems to have forgotten
what he'd started.

Elko drives on. "My client, with good reason, is worried about her
husband's life," Elko offers. "If I've made it sound more complicated
than that, I'm sorry. But that's the bottom line."

"Well—" Meat Neck clenches his teeth, blows breath heavily between his nostrils like a rodeo bull.

Elko waits. He tries to put on his most compassionate face.

"What's your client's name?" Meat Neck says. Then he revises his
question: "More to the point, her husband's name."

Elko tells him: "Mark Goodson."

He nods. Elko can see somewhere back in his brain a scheme is
being born. "Do you have ten, maybe fifteen, minutes?"

Elko tells him, "Of course."

He says, "I'll page. Listen for a page," and he ushers Elko out of
the Player's Club office and onto the casino floor.

Elko needs a drink. He goes to the Fleur de Lys Lounge and gets a
Tanqueray Ten, a double, on the rocks. He finishes it, orders another.
If Betina-Betina were sitting beside him, she'd cock her head, pull her
glasses down over the bridge of her nose and say: "Elk, darlin', you
have a drinking problem."

And he'd look at her the same way, same glasses slid down on the
bridge of the nose, and he'd say, "Betina, baby, it's no problem. It's
easy."

Ten minutes go by, twenty. He's beginning to think about getting
a third Tanqueray Ten when Shirley MacLaine comes up and orders
a banana daiquiri. Her red hair has more highlights than the evening
news. "How're you doin'?" she looks over and says.

"I could use some channeling."

It doesn't appear that she gets it.

Elko hears his name being paged: *Elko Wells to the Player's Club.
Elko Wells.* He gets up. "Take it easy, Shirley," he says.

"Bernice," the woman with the banana daiquiri corrects. "Bernice. Bernice Kelly." And as he's walking away, he hears her again.
"Room 2037. Give me a call!"

When Elko's back in the office with Meat Neck and Karla, he gets the
word. "We checked our Double Diamond winner out," Meat Neck
says.

"And?"

"It's a mixed message."

"Which means?"

"Well, the *name* we got off his driver's license isn't your man, isn't your Mark Goodson. On the other hand, the Social he gave when we checked it out *is your* guy's."

"You sure you got the license information down correctly?" he asks.

"We have a scan of the license," Meat Neck says.

Karla says, "He's two people."

"Schizophrenic," double-Rs adds.

"So who's the *other* guy?" Elko asks.

"What other guy?"

"Well, the Social was for my man, Mark Goodson, right? Who's the *other* guy? Whose license you got. He would have to have a name. Can you share it?"

Meat Neck and Karla look at one another, but say nothing.

"It appears as if my client's husband, Mark Goodson, is using another name. Who knows why? Somehow he's gotten ahold of an alternate ID. What's the name?"

"I don't think we're at liberty to—"

"Do you want my client's husband to *die?*" Elko asks.

"No. Of course not," Meat Neck says.

"The driver's license name is going to help me find him," Elko presses and feels that he's, somehow, uttered the sentence in Arabic, because both Karla and Meat Neck look flabbergasted.

"I'm sorry. Forget it. Erase it," Elko says. "I'm pressing. Pressing unnecessarily. Let me ask another question."

They wait.

"Did you, perchance, check to see whether *either...either* of these guys—the license guy or the guy I'm chasing, Goodson—was staying here? Either at the Mandalay or at the Four Seasons?

Meat Neck nods. He nods some more. "Yeah, we did," he says. "We did. We checked for that."

"And?" Elko asks. "What did you find?"

"The license guy had a room here—a suite. But he checked out of it at about ten o'clock last night."

"Using a credit card?"

"Well, he used a Visa card to reserve the room. But, when he checked out, he paid cash."

"And which name did he use in his reservation? What was the name on the Visa card?"

"It was the license guy."

"Whose name you're reluctant to give to me."

"Whose name I *can't* give. I'm *not going* to give you."

Elko takes his fourth deep breath of the hour—a breath so deep that he can feel it sucking his toes up through his knees and into his thighs. He tries to be accommodating, to smile, but, instead, his lip does a kind of curl over his gums—very much like a snarl.

"You understand," Too-Tight-Shirt nods. "You understand, I hope, what our policy and point of view has to be."

"No," Elko says. "No, not really, but I'm giving it my best shot."

They see Elko out of the executive offices. Everybody thanks everybody. Robert-Richards-Richard-Roberts walks off. Karla waits until he's out of sight. She reaches into a pocket and produces a business card. "Do you have a pen?" she asks. She writes something on the card, offers it.

Elko returns a nod of gratitude and slips the card into an inside pocket. She walks away.

Five minutes later, inside his car, Elko pulls the card Karla's given him from his pocket. On the back, she's written a name.

The name is *Anthony Francis.*

Driving back to his office, Elko gets a call from Darryl Hanks, Head of Security at TI. He's been talking to his people at The Mirage. Has Elko found anything—anything at all—in the last twenty-four which might link the disappeared husband, Mark Goodson, with the possible whale-impersonation scam at Mirage? A second "hit" has just turned up. An important whale from Texas is out of the water and flopping around on the beach.

"I have to tell you that the big boys next door at The Mirage are losing their smiles," Darryl says. Whoever it is played it to the hilt and disappeared with a couple million in high value chips. They're just checking every angle: Is it possible, does Elko think—even remotely— that the magically disappeared husband might be involved in any way?

"Not even remotely," Elko tells Darryl, "This guy's a Boy Scout."

Elko tells Darryl that the word that gets used most to describe Lena's husband is the word *citizen.*

"I don't know," Darryl says. "When I think back…on all our

players who have started in on me with the line, *Listen, I'm a tax-paying citizen*, I'm not so sure."

Back at his office, Betina-Betina is just hanging up the phone. "It's gotten out of control," she says. Elko asks, what? She wants him to guess how many women have called today and said they're Paris Hilton? She throws her hands into the air in exasperation and doesn't wait for him to answer. "*Seventeen!*" she says.

"Breaks the Brittany Spears record," he says.

Betina-Betina asks what Elko wants her to do about all the Paris Hiltons. "It's too many to interview," she says. "What should I do? Have them all send head shots?"

"Have them send tapes," Elko suggests. "Tell them that their tapes will be reviewed carefully."

Elko shuts himself away in his office and pulls Mark Goodson's *Brother Anthony* e-mail file up on his screen. He scrolls it forward and back, forward and back, wishing all that time that there were a comedy club somewhere in the city that played in the afternoon. He needs inspiration. The Tanqueray has made him tired, and if there's a revelation crouched quietly at the back of his brain, he's not accessing it.

Mere weeks after Mark Goodson gets his first e-mail from *Brother Anthony*, Mark disappears and—the next day—reappears both as himself and as *Anthony Francis*. Or, another possibility, *Anthony Francis* appears as him.

Elko suddenly feels his job is both more difficult and easier. Now he's on the trail of *two* guys. And the probability is: if he finds either *one*, he'll discover the other.

He asks Betina-Betina to call every hotel and motel in town, suggesting she begin with the big places. "He's got a lot of money," Elko says. "He's probably not going to want to hole up." Elko proposes that Betina-Betina should be looking for a new registration—sometime, probably, last night around midnight. Registration name: *Anthony Francis*. Follow-up name: *Mark Goodson*. "Let me know as soon as you get something," he says.

It's entangled and complicated and feels, to Elko, like the anxiety before a playoff game. His sebaceous glands are running on overdrive. It is, precisely, what always used to happen before every big game. The two-three hours, during which he was just waiting for the starting whistle, used to make him crazy.

Elko considers calling Faye and arranging to see her, spend some time in bed, but instead, he e-mails Faye and attaches the Mandalay jackpot picture. He thanks Faye for connecting him with Lynn and testifies that Lynn kept her hands to herself and was very helpful. He asks Faye to put the new picture out on the Bloody Marys' network, see what it stirs up.

Betina-Betina knocks, opens the door, walks in. "Interesting," she says.

"Find him?"

"Anthony Francis checked into the MGM about twelve thirty this morning. He checked out about an hour later."

"Didn't like the bedspreads," Elko says. Abruptly, Elko has an idea. "He seems to know people are looking for him. He's going to be someplace where he can just pay cash and not have to show any ID."

"Like where?"

Clearly Elko's on the trail, but it's the trail of a moving target. And it would seem that his target doesn't have a full pocket of IDs. He's just got *one*. And he wants to use it, but it makes him nervous. He checks, and Faye's e-mailed that another one of her Bloody Marys named Leticia served a mimosa in the Bellagio coffee shop just that morning to a guy who resembled the guy in the photo. Letitia remembers him because he tipped her a twenty. Faye says Leticia's off now— her shift bridges graveyard and day—but she's willing to help in whatever way she can. At the bottom of Faye's e-mail is Leticia's cell phone and e-mail address.

Elko calls Leticia. She sounds Jamaican. He identifies himself and apologizes for breaking into her day. Then he cuts to the chase— thanking her for helping out and coaxing her for details: "Anything you can remember," he says. "I'll be grateful."

She sketches a visual thumbnail and it fits for a possible Mark Goodson. *What was he eating?* Elko asks, and she says that what she remembers is: steak and eggs. "I remember meat on his plate," she says.

"How did he seem? Relaxed? Anxious?"

"He was looking around a lot," Leticia says. "Like he was there to meet someone and was afraid the person wouldn't see him, recognize him."

"Or maybe *would*," Elko says.

"So...Faye says this guy is *missing*?" Leticia asks.

"That's the report: missing from action. Missing *something*."

"If I see him again—I'll call," Leticia promises.

Elko thanks her and hangs up. He replays Leticia's words: *like he was there to meet someone.* Something like a dust devil moves counter-clockwise in Elko's brain.

"You're having an idea," Betina-Betina says.

He nods.

"Thank you for sharing," she says.

He lists the five things he thinks are likely:

1. Mark Goodson's on foot; the Mandalay jackpot and his possible photograph have spooked him; he doesn't want some cabbie saying, *Oh, yeah, I recognize him; I picked him up at…*

2. Because he's on foot and because he was eating breakfast at the Bellagio, he probably found himself a room at some place between the Bellagio and Mandalay—there are a good half-dozen possibilities.

3. He won't be using the *Anthony Francis* credit card for wherever he's staying for fear of being *located.* But he may very well continue to use it around town, where he can hit and run.

4. The very fact that he's still in town says something about his marriage to Lena; he can't just run. He may want to, but he can't. Something holds him.

5. The twenty-dollar tips telegraph that he's a boring guy who's experimenting with extravagance.

Elko makes a mental note: *think about and be on the alert for a trail of big-spender experiments.*

Elko's not proud when he does a criminal thing, but he justifies it: people who have intelligence—even if the intelligence is transgressive—should use it. *Never waste your gifts under a barrel,* or however the expression goes. So, he hacks into the MBNA Visa card files, enters the Anthony Francis card number, and sets up an alert system. Any time from now on that the card is used, he'll get a message and be able to check.

And while he's at it, he checks the recent uses. The last one was at MGM. Before that, Mandalay Bay. The next three back are all airline charges—two at Delta, one at Aero Mexico—all three purchased the previous day and within the same afternoon hour at McCarran Airport.

So, okay: Mark Goodson bought three airline tickets and didn't use them. Interesting. The scent of the runaway fox is dilating Elko's nostrils; it's in the wind, in the air—thick and heavy. Now the bread crumbs on the path are an angel cake! Okay! This is good! Yesterday afternoon, Mark Goodson had an impulse—in triplicate!—then, for whatever reason, turned away from it.

Yet another question occurs: What was the reason for Mark's turning away? Elko uses the Internet for help—any news item, yesterday, that involved International or domestic flight?

And in a snap of his fingers: *bingo!* MAN SAVAGELY STABBED TO DEATH AT MCCARRAN. There's a sketchy account. There's the man's name, Parker Childs. And there are two pictures: one of Parker Child's body spread out on the mosaic floor and the other of the same man as he might appear as an executive in a company report.

Elko studying the visage of Parker Childs thinks—*I have never seen the face of a man who appeared to be so harmless!* Except, of course, it's not true. He's seen the face of Mark Goodson.

Now he thinks he may have *too many* leads. Now the simple scent of Mark Goodson is a stench, and the trail he's on becomes one that branches and branches of branches. And every branch in the trail is thick with bread crumbs.

So, he devotes the rest of his afternoon to arranging and rearranging all the new details. His objective is to achieve a design that's neither disturbing nor confusing. Playing faintly on the screen of his brain—like a ghost video—is the moment when he will sit down for dinner three hours from now at Ellis Island with Lena and lay out all of the day's revelations and possibilities, unwrap them with a particular flourish and in a pattern alive with both grace and charm. "I knew you could do it!" is what she'll say. And then she'll kiss him—half on the cheek, half on the lips—a calculated mistake, a *we-almost-went-to-bed-together-didn't-we?* kiss. And they'll both smile—first one and then the other, but it will be the same smile. It will be an *I'll-bet-it-would-have-been-good* smile but, secretly, they'll both know that—now that Mark seems close to being returned—it's too late. And there will be just a twinge of lust overshadowed by virtue, and that particular combination will key both of their appetites and they'll devour their steaks.

19 ♦ Rage in Pursuit

At 7:25 AM, on Thursday, September 20, J. Bob Marshall, dressed in a dark green leisure suit and gripping an alligator carry-on, boards his private Gulfstream to Las Vegas at the Dallas Executive Airport. The minute he's buckled in, he orders a Maker's Mark.

"On ice, right?" His personal attendant is wide-hipped and red-headed. When he's not calling her his *roan,* he calls her *Red.*

"On ice, so nice!" J. Bob runs his knuckles up and down Red's spine. She's dressed in denim and suede, her long mane knotted in the back.

"And double." She does something with her eyes, then lips.

"Red, honey, just pour. Just put the ice in and fill the fucking glass. I'm in a mean, longhorn mood. This is going to be, quite possibly, the cruelest day of my life. It's a short trip. Lubricate me. I'd feel badly to have you at the receiving end."

Buckled in and nursing his Maker's Mark like an escort's rack, J. Bob is playing a mental game. He's imagining people who impersonate other people for profit and, if they were an animal, what kind of animal they might be. He decides either a tapir or a hyena.

At 11:10 AM, on Thursday, September 20, Darrin Folger starts to slip his canvas carry-on under the forward seat on his Southwest flight to Las Vegas from New York's Kennedy. He's wearing a UConn athletic jacket, Levi's and a pair of Adidas. Before he lets the carry-on go, he runs the tips of his fingers across the grainy canvas of a side pocket from which, earlier, he removed his father's adz and repacked it in his checked baggage.

In the fever and blind intent of his mission, he'd forgotten about security, which, had he not repacked it, would have certainly confiscated such a brutal weapon and, quite possibly, isolated him for interrogation. Darrin believes he can actually feel the cruel tool's absence, the impression it's left in the fabric. His heart races. He imagines himself face to face again with the square-jawed man bearing either the first or last name of *Anthony.*

20 ♦ On the Run in Paradise

When the third of the Mandalay Bay Double Diamonds drops into place on Mark Goodson's machine, it seems, briefly, that the entire casino's lighting has changed. There's a kind of pulse and then a flicker and then a flash finishing off with a rumble.

Nearby players leave their machines and crowd around.

People are saying, "Way to go!" and touching him.

Mark's the center of attention.

Mandalay suits with nametags arrive smiling, their voices coming at him like a dentist's drill. *Congratulations!* The word sounds like some kind of soundtrack reverb, trapped in an echo chamber. "We just need some information." A woman in a green blazer appears from nowhere with a camera: "C'mon, sweetie, gimme a big winner's smile!"

In the film fast-forwarded in his head, he grabs the green-blazered woman's camera and smashes it against the bank of slots with such ferocity that there's a cascade of sparks.

The fast-forward-film-in-his-head spools even faster. It's all velocity. Mark needs to escape.

Except!

Except now, *more* people are crowding. His cocktail waitress arrives with his drink.

Someone points up at the progressive readout: $367,224.70.

More people in blazers, suits. He's hyperventilating in ragged surges. *$367,224.70!*

Mark tries to set a keel—somewhere, anywhere. Find a gyroscope.

$367,224.70! How could it be that these things are happening? Jesus! He's a man who balances people's books, whose advice on any client's investments is to the right of conservative.

At the cage, he's asked for his Social. Boy Scout that he is, he recites it. *Fuck! Why'd he do that?*

The clerk asks for a driver's license, and he produces his brother's Florida license.

Now, in the film in his head, security staff arrives—all talking at once, so he can't understand them, but he can understand that they're asking questions.

He starts asking his own questions, all starting with *What if?*

What if the man who'd killed the other man—the man who dressed as Mark usually dressed in a blue blazer and khakis—at McCarran Airport has followed him here?

What if Mandalay security is—right now—trying to track down the discrepancy between his driver's license and his Social Security number?

What if he checks out of Mandalay and goes somewhere else— walks down to the Luxor or, across the Strip to the MGM *or the Tropicana, and someone drops him on the sidewalk and speeds off with his satchels of money?*

What if he takes a cab somewhere—further away, at some distance, possibly Caesars—and there's an APB *out for him, and the smarter-than-your-normal-cab-driver figures out who he is and called him in? Or tries to extort him?*

What if? What if? What if?

In the film-in-his-head, Mark feels paralyzed, but realizes paralysis isn't really a plan.

Any connection with another person—other than the most casual—only creates a record, sets down footprints. Already, here—having won—he's in trouble.

Almost slow-motioned now, Mark sees Lena, still in town, walking through the Mandalay and seeing his picture on the casino's Wall of Fame, the slot-winner wall, *with the name Anthony Francis!*

Maybe he should just go *back*—rewind these last days—to Lena: tell her everything and hope for the best.

Even if she'd meant what she'd said—*You mean nothing to me*—Mark knows she's not a person to mean cruel things for long. Cruelty, most times, she regrets and takes back. And—face it—she's all he has; beyond her, there's no one. She's his only out from being an orphan.

Back in his room, Mark opens his safe, stuffs his bags with the money and chips. At the door to his room, about to leave, he feels panic. He has to get from *here* to *there* now. He can't stay *here* now; people know him. He's…*traceable. Recognizable.*

Forty-five minutes later, Mark's in an even larger suite at the MGM Grand, standing at his locked door and experiencing even greater waves of panic. He's gotten *there*, but now *there* is *here* and it's not an iota better. In the elevator, riding up, it had occurred to him that he'd made an enormous mistake, registering with his appropriated credit card. Of course, *Anthony Francis* isn't really him, still *Anthony Francis* is a *somebody* and not just any *somebody*, a *somebody* who's now been recorded—less than two hours ago at Mandalay Bay—as winning over three hundred thousand dollars. How can Mark be sure that his phone won't begin ringing *here*? At which point, of course, it rings.

He doesn't answer it; instead he rides the elevator down and checks out. "Did you enjoy your stay with us, Mr. Francis?" the front desk clerk asks.

"I always tell people: the MGM never lets me down," Mark says.

"Well, we're glad to hear that."

Twenty minutes later, Mark's using cash to register at Planet Hollywood. "If you have a suite, I'd prefer a suite," Mark says.

Their available suite was $599, plus tax.

"If we could have a credit card, please."

"I'm sorry, I said cash."

"That's fine. You did. We'll use the imprint—in the event there are incidentals."

"Hey, listen, why don't I give you a thousand."

"We'd prefer—"

"Two?" Mark peels off bills.

The clerk calls over a supervisor and the two mumble together briefly before the supervisor walks away.

"Two thousand's fine," the clerk says. "Any money you don't use, we will, of course, return."

"Excellent."

"I will need a photo ID, Mr. . . . ?"

"Don Quixote," Mark said.

The clerk lowers her glasses down to the bridge of her nose, looks at Mark. "If I could just see an ID, Mr. Quixote," she says, "then I can certainly accommodate you."

Mark draws a wide breath, holds it, tries to imagine himself as fearless and criminal. He reaches into his blazer pocket where he has a thick packet of bills. He peels off ten, pushes them across the counter to the clerk. "I'm not sure which one, but I know my picture ID is on one of them. Why don't you keep them all; you know, for future reference."

The clerk draws her own wide breath. She looks to either side to assure she's not being watched then slides him a key packet and nods. "Welcome to Planet Hollywood, Mr. Cervantes," she says.

In his room, Mark staggers to the safe with the weight of his wealth and locks up his money, stretches out on his California-king bed and— perhaps for the first time in three days—begins to relax. It's nearly midnight, and he calls room service. "I'd like three or four shrimp cocktails and a tray of mai tais," he says.

"So, how many is a tray?" the room-service person asks.

"Well, in cards, it's a *three*," Mark says. "I don't know, *you* decide. A *tray*." It feels good to be whimsical and cryptic and offhand. Mark thinks he understands maybe just a bit of what it must be like to be Lena.

He activates his video, peruses the menu. Maybe he'll watch an adult movie. Why not? Maybe, after his mai tais and shrimp cocktails, he'll go down into the casino and gamble. He's never played craps. Only blackjack and slot machines. Maybe he'll throw the dice and shout, "Baby needs a new pair of shoes!"

And tomorrow, he'll maybe buy himself a bathing suit, a bunch of Tommy Bahama shirts, some five-hundred-dollar sunglasses. He'd slop himself with sunscreen, buy an expensive cell phone, pretend to be talking on it in a loud voice while sprawled in a large lounge-chair, poolside. He'll invent business, make his voice bark, pretend to be making hugely-capitalized deals. He can sit there and buy and sell office buildings in Houston or Atlanta. He can be *anybody!* A senator! He could shout things like, "I say we go in preemptively! Bomb them!" and then, after a short pause, say, deferentially but loudly, "Absolutely, Mr. President!" He can hear himself, snatching up his towel and stomping off, yelling, at the top of his voice, "Then we need to close down every airport in the country immediately!" and then disappearing through a hotel door, inside.

Forty-five minutes after J. Bob Marshall lands at McCarran, he's sitting in a room with The Mirage surveillance shift manager, Harlan Cobb, watching tapes of his impersonator.

"Fuck!" he keeps saying. And then, "Fuck!" and then "Fuck!" again. "Fuck, this guy's good," J. Bob Marshall says. "Fucker's *nailed* it! Looks just like me. Not quite as macho…Still, dresses just like me. Has my little…gestures, wardrobe. Guy's an *actor!*"

"Certainly fooled us," the surveillance manager, Harlan Cobb says.

"Except I never wear a vest."

"Sir?"

"Except I never wear a vest. See there?" And J. Bob points. "Zoom in? You can see it just at the corner of his lapels. Right there. A kind of—"

The camera zooms, then zooms again.

"Yeah, you got it; that's it. A kind of funny little…vest-thing underneath. Strange sorta. Like…I don't know, a *ski* vest, not a regular vest; it's stitched."

Somebody in the room asks, "Is that a zipper?" He hits it with a pit light. "There? Running horizontal?"

Again, the camera zooms, fumbles around a bit for the precise place and image resolution.

"Looks like a zipper-*pull* certainly," someone else says.

"What kind of undervest has a zipper?"

"A money vest?" Harlan Cobb asks.

"Why would he—" J. Bob Marshall begins.

"He's playing with your chips, not putting them back into your account. It makes sense. Brings them to the cage, converts some into cash. Then stashes it all in the vest. Puts a little weight on him. Makes him look more like you."

"Fucking fuckhead!" J. Bob Marshall shouts. "Fuck!"

The tape is rolling again, moving forward.

"Wait! Go back! Go back!" J. Bob sees something.

Harlan Cobb pauses the tape, runs it back.

"Now forward!"

"See that?"

Again, Harlan Cobb pauses the tape.

"Are you *seeing*? Are you seeing what I'm seeing?" J. Bob asks again.

"I'm not sure. *What?*"

"Him! The guy! He plays with his chips, manipulates them the same, exact way I do! Between his fingers, rolling them. See that?"

Harlan Cobb slows the tape down to half-speed, moves it forward, back.

"So, where did he *learn* that? Huh? How's he know to *do* that? The fucker's studied me." J. Bob looks—one to the next—at the four other people in the office. "Seems to me..." J. Bob stretches a hand out toward the tape. "Seems to me—am I outta line here?—that, whoever the guy is, he has to be somebody who has access."

"You suggesting *inside*? Somebody *inside*?" Harlan Cobb asks.

"I'm suggesting..." J. Bob sucks a deep breath, one he hopes will prevent him from killing someone. "I'm suggesting, this guy is somebody who's had the opportunity to watch me play *close up* and *in detail*," J. Bob says.

Harlan Cobb leans into the screen. "Whoa! Catch that! I hadn't seen that before," he says. And he positions a small, green-lit pointer-dart on the J. Bob impersonator's right hand.

"Look at that!" Harlan Cobb says. "There. Right thumb," Cobb says. He points.

J. Bob removes his glasses, puts them on again, squints. "I'm still not— What? He's got it bent. I can't see half of it."

"And that's because it's not bent," Cobb says. Then adds, "It's not *there*. It's a half-thumb."

J. Bob leans forward and sees that Cobb's right. "Son-of-a-bitch!" he says. And then, "Fuck!"

"Half a thumb," Cobb repeats.

"I shake hands—next little while—with anybody wearing a zippered vest who's got only half a thumb: he's dead," J. Bob Marshall announces. "Dead. I'm gonna kill him."

By the time Mark Goodson has finished half of his shrimp cocktails and drunk two of his mai tais, he's feeling frisky. So he pulls a couple thousand out of his stash and rides the elevator down to the Planet Hollywood casino.

It's two in the morning, and the floor is quiet. It seems a safe hour to do something that the CPA, Mark Goodson, would never do. Not many people around—no one who can possibly know him.

But what is it that not-Mark-Goodson might enjoy? A drink at the bar? He's done that. Playing dollar slots? He's done that, too.

He finds an open craps table. A young college couple is playing. And an old man who coughs a lot. At the far end of the table are two men in silk suits and florid shirts who look Polynesian. They're talking animatedly in a language Mark can't understand. They seem happy, even silly, and Mark takes it they're winning.

Mark studies the layout. "What's a big six?" he asks a dealer.

"You bet it, six comes up: you get paid even money."

"But why is it *big*," Mark asks.

"Why is grass green?" the dealer says. "Why is the Big Easy the Big Easy? Because it's not the Little Easy. Would you want to make a bet if it said little six?"

"Possibly not."

"There you go," the dealer says.

Mark pulls the two thousand from his pocket and holds it out.

"Drop it on the table," the dealer says.

Mark drops the sheaf of bills. The dealer picks them up, then lays the bills out in two rows of ten. "Two thousand!" he announces, and when another man, wearing a suit and sitting in the middle of the table, echoes *two thousand!* he bunches each pile around a plastic plunger and forces them down through a slot in the table. Then he slides two stacks of chips—one black, one green—across to Mark. "Two thousand," he says.

Mark picks up his chips, drops them in his rack. "I'll just watch," he says.

One of the Polynesians rolls the dice—a six.

The dealer points. "That's a big six," he says.

"I'm learning fast," Mark says.

The Polynesian rolls the dice again. "Nine!" The old coughing man just down from Mark has some chips on the nine, and the dealer pays him.

"What's the best bet on the table?" Mark asks.

"Seven."

"Where do I bet it?"

When the dealer points to the come line, Mark lifts all the black chips from his tray and sets them there. The dealer books the bet: "Fifteen hundred! Coming!"

The Polynesian rolls—a seven!

Mark grins, but the Polynesian slams his fist on the table.

"Why's he angry?" Mark asks.

"He sevened out."

"But you said—"

The dealer waves Mark's question away. He slides Mark his stack of blacks and a second stack equal to it.

"How much did I win?" Mark asks.

"Fifteen hundred," the dealer said.

Mark feels pleased with himself and wishes Lena could be beside him, just for the moment. It would excite her. "Pretty good, huh?" Mark tries for a chumminess with the dealer.

"It'll buy you breakfast," the dealer says.

Mark feels annoyed. He's trying to have fun; he's trying to be nice; he's trying to be amiable. And anything he says the dealer acts bored and snotty.

Now another dealer is giving a tray of dice to the girl of the college couple.

"So, if seven's the best, what's the worst bet I could make?" Mark asks.

"Twelve or two."

"Either?"

"Either or both."

"I'll bet both."

"It's called hi-lo."

"I'll bet that."

"Drop whatever you want to bet."

Now Mark's starting to feel pissed. "I'll bet everything," Mark says.

The dealer nods toward the felt, indicating that Mark should drop his chips.

Mark scoops all of the chips out of his tray and drops them, scattering them.

The expression on the dealer's face clearly says *asshole*! Instead, he presses his tongue against his upper lip, gathers the chips and stacks them in the appropriate box.

The college girl rolls...a two!

"Hey!" Mark calls and raises a fist in the air.

"Hey!" the dealer—underscoring *boring*!—echoes.

Back in grade school, Mark had his fill of mockery. It had come at him from all directions. He'd been the kid who always did everything he was supposed to—all his homework and more, passing the milk, the best art work. Now, as an adult, he's sizable, even formidable. But, because his growth spurt had come late, when he'd been ten, eleven, even twelve—anyone, pretty much, who wanted to could have at him without response.

And it had been painful, which was why now, here, not even Mark Goodson anymore, it's a different story. Mark hears the dealer's mocking *Hey*! and, in a reflex, reaches across, grabbing the man's shirt, pulling it entirely out of his black trousers.

The dealer backs up. Then, before Mark can do anything else, two Planet Hollywood security guards—a lean black and a fleshy redhead—are on him, clamped on his arms. "Settle down, buddy," the fleshy redhead says. "Don't do anything you'll regret," the black security guard says.

Mark hasn't had feelings like this for almost thirty years. He wants to smash the smug dealer's face into a stone wall. He wants to take a jagged rock and underhand it between the man's legs.

"Chill, okay?" The redhead is trying to make his voice reassuring. "No need to make something out of nothing," the black guard says.

"Color him up, then he's done," a man with a nametag and a suit is saying behind the table.

The dealer Mark had grabbed slides an assortment of colored chips in front of Mark. On the dealer's face is a malignant look. "Fifty-two thousand, five hundred" he announces.

"The two is thirty-to-one," the man with the nametag and the suit says.

"Pick your chips up," the black security guard says.

Mark gathers them.

"Why don't we walk you over to the cage?" the fleshy redhead suggests.

Mark in the center, the three walk silently to the casino cashier.

"You going to be all right?" the redhead asks.

Mark nods.

"You in town for the fight?" the lean black officer asks.

"No," Mark says. He feels ashamed, but he still feels angry.

"That's a pretty nice win," the lean black notes.

"I'll take it," Mark says. He can feel himself relaxing—just a hair, just a bit.

"You staying at the hotel?" Red asks.

Mark lies. "No."

"We're going to make a request." It's the black officer. "We're going to ask that—after you cash in—you stay away from the tables."

"Are you throwing me out?"

"Just for tonight. We'd like you to calm down, cool off."

"And we don't want to embarrass you, but if you go up to a table again tonight—" And the officer points up, indicating one of the surveillance globes in the ceiling. "We got you on tape."

"Now this is all just information, sir, not a threat. Okay? But if there are any further problems, it's all going to be—you can understand—far less friendly."

"I understand," Mark says.

"May I see your ID, sir?" says Red.

"I don't have it with me."

"Then I'll be happy to escort you to your vehicle. That's a lot of chips to be carrying around. And next time, by law, you cannot play in this casino without your identification on your person. State law."

The three arrive at the cage.

"I have to cash in," Mark says, then quickly adds, "and I came in a cab."

The chips in Mark's fist feel like some gear mechanism. When he sets them down in front of the smiling cashier, her eyes move back and forth between him and what he's laid down. "You understand, for that amount...I'll have to see a photo ID and check your Social," she says.

Mark's jaw moves, but no words come.

Red smiles. He knew that was about to happen.

An hour later, after a cab ride he didn't want, a return to the Planet Hollywood hotel, avoiding the casino, then another cab ride, Mark is lying in bed—in another suite he's paid cash for—at Bellagio. His Planet Hollywood chips lie scattered in his safe with all his other chips and bundles of hundreds.

It's Darrin Folger's first time in Las Vegas. All forty-four years of his life have taken place, essentially, between Bridgeport, Connecticut and Hempstead, Long Island—almost always along railroad lines and in gritty blue-collar communities. And now, arriving on McCarran's first red-eye from the East Coast, Darrin—standing outside the terminal in the morning's clear-as-water light—is a bit dazzled and punch-drunk.

He still wears his UConn jacket and carries an Adidas bag with some clean shirts and socks. He's sewed his father's adz into the ribbing of the bag where it would be least detectable. And the ruse had worked. In a separate case, he carries his laptop. "Take me to the hotel called the Mandalay Bay," he tells the cabbie. Then, traveling west on Tropicana—his face almost pressed against his backseat window—he stares out and asks, "What's that?"

"MGM Grand," his cab driver says.

"The whole thing? All of it?"

"Whole-thing-all-of-it," the cabbie says.

Though he's spent time in and out of New York's Manhattan, Darrin has never seen a building like it.

Waiting to turn north onto Las Vegas Boulevard, Darrin finds himself staring up and out and asking, "What's that?" and then "What's that?" again. And again.

"The Tropicana...Excalibur...Luxor."

Darrin promises himself that he'll bring his children here—after he finds his tall, square-jawed Opportunity Man, his Anthony Frank or Frank Anthony. In the backseat of the cab, he stares down at his hands. Once he's found his man: if he fails to get all his money back, can he kill him? And if he, in fact, stops saying *No* to the violence of his father living in his hands, will he be able to refuse his hands after that? Or will their inbred brutality have a life and weather of their own?

Still—maybe next year, maybe the year after—he'll have to bring his family to this place. Lisette, especially, would love it.

"A lot of dancers here, right?" Darrin asks the cabbie.

"Wine, women, and song. A lot of everything."

"It's sort of like New York."

"Hey, I grew *up* in New York!" The cab driver talks to Darrin in his mirror. "Gimme a break! *Nothing* like New York. See that casino there?—New York New York's *nothing* like New York. They got their heads up their asses out here."

"I just thought—"

"Listen, like I said, that place? New York New York—" The cabbie points. Darrin takes in the tug boat, the Chrysler Building, the Statue of Liberty. "You go in there, it doesn't even come *close*. Listen, don't get me started. I drove a cab in Manhattan for almost seventeen years. You think you can get a good bagel in New York New York? You think you can get chopped liver? Piroshkies?"

"I'm from Norwalk, Connecticut," Darrin says. He's hoping he can forge a link, establish himself as East Coast.

"I know Norwalk," the cabbie says. "Look, a word of advice—" Darrin's cabbie holds a hand up. "Get whatever you came here for done—then get the earliest plane back to JFK. This city's like a young whore on mushrooms. Don't ask me what I mean. Let's just leave it at that."

When they pull up under the Mandalay Bay porte cochere, Darrin pays the cabbie. "Thanks for the tour, and thanks for the advice," he says.

"Advice and sad stories—always free," the cabbie says. And he drives off.

A half hour later, Darrin is in a room that costs him less than he expected. He opens his laptop then stares again at his hands. He once drew with them; he still has the ability. He has never used them to hurt; he has never used them for violence. If he gives his hands permission, if he lets the storm fronts in them loose...Then what?

He checks his laptop's program for any new charges made by Frank Anthony's credit card. Good! There is one. *Excellent!* That means the card hasn't left town; it's still here! Its cluster was still a growing cluster: Las Vegas!

What Darrin finds out, though—in the logged record of the new Anthony-Francis/Frank-Anthony transactions—is confusing. There are two consecutive charges, both the day before. The first, Darrin has seen. It was for a room here at the Mandalay Bay. The second— only four hours and forty-five minutes later—is for a second room at the MGM Grand.

Why would a man stay at two hotels in so short a time? It's a bit like open-field running: weaving and dodging. But where, if anywhere, is his end zone? Which hotel will he land at next?

Darrin opens his Adidas bag, withdraws his father's legacy, the adz. It seems an almost foolishly simple tool: a large nail, a tent peg, a spike. Why would someone even invent, let alone put to use, a tool that seems so much like a found object, like a green branch broken from a birch tree? Still: isn't this the sort of instrument in all the stories that finally ends the thirsty life of a vampire? A stake? A stake through the heart? And isn't that precisely what the square-jawed Opportunity Man, Darrin's Frank Anthony, has been? A vampire. Bleeding Darrin and his family—his children—of their lifeblood, their savings?

Still, who'd ever think you could carve open the oak-paneled walls of a workshop, gut it of wiring with what is essentially a tent stake? Yet Darrin has seen that happen, has even made the same moves himself on the phantom air, trying to experience, in mime and solitude, what it might be like to be his father. He'd carved many of his own drawings up with a no. 4 pencil until the age of about fourteen. So, he well knows that the potential savagery of the simple tool is true.

Sitting on his Mandalay Bay bed—forearms on his knees—Darrin holds his hands in front of him. He studies his palms first: the crosshatching of their lines. Then he follows the calloused, rose-yellow skin out to the tips of his fingers and studies them. Darrin spreads his fingers apart, webs them together again, spreads them. Hands are miraculous, really. Hands are sacred. You can be touched by another—as he has been touched so dearly by his wife and children; you can be touched and tremble. Darrin moves his open hands so that they are set together. To them, *at* them, he whispers the word, *No*.

Darrin sets the adz to one side, stands. He strips the fitted sheet from his bed, opens it on top of the bedspread, stretches it down tight like a canvas. From the earliest age, Darrin has had a talent for art, a gift for likenesses. Prismacolor drawings of all three of his and Annabella's children hang in their Norwalk living room.

Now Darrin removes a penknife from his bag. He thinks of saying the word, *No*, again and again to himself. Instead, he opens the small penknife and stares at its small and innocent blade, a blade no longer than three inches, no wider across than five-eighths of an inch. He pushes the tip of the blade into the palm of his left hand. Then he slices—left to right, right to left—an x. Not too deep. Then he dips the tip of his father's adz into his own blood, studies the canvas of his sheet, and begins to draw.

21 ✦ Elko Struggles with...Lots of Things

Lena sits crouched on the passenger seat. "Okay, so, what happened? You're acting like—after you left me this afternoon—a lot happened."

"It did," Elko says. He nods. "Or *may* have."

"Has someone seen him?"

He's about to tell Lena what he knows when his cell rings.

"Amuse yourself," he tells Lena. "I need to get this."

It's Faye. She says, *hello, darlin'* and then tells him, "I've just sent you a couple of new sightings. One, especially, at Planet Hollywood. When you're in your office, check them. But something else has just come up back at Mandalay. Not through cocktails, not through the Marys directly, but through housekeeping. Through laundry."

Elko wonders if he's heard her correctly. "I'm sorry, you said...Did you say, *through laundry?*"

"It could be big possibly," Faye says. And then she gives Elko the name of her housekeeping contact, a floor manager named Rosy. "I'd get over there right now," Faye says.

Who is it? Who is it? Lena keeps nudging him and asking.

"I was actually heading out to dinner," Elko tells Faye.

"I'd go to Mandalay first," Faye says. And then she asks, "Are you free some time tomorrow. It's been too long. I miss your body."

"I miss your body too," Elko confesses.

"Rosy," Faye reminds him. "Eleventh floor. Housekeeping."

"Got it," he tells her.

"Call me in the morning," she says.

"I will," he says.

"This is a call for *help*. This is a *please*."

"I'm hearing you," he assures her, and they hang up.

"So, whose body is it, that you *miss so much?*" Lena says. "Who's the lucky woman?"

He smiles. "Her name is Faye. She says I should get over to Mandalay Bay, pronto," he says. "She says there's something that's come up there that might be important."

Elko tries to explain about Faye and the Bloody Marys. He underscores the point that he's very left-brain/right-brain. "Sometimes I'm in cyberspace, sometimes just in space. I can break into almost any information bank I need. When that doesn't work well, then I try my own form of electroshock, usually through laughter. Sometimes losing my breath makes a flash-connection for me." He tells her about his head injury when he played football.

As they're driving up Paradise, so that they can cut back west to Mandalay, Elko lays out, one by one, all the various afternoon fragments and shards that he's collected.

Lena's thrilled that Mark has won a jackpot for over three hundred thousand.

She has never heard the name, *Anthony Francis.*

She rejects the *brother* idea totally, almost to the point of being angry. "That's ridiculous," she says. "Please! That's just stupid! Mark's an only child."

"But an *adopted* only child."

"What's your point?"

"My point is, his mother could have had others."

"Mark doesn't have a brother," Lena insists.

"So then, who's *Anthony Francis*? And what's Mark doing with Anthony Francis's credit card?"

"These things happen," Lena says.

They pull into the Mandalay Bay valet parking lane. A valet in safari shorts opens Lena's door; another parker on Elko's side opens his. Elko gives him his name, takes his claim check and walks around to the other side of the car.

"Let's find Rosy," Elko says.

The elevator opens on the eleventh floor, and they step out, check the corridors, find the housekeeping room, and knock. When a Latina comes to the door, Elko starts in with his bad Spanish and can see the woman straining to understand him, but then Lena, with Spanish that's surprisingly good, intervenes, and suddenly the woman is nodding vigorously and smiling. "Ah! Rosy! Si, Rosy!" she says.

She motions them into the room which is a large storage room for linens and then holds her hand up, signaling that they should wait. She picks up a beige wall-phone, dials some numbers. There's a wait-in-silence, then the woman is off-and-running again, bubbly and nasal. When she hangs up, she redirects all of her energy and chatter to Lena. As much as Elko would hope to, he can't translate what she's saying, but he *does* hear that it's interlaced often with the name *Rosy.*

Lena turns to Elko. "She says: *Wait here. Only a minute. Rosy will come.*"

And, promptly, Rosy arrives—red faced, matronly. Her English, Elko thinks, is possibly better than his own. "I'm sorry," she begins.

"I would have given you directions down to the laundry. But I was afraid you might get lost."

Elko thanks her for her trouble.

"What I need to show you is there," she says. "In the laundry. I didn't want to bring it up."

Lena thanks the Latina woman. Elko Spanglishes his own gratitude then they're off, riding a service elevator down.

As they cross the laundry—between the tumbling of dryers and whooshes of steam—Rosy turns to Lena.

"You're the wife?" she asks.

"I am," Lena says. "True. My title: wife."

"This may be disturbing to you," Rosy says. "It was to me."

They reach a side office. Rosy knocks and someone answers in Spanish. Then Rosy answers the Spanish with her own Spanish and opens the door. A woman in a maroon blazer is sitting at a computer. There are linen samples tacked to burlapped corkboard across one wall. There are drawings of logos done on graph paper. There are embroidery swatches.

Rosy walks them across to a large table. She takes a folded piece of linen from a nearby shelf, sets it down. What it looks like—folded as it is—is a sheet, except it's dotted with red.

"Maybe you should sit down," Rosy tells Lena.

The housekeeping executive in the maroon blazer brings a chair over for Lena, and Lena sits.

"Okay," Rosy says. Her hand is on the sheet, and she checks both Lena's and Elko's faces. She opens the sheet—fold by fold. They can see it's daubed and they can see the daubing looks like blood. Rosy pauses, sensing, in her own way, that hers is a shroud ceremony. Then Rosy continues the unfolding.

On the sheet is a king-sized portrait, in blood, of what appears to be Mark Goodson's face. The Shroud of Turin meets *Friday the 13th*.

Lena screams, slumps. Elko takes hold of her shoulders, talks softly. "Hey, it's just a drawing," he says, trying to keep his voice even. "It's just an image. It's not Mark. Okay? Not a body, just a sheet."

The sheet's fully unfolded. Lena's moaning, rocking; her eyes are shut. Rosy doesn't know what to say. "I'm sorry," she tries.

"Where did you find it?" Elko asks.

"It was mounted on the wall with push-pins in one of our rooms," Rosy says. "I reported it to management. The police came to look at it, but they didn't do nothing. The man checked out already. They know who he is, but they think it's just a prank. If the stains don't come out, the hotel will send him a bill."

Lena's eyes circle and float wide. She looks almost in an epileptic trance.

"I'm so very sorry," Rosy says. "So very sorry."

"Look, you did what was right," Elko tells her. "And we appreciate it."

Lena's eyes are shut again. She's leaning back into Elko's hands; he's supporting her.

"Oh!" And then Rosy suddenly taps her head. "Stupid-stupid!" she says. "Stupid me, I almost forgot." And she reaches into her apron and produces a Mandalay Bay envelope. "I got you a copy of his billing statement. The guest. Don't tell anyone."

Elko takes the envelope, opens it. He's hoping to see the name *Anthony Francis*. Instead, it's a *Darrin Folger* with an address in Norwalk, Connecticut. Elko slips the statement back and pockets it.

"You went out of your way," he tells Rosy, slipping her a twenty.

"I have a friend in registration," she says. "We try to help each other. We do favors."

Elko slips her another twenty. "For your friend," he says.

Suddenly, as though some kind of high-voltage has hit her, Lena startles, then calms. She focuses on Elko...then Rosy. "Thank God!" she says. "He's all right."

Elko decides he won't press. He'll leave well enough alone, won't presume to question.

"He's all right," Lena says again, her voice liquid, a wake buoyed and braided with both spent grief and liberation. "He's scared...he's excited; he's very hungry for stone crab. But he's all right."

Both of them thank Rosy. Lena gives her a hug. "You have three children, don't you," Lena says. She has one hand on either of Rosy's shoulders.

"Si," Rosy says.

"And one of them is not well—seriously."

"Si."

"Your youngest."

"Si."

"Daughter."

"Si."

Rosy's face has taken on a look that is half the expression of a person who's terrified and half the face of a profound believer, a person who is ecstatically devout.

"You need to have much courage," Lena says.

Rosy is nodding.

"Grande couragio."

The two, again, hug each other.

The entire way from the laundry to the valet pickup, Lena and Elko walk in silence. He's carrying the refolded bed sheet, which Rosy had placed in a large plastic envelope. It had cost Elko another twenty to get the sheet.

His car comes. The attendant pushes the passenger door open for Lena. Elko holds it. She gets in. He trots around the car, tips the young man five, gets in, tosses their trophy sheet into the back seat, pulls slowly ahead about fifteen feet when Lena, who's slid close beside him, breaks out in sobs that seem to pour from some enormous underground cave. He eases over, flips the car into neutral, pulls the brake on and holds her.

"You owe me another sixty bucks," he says.

In the husk of his car and in what, in Vegas, passes for dark, Elko understands that Lena's visitations, her sixth sense, are very much like his own—sudden film-clips that unwind onto the brainscreen at freakish moments of their own choice.

"*Sometimes,*" Lena says, "I hate all the carnival music and future voices inside me. *Sometimes*...Mark makes me feel like the needy predator that I am."

She tilts her head back, eyes wide, and looks up, it seems, through his Z's roof. "Her daughter's going to die," she says.

"Rosy's?"

"Yes."

Elko doesn't know what to say next, so he waits.

"It's going to be awful," Lena says.

He waits again.

"The disease she has, it's not exactly cancer, but there's a tumor—it will attack her brain. Will travel there. I think in her blood. And she'll be a crazy child...maybe even for as long as a year. And then she'll die."

"I'm sorry," Elko says. He asks her where she'd like to eat, what kind of food she's hungry for.

She tells him, "Anything spicy."

22 ✦ Billy, Billy, Billy!

It took well over an hour after Billy Spence stabbed, grabbed, and ran at McCarran Airport for him to realize he killed the wrong man.

Billy's an epigram man. Now and again, he coins certain rules for life, writes them down in black marker, tacks them to his walls. One is: *Always be moving. Never be a target.* Another is: *When there's heat, change directions.*

So, first he dashes through an airport steel door into a Restricted Zone where he's told by an armed security guard that only airport personnel are allowed.

"You're not supposed to be able to get that door open from the outside, anyway," the guard says. "It needs an electronic card!"

"I pushed it and it opened," Billy says.

"Well, push it out, then, the other way."

He rides up an escalator, down an elevator, goes in one door of a men's room and out another.

At every twist and turn, every entrance and exit, Billy hears commotion. He hears the bleating of emergency calls. Employees in uniforms and official vests hurry past him. He ducks into a VIP business lounge, is asked for his card, fumbles in his pockets, fails to produce one.

"We can look you up," the lounge clerk offers. "All we need's a picture ID."

Billy checks his watch. "Actually, it's pretty close to boarding time," he says.

He leaves, goes into an airport New York New York shop, mills with the crowd. He buys a stuffed Statue of Liberty, which is difficult to carry together with his stolen briefcase and valise. Still, it makes him look like a tourist.

"Somebody killed somebody!" he hears a woman shout.

Good, Billy thinks, *We're starting to get panicked!*

"Somebody's got a bomb."

Perfect! Billy thinks: *rumors!* And he seizes the moment and bolts outside, grabs the first stretch limo. "The Hard Rock," he says.

"Café or Casino?" the driver asks.

"Casino," Billy says.

"I like your statue," the driver says.

"Listen, you have somebody in your life who'd appreciate it, it's yours," Billy says.

"I'm gonna send it to my mother," the limo driver says. He seems delighted. "She's ninety-four years old. Lives on an island, Karpathos, in Greece; village called Aperi. She loves America."

They pull up. Billy pays the driver. "Give me your tired and your poor," Billy says.

"And the same to you," the limo driver says.

Still unaware that he's slashed hastily and snatched blindly, Billy goes inside.

Jesus Fucking H. Christ! how he wants to open the two carrying cases that he has! To at least *see* what he believes to be his money. Billy still thinks he stabbed the right Mr. Blue-Blazer-Khaki-Pants. But this is neither the time nor place for money gazing. People, possibly, are still on his trail from McCarran. Odds are he's being chased. But he's been chased ever since he was a kid. Over twenty years—and he's gotten away; he's managed! Billy Spence is *Mr. Slippery!* He's a will-o-the-wisp—appearing, flickering, dissolving, taking on apparent substance, then dissolving. *Mr Slippery.*

He goes into Nobu and asks a manager who's working on the night's seating, "Can I just see your kitchen?" He doesn't wait for an answer; he just walks in. A culinary assistant asks what he's doing there. He says, "Everyone who gives me business in Las Vegas, I take to Nobu!" Then he goes into a little soft-shoe: "You're the top! You're the Eiffel Tower!" The assistant stares at him as he dances, looks both irritated and confused. Billy ends his performance with a flourish, says, "Thanks." Then, "Is there a service entrance?"

Outside, he sprints over to the cab stand. "Downtown," he says. "El Cortez."

Billy circles the El Cortez floor three times, rides up and down twice in elevators, then catches a cab out to Henderson. *Mr. Slippery!* "Sunset Station," he says. He doubts anyone can still be on his trail, but, if they are, he'll lose them. *Always be moving. Never be a target.*

At Sunset Station, he has a glass of merlot at the Gaudi Bar, disappears into the bowling alley, takes his shoes off, puts some rented bowling shoes on, takes the bowling shoes off, puts his own shoes on again.

He goes into the Sunset Station Cineplex and watches no more than seven minutes of a movie starring Tom Hanks. In three consecutive scenes, Tom Hanks is: marooned on an island; in a JAG courtroom; and, sitting alone at a bistro table in New York City. I think I've seen this film, Billy thinks.

He leaves the theater. No one is following him now.

He catches a cab back to his apartment at Vegas Towers. In the cab, he has the impulse to unzip the valise, reach in, touch his money. He's being surreptitious and he's drawing the zipper slowly. Slowly. How much had been in the vest? He works the abacus in his head: a little more than three million? When you really thought about it, it was modest. For performances like his? Christ: what does Tom Hanks get for a film performance? Ten million! Twenty! In the larger scheme of things, Billy's take is reasonable!

The zipper slides back, and there's room for Billy's hand to slip in. It's erotic. The cab is moving along the Henderson Highway. Billy can feel the veins at his neck enlarging. He slips his fingers into the valise—over the small metal teeth of the zipper, and in. Slowly—sensually.

And then his fingers encounter fabric. They hit something that feels like balled socks, then something else feeling like jockey underwear. Very clever! Billy thinks. His man has covered up the money with clothes: smart. Well, Billy can wait. Another ten, fifteen minutes, he'll be back at Vegas Towers, and then he'll empty the whole of his three-plus million onto his bed, take his clothes off and roll around in it. Alas, he still hasn't realized that an hour ago at the airport he killed the wrong Blue-Blazer-Man.

Now they're heading west on Flamingo, and Billy directs the cabbie: "Left lane at the light; then make a U-turn."

Inside his apartment, Billy double locks his door, then leans against it with his eyes closed and breathes deeply. It's exhausting, this life of scene-after-scene, this masked life of intrigue and adventure.

But this is home and safe. He opens his eyes and feels that vast relief any performer feels finally, again, back inside his dressing room, after any long and demanding performance. There are his flowers. There's his dressing table. And his mirror. And his lights. His wardrobe brushes, latex, wigs, body pads. He should send telegrams to himself, wishing himself good luck—"A Fabulous Opening!"—then tape them to his mirror.

Billy visits his bathroom, pees, studies himself in his bathroom mirror. He runs through a half-dozen dramatic faces—highlights, as he imagines them, from the last couple hours. He's been terrifying. He's been naïve. He's been sophisticated. He's been utterly common. How little it took! Yet how complete each transformation!

Now, though, he's ready to satisfy himself. It's *Billy Time!* So he carries the stolen valise and attaché into his bedroom where, with a theatrical flourish, he unzips the valise then unsnaps the attaché. *We open!* He thinks and inverts the attaché over his bedspread, and papers and file folders, documents, yellow pads, note cards, assorted pens, a toothbrush and toothpaste, vials of medication tumble out. *Whoa! Wait a minute!*

Billy can't believe it! *Where?*

He dumps the valise. And its socks and underwear! Polo shirts and ties! Clothes only! Only clothes!

THIS IS IMPOSSIBLE! A TRICK! SOMETHING'S GONE WRONG! HOW COULD IT BE? FUCK!

Billy slams a fist into the wall of his bedroom. His fist breaks open the Sheetrock.

He paces and pants, hyperventilates, screams GODDAMN! and FUCK! a dozen times.

He's killed the wrong man! He's killed the wrong man! He's killed the wrong man! And the wrong man had nothing! FUCKING NOTHING! Billy screams. FUCKING NOTHING!!

He sits down by his makeup mirror, throws his head back, rolls his eyes to the ceiling, breathes in, lets the breath out, breathes in again. He puts his head in his hands, shuts his eyes, tries to think.

Billy, Billy, Billy! Billy, Billy, Billy: what do you do now?

He starts doing warm-up vocal exercises: *Pa-pa-pa- Ba-ba-ba—* Then he stands and starts doing limbering exercises—rolling his neck, shaking out his hands. *An actor prepares,* he thinks. It's a crazy thought, but it's a crazy moment. Billy thinks he needs lithium.

Okay— Okay— So he's killed the wrong man. Okay. Mistakes happen. Sometimes you pick up the wrong prop. Forget your lines. Okay. Sometimes what's most exciting about theater is the accidents.

Billy untacks J. Bob Marshall's picture from his wall. J. Bob has been his best and his most profitable performance during the last week. So— He will just reprise it. Stun the world! If there'd been reviews, the reviewers would have used words like *Unsurpassable! Unrepeatable!* But what do reviewers know? C'mon, they're *scribblers! Hacks!*

Billy lifts the J. Bob wig from its Styrofoam head. He holds it, like Yorick's skull, out in front of him, and it's as though Billy's half-thumb were a stray tooth in the skull's jaw.

Tonight he'll stun the casino and larger world a second time! Tonight, Billy will give a two-million-dollar performance and be a J. Bob that would make even the eyes of J. Bob himself go wide in amazement—a performance to die for!

23 ✦ Elko Wonders and Gropes

Inside the Lotus of Siam, Lena asks the waiter if they have anything spicy with raw oysters. He says, no, but they do have a dish with raw shrimp. She says she wants it. Elko orders tom yum and a Thai sausage appetizer, also a noodle dish with lamb, pistachio nuts, and cilantro.

"Make it hot," Lena asks. "Very hot; four alarm, the hottest."

The waiter smiles.

"Just medium hot on the tom yum," Elko says. "And on the lamb dish. I want something I can eat at this table. I'll enjoy watching her eat the shrimp. You better bring a chilled bottle of Muller Riesling, too."

Lena catches Elko looking across the table at her. "So tell me what you know," she says.

He pulls the Mandalay-room statement from his pocket, unfolds it, points to the billing name. "Anyone you know?" he asks.

Lena shakes her head.

"No knowledge of either an Anthony Francis or a Darrin Folger?"

"None."

"So this Darrin Folger guy is doing blood-pixel portraits of your husband, Mark, on his bed linen? I'm hoping that's just paint. The police, obviously, did not think it was blood enough to even have it examined. But why would this Folger guy be doing that? Is it some kind of threat?"

"I don't know."

"How about: Maybe the blood-pixel drawing isn't Mark?"

"Oh, it's Mark."

"Maybe it's his brother."

"Hey, we've been there and done that. Mark's an only—"

"Child. Right. You've said."

The waiter brings their wine and appetizer.

After the wine is poured, Elko begins by reviewing what he believes are the facts.

Facts: Lena's husband, Mark, stepped into a magician's box Tuesday night and disappeared. Early Wednesday afternoon, a man dressed the way Mark frequently dresses—tan khakis and a blue blazer— was brutally stabbed to death at McCarran Airport. Just prior to this stabbing, another man—identified through his credit card as *Anthony Francis*—bought three one-way tickets to Hawaii, Mexico City, and New Orleans and then, according to the flight records, used none of them.

"*Anthony Francis,*" Elko throws out, hoping he'll see some spark of recognition. He reminds Lena that within the year Mark has had a substantial e-mail correspondence with a *Brother Anthony*.

Lena insists that she hasn't the vaguest idea about any *Anthony*

Francis, or where Mark might have ever gotten an *Anthony Francis* driver's license. The name's *totally weird,* she says, totally unfamiliar. "Sounds like the names of two *saints,*" she says.

"Nevertheless," Elko begins and goes on to remind her that at around midnight, Wednesday night, *whoever* this guy is—*Anthony Francis, Brother* Anthony—he shows up again at the MGM but then, almost immediately, checks out. Curious move. Elko further explains that *Faye* reported that there have been two other recent *Mark Goodson* sightings by Bloody Marys—one in the early morning hours at Planet Hollywood, the other having Thursday-morning breakfast at the Bellagio coffee shop.

Finally—and this she's seen firsthand—at about the same time as the last Bellagio sighting, yet another man, who's since been identified as a *Darrin Folger,* checks into Mandalay, creates a striking likeness of your husband in what appears to be blood on a bedsheet and before he checks out, tacks the Mark-Goodson-likeness to the wall of his room.

With Elko's bedsheet reminder, Lena snaps open her purse, draws a pair of large-lens sunglasses and dons them. Her eyes disappear. Elko believes her to be staring at him, but it's just as possible she's not.

"Exactly, what are you saying?" she asks.

"So, *Darrin Folger,*" he says, ignoring her question. "Help me. Focus. *Darrin Folger.* The artist. The name—you're positive?—rings no bell?"

Lena shakes her head.

Elko summarizes that around the edges of all these confusing Mark Goodson/Anthony Francis/Darrin Folger sightings, con artists are impersonating whales and scamming the big boys at MGM/Mirage for several million dollars.

"It doesn't make sense," Lena says.

Their noodles and raw shrimp arrive. Lena acts the hostess, serving portions onto Elko's plate and then hers.

"Explain this: You can see into Rosy's life—her family, the death of her daughter—but nothing in any way cohesive comes at you out of all these various sightings?"

"All I can see is what I see," Lena says.

"Even when it's your husband?"

She removes her sunglasses and Elko sees her eyes starting to tear up.

"You're crying," he says.

She looks down at her plate. "It's the shrimp sauce."

"Let's say he *wants* what's happening," Elko says. "Just for the sake of argument. Let's say he *wants* to be there/not-there, visible/invisible."

"Then?"

"Then, I'd say, part of him wants to keep being who he's been—your husband and the CPA Boy Scout. But another part of him doesn't. There's a fair chance that he could be working on his Bad Citizenship merit badge."

"Mark?"

"Well, this is a great city in which to act out ambivalence," Elko says. "While you're here, in any twenty-four-hour period, you can be one of the Apostles and a serial killer. Simultaneously."

"So, okay. Slowly and in a single sentence," Lena says, "tell me your theory about Mark—what's happened to him, where he might be."

"I think he's on the run," Elko says.

"Finish the sentence."

"I think he's on the run *from* himself—but also from someone else."

"Who?"

"Whoever carved up his body-double at McCarran," he says. "What's slowly coming to me is that this is very much a case of people being mistaken for other people."

"Mark's being mistaken for someone else?"

"Mark's being mistaken for *at least* one *someone else*. And very possibly, someone else is being mistaken for *him*." Elko describes to Lena what he's come firmly to believe. "Nobody in the world owns either his body or his face. There's always at least one other person who looks like you or me…or Mark, and who, with just a little work, can *be* us. I have some pictures—surveillance photos of Anthony Francis collecting his slot win at Mirage." He takes an envelope from his inside jacket pocket and sets it in front of Lena's wine glass. "These were taken at the cashier's cage," he says. "Excellent lighting."

She picks up the envelope, opens the flap, and looks inside without withdrawing the photos. Then, with a blank expression, she recloses the flap and sets the envelope back on the table in front of Elko.

"Well?" he says.

"Your food's getting cold," Lena says.

And Elko knows for certain that Anthony Francis is Mark.

"All of us are ourselves, obviously" he says. "But then we're also at least one other person. Sometimes that fact ends up in confusion. Sometimes it offers a huge opportunity. A man dies in an airport because of the way he's dressed. Another man with an uncanny resemblance to your Boy-Scout husband walks out of The Mirage with almost a half-million dollars."

"Mark's not that complicated," she says.

"Don't underestimate. He could *be* complicated."

"He's not."

"What I mean is: he could *get* complicated."

"By?"

"Whatever. Things beyond him. People. Outside forces."

"This your conspiracy theory?"

"This *city* could complicate him—without his consent."

Lena waves what he's said away. "Go back," she says. "Say the *on-the-run* sentence again."

"I think Mark's on the run," he says. "From himself. And toward some *other* Mark he thinks, maybe, he'd like to be. But also from at least one other person."

"Who?"

"Who do you think?"

"Me?"

"It's possible. You could be one of his possible pursuers. But you're not the one I'm worrying about."

They finish their meal halfheartedly, with no further discussion. In the Z, Elko can smell Lena sweating Thai peppers. "What's your secret?" he asks. "Where did you learn to eat those Thai peppers?"

"I have a broken thermometer," she says. "I'm spice insensitive."

The Comedy Improv's only half full, but it doesn't matter.

"I don't think I get why we're here," Lena says.

Elko tries to explain, reminds her how he's inspired by stand-up comedy. "We've already had this conversation," he says. "Yesterday at lunch. Remember? *Voices.*"

Lena shakes her head.

"Different people access their voices differently. You put your hands on Rosy's shoulders, and suddenly—who can say? from somewhere—you're getting messages about a dead daughter. For you, it's touch; it's contact. For me, it's listening to bad stand-up."

The lights in the small showroom begin to dim. A spot hits the stage. A man in a black turtleneck walks out. Welcomes everyone. He says that the rules of the game are that one by one, over the next hour and a half, he's going to introduce a series of stand-up comics.

Each comic will start off his or her routine. *At any point* a member of the audience can shout out a specific topic—"Doctors!"—and the comedian at the mic has to, *on the spot,* switch to jokes about doctors. It may be a guy and he may be telling a wife joke—somebody yells *Doctors!* and the wife joke has got to *become* a doctor joke. Everybody on board? Okay? Got it? Great! Let's go!

The first comic is a woman—about thirty five, a redhead. Her name is Rhoda Frost and she starts off telling *fat* jokes.

My boyfriend says I'm so fat that...when I approach the buffet table, the staff unsheathe nightsticks and put on riot helmets!

I'm actually one of the few people you can see from space.

For Elko, it's perfect. He catches Lena looking at him with a look that says, *Are you serious?* He's smiling, nodding, chuckling. He can feel his brain fill up with bubbles.

Rhoda Frost moves from fat jokes to sanitary napkin jokes to plumber jokes.

A man in his forties named Kelso McGuire strides onto the stage next and starts off with *geriatric* jokes.

She's so old, when she was born, Captain Crunch was still a private! Old is when your friends compliment you on your new alligator shoes and you're barefoot. My grandfather's so old his doctor doesn't give him x-rays anymore, he just holds him up to the light. When she was young, the Dead Sea was only sick.

Lena leans in to Elko and asks, "Are we there yet, Daddy?"

He whispers back, "Ten more minutes."

The third comic's extremely young and looks like every goofy classmate you remember from high school. His hair is red and not really combed. He wears his pants somewhere between his waist and chest. His teeth look a little crooked and he has a weird nervous laugh that makes you embarrassed for him. He starts out by telling *acne* jokes.

You think my face is bad now, but last year I went camping and the bears built a fire to keep me away.

"Anthony Francis!" Elko yells out. Beside him in the dark, Lena tilts her head, cocks her eyes.

We have a class bully at our school. Name's Anthony Francis. He's so cruel, he knows the words to the Bronx cheer. I'm not saying he has no friends, but...

"Disappearing husbands!" Elko yells.

My mother's a single parent. My father disappeared—just not early enough, she said. They split the house in the divorce: he got the outside. What do you call a woman who knows where her husband is every night? A widow!

Somewhere inside Elko's brain, a bulb flashes, and he thinks that, quite possibly, he's got it—certainly he's got something. So he nudges Lena with his elbow and nods okay. He wraps his hand around Lena's upper arm, nods to her, elevates his eyebrows and the two of them slip as quietly as they can from their row and up the aisle. Behind them, the goofy, acned kid has their escape in his cross hairs, and he chases them with his last disappearing-husband joke.

Why did the husband disappear from the Comedy Improv?

They push quietly through the small second-floor showroom door. The casino sounds percolate up from below them.

"Well, that was certainly side-splitting," Lena says.

"I think it did what I needed it to do," Elko says.

"Make you glad you escaped high school?"

Elko puts his hand on the flat of Lena's back and guides her toward the down escalator. After she visits the lady's room, they exit the casino.

Elko gives the parking attendant his claim check and the attendant tears it, points to some benches. "Your car will be right up," he says, "you can wait over there."

They cross, sit. Lena studies Elko—her eyes, quizzical.

"Two things," Elko says to her. "Two things I will make a bet on. One, if you go through Mark's hospital-of-birth records for the day he was born, you're going to find that there was an Anthony Francis also born there, pretty close to the same time. And two— two's harder to put into words. But it goes something like this: Mark went down the rabbit hole...and came out the other side."

"Mark went down the rabbit hole, and...you're saying he?"

Elko's Z arrives. They both get in, buckle up. Elko picks up where he left off. "Okay, my theory is: he went in as *Mark*, but came out as *not-Mark*. And there's some money involved. Odds are...a lot."

"Well, he won the—"

"Doesn't count. That was *after*. More money. Earlier money. Money he had when he came out. And even though it's in his possession it's not his, not Mark's."

"I'm sorry: Because?"

"Because it's *not Mark's*."

"Say again?"

Elko confesses that, right now, he can't come any closer. He says it's some combination of the redheaded kid's jokes that triggered the theories, the insights. Elko says that up until the comedy flashes he didn't think that Mark was in trouble, but now he's sure he is. "I'm seeing in infrared," Elko tell her. "And my infrared's warning me that the other side of the rabbit hole is a dangerous place. Black. And violent."

"So, what do we do? How do we find him?" Lena asks.

Elko pulls up under the TI porte cochere.

"Park the car; see me to my room," Lena says. "Please." Her eyes are red in the available light.

Something inside Elko gyroscopes—like a china plate on a juggler's finger. He kills the engine, steps out, gets a ticket from the valet. Lena waits for whoever's available to open her door.

They walk inside, neither one saying anything. In the elevator, Lena hugs him, burrows in—not the drawing-close of a would-be lover; more that of an abandoned child. She smells of all the lubricants of her body, and a low voice in Elko's head quietly warns, *Slow, Elko. Slow, man. And careful.*

The elevator arrives. They walk down the long corridor, arrive at her door. She turns. "We're very much alike," she says, then slips her room key into the lock, cracks open the door. "Goodnight," she says. "Goodnight, Elko."

And she disappears.

Elko drifts over the casino floor, badly needing something he doesn't have. It would be nice to name it, sweet to have it on the tip of his tongue. But that's not to be. Not tonight. He decides to wander over to Bellagio—the place of Mark Goodson's most recent sighting. Maybe his lost words will—with the necessary clarity—bubble up to him there. And if not his lost words, Lena's lost husband. Mark. Or, more probably, *not-Mark*.

24 ♦ The Orphan in a House of Mirrors

Whatever it is that might, ultimately, happen, whoever it is that he might, finally, become, Mark Goodson feels at home in Bellagio. He's been there for less than twenty-four hours, and yet he feels, strangely, that he's *grown up* there—had all of his early birthday parties in the Candy Shop; gone trick-or-treating costumed as a skeleton or made up as Frankenstein, along the Via Bellagio. It seems that the Conservatory and Botanical Gardens have been his backyard. He believes that he has vague memories of a tree house up near the skylight, recollections of playing hide-and-seek there, of sailing leaf boats along the water that flows under the wooden bridge. And—is this wrong?— doesn't he remember helping his father mow the lawn, holding the trowel for his mother while she plants tulips and daffodils?

Even the casino seems more a neighborhood than a gambling floor. People are so friendly. Half the time, he swears he can hear dogs barking, friends from school practicing their piano lessons. And there are the bass-reverb sounds of boom boxes. Television programs drift through open windows: *Wheel...of...Fortune!* Mark can hear the summertime sounds of ice-cream trucks. Hasn't he had a paper route here? Isn't the sports book where he's had football and basketball practice?

So many people smile. So many people seem to know one another. There's nothing inside Bellagio—as Mark experiences it—that seems like Ratrace, USA. Mark imagines the crime rate here to be close to zero. Here's where your mother—or *some*body, *somebody's* mother, lots of people seeming very maternal—cook anything you want. You can have peanut butter and jelly if you want peanut butter and jelly. You can have a hamburger if you want a hamburger. You can have Dover sole or a California roll or gnocchi.

And you can stay up as late as you want, watch anything you feel like on TV, stand in a really hot shower and nobody will say, *Turn the water off!* And people appreciate you. If you hit on a fifteen and get a six, dealers will say, *Hey, dude: nice draw.* If fact, the whole table will cheer when you make your number in craps. Mark wonders what it would cost to *buy* a room at the Bellagio. Of course, it will have to be a suite, because that way—if he chooses—he can cook when he wants to, have people over. Or maybe he can lease with an option to buy—give it a try for a year or so.

For Mark, Bellagio is peace, prosperity and the pursuit of happiness. Everybody there greets him when they see him. Everywhere he walks, it's all friendliness without responsibility. Nobody asks, Mark would you walk the dog or pick up the cleaning because nobody there knows his name.

It's nine thirty, Friday evening, September 20 and for the first time since he's disappeared, Mark feels a sexual restlessness. He misses Lena. She can be cruel, but even her cruelty has such heat. His neck suddenly feels tight and the armature of himself feels like it's bobbing on water.

Mark threads the floor until he finds the Fontana Bar, where he sits at a table and orders a Manhattan. He's abandoned mai tais and is in the process of running through all the other drinks whose names he's heard but has never tasted. He's had a whiskey sour with his dinner at Cirque and rather liked it. So now he'll try a manhattan.

There's an attractive woman—Mark judges her to be in her early fifties—at the next table. She smiles at Mark. "Quiet night," she says.

"It is," he says. And, as he says it, the casino, suddenly, seems to grow quieter. And he swears he can smell an offshore breeze with just a hint of diminishing tide.

"How's your luck been?" the woman asks.

"It's been good. Actually, very good. What about yours?" Mark asks.

"Not so good. In fact: terrible," the woman says. "So maybe I should latch onto you. Maybe I need a good luck charm." She smiles. "I certainly need *some*thing."

His manhattan arrives. He pays for it, tips the waitress a twenty. He likes the pleasure-surges he's found in cocktail waitresses when he tips them twenties. He takes a sip of his drink. Not bad. Now his cocktail waitress is holding an open cocktail napkin in her hand. She looks at Mark, looks at the napkin, looks at Mark and then the napkin again.

"Yes?" Mark says.

"I'm not sure I get this," the waitress says, "but I think maybe you should see it." When she spreads the napkin on the table, Mark sees that it holds a ballpoint rendering of a face and that the face is his. "So, what's the deal? Are you somebody famous?" the waitress asks. "Are you somebody I should know?"

Mark can see that the woman at the next table is attentive, listening.

"Weirdest thing is," the cocktail waitress goes on. "The guy who drew this was sitting way over there." And she gestures to the far side of the lounge. "And he *left* just before *you* arrived."

Mark studies the drawing, aware of the woman at the next table studying him.

Mark looks up at the waitress. "Can I have this?" he asks.

"It's why I brought it," the cocktail waitress says.

"Thanks," Mark says. And he begins—slowly, carefully—to refold the napkin.

The waitress lingers. Perhaps she's hoping for another twenty, but when Mark simply smiles and nods, she says, "Take it easy," and hurries away.

"Are you somebody famous?" the woman at the next table asks.

"Not that I can recall," Mark says. He slips the napkin into an inside pocket then sits and turns the glass holding his Manhattan on the table in front of him as if he were unscrewing it. *Why would somebody be drawing him?* And then, *Who would the person who had made this drawing be?* He takes a drink. An idea occurs. He takes the matchbook from the ashtray on the table in front of him, opens the cover, finds a blank spot and writes his Bellagio suite number on it. Under the suite number, he writes *Tony Bennett,* which is the name—using cash only—he first tried registering under...until it was clear Bellagio would have none of it and he instead used his twin's driver's license and Visa card.

Abruptly, he's aware that the woman from the next table has just sat down at his.

"Suddenly, you're a man of mystery," she says.

Mark stands, reaches into his pocket, "Look," he says. He pulls out a wad of hundreds, peels two off, holds them out. "Get into a good game of blackjack," he says. "Be lucky; think of me."

"Hey, a couple more, and I'm yours for the night," the woman says and smiles.

He drops the hundreds. "Win big. Win a fortune," he says.

He walks away and spots his cocktail waitress, serving drinks to a distant table. He catches her on her way back to the bar. "Excuse me..."

"Ginger." She smiles.

"Excuse me, Ginger," he says. "And thanks for—before—bringing me the sketch."

"No problem."

"Can I ask a favor?"

"Ask away. I'll certainly try."

From one pocket, he pulls the matchbook on which he's printed *Tony Bennett.* From another, he pulls yet another hundred. "If you see him, see the man," he begins, "you know, man who did the sketch on the napkin: give me a call, okay? In my room." And Mark points to the matchbook with his room information. "And...it doesn't matter how late—any time, whenever—if you see him again, I'd appreciate it if you'd just call and tell me...you know...where he is, what he looks like, what he's wearing, where I'd find him. Can you do that?"

"Sure," the waitress says.

"I'd appreciate it," Mark says.

"Thank *you,* Mr. Bennett," she says.

25 ✦ Billy Spence Lap Dances with Hubris

Which does Billy love more, money or performing? It's hard to say. Which is why, probably, he's combined them. He's a talent beyond *Star Search*, beyond *American Idol!* He's a Legend in Concert without the concert. Or...he would *be* a legend! *Should* be. Never mind the Bugsy Siegel stories, the Benny Binion and Elvis and Frank Sinatra stories. After his *encore*, J. Bob Marshall performance tonight, they'll be telling the Billy Spence story into the next millennium. *Did you hear about the night—I think it was at The Mirage—when this guy walked in impersonating one of the casino's high rollers—one of their whales—and walked out with three million? No one knows who he was! No one ever found him!*

Billy studies the J. Bob blow-ups he's taped to his mirror. He studies himself. He's almost ready; it's almost time! He looks back at the photos...himself. Again. How has he done with the cheekbones? Pretty much on the mark! And he has the right waves in the hair, the right salt-and-pepper. The chin? Pretty good; pretty close, but he can square the chin up just a little bit and be closer. And...wait a minute. He looks at the left side of J. Bob's neck, takes his magnifier up, looks closer. Was that? How had he missed that? A scar running from just below the left ear, diagonally back, to the back of the neck. Okay! Okay! He can do that. Piece of cake!

Twenty minutes later, he's ready. He's sewed himself another quilted silk-lined money vest and put that on. Then he's slid on a chocolate-colored suede jacket, adjusted a bolo tie with the rock-turquoise tie-slide. Added the hat. The MGM/Mirage file on J. Bob says he never wears his hat inside except when he's losing—*steaming* is the word in the file. *If he's wearing his hat, he's angry,* the file announces. *If you see Mr. M. with his hat on, double up on the hospitality.*

Double hospitality! That might be interesting: show up with the hat on, get some perks, get spoiled a little—maybe a midnight dinner at Renoir—then move on to the tables.

Should Billy play in the High Limit room? He liked it better when it was by the Baccarat Bar and elevated—that sense of being above the other players: those common stragglers in tank tops and Hawaiian shirts, the business men in their suits, there for conventions. Point of information: J. Bob never plays the High Limit—though he does play in the middle of the night. "Ah think—for the hell of it—ah'm gonna play in your High Limit tonight." Billy tries the sentence in the burnt air of his Vegas Towers studio. He lowers his voice, slows the sentence, almost sucks on it as if it's a cube of ice, then tries it again.

Where might he attract more attention? On the floor or in High Limit? Does he *want* attention? Does Al Pacino want an audience? But...okay, let's get serious here: Does he want attention? Well... no; not attention exactly; not public attention, really. But certainly— it's critical that he have an *audience.* All of the money that he hopes to walk away with is, ultimately, the payment that he is worth for a great *performance.*

Still, there remains a compelling question: What is the difference between *attracting attention* and *having an audience? Attention* is more accidental, Billy thinks: attention's more random—you're look- ing elsewhere and then something *catches* your attention. Or you *catch* somebody's. An *audience,* well, they're there; they're assembled for the performance; they've paid for...and have you in their crosshairs from the get-go.

And, truth of the matter: I'm an audience person, Billy thinks.

He tries his left profile in the full-length. He tries his right profile. He tips his Stetson to himself, gives a thumbs-up, which shows off his stubbed second finger. Even with his new money vest, he doesn't have the full heft and chunkiness of the living-breathing J. Bob. But it won't get noticed.

Perhaps he should take a picture of himself all dressed up like this. J. Bob might like a keepsake of Billy's performance. Billy could even deliver it to J. Bob at his ranch outside of Dallas—costume himself as a postman, say it's a special delivery. It would be a thrill to stand only an arm's length from the man he's so brilliantly scammed out of almost two million dollars.

Billy writes the dialogue.

—*Afternoon, sir.*
—*Afternoon. You got something for me?*
—*You expecting something?*
—*Boy, I'm always expecting something.*
—*Hard to surprise you then, I guess.*
—*No, I don't like surprises. Fact is, I take badly to them.*
—*Is my life in danger, then?*
—*Hell, you're just the messenger. I don't shoot the messenger.*
—*But if a person does you dirt*—
—*(Pointing off to a barn) See that fertilizer?*

Something like that. Something along those lines. How would J. Bob know? Some guy in a US Postal Service uniform arrives at his door with a Priority Mail envelope. Even if he opens the envelope right there and sees the glossy of Billy all decked out as J. Bob himself he'll never connect it with the mailman, even if, by that time, he knows about the skimmed three million dollars.

Maybe Billy should do that. It'd be a rush—talk about meeting your audience!—to stand face-to-face with one of the great acting challenges of his life!

26 ♦ How Do You Get from Mark to Not-Mark?

Back in his suite, Mark finds himself roiling again—a combination of restless and sexual energy. Walking Las Vegas Boulevard, he had taken a pamphlet from a Latino who was slapping them into the hands of whoever would take them. It's in his inside jacket pocket, and he pulls it out, thumbs through it, forwards and back. There are pictures of sluttish-looking women, telephone numbers, listed websites. A regular client whose taxes Mark's done had once rambled on, angrily, about escort agencies in Vegas—*Rip-offs! Total rip-offs!* he'd said.

Mark turns the pamphlet's pages slowly. He's never paid for sex; it has never even occurred to him. But if he's going to spend the rest of his life being not-Mark, what's there to do? What's the alternative? He's a man. When he and Lena have sex: sure, sometimes it's a bit extreme, not always scenarios he would have chosen; still, almost unfailingly, it's good. And, yes, sometimes he feels even a little ashamed and certainly exhausted after she's had her way. Nevertheless!

He finds the website for *Exotics-Vegas* and, using the computer console in his suite, accesses it. The site offers choices: *Massage... Escorts...Fetishes.* He goes to *Escorts.* There he can choose by hair color, age, body type. Once within a category, he can scroll through pictures. If he double-clicks any picture, he will get a larger picture and a box of information.

Many of the women on the website look, in their way, pleasurable—not at all like the cheesy photos in the pamphlet. They actually look tempting, friendly, playful. Some even look sympathetic and interesting. Mark writes down the contact information for three of them: Brie, P. J., and McKenzie.

McKenzie is a redhead who reminds Mark, just a bit, of Lena, and he tries her first. Her phone rings three times, then her husky voice comes on: "I can't come to the phone right now, but if you leave a message I'll be glad to..." Mark hangs up.

Brie is booked for the evening; does he want to schedule for tomorrow? Mark says he's hoping for tonight, and they hang up.

P. J. says she's on her cell, heading to an appointment, but she'll be free somewhere between twelve thirty and one; how many hours would he like to schedule? Mark says two. "You understand: seven hundred?" P. J. asks. Mark says that's fine, gives his Bellagio suite number, and they hang up.

It's quarter to eleven. Mark paces his suite, stopping, with each sweep, to stare out his window. How is a man supposed to proceed with an escort? Are there certain expectations? Will he expose himself as a novice? Will he be able to perform? There've been so many times with Lena when he's felt he hadn't measured up to her need. "It's okay." He's spoken the words to himself aloud. "It isn't her need—that's not the point—it's yours." He sucks in his breath, hates his nervousness, isn't so sure he can last the next two hours.

How does a person *wait* for such an event? And is it an *event* that he's waiting for?

He decides it might be good to take a shower, soap his body thoroughly, be fresh. And so, he does that, using both soap and body gel. Then when he's stepped out and is drying himself, Mark notices that his message light is on.

Sure at first that it's P. J. canceling he retrieves his message. Instead, it's the cocktail waitress, Ginger. Ginger says that she's spotted the man—the caricature/artist man—playing a Deuces Wild poker machine which is right next to the lounge. The machine number—she's checked it—is 8712. "He's sort of dark-skinned, sort of thin. His hair is black—slicked sort of—and he's wearing a sort of dark gray—maybe synthetic-fabric—sports coat. I hope you get this message and find him." The hotel service voice says Mark's message has been delivered at 10:56; it's now 11:03.

Mark dresses quickly and rides the elevator down to the hotel lobby. At first, he struggles for direction—where the lounge he had his drink in is located—but then he remembers, heads off, finds it. He spots Ginger, walks slowly and cautiously over to her.

"Thanks for the message," he says. "I appreciate it."

"Listen, no problem," Ginger says. "Is he still there?"

"I haven't checked yet," Mark says.

Ginger cranes her neck. "I think I see him," she says. "Yeah, it's him. Same machine."

Mark slowly pivots, follows Ginger's eyes, sees the man working his Deuces Wild machine; his back to them.

"So, do you know him?" Ginger asks. "Do you, like...recognize him?"

"I don't think so," Mark says.

Ginger volunteers: "Well, I can go over and ask, you know, if he'd like a drink, get him to turn toward me, maybe you can see," she says.

"Well then, also, could you..."

"What?"

"Also, maybe, get some information?"

"I can try."

"That would be great; that would be fabulous," Mark says. "Because he could be, possibly, someone I should be aware of. You could, maybe, be friendly, flirt with him. I could/would...pay you for your doing that, your time."

"You don't need to."

"I know that, but—"

"What are the questions?"

"Well..." Mark's brain circles a roundabout, finds direction. "First, I guess, it will help to know his name. Also, I'd love to know where he's staying; what hotel. Then, if you can find out...anything else, that would be...well, that would just be incredible."

Mark sits at a lounge table where he can obliquely observe. Fifteen minutes later, Ginger walks by and, over her shoulder, says, "Lots of stuff. Follow me."

He rises and follows until they're both out of sight and beyond earshot of the gray-jacketed man.

"I really appreciate this," Mark begins.

"God, he's a regular chatterbox—a whatever-they-call-them... *walkie*...Talker! I just started him going, and he talked and talked. I was lucky to get away!"

"So—?"

"So, okay! I just hope I can remember all this stuff. I was trying to, you know, sort of, write it down. In my brain. Okay! His name is...Darrin Folger. He's from...just a minute; it's Connecticut. North...No. Norwalk. Norwalk, Connecticut. He's staying at Mandalay Bay. He's here in town looking for...He used the words *business associate*—a *business associate*. And it's you, right? Or it's the guy in the picture—sketch, drawing—he showed me another one—same face. So, do you—"

Mark shakes his head. He takes the man, *Darrin Folger,* in.

"So, you don't know him?"

Mark shakes his head again.

"Okay!" Ginger seems especially energized. "I'm not done. There's more. He's here looking for this *business associate*—whose name is... *Francis, Anthony Francis.*

Mark freezes.

Your first name is *Anthony*, right?"

Jesus, his twin! Mark shakes his head.

"*Bennett?* You said: *Tony Bennett. Tony—Anthony?*"

"Oh, yeah; right," Mark says. *The man is looking for his twin!*

Ginger rattles on. "So, he said this *associate*—Anthony Francis—was supposed to meet him at Mandalay Bay, but that he's checked out."

"And *now!* Are you ready? Do you want to hear the absolutely weirdest thing?"

Mark forces himself to center again, focuses.

"This is, like, totally bizarre."

"Thank you. Good."

And *then*! Ohmygod! Then he reaches into his inside jacket pocket. And he pulls out this, like, *spike*! I'm serious! A spike—metal thing—about this long."

Spike?

"And then he asks me: *Do you know what this is?* And I say: *Well, yeah; it's a spike.* And he smiles, shakes his head: *No, no, it's a tool,* he says, *it's called an adz.*"

Okay, wait a minute. So how was the man—dressed like Mark—at McCarran airport killed? Wasn't he...stabbed?

"And I'm getting more-than-a-little creeped out at this point. So, I tell him, *Listen, I'll be right back with your rum and coke.* He's drinking rum and coke. And that's that."

Mark feels gathering clouds being blown across the open sky of his brain. He scans, hoping to catch sight again of the man, the stranger, here on his stalking mission. For the first time since Tuesday, Mark wishes that he'd never stumbled onto the three-million-dollar vest in The Mirage men's room. Instead, he wants his life to be back in place: Lena to yell at him, call him an idiot, laugh out loud at any one of his many fears, grab him by his hair and pull him down on their bed.

At the same time—crazily—Mark wants to stroll over and stand before this Darrin Folger, this man with a spike. An adz. He imagines all that he might learn about himself—the self that he just as well could have become, the dark self—by simply rising from his chair, taking forty strides, standing face-to-face with the man and asking, *Were you looking for me?*

"Listen, you okay?" Ginger asks.

Mark reaches into his pocket.

"Sir? Mr. Bennett?"

"You've done a terrific job," Mark says, and he begins to peel off bills.

"Oh, listen, you don't need to—"

"Terrific job. I appreciate it. Outstanding." It's possible, he understands, that Ginger's saved his life.

"Listen, I'm happy just to—"

Mark hands her—without bothering to count—hundreds. "I mean it. You're a good person," Mark says. "You work hard; you care about people; doing the best job you can is important to you." He extends the money.

Ginger takes it. "You seem upset," she says.

"Have you ever disappeared?" Mark asks.

27 ✦ Identity on the Rocks

Elko decides to walk from TI to Bellagio. He needs the exercise and the air. The volcano is erupting at The Mirage as he threads his way through the crowd—through the *ooo!*s and *wow!*s—smelling the spectacle-hydrocarbons. And something in the heat, something in the black water on fire pricks a need in his brain. So, he stops under a palm shadowed between the moving sidewalks—one into Mirage, the other into Caesars' Forum Shops—and he calls Faye. "I know it's late," he begins.

"It's late. I'm in bed. And I'm drinking your wine," she says. They have a joke: that Elko doesn't have to drink so much if she drinks some for him.

"Hey, it was an impulse. I'm sorry," Elko says.

"You sound sad."

"Well, no, not sad."

"You're right. I didn't mean sad. I meant something else."

"More, probably, *hungry*."

"Horny?"

"We've established the ballpark."

"So, have you found Mr. Disappeared?"

"No. But I think I'm close."

"How close?"

"Not exactly sure. But I'm on my way to Bellagio. That's the last place he was spotted."

"You *always* find the people you're looking for. You've never *not* found someone."

"Well, I've been lucky. I've got good scouts, thanks to you and a few others."

"Do you want me to get dressed and come over?" she asks. "I'll do that."

Elko tries to be honest. "I don't think the timing's right," he says. Faye can never entertain him at her home. She has a husband. She and her husband used to be swingers, but he developed diabetes and lost the bulk, so to speak, of his swing. Faye's a Queen, an absolute Queen of a woman who could have been anything—small-business owner, lawyer, painter, ceramicist, floor manager at a casino. She does a little bit of all that anyway. But what she, in fact, chose for herself was to be a cocktail waitress, stride the floors of Planet Hollywood, the MGM, Caesars…delivering drinks to the high and low rollers without the least taint of judgment. She said once she wished she'd been alive to serve Elvis's wedding reception. She served the down-and-out who couldn't scrape up a tip. She graced downtown- and strip-casino floors with her long legs and fine boobs until her back gave out and then she quit. "It was the best way to work off my sexual energy," she's told Elko. "All those players—all those men—their eyes on me. I could fantasize."

"Call me if you change your mind," Faye says. "Or if your *friend* changes his."

"Have a Crown Royal on the rocks for me," Elko suggests. They've been known to drink Crown Royal before and after. "And remember. Or imagine."

"Can I do both?" she asks.

"Be my guest," Elko says. And they hang up.

But something's still making the back of Elko's neck buzz—the sense of a shadow about to tangle with, and blindside, him. And if the shadow isn't sex—not a rushed plunge with Lena or the kind of *going-missing* that he cherishes with Faye—what is it? What's its name, exactly? What's its schedule?

Something—a voice—says: *don't go to Bellagio alone.* Elko lets the words sink in. He doesn't move; he pays attention. Sometimes when a voice calls and leaves a message, it takes a breath then goes on. This time, that's it. *Don't go to Bellagio alone.*

So, he lifts the cell phone in his hand and dials Shaq, then, when he only gets Shaq's message, he dials Amana. Amana's downtown at the El Cortez playing poker. "I've got Jackie Gaughan sitting next to me!" he says. Jackie Gaughan owned the El Cortez; he's a legend. Every once in a while, he appears and plays at one of his own tables, and those are usually fabled nights.

Elko tells Amana that he may need some backup and muscle at Bellagio. "It's just a feeling," he says. "I can't tell you any more than that."

Amana says he'll be right up. He'll find Elko on the floor; give him, maybe, twenty minutes. "Maybe I'll round up another of the guys," he says, "but count on me."

They hang up and Elko begins to flow with the crowd along the sidewalk. Something seems off. He mounts the escalator to the pedestrian bridge over the Flamingo and immediately feels better. He stops; he breathes; he lets the night be lights. How long, he wonders, will it take Amana to make it up here? He estimated twenty minutes. But when Elko measures the pace and movement of the traffic below, he has to guess that Amana will take closer to an hour.

Once he's on the floor in Bellagio, Elko starts showing Mark Goodson's photo around—to dealers, floor managers, cocktail waitresses. At first, it's mostly *Sorry* and *Can't help you*—though, every once in a while, there's an *It's possible* or an *I may have*. No one wants to commit. *This is a big place,* he hears repeatedly, and *a lot of people.*

But then he hits a floor manager named *Larry* and his luck changes. When Elko shows him the pics of Mark, something behind the manager's eyes lights up, and he takes them from Elko's hand, studies them, and spreads them out on an unmanned blackjack table. Then he reaches into an outside pocket of his uniform blazer and removes a folded napkin. He spreads the napkin beside the pictures, and there's no question: it's an ink drawing of Lena Goodson's husband. "I found this beside a Deuces Wild machine," Larry says.

Then he reaches into his side pocket a second and third time retrieving two other napkins and spreading them. "This was beside a Double Diamond," he says. "This here was at a Multigame at the Noodles Bar."

All three are Mark Goodson. They're swift, of course. They're sketches; the ink's bled into the napkin, so the lines are fuzzy. But the face is unmistakable.

"Someone's using your man as a model," Larry, says. "Has he done something he shouldn't have?"

"Depends, probably, on your zip code."

"Zip code? What'd he do?"

"Disappeared."

"Well, he's being remembered." Larry sweeps a hand across the sketches. "I mean, at least by someone."

Elko asks Larry for the sketches, which he gives, after which Elko thanks him and leaves. As Elko's peeling away, he notices a man in a tan cotton jacket who's been rubber-necking his negotiations with Larry. The man's maybe five ten, thin; small, but in the way hockey players are sometimes small. His neck muscles are like rope and his hands are like a riveter's. He tries to act embarrassed and apologetic for his gawking, but Elko doesn't buy it. Something in the small rope-necked man's eyes tells Elko to pay attention. He senses that whatever it is, there's a Mark Goodson connection.

"I'm an art dealer," Elko announces before the man can say anything. "I trade in sketches."

Elko watches his hockey player scramble for a reply. He can't find one. He tries to smile, but Elko sees the smile break up like river ice the minute it's formed.

He pushes his luck and opens one of the napkin drawings in front of the man. "Anybody you recognize?" Elko asks. "Friend? Enemy? Relative? Business associate?"

The hockey player's got the bait in his mouth, the way a cutthroat will sometimes tease a fly. Elko stands there, watches him, waits.

"Your artist's not a bad artist," he says. "I do some art. He's not bad. Gets the look—not too many lines."

"Matisse," Elko offers. "Picasso."

"Well, he's got a way to go before Matisse or Picasso. But let's just say he can nail his subject." And, with that, he turns and begins to walk away.

"So, you seen this guy?" Elko calls after, but the guy just keeps walking.

Elko strolls over to the Noodles Bar, where one of the napkin sketches showed up. He asks the bartender, Chad, if he's seen the guy in the sketch.

"No, but I've seen the guy who drew it," Chad says. "And so have you."

"Meaning?"

"You were just talking to him. Over by the bank of Cleopatra machines. Wiry guy. Tan coat."

Chad obviously means Elko's hockey player, so Elko spins to see if he's still in the viewfinder. He isn't. "What was he drinking?" Elko asks Chad.

"Coronas."

Elko thanks Chad and heads back onto the floor, hoping Amana will arrive and give him some backup. He's developing an uneasy feeling about the hockey player.

It's an uneasy feeling that is deserved, as it turns out. Less than five minutes after Elko starts his sweep of the floor to see if his radar can pick up the wiry artist, he feels something sharp and metal pressed against the back of his skull.

"I can turn the back of your head into cacciatore," a voice says. "Or not. It's your choice."

"I choose shrimp scampi," Elko smart-asses and wonders if he's going to regret it.

"We're going to walk through to the lobby, take a left, go outside then across the pavement to the lake," Elko's hockey player says. "Okay?"

"Good directions," Elko says. "Now tell me the quickest way to Sunset Station."

He feels the sharp metal press harder against his skull and can almost smell the tempered steel, taste it in his mouth along his fillings.

"I get your point," Elko says, and begins to walk.

Maybe this is the phantom-in-the-night he was sensing when he called Faye.

28 ♦ A Means of Transport

At 12:50, there's a knock on Mark's door—a rap: light and delicate, and Mark opens it. The woman standing there smiles—white teeth, flashing eyes, a smile of sunlight.

"Tony?" she asks.

Mark's momentarily confused; then he remembers. "Oh, hello; hi," he says.

"I'm P. J."

"Right. Hi." And he steps aside, pulls the door wide and lets her in.

"Nice! A suite," she says.

Mark slides the door closed. "Can I—?"

Again, the smile. "What?"

"I don't know, *something*. I had it in my mind to say something. Take your coat?"

"Sure. Why not?"

P. J. turns her back to Mark and he slides her black cashmere jacket off her shoulders. Then he rolls open the entryway closet and hangs it. P. J. moves into the center of the suite's living area, stands by the bar.

"I hope this isn't too late," she says.

"It's perfect; it's fine," Mark says.

She's beautiful—much more than her picture; older, perhaps, but with features that seem classical, sculpted; eyes that seem, at once, inquisitive and lit with candles. Her cheeks are finely muscled; her mouth, balanced and full.

Mark's already set fifteen hundred-dollar bills inside a Bellagio stationary envelope and written *P. J.* on the outside. He points to it, slides it toward her. "There's a little extra in there," he says.

"Don't be nervous," she says, moves in and puts a hand on his shoulder. "I have some music. Would you like music?"

"Sure."

P. J. reaches into her capacious bag and withdraws, first a CD player, then a small packet of discs. She sets the player on the bar and is about to insert a disc when Mark puts his hand lightly on her arm to stop her.

"There's a stereo console in that cabinet beside the bar," he says. He walks over to the cabinet and opens the door. He finds the ON button and turns it on.

P. J. smiles and inserts her disc. As Diana Krall's voice pours like liquid from the surround sound speakers, singing "Mood Indigo," P. J. says, "Nice place you got here."

"Can I get you a drink?" Mark asks. "There's a bar here. Pretty much anything."

"What are you having?" P. J. asks.

"I hadn't actually thought," Mark says.

"Well, if there's some cabernet...and it's not too much trouble opening some, cabernet would be lovely," P. J. says.

"Consider it done," Mark says. And he searches around, finds the cabernet, finds an opener, finds some wine glasses, goes about preparations.

P. J., in the meantime, is moving to the music, circling. "I love these Bellagio suites," she says.

"You've been here before?" Mark asks. "I don't mean this exact suite. But—"

"On occasion," P. J. says.

"I'm married," Mark says. Then he tries to backtrack: "Well, in a way; sort of."

"I saw the ring," P. J. says.

He brings their wine. She nods to the long couch, and they move to it. "I don't have any...coasters," Mark says. "For the glasses."

P. J. sits, sets her wine on the glass coffee table, pats the place next to her, where Mark sits. She lifts her glass. They toast, drink. "Mmmm. Very nice," P. J. says. Then she sets her glass down, stretches her hand out behind Mark's neck and pulls him to her. They kiss. Very, very soft; very, very long: Mark thinks it a beautiful kiss, not the sort of kiss—paying, as he was, for sex—he would have really imagined. Cherishing. Sweet. "Hello," P. J. says when it's over.

"Hello," Mark says. His throat is dry from the tannins in the wine.

"Is that better?" P. J. asks.

He smiles. "It's a start," he says.

They talk about Bellagio as a resort. They talk about Las Vegas. When P. J. asks Mark what it is he does, he stumbles at first and then says, "Finances."

"I don't mean to pry," P. J. says.

"I'm not really sure who I am...is the truth tonight," Mark says. "Something's happened that I can't really tell you about. But I'm not the person I was. And I'm not sure I know the person who I will be."

P. J. smiles her beautiful smile, takes a very long full drink. "That's sort of the way it was for me. When I first went into...what I've been doing for the last fourteen, fifteen years. Not the person I was—not really sure who I would be. I like the way you put that."

They kiss again.

Then she tells him about where she'd grown up. "The name of the town's really not important. It's at the edge of Cape Cod. My family—parents, grandparents—were all very brilliant people. They discovered cures for diseases, wrote books, traveled abroad." P. J. laughs, but it's an uneasy and rueful laugh, one that threatens, midcurrent, to become something else, but doesn't. For a moment she simply sits there, stares straight ahead. "Important and brilliant people," she says. "Not people to have raised a hooker." She laughs.

"I wouldn't...I don't know...characterize you that way."

"So how would you...*characterize* me?"

"...Beautiful."

"Okay. That's fair."

"But no; I don't mean just that. *More* than beautiful. I would say..."

P. J. waits.

"I'm sorry. I'm under some pressure. I'm just babbling."

P. J. looks rueful. "I have no idea why I started in on the town where I grew up and my family. It just came into my head. Maybe it's the wine. Maybe it's your being such a sweet man."

Diana Krall is singing...P. J. takes one of Mark's hands in hers, rises. "So, shall we?" she asks.

Mark rises beside her.

"Take your wine," she says.

P. J. walks him into the bedroom, draws the spread down, comes close. She undoes a button of his shirt, then another. She reaches inside, puts a hand flat on his chest.

"Your hand's warm," he says.

She spins, almost a dance step, presents her back. "Your turn," she says.

Mark sets his wine down and begins to undo the hooks on the back of her dress. One, two, three...

She rotates back. "Now slide if off of my shoulders," she says.

Mark does. And when he does, P. J. shivers in place, and her dress drops to the carpet. "I'm a snake," she says. "See how easily my skin slides away...when I don't need it?"

Mark's throat is dry. P. J. wears no bra. Her breasts are so firm and lifted that she has no need of one. Her scant panties are green and lace. She's stunning, breathtaking.

And now she's back unbuttoning him. "Let me," she says. "Let me do what you need. What's necessary?" She pulls his shirt from his shoulders. She unbuckles his belt, sits him on the bed, pulls his shoes and socks off, and pulls his pants down. She's kneeling on the floor between his legs. She reaches and takes either side of his jockey shorts, pulls them down.

And now her tongue is on him, on his tip—moving extremely slowly, circling. And now he's in her mouth. Now not. Now in again. She begins biting his thighs—playfully, teasingly. Now she's back on his cock again with her tongue. Mark feels curiously held together by only the thinnest filament—and yet he feels strong.

And so it goes, for an hour nearly. On and on. Himself having new, and then newer, impulses, trying them, never feeling self-conscious or undesired. It's as though he were being allowed to discover an entire lifetime of love to a single woman in a single night. And when the end is reached, Mark discovers himself crying and laughing, breathing as though he's just finished a race—immensely grateful, entirely unbound, and completely satisfied.

For five minutes or so, they just lay there in the dark—sometimes kissing softly, sometimes taking a drink of wine, sometimes one burrowing into the soft skin of the other with a chin or top of the head. Diana Krall is still out there somewhere—circling in her music, continuing to let her voice out, weave her notes.

Then something peculiar begins to seize Mark. Something—he can't help himself. He begins to shudder, shudder more violently, then begins to sob.

"It's okay. Let go. Let go, baby," P. J. says. "Let it all out."

Mark folds into himself, rocks. P. J. holds him and, when he needs to rock, rocks with him. Finally, he slows, slows more, quiets, stops.

"I need to tell you a story," he finally says.

"Do it. Tell away. Tell whatever story you need," P. J. says.

"It's an awful story," Mark says.

"Happy, sad, awful, beautiful—doesn't matter," P. J. says. "Tell."

He feels desperate, safe, crazy. "I dug up a grave." He's a penitent, giving confession. He goes on. "Dead people are winning slot jackpots."

"Welcome to Las Vegas," P. J. teases.

"Other people are hunting them with spikes."

"I'm listening. Tell it," P. J. urges.

"One day," Mark begins. "One day, almost a year ago…"

29 ✦ Hammers and Nails

Once they are outside and overlooking the Bellagio lake, the man, whom Elko presumes to be Darrin Folger—the sheet and napkin artist—moves him around behind some cypress trees. The presumed Darrin Folger positions Elko to look out across the ballet of fountains, positions himself behind.

"I need some information," he says.

"I'll do my best," Elko says.

"What I need is better than best," the man makes clear, and Elko feels the thick, sharp edge of the steel against the crown of his skull. "Better than better than best. Remember: I can take you apart the way a good hunter dresses down a deer. I can do ten-second brain-surgery."

"Skillful man," Elko says.

The man's hand is either humming or shaking—but he's working against it. "Skillful. Absolutely. An artist." He breathes out—trumpet nostrils, like a horse.

"So, okay, what's the information?"

"Where's Anthony Francis?"

"Where's—excuse me—*who?*"

"You heard me."

"Anthony Francis?"

"Careful!" And if he's nervous, he overcomes it, because he slams the side of Elko's head with the shaft of his steel which gashes a small opening and Elko can feel blood—warm in the mist of the fountains—seeping, first, into his hair, then down his cheek. "First time, all you need is a butterfly bandage—not even stitches," he says. "Second time, what you'll need is a transfusion. Third time…" And he takes a finger, dips it in the blood, and wipes it across Elko's lips. "Third time, that will be the only taste you'll know for the rest of your life."

The music under the dancing fountains is Frank Sinatra: "Come Fly with Me." Something's shifted in the man behind; something's descended and gone black, so Elko decides to cooperate, give information, tell him who he is, why he's there, what he knows.

Elko licks his own blood from his lips and explains that he's a PI, hired to look for a man who's probably the twin brother of the man the spike-holder's looking for. Elko starts to fill in the puzzle, until it occurs that the metal which has been pressed menacingly against his head feels not to be there. At first, Elko thinks: *Good! I've got Darrin Folger's attention.* So, he picks up the investigation thread he's left dangling, but then senses that the body behind him isn't a body behind him anymore and that he's talking to himself. So, he stops.

He thinks: *If I pause and he's still there, the guy will prompt me. In no uncertain terms.* But there's no prompt, only the *whoosh* of the fountains and Frank Sinatra cresting with *Come Fly with Me,* traffic, and casino ambiance. Then, when he stops to listen carefully, Elko swears he can hear nearby body-sounds: thuds, thumps, and groans.

So, he turns behind him and, when he does, sees Amana and another AA buddy—an ex-American-League pitcher (mostly for Cleveland) named Sandy Stubbs—laying Darrin Folger out. Amana is beaming.

"Just the way I always be," he grins. "So big! So fast! So silent!"

Darrin Folger is out cold, not even twitching. Elko walks over.

"Hey, Elk!" Sandy Stubbs says. And now it's his turn to grin. He stands up, raises his arm. "Hi! My name is Sandy Stubbs, and I'm an athlete."

Amana holds up the adz that had opened the seam in Elko's head. "Roughing the PI," he says. "Ejection from the game…and a loss of down." He laughs and his laughter sounds like wine barrels being rolled across a plank floor. "We spotted you inside," he says. "Just as this dude was puttin' the silver spike to your head."

"So fast! So silent!" Elko remarks admiringly.

"You need to see a medic?" Amana asks.

Elko touches the side of his head, brings his fingers forward, reads the blood. "I don't think so," he says.

In Darrin Folger's pockets they find a wallet and a room key. The wallet confirms that he is, indeed, Darrin Folger—all the way from Norwalk, Connecticut. The room key is still in its Mandalay Bay registration envelope and it lists his room number as 1523.

Amana's Jeep Cherokee is still in the valet to-be-parked line. Sandy pulls Darrin Folger into the back seat with him, and they drive over to Mandalay Bay. They tell the valet parker that they've got a drunk friend.

"Hey, it happens," the young valet says.

"Yeah. Outta control," Amana says.

"We'll get him to the room, he'll be fine," Sandy Stubbs says.

Darrin Folger is groggily regaining consciousness, being held up on either side by Amana and Sandy Stubbs, when they go by the security officer checking room keys by the elevator and offer him the same routine. He tells them: "Hold on. Wait a minute."

"We just want to get him off the floor and where he won't hurt anybody," Elko says.

"Who's the room registered under?" he asks.

Elko tells him: "Darrin Folger?"

"What's the room *number*?"

Elko tells him and the officer gets on his walkie-talkie to the front desk, asking who they've got listed in room 1523. He puts his hand over the mouthpiece. "It's not that I doubt you," he says. When the name checks out, he lets them pass. "All four of you in the same room?" he asks.

"That's a rhetorical question, right?" Amana shoots back. He laughs; the guard laughs; the elevator door opens and they move in.

Upstairs, after laying out Darrin Folger on the bed, they raid his minibar. Amana rips open some cashews and a can of Miller. Elko pulls two mini bottles of Tanqueray and one Jose Cuervo. Sandy Stubbs pulls a can of Pringles and bottle of Columbia Crest cabernet.

"Did I thank you?" Elko asks his friends? "I mean, for saving my life?"

"Tell the story in our next meeting," Amana says.

"Shaq would've thought this was cool," Sandy Stubbs says.

"Shaq, I think, would've killed the guy," Elko says. "Shaq has an anger-management problem."

Within a few minutes, Darrin Folger begins to twist and stretch. His eyes flicker, open. He takes in the room and all three of his captors.

"Chill, my friend. Okay? Chill," Amana greets him. "Think before you do anything. There are three of us dogs. And some of us dogs are very big. And all of us—you can count on this—are strong."

Elko waves at Darrin over the heads of Sandy and Amana. "Hey, I don't begrudge you the cracked head," he says.

Darrin turns the color of shame.

"But I do have some questions," Elko says.

"We're the witnesses," Sandy Stubbs says.

"Witnesses—hallelujah," Amana says, and tambourines his hands

"Those are some nice-looking children you have pictures of in your wallet," Sandy Stubbs says.

"This is a great minibar," Elko says. "Anything you could want. Plus ice. Can I get you something?"

Darrin asks whether there's any Johnnie Walker Red, which there is. Elko pours two minis into a glass with ice and hands it to him. "To family life," he toasts, and they clink glasses. "In our time...as we know it."

"To family life!" both Amana and Sandy Stubbs echo in concert. And drink. Darrin's a bit slower. His eyes look skeptical.

Elko announces that he's going to finish his story—"the story that was so rudely interrupted," he says, winking at both Amana and Sandy— and then, he says, he needs Darrin to give him some information.

"I'll tell you what I can," Darrin Folger says.

"Better, you tell him what you *know*," Amana suggests.

"You were chasing the wrong fox. I'm a private detective," Elko begins. He says he's looking for a man who's a dead ringer for the man Darrin's been drawing.

"Don't say *dead ringer*. It might be bad luck," Sandy Stubbs says, and smirks. "That spike looks like it could be used in horseshoes."

Elko exits into the bath, wets a facecloth, balls it up, brings it back. In his other hand he's got Darrin Folger's Colgate foam-shave can, with which he draws a strike-zone box on the wall. Elko hands the balled-up facecloth to Sandy.

"Here. See how many inside corner strikes you can throw. And, while you're at it, shut up for the next fifteen minutes. Okay?"

Sandy smiles, nods, stands, checks the runner at first, throws. He's still good. Elko goes back to correcting Darrin's wrong impression by filling in his own backstory. When it's over, Darrin understands that the man he's after, Anthony Francis, and the man Elko's after,

Mark Goodson, may be twins. Elko tells him that he's pretty sure that *his* man and not Darrin's is the one people are spotting and that— however it's happening—he's using his twin brother's credit cards.

Elko asks Darrin why he wants to take Anthony Francis's head apart with an almost-surgical claw hammer.

"Because he's a fuckface," Darrin Folger says.

"Okay, *fuckface* is within the realm," Elko concedes. "But if there could be just a few specifics. Help me out a bit."

"Money," Darrin Folger says. And then he tells the story of how he was drawn in, how he gave over, first his trust then almost all of the savings which his family had, savings they'd earmarked for their children. Darrin speaks about his wife and daughter and begins to sob.

"Fuckface is the word. Fuckface may be too generous." Elko's heart drops; he feels terrible. "Sandy!" he calls over. "I need your baseball; bring me your baseball!" Sandy does, whereupon Elko hands it to Darrin, who opens it and uses it to wipe his face.

"I'm sorry," Darrin says about his tears.

"Hey, don't be sorry," Amana tells him. "Every time I think about the Super Bowl XII ring that I missed by a field goal, I'm the same way. *I* cry."

"To what-we-almost-had-in-hand!" Sandy Stubbs toasts. And they all raise their glasses and drink.

Elko can feel the Tanqueray sliding down his throat with its slick and wonderful cool burn, and he's ready to feel the burn again when his cell phone goes off—the opening bars of *Eine Kleine Nachtmusik*. He pulls the phone out of his jacket, checks the number, but doesn't immediately recognize it.

It's Michael Vincentes, his host connection at Mirage. "So, you still looking for the husband who disappeared at the Lance Burton magic show?" he asks.

"Yes," Elko says. "Absolutely."

Michael Vincentes reminds Elko that the two of them had speculated about a possible connection between Mark Goodson and the high-roller impersonations that had taken a significant bite out of a couple of Mirage whale accounts. "I don't know really whether this is a piece of the bigger puzzle," Michael Vincentes says, "but we've got something very strange going on here tonight, and—if you can—you might want to drop by and check it out."

"So—" Elko says. "Can you describe—?"

"Well, one of the targeted whales—a Mr. M. from Texas—flew up here late last night. And he was pretty much choked up on raw vengeance—spent hours watching his double on surveillance tapes. A lot of fire in his eyes, bile on his tongue."

"And—?"

"And tonight...I just got in, but word is that there's a lot of Mr. M. activity and action. Eating in two restaurants—Renoir and Onda— almost at the same time. It's like there were *two* of him."

"So you think your double's back?"

"I'm just a host, Elko. Surveillance doesn't talk to me about anything. And don't expect them to tell you anything either. But I think it's possible."

"I'll be right over," Elko says. And he breaks the call and looks around the room—at his friend Amana, his friend Sandy Stubbs, at Darrin Folger. "Well, the night's heating up," he announces.

"To heat!" Amana raises his glass.

"To heat!" And they drink.

30 ◆ Heat and Broken Mirrors

With P. J.'s head resting on his bare chest, this is the story Mark tells.

He says that one day, in late May of the previous year, he had received an e-mail at his office. It had been strange, sinister to a degree, allusive. It had hinted that Mark and the e-mail's writer shared a hidden connection, a past. Mark tells P. J. that he chose not to answer the e-mail. But then a second arrived. And a third. *We're connected!* the cryptic e-mails seemed to say. *What are you afraid of? Why are you afraid of your past?*

So, he'd ventured a response. And, with that, his conversation with a man named *Anthony Francis* had begun.

Mark had been an orphan, he confides to P. J. *Maybe still am,* he says. Then, *Forget that.* Orphan. Until twelve, when Hank and Charlene Goodson adopted him, *home* meant only foster-care—sometimes with individual families, more often in larger care-center facilities. "I got moved around," Mark tells the woman he's known barely two hours. "I tried so hard to be good—with the families that took me in—that I think I scared them. One dad said to me, *I keep waiting for you to stop being so good. I'm afraid of what it will be like.*"

When Hank and Charlene Goodson adopted him, Mark says, they told him the few things—from his records—that they were allowed to: the city that he'd been born in; the name of the hospital; his mother's nationality listed as Lithuanian; and the fact that he'd been followed in birth by a twin brother.

Where's my twin? Mark had asked.

The Goodsons had had no idea.

What's my brother's name? Mark says he'd asked.

The Goodsons had had no idea.

"So, I'm sorry, but...the e-mail was—" P. J. prompts.

"Right. Him. Yeah. Anthony Francis. At least that's what he claimed," Mark says.

Mark slides a pillow behind his back, kisses the top of P. J.'s head, and goes on. He tells her that his e-mail correspondence with Anthony Francis had gone on for almost a year. Over those months, each filled in a history. Mark confesses that, in telling about himself, he'd felt like he was creating the history of The Most Uninteresting Man in the World—at which point P. J. stretches herself up and kisses him hard and long on the mouth.

"So, did your brother think you were uninteresting?" P. J. asks. "Because *I* don't."

Mark describes Anthony Francis as cynical, funny, and curious in his reactions. "He berated himself—said he was the *evil twin.*" And the fact was, Mark relates to P. J., that his twin had spent the better part of his life in a bit of a swamp—constructing questionable schemes, abusing the confidence of people. *When you're an orphan, you don't trust anybody,* he wrote to me in an e-mail. He wrote: *Everybody's taken over what should be your home, and you want it back.*

The statement, Mark tells P. J., had startled him when he'd read it. It had made him realize that, for himself, he'd always believed just the opposite. *When you're an orphan, you trust everybody—that* had been his own belief. *And you're grateful that—even for a couple of hours—they let you into their house.*

Anthony Francis, Mark relates, had felt fundamentally cheated— thus, free to cheat all others, whereas he himself, Mark Goodson, had felt fundamentally *accommodated*—thus, bound to accommodate all others.

You don't seem real to me Anthony had written to Mark. *You don't seem believable. What if I told you I'd killed people? What if I told you I'd incinerated people who wanted to hurt me and buried their ashes?*

They'd written about women and about love, Mark relates. He can palpably feel P. J.'s attention. *What keeps you in the same marriage?* Anthony had asked. And Mark had responded that staying is what he'd promised to do. *You talk like you're thirteen years old!* Anthony had written back.

As for himself, Anthony had married two women for small fortunes and left them both. The one woman whom he might have actually loved, he'd almost beaten to death in a fit of rage. Mark had confessed, in reply, that sometimes Lena lit into him physically, pummeled him. *But her fists are so tiny,* he said.

"So, P. J., listen: I'm sorry if I'm boring you. Am I boring you?" Mark asks.

P. J. flicks her tongue on one of his nipples and teases him briefly. "Baby, I'm here. I'm with you; you have me," she says.

"Most of this is background," Mark says.

"Nothing wrong with background," P. J. says. "Some of my best friends have background."

"I just need to get this out," Mark says. He tells her that after about a year of e-mail messages, the idea of meeting one another face-to-face crept into their exchange. He can't remember which twin had raised it. It seemed, in retrospect, that both had e-mailed each other of the possibility on the same day.

Then they'd moved from the *notion* of meeting to the *possibility,* then to the questions of *where* and *when.* Anthony seemed always on the move. One week he'd be in Montgomery, Alabama; the next week in Evanston, Illinois; the week after in Stamford, Connecticut. *I'm pursuing the Holy Grail,* he wrote, *but they keep relocating it.*

At last, they'd agreed on Sun Valley. Mark had always wanted to fish there; Anthony was tracing a general movement west. And though Mark almost always fished with Lena's father, he'd seen an ad for a fly-fishing camp in a magazine and had used that as his excuse. So, a meeting of the twins had been set up less than a month ago.

"The plot thickens," P. J. says and burrows into him.

"Thickens doesn't begin to cover it," Mark says.

Mark tells P. J. he'd e-mailed his brother: *I think I need to level with my wife.* THIS IS BETWEEN US! Anthony had e-mailed back. *What I ask you to remember is: I'm a person without principles. We have only a few rules—and if you break my rules of* SILENCE *and of* SECRECY, *I warn you: anything can happen.* So for reasons of safety and sanity, Mark had dropped any disclosure to Lena.

"You wife's name is—?"

"Lena."

"Lena the hyena?" P. J. grins.

Mark goes on. In the months just before the brothers were to meet, Anthony began shifting ground unpredictably, sometimes explosively. One day, he'd cancel the plan. The next day, he'd beg Mark to not opt out: *Please! Don't back out! Do this! I've been a terrible person! I need you to meet me! I need to come face-to-face with who I might have been!*

"I didn't know whether he'd show up," Mark says, "and, if he did, what kind of shape he'd be in." Mark says he'd never lied to, or kept a secret from, Lena—but, with this real—and at the same time phantom—brother, he'd felt he had to.

"You never kept a secret from your wife?" P. J. says.

"Until then."

"That's kind of hall of fame, you realize. *Guinness Book.*"

"It's just...how I am. Or, I guess, now maybe, was."

Mark tells P. J. that he and Anthony had planned to meet in Ketchum, Idaho, near Sun Valley, at a place called the Pioneer Saloon. "It was old west, but yuppie at the same time," Mark says. He tells P. J. how he'd gotten there at least a half hour in advance and secured a table. "I thought, *I shouldn't have a drink* and then *I need one.*" *I need one*, Mark tells P. J., won out.

"Need'll get you every time," P. J. quips.

Then, Mark goes on, when the hour-to-meet came, Anthony wasn't there. And he wasn't there fifteen minutes, a half hour, an hour later. Mark had had one, two, *three* Samuel Adams and began to find himself starting to cry about moments in his life which it had never occurred to him to cry about before.

"Oh, baby!" P. J. puts the hair of Mark's chest into her mouth and began to roll it around there. "Oh, dear; baby, baby!"

Out of the blue, Mark tells her, suddenly and without warning, Anthony was there—in the smoky and dappled dark between the Pioneer's front door and the far end of the bar—scanning the place, squinting. And it was huge and terrifying, like looking into an exploding mirror. *You see yourself*, Mark explains, *but it seems like shards of glass are going to make a butchery of your body.*

Mark says that he raised a hand, and Anthony saw it and waved. He began crossing to Mark's table. Then, out of nowhere, a drunk student wearing a Michigan State sweatshirt backed into Anthony and accidentally knocked him down—and Anthony was up like fire, grabbing the drunk student, slamming him against the wall, driving a fist into his mouth, splitting his lip open like a melon.

P. J. presses the flat of her hand between her breasts: "Good heavenly Lord!" she says.

Mark nods his head and says that he threw two twenties onto the table where he'd been drinking, moved, and grabbed his twin brother by the arm. *We need to get out of here!* he'd said. And the two—like looped broken-field runners—wound a path to the south end of town, until they found themselves in front of a restaurant six storefronts beyond the Pioneer Saloon.

Mostly the first talking came from Anthony who alternated between caustic interrogation of Mark about his good life and the confessional spilling of his own. *What can I say? I'm a bad person. I don't trust anybody. Including you. It gives me almost infinite pleasure to damage and wound people. It feels like I'm swinging the pendulum back.*

Mark had rented a condo in an area north and west of town called Warm Springs. After their food, they'd gone there, drank whiskey, and talked all night. When the dawn came, Mark had never felt—at the same time—more clean and dirty. "It was so odd. I felt like some insect or lizard," he says. "But like an angel, too."

"Welcome to the human race, Sweetie," P. J. says.

Mark goes on. He and Anthony had talked for two days, he says. On the third day, they'd taken Mark's rental car up over Galena Summit then driven down into the Sawtooth Valley. Driving in the shadow of the Sawtooths, Anthony had told Mark: "I have no friends. No family. The law wants to put me away forever. Many people want me dead."

When, with P. J.'s head still pillowed on his chest, Mark describes the beauty of the Sawtooth Valley, his voice catches; his jaw works back and forth on its hinge, trying to avoid tears.

"If you need to cry, cry; if you need to scream, scream. That's why I'm here," P. J. says.

Mark rambles about Black Angus in the fields, elk sometimes on hillsides in the distance, hawks and osprey circling in the sky, fly fishermen—every now and again—working the Salmon River. Anthony, he says, had grown silent, even angry, in the incessant presence of the beauty. Finally, he'd slammed a fist against the car door. "I don't belong here!" he'd said. "I don't know why I came!"

They'd started seeing signs for a Redfish Lake. It was getting dark. When the lake turnoff arrived, Anthony snapped at Mark that he should take it. "Go in here!" he'd yelled. "Go in here, you asshole! It's getting dark. I'm hungry; I'm tired. If there's a lake, there'll be cabins."

And there had been cabins, and a lodge—Redfish Lodge. So, they'd rented a small cabin and had dinner in the lodge dining room. Anthony had ordered a sixteen-ounce porterhouse and, without conversation, finished it in ten minutes. He'd drunk three Jack Daniels on ice in that same time. Then he'd told Mark he was going to the cabin. "I need to sleep for a couple of days," he'd said. "The air here is too clean. It's fucked up my system."

Mark pauses.

P. J. looks up. She smiles. "And—?" she says.

"Right. I'm getting there. I'm close. I know it seems like I'm just talking, going nowhere. But I'm close."

"It doesn't matter...close...far away—I'm taking the ride. I'm listening," P. J. says.

Mark tells P. J. that when he'd finished his own meal and gotten back to their cabin, Anthony'd been asleep in his clothes on the bed. "He just looked like some kid," Mark says. "Like some kid at camp or some place." He tells her he'd pulled a chair up and studied his brother's face.

And then, in some weird way, it became a mirror. He saw himself at the ages of seven, ten, thirteen, seventeen, twenty-two—a catalogue of moments in Mark's growing-up, moments which could have slipped to either side of a particular decision. He could have run away from home. He could have taken the forty dollars that his mother had forgotten to pick up from the kitchen counter. He could have touched Maggie O'Brien's breast. He could have taken the sex offered to him by Karen Paisley and then broken her heart. Watching his twin brother sleep, he tells P. J., he'd realized that the difference between *yes* and *no* was so small, so slight.

"Amen," P. J. says in a near whisper.

"Amen, true," Mark quietly echoes. He says that he'd studied Anthony's face, found it *his* face, except...Except his own face wasn't quite so marbled, quite so folded and mottled with the colors of bruise, the small islands of violet and green on the skin.

Something about Anthony...Mark struggles to find the words. Something about Anthony—he looked like every day of his life he'd been in a fight. Even the expression on his face as he *slept*.

Mark starts breathing harder, talking faster. P. J. takes his hand. He tells her that the next morning, Anthony had woken as though out of a nightmare. His first words had been, *I have no fucking value.* At the lodge, he'd stuffed himself with sausages and pancakes the way he'd stuffed himself with steak the night before. The day had been clear—solid blue sky—and hot. Mark had suggested that they rent a boat or go swimming. His brother had sneered: *I never made friends with the water,* he'd said. *I can't swim.*

Anthony had gone back to the cabin and slept all day. Mark sat on the cabin's front porch and tried to finish a James Lee Burke novel that he'd bought at the airport. Inside, Anthony would sometimes make cornered-animal noises in his sleep. "Sort of like sex, but not sex," Mark says.

That night, that same night that Anthony had slept almost all day, the two of them had driven into the town of Stanley and had had dinner at a roadhouse called the Jack of Clubs. Anthony had drunk heavily and demanded that Mark keep up with him. There were some cowgirls at the bar. *Dancing time!* Anthony had announced, and he'd insisted that Mark join him in getting the girls to dance.

They'd danced. Anthony had been all over his partner, Karen Jane. Mark's partner, Sharon, had been all over him. Mark said that, in his head, it had all been like some dream of sex—himself and himself and two women—one pulling away and laughing, the other coming at him.

When the girls said they had to leave, Anthony'd insisted: *Follow them!* After which, there'd been a kind of chase. "It was sort-of a chase, but *not* a chase," Mark tells P. J. Finally, he says, the girls had pulled their pickup onto a ranch road that had crossed a small bridge over the Salmon. From the other side, they'd hoisted the drawbridge they'd crossed so that the two brothers couldn't follow. And then they'd laughed and laughed and driven off spilling dust then arriving at a small, nearby log house.

Mark says that he and Anthony had stood at the river's edge and watched the girls exit their pickup, enter their place. In the cool, crisp night, they'd heard the doors swinging shut, seen the cabin lights flare on, and heard laughter.

Hey! You with me? Anthony had called over his shoulder and then lurched, stumbling down the bank to the water's edge.

Don't be stupid! You can't swim! Mark had called.

They think they're fucking free! But they don't realize: Nobody's fucking free!

Where are you going?

Anthony had started to cross the river. Mark had bolted down the bank, moved into the current, and grabbed him. *This is fast, deep water!*

You heard them? You heard them...laughing at us?

Mark says he'd suggested they find the girls the next day. *We don't have to go there now!*

But Anthony had kept bulling his way forward. He had not been a person to be turned back. He'd had to finish something with the women, not be the object of their laughter.

They'd found themselves midriver—the fast water, ripping and tumbling around them. Mark had grabbed Anthony by his belt. *Steady! Steady!* he'd said. *Just stand where you are! I've walked rivers like this before. Let me go first!*

And Mark had slipped around so that he was in front, told his twin to grab tight hold of his belt. *I'll tell you where to step! I'll tell you where the rocks are!*

And they'd begun that way—moving slowly, carefully. From the unstable dark behind Mark, Anthony had growled out: *So you're the big leader, right? You're Mr. Scoutmaster, the big leader!*

Then, suddenly, there was a low pocket in the stream, a trough Mark hadn't anticipated, and he lost his balance—at which point, he could feel, behind him, Anthony losing his balance, screaming out *Shit!... Shit!* Then Mark had felt his twin's hand rip away from his belt.

He'd heard the splash. He'd heard his brother call out, *Christ! Mark!* then seen, like faint phosphorous, his brother tumbling downstream in the water that folded over and over him.

Mark finds himself breathing heavily.

P. J. sees, slides an arm behind him to hold him.

"I thought, *That's it,*" Mark says to P. J. "I mean, I *knew*. I *knew* he couldn't swim. He was afraid of water. I *knew*."

Mark can't continue. He's spent. He cries softly while P. J. holds him. She brings him the last swallows of their wine. Mark drinks, drinks again. He draws deep breaths, quiets.

"I walked the bank," Mark finally says. He pauses, takes a couple deep breaths. "About a mile and a half down, I found him, his body, stretched out along a mammoth log. He was dead. Drowned. I pulled him to the shore. Laid him out. Looked at him. He'd said that everyone he'd known had ended wanting him dead. He'd said that he'd only injured people. He'd said that he'd never done a good thing in his life.

"I pulled him back across the river, went back and got the car, got him in the back," Mark tells P. J. "Then I drove back to our little cabin at Redfish, pulled him inside, and laid him on his bed. Except for the fact that he was drenched...and dead...he looked pretty much the way he'd looked the night before.

"I emptied his pockets. There wasn't much. A driver's license. A Visa card. A little over a thousand dollars.

"I studied his picture on the license. I pulled my own license out. It was the same person. As far as the world could tell, there wasn't a difference. I have a belief. And it's that there's a moment—somewhere very early in your life—and you tip one way or another. I tipped toward Boy Scout; he tipped toward criminal. But it could, just as easily, have been reversed.

"So, at the end of the day...I'm my brother." Mark starts to cry again. "My brother," he repeats. "I'm a criminal. It's in my blood. I'm a thief and a heartbreaker and a killer."

P. J. starts to protest. Mark puts up a hand to stop her.

"So, I put everything there was of my brother into my pockets, and I've carried it with me ever since. Because there had to be a day when he would be resurrected in me. And he might need them: his license, his credit cards, his cash. I sat by him and watched him all night. He looked peaceful. Maybe what might be called the *good* in me had entered him. Maybe somehow, in the river, our souls had mixed. I cried for him. I cried for myself and for my..." Mark hesitates.

"Wife? Cried for your wife?" P. J. says.

"Yes."

"Men have wives. I understand."

"Early the next day," Mark says, "I dragged him out again into the car and drove out on an old logging road I'd found to a remote place where there was a beaver pond. I pulled him into the water and stuffed him under a beaver dam. I said a prayer. *Goodbye, my brother.* And that was that."

The Bellagio suite is quiet. Only the cooling system makes the tiniest hum. P. J. seems to be waiting for Mark to say or do something before she takes any initiative. But he doesn't. He just sits with his back against the headboard, breathing deeply.

"Are you tired? I'll bet you're tired," she finally says.

"I am," Mark says. He tries and almost smiles.

"Is it time, then?" she asks. "For me to...you know, slip away?"

"I suspect," Mark says.

"Is that a *Yes?*"

"It is."

"I thought."

"Though it's a 'Yes' *sadly.*"

"You're a dear man."

"I don't know."

"I do."

"Less dear, I suspect, than you."

"Five words." P. J. looks serious, like she's going to deliver a speech.

"Five words?"

"Five words."

"Which are?"

"You are not your brother."

Mark's spine shivers. He smiles. "Possibly," he says. "Possibly. The jury's still out."

"No."

"No?"

"No." P. J. brushes the tip of her nose against his. "No, I'm the foreman—foreman of the jury. And I say, *No. Not in a heartbeat. Not Guilty.*"

Mark breathes in. He swallows. "Thank you," he says. "Thank you. I guess we'll see."

They kiss one more time—long, sad; the kiss of lovers who have agreed: they will never see one another again.

Then Mark helps P. J. on with her coat, undoes the security latch on his door, opens it, watches her slide out and disappear. "Thank you," he says to the space-that-had-been-her.

And then he moves back and stands in the center of his suite. The night is not over for him—it has that feel. He feels new life, new direction.

Maybe he'll go back to Mandalay Bay and see if he can win another jumbo slot jackpot. Or maybe—funny he should feel this—maybe he'll stroll down through the Las Vegas night all the way to Treasure Island, knock on Lena's door, enter her room, make love, then leave and tell her he'll be in touch. Maybe he'll call the shots, be dominant, show her he isn't always a Boy Scout.

31 ✦ Double or Nothing

Though it is now sobering hours later, Darrin Folger—now strapped to the bed—is still scared and incoherent. He talks Mobius strips about his wife and children. His hands keep closing and unclosing. Like a nervous child, he bites them. When at one point he draws blood, Elko suggests that he call room service and order some Tylenol PM. "Try to sleep," Elko advises. Elko warns that if he runs into him on the loose, finds the least evidence that he's acting on his own, he'll haul him in, and he can be assured that it will be a long time before he's reunited with his wife and children.

"Listen to White Elk," Amana advises Darrin. "White Elk is a wise man."

Elko waves Darrin's wicked adz which he's confiscated—waves it like the stick of a flag—and he cautions: "You don't want to scoop the limbic stem out of the wrong skull." Elko tells Darrin about the business he runs, and then, for emphasis, he repeats the word, *look-alikes,* after which he slips Darrin's adz into one of his inside jacket pockets. "There are a lot of people who look just like other people," Elko warns. "Especially in this town. You spend a little time in this town, it's inevitable. Count on it: pretty soon, you're going to start seeing double." Elko tells Darrin that the phone call he just received was from a man who'd started seeing double over at The Mirage. "Seeing double can be dangerous," Elko tells Darrin. "Get some sleep."

Sandy and Amana and Elko ride the elevator down and pile into Amana's Jeep Cherokee. Elko thanks his friends—*life-savers,* he calls them—and reminds them that it's late; they're all tired and if they can just drop him off, he'll be fine.

"You think?"

"I do—I think."

"But what about *things heating up?*" Sandy Stubbs says.

"Probably just the volcano," Elko suggests.

They pull the Cherokee in, let Elko out. "You need us, call us," Amana instructs.

Elko thanks them again, repeats that he owes his life to them, tells them he'll see them Thursday morning at their meeting. "Stay away from men with sharp hammers," he advises.

"No contest," Sandy Stubbs grins. And they pull away.

Inside, Elko finds Michael Vincentes standing near the cashier's cage, watching a lone player at a craps table. "That our man?" Elko asks.

Vincentes shakes his head, negative.

Elko reminds Michael Vincentes of his reason for calling—his spotting of the doppelgänger from Texas. "You were seeing double," he says, "or thought you might be. At least wondered."

"Right. That's right," he says.

"And—?" Elko probes.

"Nowhere. Gone," he says. "*Vanishito!*"

"That's all?"

"Listen, someone else might manage to, maybe, *look like* J. Bob Marshall. But no one else could be as vicious and mean. As his host, I could be fired for saying that, so don't quote me."

"So, when was the last time—?"

"I don't know. The two of them *everywhere*...and then *nowhere*. Something's happening."

"Maybe they met each other."

"I don't even want to imagine it."

"Why is that?"

"J. Bob's not in the best of moods."

Elko asks Michael Vincentes if he can produce a decent photograph of J. Bob. "Or his reflection," he adds. "Either one. Best-case scenario: both."

Michael Vincentes retreats, almost disappears between his shoulder blades. He's hesitant. "I don't know," he says.

"Look, I'm just trying to help out," Elko says.

"I know...and I appreciate it. Except—the thing is—it's not in my job description," Michael Vincentes says.

"Meaning?"

"Meaning, we don't send out headshots of our whales to fans."

"Hey, I'm just trying to compare Narcissus to his reflection."

Michael Vincentes considers; he nods. He sets his jaw, nods more, and motions for Elko to follow. When they reach a private elevator, Michael Vincentes makes a quick call on his cell and when whomever answers, Michael Vincentes turns away from Elko and mumbles for a full minute and a half before he closes his cell—slipping it into a vest pocket—and turns back. "It'll be just a minute," he says.

"Before?"

"Before Mickey Chase gets here," Michael Vincentes says.

"And Mickey Chase would be?"

"Security Chief. He's the man you want to talk to. Not me. And we have not discussed anything. You just told me you were a PI, and I referred you to security."

The private elevator door opens, and a lean man, looking neither like a Mickey nor a Chase, steps out. Michael Vincentes makes introductions after which Elko and Mickey Chase step back into the elevator. "Thanks," Elko manages as the doors close.

"I made some calls. Seems you have some juice," Mickey Chase announces as the elevator jolts to life.

They ride up. Mickey Chase logs into a computer, finds the file he's been cued to find. He brings up images: full body, headshots. "Tell me which ones," he says over his shoulder. "I'll print them up."

He moves the surveillance tapes—frame by frame—back and forth.

Every once in a while, Elko asks him to zoom in. "He looks mean," Elko says. "*They* look mean, either or both."

"Because he *is*—they *are*—mean," Mickey Chase says. "The *real* J. Bob: rattlesnake mean, but *rich*."

"Does it surprise you that your crew didn't see through the masquerade?"

"And see what?"

"I don't know. Guy playing with that much, I think I'd be watching pretty closely."

"Well, then you *do* that. You go ahead and *do* that, Mr. Investigator," Mickey Chase says and slow-motions the footage. "Go ahead. Jump right in: watch *pretty closely*."

"I regret my arrogance," Elko says.

"Apology accepted. Whoa! Wait a minute!" And he zooms in on a left hand, holds the frame, grabs a second tape and throws it into another deck and monitor. "This is real J. Bob footage, we've confirmed that," he says then runs the tape until there's a real J. Bob right hand he can also zoom in on. "You gonna pay me for this?" he asks. "Me: doing your work *for* you?"

What they see in the two right hands—side by side—is that the stage version of J. Bob Marshall has only half a thumb.

"Hey, *okay*," Elko says.

"Hey, *okay*."

They go back to running the footage frame by frame. Elko chooses six close-up face shots. Mickey Chase gives him an envelope to slip them into and they ride down. Mickey Chase is eyeing Elko. "So, you think maybe our J. Bob impersonator is possibly working *with* your vanished man?" he asks.

"I think there are coincidences," Elko says.

"Like—?"

"Like—I don't know—like people who look like other people. For now, that's as good as I can say it: *People who look like other people.* I don't think they're a team. I don't think they're working *in concert.* But they're both people who look like other people. And they were both here. Both of them keep showing up...and then disappearing. Other people want both of them dead. And—I'm guessing here, but—I think the whale-money you're missing is, somehow, the common—maybe *un*common—denominator."

The elevator door, gliding open, is amazingly silent. They move out into a casino that, at almost three in the morning, should be nearly empty but isn't.

Elko thanks Mickey Chase; they shake hands. Mickey Chase disappears behind the sliding elevator doors and rises up and into the surveillance-camera stratosphere.

Elko finds Michael Vincentes again and, strolling the floor with him, fills him in. Elko shows him the shots. "Interesting," Michael Vincentes says. "Interesting."

Elko thanks Michael Vincentes for his time and for the pictures then promises to let him know right away if anything gets uncovered. Michael Vincentes gives Elko a dummy room-key: *in case you need to go places—like up in the elevator.*

Elko wanders over to the Lagoon Saloon, sits at a far table, orders a double Tanqueray Ten on ice. Lena finds her way into his head, and he wonders if she went to sleep. Then, as soon as he wonders, he gets a flash—a lot of light and some of his *own* voices. And the flash is that Lena *didn't* go to bed.

He tries to pin a word—just a single word—to Lena. He tries *precarious*. He tries *unsettled*, then *hungry*. He ends up with *volatile*, but he's not crazy about it. What he knows, though—just as surely as he knows the twinges of his right shoulder's rotator cuff—is that it's very possible that Lena is in trouble.

Elko pulls the J. Bob and look-alike pictures out of the envelope, takes out a magnifier he always carries, and starts studying them. Michael Vincentes has pointed out that the look-alike—when you zoom in on his right hand at the blackjack table—is missing part of this thumb. Elko rechecks that. Then he studies the men's hair, their eyebrows, noses, and jaws. There's a scar on the real J. Bob that isn't there on the imposter. And the look-alike (who appears slightly shorter) distributes his body weight differently than the real J. Bob Marshall. Otherwise, the likeness is uncanny. The guy *is* good. The guy, one might venture, is a professional.

Elko sips his Tanqueray, cycles in a slow rhythm through the photographs, tries to let his mind levitate. What would be the connection between this imposter-guy and Mark Goodson? What would be the connection between Mark Goodson—or Mark Goodson's evil twin, Anthony Francis—and a man born as, or calling himself, J. Bob Marshall? What are the things Elko knows? What are the things he doesn't know?

He *knows* that both Anthony Francis and the whale-player fuck people over for money. But what does that tell him? Elko *knows* Mark Goodson—in his heart—is a Boy Scout and that the real J. Bob Marshall is meaner than a hive of killer bees. Elko *knows,* as well, that the sun rises in the East and sets in the West. He *knows* that the best stand-up comics can't help themselves. He *knows* that, at the end of most days, he has a loneliness larger than Australia and that his body hurts as though he'd played sixty minutes of a game without painkillers.

And—Tanqueray or no Tanqueray—Elko suddenly feels tired and slow. His brain's wallowing in a peat bog, and it's like he's staring into a mirror and not quite able to come up with the face that's staring back. He thinks maybe he'll call Faye. But, just as his groveling libido starts kicking in, he looks out across the floor and sees either J. Bob or the man who's made himself up as J. Bob. The guy's standing, cleaning a pair of glasses. His hair looks like bale wire in a wind-tunnel. There's a long, scabbed-over scratch on his face. The man finishes with his glasses and begins to move.

Elko grabs his Tanqueray and follows. His man's heading toward the elevators, but stops and stares into the empty Samba Grill. He pulls a cell phone from his suede jacket, opens it like a compact, stares in, dials. Whoever answers doesn't seem to understand, because he looks to be repeating himself. When Elko's close enough, he hears him say: *Never enough blood.*

Elko passes and tries to see whether the hand that's holding the cell phone has part of its thumb missing, but the way it's curled, he can't get a read. The man catches Elko staring, so Elko says, "How's it going?" and moves on. A minute later, they're waiting at the same bank of elevators. When a door opens, Elko lets his target drift in first, sees him push twenty-seven. Elko nods and tells him, "Same destination." He tries a second time to check both of his hands which are balled into fists, but can't tell anything.

Just out of the elevator, Elko watches the man slip a card keyed to the suite lock on room 2703. As he passes, Elko hears the man's door shut—at which point, he reverses field and moves to the house phone in the elevator foyer, where he places a call to Michael Vincentes.

"So, okay; which of your two J. Bob Marshalls would be in room 2703?" Elko asks.

"Again?"

"Room 2703. Which one of your Marshall-twins have you got registered there?"

"Hard to say," Michael Vincentes says.

The words, *Never enough blood,* echo in Elko's head, and he asks Michael Vincentes if he'll do a favor: "Call over to room service and see if 2703 just placed an order. My guess would be a steak—rare. I'll hold."

A minute later, Michael Vincentes is back on the phone. "Chateaubriand—rare," he says. "With a twice-baked potato and onion rings. And a bottle of Maker's Mark."

Elko thanks him and promises: "Last favor of the night."

"I'm all yours," Michael Vincentes says.

Elko asks if he'll call room service again and talk to the server who's going to be bringing the order up. "Tell him what you need to— but, basically, that I'll meet him at the service elevator and that The Mirage needs his help. Don't scare him, but make him curious."

"Do you realize I'm just a host here?" Michael Vincentes says. "I'm supposed to be serving my players' needs. Not spying on them. You're going to get me fired."

"Last favor of the night," Elko says again.

"I ought to have my head examined."

The room service waiter's name is *Robert*. Michael Vincentes has done a good job prepping him; his eyes are like light bulbs. He lifts the lid and shows Elko the Chateaubriand, and it's like open-heart-surgery rare. Elko tells Robert he shouldn't worry; he's not in imminent danger, but it's possible that he's about to serve one of the FBI's ten most wanted. "All we're asking," Elko says, "is that you be our videocam—take in everything you can."

"Hey, no prob; I'm cool. I'm aboard!" Robert says.

"Anything strange, anything unusual, anything out of the ordinary— make a mental note."

"I'm aboard. I'm in! I have a brother who did reconnaissance: I know that shit," Robert says.

"This is invaluable," Elko assures Robert. "This is gold. You be our man. You be our eye in the sky. Especially—if you can do it— check the bathroom." Elko tells Robert that bathrooms are sometimes the places where people put things that they don't want anybody else to see.

"I'm aboard!" Robert says yet again.

They agree to meet back where they're now standing, at the service elevator, and Robert's off. Elko paces and thinks of calling Lena, thinks of calling Faye. He thinks of waking Shaq in the middle of the night and asking him to be on call. But for *what*? To get the rebound? To play the post? To catch a lob and slam it with two tenths of a second left?

Then, before he can call anyone, Elko hears Robert's cart. And when Robert arrives, he's the color of the ash-gray brocade vest he's wearing over his server's shirt. His hands are shaking on the handle of the cart.

"So, you okay, man? What's the word?" Elko asks.

Robert takes a breath, almost says something, doesn't, exhales, takes another.

"You all right?" Elko again asks.

He nods. And the nod says, *Yes,* but he's being brave.

"Go slow. Take your time," Elko says.

Robert does his breathing/almost-talking/letting-air-out a couple more times. Then he begins: "I took your idea," he says. "The bathroom. Getting into the bathroom."

"You're a good man," Elko says.

"I tell him...the guy...Mr. Marshall/whatever...that I'd been having, you know...*problems*. Did he mind? Might I use—? He says, *Go ahead, Be quick.* He gives me a book of matches and asks me to light one when I'm done. So I go in. Shut the door. He calls, *be sure that, when you're done, you wash your hands.* So I lock the door, run the water. Make sounds. Snoop. He has some prescription stuff—nothing heavy. Just...normal stuff: Lipitor, one other. Then I see that there's a hand towel. Looks like there might be something under it."

Robert starts hyperventilating again. He twists his head on his neck, like an actor doing warm-ups.

"Hey, it's okay. Take your time," Elko says.

Robert blows breaths out like he's firing embers.

"It's good. You've got my interest. *Hand towel,*" Elko prompts.

"Right," Robert says.

"Under it."

"Right, under it...is this other towel, washcloth—really bloody. And in the washcloth..."

"In the washcloth?"

Robert takes a deep breath, holds it, then says: "Somebody's finger."

32 ◆ Billy Spence! Give Him a Hand!

It's still early in the evening. Billy Spence is up thirty thousand on his second J.-Bob-Marshall-marker for three-hundred thousand when he feels a hand on his shoulder. But because he's about to split sevens against a dealer's four, he waves off the interruption. Except, whoever it is behind him squeezes Billy's shoulder so hard that the available casino light suddenly has blood vessels in it.

When Billy turns painfully and looks up, he's face-to-face with himself. Or perhaps more accurately, he's face-to-face with *not-himself*—the *Other*. It's as if playing the lead in *Death of a Salesman* and late in the second act—planting carrots by flashlight at night in his weedy back yard—Willie Loman feels a tap on his shoulder and when he looks around, instead of his son, Biff, it's was the *real* Willie Loman standing above him.

It occurs to Billy that he may be imagining a parallel reality, a parallel universe! Or be *in* one!

Or—a new pain-flash in Billy's brain—it's like what's on either side of the fold in a Rorschach. How do you tell the first ink from the inkblot? And what do the two of them—facing each other across the crease—mean? What do they remind you of? And what difference does it make if you say a *butterfly* or a *woman's clit*?

It's all echo and mirror and reflection. This pain-moment-flash. Weird. Dangerous. The man hunched and shaggy above Billy has the same nose, same chin, same weather-etched lines on his forehead. His hands are rougher, meatier—Billy can see that. Feel that. But—it's amazing!—they're wearing the same Western-style suede coat. Except Billy's is chocolate and the man mimicking his grimace above him wears a coat more the color of dusty earth.

Someone watching might have thought, possibly, it was a joke, a lounge act: two identical men—each looking just a little too Dallas, a little too Oklahoma City Cowboy Hall of Fame. For just the creased shade of an instant, there's the expectation that one of the two will say to the other: *What's the last thing a cowboy says to his horse at night?* Or maybe one of the two will pick up a fiddle, and the other will pull a harmonica from his pocket.

These imaginings, though, *aren't* the reactions of Charles, The Mirage dealer, who has—just ten minutes before—signed off on a three-hundred-thousand-dollar withdrawal on J. Bob's credit line. Charles's eyes spin like pinwheels, and his mouth goes slack. Someone listening carefully would have heard him mutter, *Fuck!*

These imaginings aren't, as well, the reactions of Karen, the nearby floor supervisor—frozen in place about twenty feet away. What Karen does is roll her eyes upward toward the cameras, roll her palms up in a gesture of helplessness—hoping surveillance is catching this and, in turn, putting in a phone call to security. And Karen is also thinking, *Where the hell's the pit boss? The shift manager? Maybe I should drift over, pick up the pit phone, signal security,* but the scene has her nailed in place. For all its calm, it has all the ragged and bloody charge of the worst violence.

"Play the hand out. Split the sevens," the standing J. Bob Marshall says to the seated one. "We're playing the hand out," the real J. Bob says to the dealer, Charles. "Then we're cashing out."

So, how might Olivier play Othello to Othello?

Charles hits the first seven with a four.

"Double," J. Bob instructs Billy.

How might Brando play Stanley Kowalski to Stanley Kowalski?

Billy adds a second five thousand to the first. Charles hits the two cards with a nine. Then he hits Billy's second seven with a three.

"Double," J. Bob again says.

"My big brother," Billy tries pointing over his shoulder.

"You shut the fuck up," J. Bob says.

"Sorry about his foul mouth," Billy says, and he feels something in his neck go out like a light as J. Bob squeezes. "Double!" J. Bob barks.

Billy doubles. Twenty thousand, now, rides on the hand. Charles hits Billy's ten-count with a queen. Then, when he turns his hole card, it's a four. *Fuck!* Billy hears J. Bob say. Not missing a beat, Charles hits his eleven with another seven. *Yes!* J. Bob, behind Billy, barks again.

"We're going to play the next hand for a hundred thousand," J. Bob announces to Charles. Charles makes eye contact with the hovering Karen. Karen nods assent. "Twenty gold," J. Bob instructs Billy. Billy counts out twenty gold and slides them into the circle.

How would Sir John Gielgud play Hamlet to Hamlet?

Charles deals Billy a natural. Billy feels J. Bob's hand on his neck tighten with excitement.

"I'm on a roll!" J. Bob croons.

"*I'm* on a roll," Billy says.

"You're on a fucking morgue slab," J. Bob whispers into Billy's ear. And then he indicates the two hundred and fifty thousand in the betting spot. "We're gonna let it ride," he says.

"I don't think that's a—"

"What you think doesn't amount to mosquito piss in the wind," J. Bob says. "Let it ride," he repeats.

Again, Charles gets confirmation from Karen. He deals Billy an ace and a seven. He deals himself a five, a three, and a king. "Push," he says.

"Let me think," Billy hears J. Bob behind him announce. "I never like the hand after a push."

"Listen, sit down; be my guest; take over," Billy says, and starts to rise.

J. Bob shoves him back down into the chair. "Whoa, Charlie. Just whoa," J. Bob says.

This is a Western, Billy thinks. *It's not Othello or Hamlet or Death of a Salesman, it's a Western!*

"Okay, slide all your chips forward," J. Bob Marshall says to Billy Spence.

Billy doesn't argue. He'll play the Quiet Stranger who the Evil Cattle Baron underestimates the power of. He cups his hands around his stacks and slides them forward.

"Tell Charles that you want to sign off on your marker. Any money left over, put it into your account."

Billy complies. He has his actor's take now, his through line: *He was the quiet, genuinely powerful character who the audience couldn't keep their eyes off. It would just be a matter of time before the stage would ignite with his electrifying performance.*

Charles and Karen are counting and recounting the chips—setting them out clearly in stacks of twenty for the cameras. Each is backing the other up with the paper work.

An impatient drunk who's come to the table during the count, squirms a bit in his chair to get comfortable, slides a green chip forward, waits, squints at all present and blurts, "Hey, Charles! You through with the Bobbsey Twins? C'mon: deal!"

J. Bob slides a lilac five-hundred chip over in front of the drunk, then puts a hand at the back of the drunk's neck and squeezes. Instantly, the drunk's eyes go white and wide. "Slow, partn'r. We'll just be another minute," J. Bob tells the drunk. "We appreciate your keepin' your pants on."

"Thank you, Mr. M." Charles slides the paperwork across to Billy.

"Pick it up," J. Bob whispers.

Billy picks the transaction receipt from the table. *Lay low... find your moment... then explode,* he thinks.

"Now slide your chair back, we're goin' for a walk," J. Bob says.

When Billy slides off his stool, the mirror image becomes, suddenly, even more warped and comic. Though the two men appear to have the same faces and though they wear essentially the same clothes, J. Bob is a good three inches taller than Billy Spence. And their necks aren't the same necks. Billy's collar's a fifteen; J. Bob Marshall's must be a good eighteen. And J. Bob's hands seem twice as large. And they are intact. Still, in the flesh—pocked and windblown as it is—the man is a caricature, a muscular brainstem without a brain. Total community theater!

Hell!—it wasn't a matter of Othello or Hamlet. It would be Olivier playing Jed Clampett to Jed Clampett.

Billy is in some spin-cycle of self-amusement when he takes in two security staff in gold blazers who have just arrived. "We're going to ask that you two gentlemen step away from the table, please?"

J. Bob looks like he might explode a bomb wired around his waist. He chews on his cheek briefly, eyes the two security guards, and takes a half-dozen steps into an alcove of slots. Billy gauges his chances for escape but, pressed in by security on either side, decides that a four-character exit scene would be better than one with just two characters and moves in beside J. Bob.

"Be quick," J. Bob instructs the security guards. He looks, in turn, bored, enraged, hypervigilant. "Be quick. I'm an important player— and I'm impatient."

"Sir, we're just trying to sort what's happening out here. You're Mr. Marshall?" the taller of the security guards questions J. Bob.

"Look, I tell you what—" J. Bob's voice moves like a Gila monster over gravel. "You get to ask a question, then *I* get to ask one. Okay?"

The tall security guard looks like he was going to say one thing, then chooses another. "Sounds fair," he says.

Billy likes the attention on him being deflected. He knows magic; he's done magic, and he knows the potential of misdirection. *The vanish!* he thinks—the surprise exit that catches the audience off guard and has them asking, *Where did he go?* But when he tries to back out and away invisibly between two slot machines, J. Bob hooks him by his shirt front. "J. Robert Marshall," J. Bob says, nodding to the security man's opening question. "And this here is my little brother. *Ringer.* We call him *Ringer* on accounta he's always going off. When he goes off too much, we call him *Dead Ringer.* So, that's *my* answer to *your* question. My name is J. Robert Marshall. Now, the question's mine; it's my turn."

The security guards eye one another. Each nods. "Go ahead," the taller says.

Billy can still feel J. Bob's hand, like a claw, curled around his coat collar at his neck.

"Go ahead," the second repeats.

"I will. I'll do that, I will. Who is it that you answer to?" J. Bob asks.

"Who is it—?"

"Your superior. Both of you, either of you. Who is it that you answer to? Someone here at The Mirage instructed that you come over to where we are and pull us aside and talk to us. So, who would that be? Who do you answer to?"

The guards check each other. The one with the tan fields the probe. "That's really not the—"

J. Bob dials his sound up two points. "I said: *Who asked you to come over? Who do you answer to?*"

"I think we should go somewhere more private," the taller security guard says out of the side of his mouth to the tan one.

Billy likes the scene now. The script's got juice; he's involved. He likes J. Bob's *heavy* and has a sudden and wild improv idea, a way to redirect the scene. "We were testing your surveillance," Billy cuts in. "We're casino industry consultants—hired to see how quickly staff at the—"

J. Bob doesn't blink; he slams Billy's head into a Wheel-of-Fortune machine. Bulbs exploded. Sound tracks repeat themselves in a loop. The casino swims. Only the Wheel-of-Fortune housing holds Billy up.

"Mr. Marshall—!"

"You need to get Whoever-You-Answer-To on your walkie-talkie— okay?" J. Bob says. "And I'm talking *Now.* You understand *Now?* You understand American?" His patience is in the debit column. "You tell whoever-you-answer-to who you have here. *Remind* Whoever. Then you need to suggest to him—or maybe it's *her* and maybe she's *Black* and a fucking *lesbian*—it's a modern world—but you need to suggest to *Whoever*...that my account be brought up on the screen and that the money I've spent here for the last three years be carefully eyeballed. On accounta I can always, you know, go be a Diamond Player at Caesars. And then you need to inform *Whoever* that Mr. Marshall just isn't in the mood to talk right now—here on the floor or in a private room or anywhere. Then we'll see what *Whoever* says."

The space is silent. The two guards eye one another like ferrets, like gophers...sniffing the air and on their haunches.

Something like residual adderall kicks in in Billy's brain. *Whoa!*

Good moment, he thinks. *Nice focus; nice timing.* Good! So, he's in a better play—with a better supporting cast—than he originally thought.

"Hello? Boys? Whaddaya say? What's your call?" J. Bob has the two guards leaning forward. "You want to lose MGM/Mirage ten, maybe twenty million a year...or do you want to make a call?"

The guard with the tan reaches for his phone.

Billy touches the back of his right hand with the fingertips of his left. He wants to see if his skin is, in fact, as cold and rutted as it has begun to feel. It is. He raises the back of his hand to his nose; it smells corrupt, like mulch. The play has him, though; the play holds him now. Still, he has a bad feeling about the script.

The guard with the tan talks in low tones into his phone. The taller guard keeps prompting, *Tell him...Tell him...*but never finishing his sentence.

Billy swears that the casino floor of The Mirage is beginning to tilt. Most times Billy likes it when the play plays him, when he's immersed. This time, though, there's something not quite right about the scenario.

The guard with the tan hands over his phone to J. Bob. "He wants to talk to you," he says.

The two guards and Billy listen and watch.

"Hello," J. Bob says. And then he says, "That's right," and then, again, "That's right," and then, again, "That's right." He nods. "Arapahoe," he says, and then, "Cartwright." Then, for a while, he listens. Finally, he smiles. "That's all I'm asking," he says.

Billy thinks he hears flies circling around his head.

J. Bob hands the phone back to the tan guard. "Your turn," he says.

The guard takes the phone. "Yeah," he says. And then, "Right," and then, "Right," again and then, "Okay." He lowers the phone, slightly, switches it off, stares at J. Bob, then—briefly, nervously—at Billy Spence. "Have a good night, Mr. Marshall," he says. And then he nods to the taller guard and they both stroll away.

"So—" J. Bob moves in, flattening Billy against the Wheel-of-Fortune machine. "Here we are. Face...to...face. Ringer and Dead Ringer. The *Bobbsey Twins.* Whaddaya got to say for yourself, Pard? What do you say?"

Billy feels he should have a line here, but he can't find it.

"You know: you can go to the well...but you can't go to the well too many times. Right? Because if you do: either the well runs dry—that's one possibility. Or you drown. Or maybe a strike of lightning hits the tin pail you're carrying…and you get fried. Whaddaya think?"

Billy *knows* there's a line. In this crazy theater performance of his life, after J. Bob's *Whatdaya think?* and after the PAUSE and as the lights start to dim, Billy knows: it's the denouement; it's his line; it's *his* turn. Here it is! The moment! The twist! The reversal! He has a line. And it's a killer line—a breath taker—the last line of the scene— he understands that. It's the zinger that's just before the blackout. But, good as he is, try as he might; tip-of-the-tongue as the word certainly must be, he can't find it.

33 ✦ Finger Food

Standing by the service elevator on The Mirage's twenty-seventh floor, Elko schools Robert about mantras and meditation. He assures Robert that there are worse things than half-hour-old still-bleeding fingers under washcloths. He says: "Think about being a suicide bomber and what that must feel like when the bomb goes off and you come apart."

Elko hopes he's helping Robert see the other side. It's what he and his friends like Shaq and Amana do in Athletes Anonymous. They walk around to the other side of the glass. They look through. They see themselves looking at themselves. Something like that.

Elko and Robert ride the service elevator down—all the way to the kitchens. Now *Elko's* hungry and has one of the room service staffers make him up a BLT.

He thanks Robert and goes out through the service exit, stands in the mossy dark near a black man in whites who's there smoking. Elko has his snack. The lettuce tastes too crisp; the bacon, too greasy; the tomato, like suet. The bread's too dry, and the mayo tastes like a butter substitute. Elko understands that all the wrong tastes are imaginings; they're in his head. But so is a lot of other stuff: Lena; the man whose icepick of a hammer Elko still has in his inside pocket; Lena's husband, Mark; The Mirage's whale or whale-wannabe twenty-seven stories above him, who, by now, has probably finished his room service and started in on the finger. Elko's head is like bad channel-surfing. He can't sort imagination from memory. Things tumble, wash out, appear out of nowhere.

He imagines a scene—maybe an hour earlier—when the two J. Bob Marshalls—one real, one unreal—are alone in the shadows of this same hotel—in an even mossier and more underwater dark. One or the other has a long filleting knife in his hand. One or the other is up against the building. It's like a man who has hated the way he looked all his life being given the opportunity to kill his image in the mirror.

And as Elko stands in the Las Vegas night and imagines this scene, it's the *Unreal* J. Bob, mostly, who's talking. Well, not *talking*, really—not lining words up the way they'd be in sentences. Not that. Closer to *grunting*. Making body sounds that only come *close* to words. Words like *Please!* and *Don't!* and *Nopleasedon't!* And the *Unreal* J. Bob's eyes are in a panic—the way any image-in-a-mirror-that-understands-it's-going-to-be-broken must feel, tasting the scream rising in its throat.

And the man who's not the image—the *Real* J. Bob—has got this smile. Cruel. Distorted. And he moves the filet knife that he holds around, so that it pricks the skin of the *Unreal* J. Bob, the reflection... *here!* now, again, *there.*

And it's all—this scene that Elko imagines—a nightmare, really: moment after moment, each frame/image/cell getting worse, each one making less sense than the one before it, each one opening wider and wider to the world of monsters and demons.

And it's when the *Real* says to the *Unreal*, "I think it's time," that Elko begins to really sweat and choke on his last piece of dry sandwich bread and rancid bacon... and that his cell phone rings. And like the *Unreal* J. Bob pinned against the building and squirming for his life, Elko—his voice crusted and greased at the same time—chokes out the only syllable he can: "Yeah?"

"Well, *you* sound like shit. Have you found Mark yet?" Lena's voice drifts in.

"What—?" Elko hears other voices, interference, ambient sound. "Where are you?" he asks.

"You sound like a frog," Lena says. "What're you doing?"

"I'm leaning against the delivery entrance wall of The Mirage, choking on a sandwich and having a nightmare about surgery."

"Have you found Mark yet?" Lena says.

"Where are *you*? What's all that noise?"

Elko hears muffling—the kind of sound that's a nonsound, like sheets being lifted from a bed. And then he hears Lena's voice, sounding like she's a half-block away, asking somebody, "What's this place?" And then he hears a man saying, "The Bruised Bronco."

"The Bruised Bronco," Lena says.

"It's the middle of the night," Elko says.

"Have you found Mark? I'm worried to death about him. I can't sleep."

Elko stretches—his neck first, then reality: "Almost," he says. "I'm close."

"How close?"

"An hour...two hours...a year."

"You have to touch base with me more often. I can't take this waiting."

Then Elko hears her cut out. The line goes dead. Did she hang up?

Elko switches channels, imagines another scene. In this one, *Darrin Folger* can't stand the itch. He's heard the look-alike story. Part of him buys it; part of him doesn't. How can there be *another* Anthony Francis? And who did those three guys looking like refugees from the Arena Football League think *they* are, anyway? Fuckfaces! Assholes! He was *this close* at the Bellagio to finding the object of all his rage. *This close!*

He's had a couple more scotches, taken a shower and studied himself in the mirror and thought about his family. But nothing can subdue the sense of vengeance that propelled him to Las Vegas and so, spike or no spike, he leaves his room and heads down into the world he was warned not to reenter. *I don't care!* he thinks. *I can't help it!* he says aloud to himself in the elevator. Elko imagines Darrin Folger crashing out of the elevator when it hits the casino level and grabbing a cab to Bellagio.

And in this intuition or fantasy, Elko imagines that, independently, Mark Goodson—having no idea whatsoever what to do with this new Himself or Not-Himself—has also chosen the middle of the night to be wandering the Bellagio floor. Elko imagines that Mark's pouring hundreds-at-a-time of what must seem to be an inexhaustible *body bag* of money into a Megabucks machine. Elko imagine him downing whiskey sours—drunk out of his mind—talking to himself, talking to the machine, talking to anyone who will listen, feeling himself, for the first time in his life, *on stage* and attended to by a willing audience.

And then, of course, in the way that Life is *only* intersections, Elko begins to imagine the intersection of Darrin Folger's *hunt* and poor Mark Goodson's *play*. But exactly what's happening isn't clear. Is it all dance? All preliminary? Are they still on the floor? Outside? In a room somewhere? Elko's imagination breaks up like a cell phone, and it's all very nickelodeon.

He shakes his head, covers his eyes. He tries rewinding the Darrin/

Mark scene to where the tape doesn't stammer and flip, maybe to the moment where Darrin first spots Mark—who he thinks *has* to be Anthony Francis, *can't* be anyone else—and freezes. But it just breaks up again, comes apart.

Then, his cell phone rings. When he pulls it out and checks the number, it's Lena again. But when he switches it on to answer, she's gone. All there is...is dial tone.

34 ♦ Lena Sings the Blues

Having unannounced psychic episodes—sometimes searing mixed-media voices and images—carries a cluster bomb of pain and burden for Lena Goodson. In less than a week, she's made her husband *choose* to disappear and raised a dozen red flags with her PI. Why does it so often seem that her shortest path to satisfaction involves a floor routine of self-destruction?

The dingy bar Lena has drifted into in the middle of the night, the Bruised Bronco, is on Industrial Road, a place with light the color of a midafternoon cyclone and the thick, pasty redolence of an abandoned meatpacking plant. It had served, first, as a Korean market then as a donut factory and is now an all-night bar unable to make up its mind between "country & western" and "tits & ass." There are stages and girls, but all the girls wear Stetsons and all their bras and panties are soft leather with fringe. Lena sits at the long, snaking oak bar and orders Southern Comfort after Southern Comfort.

"I'd be careful of that stuff if I were you," the cowgirl bartender warns.

"It's my Daddy's drink," Lena drawls.

"You're alone?"

"My husband disappeared."

"It happens. You come here with him?" The cowgirl twists open a Dos Equis.

"I came with him to Las Vegas."

"But not this bar."

"Not this bar."

"Be careful."

"I will. I'll be careful."

The cowgirl bartender brings the Dos Equis to a customer at the other end of the bar.

A man with skin like a Gila monster slides onto the stool to the right of Lena. "Name's *Trent*," the man says. He holds his hand out.

Lena nods.

The cowgirl bartender delivers Lena's Southern Comfort. "Remember my advice," she says, and nods toward Trent.

"I'm a big girl," Lena says.

"I can see that," Trent smiles.

The cowgirl bartender walks away.

"You by yourself?" Trent asks.

"I'm waiting for my husband," Lena says.

Patsy Cline's "Crazy" is playing over the sound system.

"So, are you early?... Or is he late?" Trent asks. And he puts a hand, briefly, on Lena's back.

"He's late," Lena says. Curiously, though she feels sober in her brain, her mouth has trouble shaping words.

"Maybe he's not coming," Trent suggests.

"Maybe he's not," Lena says.

"Maybe you're free."

"I'm never free. There's always a price."

Trent's smile says he feels cocky. "So, has your husband paid the price?"

"Oh! Oh, yes. Many times," Lena says.

"Family rate," Trent smirks.

Lena ignores the comment and takes another hit of Southern Comfort. Suddenly, a sadness she hasn't seen coming blindsides her, and she feels her jaw quiver; her eyes abruptly pool.

"Hey, you okay, Babe?" Trent asks, gliding the tips of his fingers down her spine.

"Whoa! Whoa, Cowboy," Lena says.

Trent pauses then takes his hand away. "You say *whoa,* and that's fine. But I have to tell you: I can read women."

"Can you?"

"Like a book; like a Bible. Yes, I can."

"So, what does *my* book, my Bible, say?"

"Your book's open, open to the crucial page. And the crucial page tells me you want a man inside you tonight."

Lena doesn't respond; only *thinks* responses, one of which is rubbing ground glass into Trent's face.

But the man with the Gila-monster skin beside her isn't to be stopped. "It says you want a man badly, really badly, and it doesn't really matter much who."

"Well, that's where you're wrong," Lena says.

"Am I?"

"Yeah." Lena takes a long, long pull from her Southern Comfort, finishes it, raises her glass, and catches the attention of her cowgirl barmaid.

"So then, who's the lucky guy?" Trent asks.

Lena's cowgirl barmaid arrives with another drink. "And what about you? How're *you* doing?" the barmaid asks Trent.

"Cowboy, here, says he's reading me like a book," Lena says.

"I'll have another Cuervo—wedge of lime," Trent says.

"Take it easy on this lady, okay? You hear that?" The barmaid wags her finger at Trent.

"Hey, always. Always," Trent tosses his words back and grins. Then he swivels to Lena. "So! Fill me in. Who's the lucky guy?"

Lena stares at herself between the bottles in the bar mirror. What she sees of her face—red and puffy—she doesn't like. She starts to cry—no sounds; no moans; just a salty wash, making her cheeks slick, collecting at her jawline.

Trent puts a hand on her shoulder. She removes it. He puts it on her cheek and tries to turn her toward him. She slaps the scaly hand away.

"Hey, come on. Give me your mouth, Sugar. That's all I'm asking. Just once. Give Trent your mouth. After that, what you do is your call."

Lena thinks of turning directly in, into him, to say what she wants to say. But she feels so tired and sad and weak and sorry that she's left her room at Treasure Island and drifted out through the night. She'd like to nail him and nail him hard, but she doesn't have the strength.

"Just once," Trent persists. "Once."

"Hear me," Lena said.

"All ears," the man with the cracked gathered skin rolls back his lip in a sneer and says.

"The man I want…" Lena begins, "…The man I want is the man you could never be. Because the man I want is the man who's gone away."

Trent begins to interrupt.

"I haven't finished!" Lena says. "The man I want is the man I underestimate and admire and get pissed off at because he's so good. Good at buying me pearls. Good in bed. Good at washing the dishes that I get tired of."

Trent throws his newly arrived Cuervo and lime down in a single shot. "Sounds like a prince," he says.

"He is," Lena says.

"Except he's not here. And I am."

"Unfortunately."

Trent grabs Lena's jaw with his big raw-grained hand and tries, in a single motion, to turn her toward him and pull her in.

"Don't!" Lena advises.

"You want this." Roughly, Trent puts his other hand at the back of her head and starts forcing her face up next to his.

"Hey!" the approaching cowgirl bartender warns.

But before the warning *Hey!* even reaches Trent's flat, elongated ears, he can feel himself being lifted—back of the neck, seat of the pants—and then thrown in a skyhook across the bar. He slams hard against a beamed wall about seven feet from the floor, loses consciousness and falls, like a sack of feed, to the ground.

The bar is still. Everybody's eyes are on the over-seven-foot black man who has just slam dunked the man on the barstool.

The cowgirl barmaid breaks the silence. "Nice shot," she says.

Lena recognizes her protector. It's the man Elko introduced her to, the man who looks very much like *Shaq.*

"Miz Goodson," says the man-called-*Shaq,* tipping an imaginary hat. "How're you doin'?"

Lena can't think of an answer.

"You all right?"

Lena nods.

Shaq explains that he'd gotten a call from White Elk. "He thought you might be in trouble."

"White Elk. Right," Lena says.

"So, what you doin' here, anyway?" Shaq asks Lena.

"I think, probably, just bad judgment," Lena says.

"Well, we all have plenty of that!" Shaq says.

The cowgirl bartender leans in: "You okay, honey?" she asks.

Lena nods.

"So, you be stayin' where?" Shaq asks.

Lena tells him.

"An' you ready to call it a night?' Shaq asks. "Cuz I got my wheels. I'll give you a ride, okay?"

"Okay," Lena says.

Trent is still in a heap, still unconscious. Shaq goes over and crouches beside him, checks his pulse, checks for breath, nods. "Tell him, when he wakes up," Shaq says to the cowgirl bartender, "Leave women-who-don't-want-him-touching-them alone. Okay?"

"Are you—?" someone at a near table starts to ask.

Shaq smiles. "No, I just *look* like him."

And Shaq and Lena leave The Bruised Bronco together.

35 ♦ Water, Water—Everywhere!

Elko's outside Bellagio watching the fountains and trying to map a next move when Shaq calls and tells his finding-Lena story. Shaq assures Elko that Lena's back in her room. "I gave her one of my little blue *sleep-tight* specials," he says. "I don't think she'll be up an' wanderin' for a while." He asks, since *he's* up—can he be of any assistance? Elko thanks him, but confesses that he's in a bit of a blur about what he needs to do next. He also tells Shaq about Amana and Sandy possibly saving his life. "Pretty close to where I'm standing right now," Elko tells him.

"We be the A-Team! The *AA* Team," Shaq says.

Elko thanks him for the assist with Lena.

"Always a pleasure to assist White Elk," Shaq says. "Stay away from troubled waters."

And they hang up.

It's late, and though Elko feels he shouldn't, he's restless and needs to talk. Faye's given him her own kind of carte blanche: "Don't ever need me and not do anything about it" is what she said. Elko tries not to abuse her buffet of kindnesses; he tries to pick his Faye moments. To an extent, given his earlier spike-to-the-head with Darrin Folger, he suspects this Faye-moment may be choosing *him*.

Faye's awake, as she often is, reading. She loves reading history. "It makes me feel I've lived longer than I have," she says.

Elko apologizes for the hour.

"What do I always tell you?" she asks.

"Get on top?"

"*Don't apologize.*"

Elko apologizes for apologizing.

"How's the vanished husband going?" Faye asks.

"I've got six different searches happening," Elko tells her. He relates that just fifteen minutes earlier, in the Bellagio business office, he had accessed and logged on to each of his various searches and checked them out. "They keep giving me dots—*good* dots, *connectable* dots," Elko tell her. "But I can't, somehow, connect them." And Elko gives her four of his hot-off-the-cyber-network dot-discoveries.

Until he showed up four days ago here in Las Vegas, Anthony Francis had disappeared from any-and-all identity-radar for just over a month.

Anthony Francis's "disappearance" occurs about two months after his last e-mail exchange with Mark Goodson.

The briefcase of the man murdered at McCarran has been found in a dumpster on Wyoming Avenue. No connecting fingerprint matches have been found, but there were traces of theatrical makeup on the handle.

The last book Mark Goodson checked out of the Naples, Florida library was an illustrated volume of *Huckleberry Finn*.

He says he thought he might find Lena's disappeared husband on the Bellagio floor but that he hasn't had any luck. "My intuitions have all gone to shit," he says. He thanks her for being awake and taking his call. "Just rambling to you helps," he says. "How, exactly, I can't say. But it does."

"Baby, you know I'm always awake for you," Faye says.

They hang up, and Elko finds himself in the middle of too many urges, too many impulses. Something in him regrets not taking Shaq up, earlier, on his offer to join up in the hunt. But what is Elko hunting for exactly? He's here, outside Bellagio, because he thought standing in the middle of the night and watching all the water might wash the accumulated crud from his brain. And, in part, he's been hopeful. Because he's had this voice that he sometimes gets, and, every minute or two, it's been saying, *water*. But all it's led him to, so far, is just that: water—water everywhere.

Elko leaves the night and goes back inside, where, at the Cirque Bar, he starts to order Glenlivet and water but ends up ordering only water.

When the bartender delivers his Perrier, Elko shows him pictures—Mark Goodson's in the wallet-sized snapshot Lena gave him and Darrin Folger's on his digital.

The bartender doesn't miss a beat. "They were having a drink together here," he says. "Half hour ago. Maybe less."

"Drinking here? *Together*?" Elko says.

"Yeah. They were yukking it up," he says. "I thought they were old buddies."

Something hard to put together and not-quite believable has happened. "What direction did they head off in?" Elko asks.

The bartender shrugs. "You know, I see people. They come; they go. When they're here, they register. When they go away, I don't—" He holds his hands out in a helpless gesture. "Sorry," he says.

Elko thanks him, starts to leave. Darrin Folger and Mark together? This is not a good thing.

"Hey," the bartender says, over Elko's shoulder, behind him. He turns.

"Your water," he says. "You forgot your water."

36 ✦ More Finger Food

First J. Bob escorts Billy up to Billy's room. "I'm curious and I want to see where I live," he says. "I want to see *how* I live—what I drink, if I'm neat, if I'm a pig. And, especially, I think, I want to open my safe and see if I've got any money in there."

For Billy, the play he thought he'd written has gotten both dangerous and confusing—too many rewrites, a new character. And is the curtain still up? Or is it *after* the show, the actor and his character going to the actor's dressing room? It's all gotten pretty...well, *Pirandello.*

So, Billy just goes with the flow—or perhaps, it's the riptide—and keeps silent.

When they get to the suite, J. Bob requests the room key, lets them in and, once inside, keeps the key, bolts the door. He tells Billy to lie down in the middle of the carpet—arms and legs spread. Billy complies. Obviously, J. Bob has moved into the role of director, and he's blocking a new scene. He tells Billy that if he moves, he'll be chicken salad. "I can dress a pheasant in thirty seconds," J. Bob says.

Billy tries to remember the penultimate scene in *Six Characters in Search of an Author.* Because there's a turning point. There's a particular way in which one of the characters takes the power away from the writer-director.

J. Bob tears through all the drawers and closets. "This is no way to live!" he barks at Billy. "One change of clothes? An empty half-pint of Baileys? Only one scrawny suitcase? Where's the Perry Ellis wardrobe? The Tony Lama boots?"

Billy keeps his spread-eagle, says nothing, tries to recall that Pirandello scene.

J. Bob stands at the open wardrobe by the safe. "I feel like I'm talkin' to myself," he says. "And, hey! I guess I *am.* In a manner of speaking. So, Yo! Myself, what're the numbers I punch in to get this safe open? I seem to have forgotten the combination to my own safe."

Billy recites the numbers into the pile of the carpet.

J. Bob kicks him in his ribs. "Missed that," he says.

Billy considers a death scene. He doesn't need to take shit like this from such an asshole! What if he dies? Characters die! So what? Instead, he lifts his head higher, coughs into the rug pile what looks like flecks of blood. He repeats the numbers.

J. Bob punches the four numbers in and the safe swings open. "Well, lookee here!" J. Bob says. "Lookee, lookee here! I'm a man of means! I'm a man of magnitude! I'm a man of money! Let's see how much." And, drawing the bundles of Benjamins out of the safe, J. Bob carries them over to the bar, where he begins counting them. "This doesn't look like..." he begins aloud, and then, "I don't think this is all that I've..." He crosses over and puts a foot on Billy's back. "We're at about ten percent here," he says.

He waits for Billy's response, prods him, then stands, full weight, on Billy's back.

Billy screams. He rolls abruptly, grabs one of J. Bob's legs, yanks it. J. Bob roars and topples. *All right! Fight scene!* Billy says to himself through clenched teeth. And, snatching at a nearby candlestick, he scrambles unsteadily to his feet. "YOU STUPID REDNECK FUCK!" he booms.

But when he arrives at standing, he discovers that J. Bob has recovered and has positioned himself—hands bracing himself against a table. J. Bob delivers a savage kick to Billy's groin. "You stupid Redneck Fuck Wannabe!" J. Bob barks.

Billy sees the red planet and all the rings of Saturn, moons of Jupiter then collapses to his knees doubled over. Somewhere in space, the performance-of-a-lifetime has collapsed into a black hole.

J. Bob approaches and stands over him. "Okay," he says, "now tell me—I'm getting so fucking forgetful—where did I put all the *rest* of my money?"

Billy makes an awful, grating sound from somewhere in his lungs—like he's a garbage disposal with a rock in it.

J. Bob waits.

Billy gasps for air—coughs, chokes, gasps some more. He keeps trying to say the word, *Someone—!*

"Someone—! Someone—! Spit it out!"

"Someone...took it."

"Hey, I *know* someone took it. That's why we're here. That's why I kicked you in the balls. I don't *do* that to just anybody. That's why

I'm reaching into my pocket for my knife. That's why all I can think of is filleting catfish."

"Not..."

"Hey! Whole sentences, you Fuck! C'mon! *Not*—?"

"Not me! Someone else took it *from* me." Billy flattens, like a planarian worm, on the shag.

"Who!?"

"I'm not sure. A *guy!*"

"You've got ten seconds!"

Billy tells his stolen-vest story. *This is the monologue that buys me some time,* he thinks. "I thought I'd gotten it back!" he begins. "I thought I'd killed him at the airport. I grabbed his attaché case, I thought it was the money. But when I got to my apartment and opened it, I realized I'd killed the wrong guy! He was a guy who sort of *looked* the same! But all that was in the attaché was a bunch of company contracts and a Ziploc bag with about six pieces of sashimi in it!"

J. Bob walks away from Billy, crosses to the suite's floor-to-ceiling window. Billy—his breathing level again—raises his head up and studies J. Bob's profile. There has to be an object, a prop, anything that he can use. The room is like a mountain clearing after a thunderstorm—ozone in the air, dead quiet. It's as if there's been a flash, a brilliant triumphant beat in the unfolding scene, and Billy has missed it. "Okay, so let's go to *my* room," J. Bob finally says.

He pulls Billy from the floor and shows him his knife. "Feel the blade. Run your finger along the blade," J. Bob says.

Billy's hesitant.

"Want *me* to run your finger?" J. Bob asks. He crouches and flicks the knife across the pile. The Berber shag falls like wheat. Weed whacker!" J. Bob says.

They go to J. Bob's suite two floors above, Billy improvising like crazy. *Give me a week,* Billy has said in the elevator; *a week—just a week. I'll get the rest back for you, honest to God.*

And J. Bob has laughed.

"How about that! We're identical!" J. Bob says, walking his look-alike through his own suite. "Same rug. Same coffee table. Same bar." He moves Billy to his wardrobe, rolls the door open. "Same costume designer!" he says. "Except I've got more to choose from. Feel that jacket!" he says and points to a hanging sport coat.

Billy fingers the coat.

"Alpaca!" J. Bob announces.

"Nice," Billy says.

"So, you want it?"

"No. That's all right."

"Try it on."

"I'm fine. I don't need to—"

"TRY IT ON!" J. Bob slips the coat from its rack, extends it. "See how a Stupid Redneck Fuck dresses."

Billy takes the alpaca jacket, slips it on.

"How does it feel?" J. Bob asks.

"Good."

"You like it?"

"Well—"

"Do...you...like...it?"

"It's a little big."

"Hey, *I'm* a little big, okay? Fact is: I'm a *big* big." J. Bob laughs. "What do you think? You could be *buried* in these threads, don't you guess? It would look great."

Billy says nothing. He's tired.

"Let's go for a ride," J. Bob says.

They ride around, directionless, in a Mirage limo. In the back of the limo, J. Bob pours them both Maker's Mark over ice. They drink in silence until their bourbons are gone, then J. Bob pours them each another. "What are you thinking?" J. Bob asks Billy.

Billy shrugs. Billy's tired of the play. "What are you going to do?" Billy asks.

"I'm thinking reparations," J. Bob says.

"Are you going to kill me?"

"Kill you?"

"Yes."

"Whoa! Wouldn't that be like killing *myself*, don't you think? TEXAS MILLIONAIRE KILLS HIS STUPID REDNECK FUCK SELF IN THE BACK OF A MIRAGE LIMOUSINE! You think I look suicidal?"

"No."

"No. I'm not. No. Not suicidal. Not close. *Angry.* I'm *angry.* Who could blame me—you know—that I've lost a couple million?"

"I'll pay you back."

"All the hurt, you mean? The heartache?"

"The money," Billy says. "I'll pay back the money."

"Do you believe in God?" J. Bob asks.

And it would have been a good play—with lines like that. Except that Billy can't summon himself any more. It's as though he's done a matinee and two evening performances.

"C'mon. C'mon, do you believe in God?"

"I believe in...I guess, a greater spirit," Billy replies.

"How *much* greater?"

"A higher being," Billy says.

"How high?" J. Bob lifts a flat hand, in several steps, above his head. "How high?" he repeats. "Higher than the Ghost Bar at the Palms?"

Billy says nothing

"Where's *home*?" J. Bob asks. "For you? Here in Vegas? You can't just spend your time hanging out in borrowed suites. Some place has got to be *home* for you—where you dream your dreams, where you kick back. Where's that?"

Billy is tired. He doesn't care. He tells J. Bob: "Vegas Towers."

J. Bob slides back the partition behind the driver. "Cletus," he says.

"Yes, Boss," Cletus says, only half of his face lit.

"Vegas Towers," J. Bob says. "We want to go to Vegas Towers."

"Great. Do you have an address?" Cletus asks.

"Do we have an address?" J. Bob smiles at Billy.

Billy gives him the East Flamingo location. J. Bob repeats it to Cletus, who says they'll be there momentarily, and J. Bob slides the partition back into place.

"I want to see how the other half lives," he tells Billy."

"You'll be disappointed," Billy says.

"Hey, you never can tell," J. Bob says.

There's no gateman in the booth at the entrance to Vegas Towers and Cletus drives a Mirage limo to a parking stall.

"Do you mind waiting?" J. Bob asks him.

"Not at all," Cletus says.

J. Bob ushers Billy from the limo. Billy uses his keys in the foyer.

"Hey, you're not going to ring?" J. Bob asks. "Maybe somebody's there; they'll buzz you up."

"Nobody's there," Billy says.

"But you don't know."

"I know."

"Maybe not. Could be—who can say?—*any*body. *I* thought nobody was there—right?—and lo and behold!"

Billy ignores J. Bob and begins to insert his key into the entry door. But J. Bob fists his hair and slams his head down into the occupant buzzers. "Ring!" he demands.

Blood gushes from Billy's nose.

"Don't wipe your nose on the sleeve of that jacket," J. Bob advises. "That's an expensive jacket. Ring."

Billy rings his own apartment. No one buzzes back.

"Guess not," J. Bob says.

Billy lets them in and they ride up in the elevator. When it stops at the seventh floor, Billy leads the way out and down a hallway to their right. He stops in front of 706. He still has his keys in his hand.

"Not as nice as The Mirage," J. Bob says.

"No," Billy says.

"How's your nose?" J. Bob asks.

"Possibly broken."

"Small sacrifice," J. Bob says. "All things being equal. You agree?"

Billy unlocks the door, and they go in. J. Bob sniffs the air, takes his bearings.

"I'm trying to think of a word," J. Bob says.

Billy closes the apartment door behind them. His brain is in a wrap of Freon, still he tries to think of what he might use as a weapon.

"Trying to think of a word. It's a word like *cozy*—except it *isn't* cozy. It's a word like *homey*—except it's not."

"I'm a starving actor," Billy says. "Not much more."

"I don't understand. You're a man of means, a man of magnitude."

Billy says nothing. He wonders about the hairspray that he uses to set his various wigs—whether he can spray it in J. Bob's eyes.

J. Bob walks the small two-room space. He examines the clothes rack with its various costumes—some of them dresses. He fingers fabrics, smiles, shakes his head. He walks over to the theatrical mirror, throws its switch, stares at its line of oversized chorus light bulbs. "*Magic time!*" he says. "I used to fuck a young actress from Dallas— Dallas Theater Center—and that's what she used to say a lot: *Magic time!*" He opens and squeezes tubes of makeup onto his hands, wipes them on Billy's face. He does the same with a large tube of latex.

Billy stands there. He knows he looks like a clown. Once upon a time, he'd had some hydrochloric acid that he'd used making masks, etching lines. If he can find it, can he throw it in J. Bob's face? *Phantom of the Opera.* Jesus, Billy feels *so* tired.

"So, in a week, you're going to get me all my money. Is that right?" J. Bob asks.

"Somehow," Billy says.

"Somehow," J. Bob echoes.

He spreads Billy on the floor as he'd done at The Mirage suite. Billy's far too tired to resist; he just wants the play to end. Then J. Bob proceeds to turn Billy's small apartment upside down, searching for his treasure. "So, if you were a stash of cash, where would you be?" he asks Billy.

"I told you what happened. It's not here," Billy says.

And it isn't.

And when it isn't, clearly isn't, indisputably isn't, J. Bob pulls Billy to his feet and cuts off his middle right-hand finger. When Billy starts to scream, J. Bob stuffs a dishtowel in his mouth.

J. Bob tosses the finger repeatedly into the air as though it were a small stone, a beach treasure, or the bone-handled knife he'd used to cut the finger off.

"Once a week," he says. "A finger a week. I'll find you, wherever you are. Until, you bring me my money, it's a finger a week. I used to collect stamps. Then coins. Then pocket watches. If you're a collector, you're a collector—it's just that what you collect changes. Right? Now it's fingers."

37 ✦ Comedy Tonight

Elko doesn't know where to look. His *intuition* is: Mark Goodson and Darrin Folger are still together...*somewhere*. But his *brain* is a taffy pull. He walks from Bellagio's lobby bar to Le Cirque and back again. He stands on the bridge in the Conservatory, looking down at the water. He circles the entire casino, and though it's five in the morning, the whole world that he's in seems like dusk. His brain feels like it's an oyster shell—except he can't tell whether it's the inside or the outside. And smack-dab in the middle of the murky oyster-shell feeling: that's when Elko see him!

It's the goofy red-headed comic with the nervous laugh from Harrah's Comedy Club. He's playing Texas Hold'em in the Bellagio poker room, sitting at a table near the rail. It's his laugh that catches Elko, who sees him fumbling with his chips. He piles them up and then his long piano-player fingers can't help themselves and begin to drum on the stacks, which spill without direction onto the table. "Call me Fingers," he says to the table-at-large, laughs his squeaky laugh. No one seems to be listening, and he piles his chips, stacking them nervously, again.

"Hey, Fingers!" the dealer says, "Thirty raise to you."

The table laughs. The comic throws his cards in. "The sound of one hand clapping," he says.

"Was that *clapping* or *crapping*?" another player jokes.

Elko moves to the rail. This kid—*call me Fingers*—somehow started Elko's engines earlier, got him going. Maybe he can do it again. Maybe this red-headed goofball can throw the *I Ching* with all that loose-floating information in Elko's head, turn Elko's mental scribbling into hexagrams.

He knocks his stacks down, builds them again. "Twin towers!" he says. Nobody laughs.

"Disappearing husbands!" Elko calls across to him.

He looks over, sees Elko, points a finger. "Tonight!" he says. "You!"

"I'm upping the ante," Elko says.

"Good. Do it. Go for it," he says.

"Okay, disappearing...cancel that; edit it; make it *invisible*— invisible husbands and the living dead!" Elko tries. He worries he's just given the young comic both too much and too obscure information.

But the goofy redhead stares.

"Go for it," Elko says.

"Hey, I'm off-duty."

"No such thing as an off-duty comic."

The goofball grins—total Howdy Doody.

"Come on, Fingers," Elko says again. "Give it a shot."

Cards are falling in front of him for the next hand.

"The thing about invisible husbands and the living dead..." he starts. Then pauses. He peeks at his cards. "The thing about invisible Husbands and the living dead...is that neither of them know where they're going to get laid tonight."

"It's on you, Red," the dealer says.

He mucks his hand. "Or!" he says, "the thing about invisible husbands and the living dead *in Las Vegas* is that...they *both* wish...they had more two-for-one coupons."

He rolls his eyes, shakes his head, weighs the air, palms up.

"Thanks, Fingers," Elko says. And the comic turns back in to the game.

They both wish...They both wish... That's the phrase! That's the message, Elko senses, that's going to finish the diagram, complete the puzzle, get him where he needs to go! *They both wish they had more...* not coupons, but...*some*thing. *Freedom? Options?*

Then suddenly a voice out of the blue whispers to Elko: *Reach into your back pocket.* The voice is faint; Elko almost doesn't hear it, but then again: *Reach into your back pocket.* He does. Yes! Of course! What Elko discovers in his back pocket is the appropriated key to Darrin Folger's room, the one he took when Amana, Bobby and himself had brought him back there. They'd fished it out of his pants pocket when he was out cold. In the interim, so much had intervened that he'd forgotten. And all the time, he had the key to the most probable place where—if the Folger and Goodson duo were still in the world, still a pair—they'll be.

Elko grabs a cab to Mandalay. In the back seat, he phones Shaq. "You know your offer," he says, "to be the go-to man?"

"I do," Shaq says.

"Well, our game just went into overtime," Elko says. "And I could use you."

"No prob. 'Cept, well, I got my black pajamas on," Shaq says. "But, hey: they look sort of like warm-ups. They be okay?"

"They be perfect," Elko says. "Mandalay Bay. Meet you by the parrot cages in the lobby. Or, if I'm not there, come up to room 1411. Don't wait to knock."

"I'm your man, Coach."

"And if you can: hurry."

38 ✦ Pursuer and Pursued

In the world of myth, the pursued and the pursuer inevitably meet. Sometimes the pursuer is successful; sometimes the pursued offers himself. Inevitably, though, the two arrive at the same still point, find themselves drinking at the same casino bar.

And Las Vegas is just the sort of place that courts this.

So, the weaponless man who has only his hands now—Darrin Folger—has retrieved the scent of the one he believes to be his square-jawed betrayer, Anthony Francis. While Anthony's surviving brother—Mark Goodson—has showered, dressed, taxied to Mandalay Bay. The two have found one another in the Flying Fishes Lounge and have constructed a cat-and-mouse, casual camaraderie between them.

Darrin has been drinking tequila sunrises; Mark has been drinking sidecars. And Destiny hangs between the bottles of Jose Cuervo and Jack Daniels. All the while, Darrin has been thinking: *God in Heaven! He doesn't even remember me!!* And all the while, Mark has been thinking: *This guy is fun. I need more fun people in my life.*

Each has reinvented himself with a new name. Darrin has told Mark that his name is Henry Moore. And Mark has told Darrin that his name—not exactly plucking one out of the air—is Tony Frank.

"Backwards-forwards," Darrin has drunkenly slurred.

"I'm not sure I get—"

"C'mon! Backwards-forwards! *Tony Frank*—backwards-forwards! Both names sound like a first name. You could be Tony Frank; you could be Frank Tony—backwards-forwards. Get it?"

"Right. Sure. I guess I get it."

"Hard to remember names like that."

Sitting at the bar, they've both acted as if everything they say is funny. "Moore Henry!" Mark has clinked his sidecar glass against Darrin's tequila sunrise, and they've both laughed. Then they've gotten the bartender to tell them his name: David Spencer.

"David Spencer! Spencer David!" they both chime and slam glasses together again.

This guy is funny! He's fun!

God in Heaven! He doesn't even remember me!

At which point, Mark's sidecar glass breaks and slices his finger. The bartender, David Spencer, acts like lightening, wraps Mark's sliced finger in some bar-first-aid-kit gauze, gives Mark a fresh drink.

"Life and death!" Darrin raises his glass.

And after they've both slammed back their respective drinks, Darrin suggests that they pick up their drinking in his suite. His room, after all, has a minibar just waiting to be taken advantage of.

"Reminds me of a girl I once knew," Mark says.

They ride up in the elevator, up the core of the central Mandalay tower. Pursuer and Pursued. They've been rowdy, boisterous. They've been best friends meeting, years later, at a reunion. But now—with both Pursuer and Pursued trying to regain some kind of focus...just before they arrive at the fourteenth floor, Darrin says, "I'm thinking about how I'm going to kill you."

"Fuck, shit—I mean, just *shoot* me," Mark says. He feels a perversity decant itself like alcohol and lift the top of his skull off. He trusts Darrin.

The elevator doors glide open.

"Well, you know, I could do that—shoot you—but I don't have a gun."

They start to walk.

"Well, then—hey!—*stab* me."

"All I have is a shoehorn."

"So stab me with that."

"I *had* something—earlier today—something *good* that I could have killed you with, but someone *took* it."

"Bummer."

"Yeah."

"Hey," Mark slaps Darrin on the back. "Hey, I almost killed *myself*—right?—back there in the bar." He laughs.

"I know," Darrin says. "I can still smell your blood."

Mark doesn't know what to say to this remark.

They reach suite 1411. Darrin fumbles in his coat jacket. He fishes around. Then he reaches into his pants pockets, front then back. Then it hits him. "Fuck!" he says. "My key. Must've left it inside. Wait here."

"Hey, we don't have to drink in your room. I got money. We can go down to the—"

"DID YOU HEAR WHAT I SAID? I SAID *WAIT HERE*."

"Whoa!" Mark backs away.

"Hey, I'm sorry."

"What—?"

"I'm sorry!...Okay? I'm sorry. I don't know why I got angry. Sometimes—late at night—it just happens. Do you mind? We'll ride down again. Together. Get my key. Ride up again. Take advantage of that minibar."

"Take advantage." Mark's voice slips from enthusiasm to weariness.

"Take advantage," Darrin repeats. "Please."

They ride down. Darrin shows his identification at the front desk, gets a new key coded.

Mark watches the desk clerk's fingertips tap dancing on the code pad.

"See? Hardly took a minute. *Open Sesame!*" Darrin shows his replacement key to Mark.

"So why did you lie to me?" Mark asks.

"What do you mean?"

"You said your name was Henry Moore. You told the lady at the desk your name was something else—Darrin Folger."

"Oh, well—it's just one of those...*you* know...Henry Moore's who I'd *like* to be," Darrin says. "Come to Las Vegas—I can be whoever I want—right?"

"Sky's the limit," Mark says.

"Still, it only took a minute. Just like I said. Right?"

"Right. Except, for me..." Mark doesn't finish the thought. Because there's a grave truth stamping itself into Mark's brain: *I get it! This is one of the people Anthony ruined!*

"And lifetime is precious. Right?" Darrin says.

Mark feels really drunk. *Must he atone for his brother's sins?*

On the way up again, Mark pursues Darrin's earlier explosion: "Why'd you get so pissed before? At me? Upstairs."

"Residual anger," Darrin says. "Residual anger," he repeats.

"Residual anger," Mark echoes. "Right. There's a lot."

"Lotta garbage," Darrin says.

"Lotta junk," Mark expands.

The floors go by: nine...ten...eleven...twelve. "So if you were me—going to kill you tonight—I'm curious: how would you do it?" Darrin asks.

"I'd've *done* it," Mark says.

"You'd've *done* it?"

"Sure. I'd've poisoned the glass—you know: the one I broke that cut me?—so that when I got the cut, the poison would've gotten into my bloodstream. I'd've used poison glass," Mark grins.

"Hard to find," Darrin says.

"Have to make your own."

The elevator slides open.

They start walking the fourteenth-floor corridor.

"So, if not a poison glass, then what?" Darrin asks. "If there were no poison glass available—"

"I think we've pretty much gone through the list," Mark says.

"I think the night is still young," Darrin says.

"The day too!" Mark says.

"You're not being much help," Darrin says.

Mark stops in his tracks. Maybe, Mark briefly thinks, none of this is happening; none of this is real. "Okay," he says. He grins weirdly; it's all sort of like a game that Lena would invent. "Okay," he goes on, "you offer me a challenge—if I were you: how would you kill me?—I'm going to step up to it." In unexplainable ways, it's in fact *fun* to be out of control, Mark thinks. It's *fun* to be on the edge of life-and-death, to be crazy. He spins on: "You don't like the poison glass idea?

That's fine; no prob. How would I kill me if I were you? Right? We've ruled out shooting, stabbing, poisoning. Did we do bludgeoning?"

"I think so."

"Okay, cross out bludgeoning...Wait! Wait—I've got it!" Mark grins.

"What."

"Electrocution!" Mark studies Darrin's face. "Perfect! Electrocution!"

Darrin nods. "Possible, but why—?"

"No! *More* than possible. Excellent! Clean! Neat! We get into your room. We sit down—take advantage of the bar—like you've said. Get a little more drunk."

"Okay."

"At some point, I say I feel a little sick. You tell me a cold shower'll make me feel like a new man. I get into the shower. You toss in a plugged in hair-drier...*Poof!*"

"But why do you find this so amusing?" Darrin asks.

Mark feels certain that Darrin is harmless. He will tell him the story of his brother and he'll understand. Maybe Mark can help Darrin financially. He feels a responsibility to this man. He is so drunk. Has his reasoning ability been affected?

The two put their arms around one another and weave the rest of the distance to room 1411.

Inside, Darrin opens his minibar, tells Mark: *Whatever he wants. Help himself.* "I'll be a few minutes in the bathroom," he says and disappears.

Mark sits on the floor in front of the minibar. He pulls out a glass, finds the freezer unit, cracks out some ice. "What haven't I had?" he says out loud to himself. "What haven't I had? What haven't I had?" He pulls out mini bottle after mini bottle until he reaches a brown bottle with a greenish label: Baileys Irish Cream.

It sounds good. Mark cracks the cap. He can hear a faucet running in the bathroom. He sniffs the bottle and it smells like chocolate milk and peppermint and whiskey. He gives it a taste, rolling it side to side until it coats his mouth. He lifts his eyebrows, smiles approval.

Then, as Mark is about to pour two of the minis of Bailys over ice, he hears a strange sound from the bathroom. And then a smell comes to him—stale, metallic, possibly electrical.

"Darrin?" he calls out.

He hears what he takes to be Darrin's voice—not exactly a word, not a true response—more his voice, or something sounding very much like his voice, making a sound.

"Darrin?" he tries again then tries, "Henry?"

The raw sound crawls from the bathroom again—less a voice this time, more like a tree shifting its weight in a heavy wind.

Mark takes a serious slug of his Baileys, shifts to his knees in front of the minibar, then, using the coffee table, leverages himself up. He is so drunk. The blood rushes from his head and he throws one hand out first to his right, then another hand out to his left in order to steady himself and keep from listing.

"Darrin? Henry?"

Something like a red warning light begins to pulse over a door somewhere in Mark's brain. He staggers backwards. The room clenches briefly like a fist, then opens up. He circles both his arms around the television console—as if it were a lover. Steadies himself, bends, scoops some ice from the tiny minibar freezer. It feels especially cold against his sliced hand. He presses it to his forehead.

There was a sentence in his mind that began with *someone else*. What came next? *Someone...else...*

39 ✦ Retribution

When Elko pushes open the door of Room 1411, there's an ozone-electrical smell that hits him. That comes first. Then he's aware of sobbing. No one's in the room. The sound's coming from the bathroom. He goes in, and what he sees is Mark Goodson—sitting on the tile, holding the body of Darrin Folger across his lap. Elko smells alcohol. He smells a *lot* of alcohol.

Mark Goodson's rocking and making whimpering-moaning sounds. He stares at Elko like a child who's broken something very valuable. "I did a terrible thing," he says.

Elko crouches in front of him, checks Darrin Folger's vital signs. There's still a pulse. "You don't know me, Mr. Goodson..." Elko addresses Mark softly. "But I know you. Your wife, Lena, has hired me to try to find you. She's concerned. She's worried about you."

"Is she okay?" Mark asks.

"She is," Elko says and then offers his name. "So...tell me what you can. What happened here?" He sees there's a plugged-in hair-drier on the floor. He sees that the shower stall door's open. He sees that Darrin Folger's not wearing shoes or socks. "What can you tell me about what happened?"

"I did a terrible thing," Mark moans, still cradling and rocking Darrin Folger.

"Mr. Folger's still alive," Elko tells Mark.

"He is?"

"He is. Pulse is weak, but—"

"I thought I'd killed him," Mark says.

"You?"

"I told him how he could kill *me*, if he wanted to. And he tried it out on himself."

Elko hears the room entry door slam the wall, and in a moment Shaq, wearing a pair of black silk pajamas and bedroom slippers, is towering above.

"Oh, my God!" Mark Goodson says. And he presses his back hard against the toilet. "What's he—?"

"Sorry I'm late, White Elk," Shaq says. He tells Elko that the Water Department was doing middle-of-the-night storm-drain work on Sahara. "He alive?" Shaq asks.

"I did a terrible thing," Mark Goodson says.

"Some days you can't hit the rim," Shaq says.

Elko sets a hand gently on Mark Goodson's shoulder. "Here's what I want you to do," he says. "Let my friend take him, okay? Let my friend take Mr. Folger from you. Take him in; lay him on the bed; check him out."

Mark lowers his cradling arms in a gesture that offers up Darrin Folger to Shaq and Shaq squats, slips his arms under Darrin like a human forklift, rises and hoists the limp body into the air. "Not in good shape," Shaq says.

"But alive," Elko adds.

Shaq carries Darrin Folger to the bed, lays him out. He checks his wrists, his neck, his eyes. As he does, Elko sketches out the probable electrocution.

"I'm going to try something," Shaq says. He stands, rotates his shoulders and exercises his fingers, tells Elko and Mark Goodson about a time—fishing with some buddies on the Salmon River above Stanley, Idaho—one of his friends, "trying to catch the big one," fished on through a thunderstorm, wading off of a sand bar. "Man caught a bolt," Shaq says. "Man caught a bolt *bad*." He describes how another one of the group—a sports physician—did something involving pressure just above the man's left ear.

"The dude was *dead*," Shaq says. "For all intents—you gotta believe me when I say this dude was in a cortege...travelin' toward the Next World. And this sports doc, he said there were these places—if you could press them hard enough, without crushing the skull—they were kind of like circuit-breakers. You could flip them on and off—get the current flowing again. He said a lot of the brain was electrical. Sort of like fighting fire with fire: you fight electricity with electricity. Anyway, he did this thing with his fingers, right about here—brought our dead friend back."

Elko shrugs, feels Darrin Folger's pulse again. It's hardly there, so he opens his hands—up and out toward Shaq as a gesture of go-ahead and steps aside.

Shaq cracks his knuckles, takes an enormous breath, rotates his neck. He sticks his tongue out and presses it down against his lower lip. He cracks his knuckles again then stretches both hands out to the left side of Darrin Folger's head. Then he positions and repositions his fingers just above Darrin's left ear. "C'mon, jumper cables! C'mon, jumper cables!" he says to himself. Then he shuts his eyes and stabs four of his fingers forwards.

Elko thinks he sees the fingers go straight into Darrin Folger's skull—though he knows they don't. Folger's whole body jumps—like a car left in gear when you hit the ignition. Shaq plunges his fingers into the soft above Darrin's ears again—and again, the shocked man's whole body startles.

"One more time!" Shaq says, and repeats his operation.

This time, Darrin Folger's body nearly lifts from the bed, almost floats, momentarily, in the air.

Elko swears he smells burnt wire. All he can think of is all the terrible-wonderful movies he saw as a kid—the ones with mad-scientist laboratories, where The-Misfit-of-the-World was bringing Scraps-Gathered-in-a-Landfill to life.

Elko hears Darrin Folger shriek—a fierce, triumphant animal roar—the thrum of a reentry from beyond the vale, a razor-cry of pain. Then Shaq begins moving his fingers through Darrin's hair. He's massaging the soft tissue of Darrin's skull, moving sensations around, ordering them. And as he does that—playing with the abacus of Darrin's brain—Darrin's roars become quieter, morph into moans of pleasure.

Then Darrin's eyes open and his visual engine starts. He sees Shaq. He sees Elko. He appears confused.

"You electrocuted yourself," Elko says.

"Oh," Darrin says.

"Yeah," Elko nods.

"So…" Darrin's corneas cloud…then clear. "What happened to whatshisname?" he asks.

"Mark Goodson," Elko instructs.

Darrin shakes his head. "No," he says.

"*Mark Goodson*: yes."

"No, it's Tony Frank," Darrin says. "It's *Anthony Francis*."

"No. *Anthony Francis* is his twin brother. His un-celebrity look-alike. True; in fact, literally," Elko says. "Badass twin brother. Evil twin."

"But he said—! I don't believe this! He *told* me. The name he used was—"

"Possibly, but that's not who he is."

"No! Listen—! That doesn't make sense! Why would he—?"

"Seems he's been curious. Been experimenting. Trying the evil twin out," Elko says.

"But I don't get it! Why would a person—?"

"Amen, Brother," Shaq says. "*Why would a person, indeed.*"

Mark's passed out beside the toilet in the bathroom. Elko, using a cold wet washcloth on his forehead, brings him to awareness gently, and when his eyes roll open, lets him focus a minute before—in a voice quieter than quiet—delivering the essential news: "He's alive. He's okay."

He can see his words resting on the tongue of Mark Goodson's brain, where he's tasting them like some exotic specialty.

"He's alive," Elko says again. "He's okay. Darrin Folger. He came out of it."

Elko runs the coldest water he can run into a hand towel then presses it into Mark's face. It shocks him at first, but then he breathes full and deeply.

Elko helps him to stand. "You need to tell Darrin who you are," he says. "He's confused. He's gotten you mixed up with your twin brother."

Mark's eyes circle wide. "How—?" he begins. "How do you—?"

"We can talk about that in a little while," Elko says. "But first, you've got to help Mr. Folger out."

Elko walks Mark out of the bathroom and sits him on the bed beside Darrin.

"Hey," Darrin says.

"Hey," Mark says. "I'm glad you're okay."

"So, ask him what you need to ask him," Elko instructs Darrin.

"Okay. What's your name?" Darrin asks.

"Mark Goodson," Mark says.

"Who's Anthony Francis?"

"He's my twin. My brother. Was. We were orphans. Never knew each other. Brought up by different families."

"But—?"

"We met each other for the first time last year. He contacted me. We met."

Mark Goodson looks over at Elko. He's not sure how much he should say. He doesn't know how much Elko knows, or doesn't know. He senses a growing tension in Darrin Folger. Mark turns to him. "Hey, truly, I'm very sorry if—I mean—"

Darrin's jaw locks. He jams a tongue in the corner of his mouth. He believes the twin story, but rage is rage. "Your twin—he fucked me over—fucked my whole family over—for a lot of money."

Mark Goodson feels ashamed. His eyes pool; his facial skin goes waxy. "How much?"

"Seventy-five thousand," Darrin says. He feels too many things: grief, anger, shame.

Suddenly, Mark's dizzy. He turns to Elko. "I'm really tired," he says. "I need to get some sleep." He turns to Darrin. "Don't leave town," he says. "I'll call you tomorrow. I'll get the money to you."

"He had no heart," Darrin Folger says. "He had no conscience."

"That's not true," Mark says. "I mean…I'm not condoning him, justifying. It's just…it's just, he had an orphan's heart—partly."

Elko asks Shaq if he can stay with Darrin until there's no question he's okay.

"Absolutely," Shaq says.

"I'm really tired," Mark says.

"Hey, I saw your wife—about two hours ago," Shaq says. "She was really tired, too."

"Were you in bed with her?"

"No. She said she missed you."

Mark smiles, or tries to. It's a broken smile. "I miss her, too," he says.

Elko thanks Shaq, tells Darrin that he's in good hands, and that, maybe, he'll see him tomorrow.

Darrin looks—at the same moment—relieved and confused.

Mark and Elko catch a cab to Bellagio. The eastern sky is the palest of pale blues; it's just after five in the morning.

Mark seems surprised when—under the Bellagio porte cochere—Elko steps out of the cab with him.

"I'm going to take a serious liberty. I'm going to camp out in your room," Elko says. "It's taken me some effort to find you. I'm not going to risk having you slip away."

"Not my intention," Mark says.

"Fine and good. Except we happen to be in a city where intentions are mutable."

"I'm here. I'm ready," Mark says.

"Lena's going to be relieved," Elko says.

And they step in under the Chihuly glass.

Elko prompts Mark to produce his room key for security. He does. They step into a bank of elevators.

"Did she sleep with the big guy?" he asks. "The black guy?"

"Shaq? No. No chance," Elko says.

"Did she sleep with you?"

"More of a chance, speaking honestly. But no."

"I'm surprised," Mark says.

"Well your wife—I would say—is a surprising woman."

"She can be amazing," Mark says.

"She can. A force."

"*I* slept with somebody," Mark says.

"I didn't hear that. It was a non-confession. Because...*what happens in Vegas*..."

Inside Mark's suite, Elko asks how Mark plans to pay Darrin Folger back the seventy-five thousand scammed by his twin brother. He doesn't know that Elko knows he's won a major jackpot.

The question stops him briefly. But Elko can see that it wakes him up as well and watches as Mark walks over to his outside wall, pulls the curtains back and stands, looking out.

"So, is that an *I don't know* move? Or is it something else?" Elko tries from behind him.

Mark stretches his arms up, high, over his head, grabs the curtains on either side. He looks like a big puppet, or a crucifixion. "I came into some money," he says.

"From your twin?"

"No," Mark says, not turning yet. "I found some."

What he's about to tell Elko is what Elko's been suspecting.

"You also won some," Elko says.

Mark Goodson turns. "How do you know that?"

"Again, *What happens in Vegas stays*—but it *moves around* here quite a bit."

"Oh."

"Over three-hundred thousand," Elko says.

"Then why'd you ask how I was going to pay Darrin back?"

"Because I'm a private investigator. I ask questions."

"Do you want to see something ingenious?" Mark Goodson asks.

Elko nods. Mark walks to a chest of drawers across the room, glides a drawer open and lifts a curious piece of clothing—a kind of vest.

"Check this out," Mark says.

What it looks like is a suede vest; what if feels like is something bulkier. The whole vest is lined with zippers. He lays the vest out on Mark's bedcover and opens it, discovering that the lining is a maze of pockets.

"Pretty neat, right?" Mark's standing beside Elko. He's a little giddy, it seems—like a kid, showing off a toy.

"Let me guess," Elko begins.

Mark grins, nods. "Over three million!" Mark says. "In the vest. Which I found in a men's room!" Now he's grinning broadly. And in case Elko hasn't registered the amount, he repeats it. "Over three million!"

"Which is where?" Elko asks.

"Which is where I put it. In my safe."

"So you found it…hanging…" Elko says, "inside a stall in a Mirage men's room?"

"How did you know it was The Mirage?"

Elko spells out the whole whale-impersonation drama. He tells Mark he's lucky that a number of other people didn't find him first, because he'd be dead, surely.

Mark sits on the bed.

"Get some sleep," Elko suggests. "I'm going to crash on your sofa. We can talk about what the next step is after we've slept an hour or two.

"So, is Lena okay?" Mark Goodson asks.

Elko tells him: *Yes.*

"I really miss her," Mark says. "I didn't think I would, but I do. She's a kind of visionary child...stuck at puberty. Which is when we first met. Middle school."

"*Life's* a middle school," Elko says.

"And when we fell in love."

"That's an interesting phrase."

"*When we fell in love?*"

"*Visionary child stuck at puberty.*"

"I guess gifted children aren't easy."

"Well, for what it's worth, she misses you, too. Get some sleep."

"Yeah," Mark says. "Yeah."

At about eleven the next morning, housekeeping raps and announce themselves. Elko stumbles from the couch and asks that they try again in the middle of the afternoon, then he wanders into the bedroom. Mark is on the bed, holding a pillow over his head. "Who was that?" he asks behind the pillow.

Elko tells him and says it's going on noon.

Still behind the pillow, Mark asks: "Is Lena here?"

Elko asks that he please remove the pillow from his head.

When he does, his face looks blotchy. Puffy. A combination of rash and anemia, a face that—with too little sleep—has reverted to baby fat. "Sorry," he says.

Elko tells him that he hasn't contacted Lena yet.

"She's probably still asleep herself," Mark says. "Sometimes she sleeps for a whole day. Sometimes two."

"Should we call her?" Elko asks.

"Let me wake up first," Mark says.

The suite has two baths. They both shower. Mark shaves and changes into fresh clothes.

They go to Café Bellagio. Mark has a ham steak, eggs, and coffee; Elko has an order of chicken livers. He asks the waitress to see if the cook can sauté the chicken livers in bourbon then asks for a double Chopin vodka. "And a small glass of orange juice on the side," he adds.

"I'll bet you and Lena got along," Mark says.

Elko waffles his hand. "Well...sometimes *yes*, sometimes *no*," he says. He pulls a folded piece of stationery from his breast pocket. "Regarding my fee, I found her to be less than astute in business negotiations."

"What is this?" Mark looks perplexed studying the notarized document.

"I believe it says I now own a beachfront condo in Boca Grande."

"She *gave* it to you? She inherited that from her grandfather. It's the most valuable thing we own. It's our retirement home."

"Relax, Mr. Goodson. I doubt that document would hold up in court. I'd probably be convicted of defrauding a poor and distressed woman. So, do with it what you will—shred it, burn it, frame it. Think of it as a testament to how much your wife wanted you back. But I would like to be fairly compensated for my time and effort, a few minor expenses."

"Whatever your fee," Mark says, unable to take his eyes off the notarized letter. "I'll pay you double. No *triple*."

"I'll send you a bill. My standard rates will be just fine. But regarding your wife...do you want to do this? Be *reintroduced*?"

Their meals arrive.

"How can you eat chicken livers for breakfast?" Mark asks.

"Ham steak!" Elko brays. He holds his nose. Then he reminds Mark that they've got more business to get out of the way: "Three agenda items by my count," Elko says. "Three big questions. First: When are you going to get Darrin Folger the money you promised? Second: How and when are you going to get the whale-account money back into the vault at MGM/Mirage? Third: What do you want me to do about Lena?"

Mark checks his watch.

"You have an appointment?" Elko asks.

"No, but do you know what I'd really love?"

"Shoot," Elko says.

"I'd love just eight more hours of this. I know that's selfish, but being someone else. Being on my own. Being a *big spender*. Eight more hours with no requirements of good citizenship. That would do it for me. I'd die happy."

"Well...Let's try to imagine how that could be done without you dying. Give me an agenda. A plan."

Mark offers a possible timetable. First: he'll give Darrin Folger a call, return the money Anthony Francis swindled from him. They'll drink a bottle of expensive something together.

Elko assures Mark that the Darrin Folger leg of the tripod is easy, a slam dunk. Elko will let Mark handle the details and trust him.

Second, Mark says he'll get the three million plus back into The Mirage conduit by gambling it away at Bellagio—huge chunk after huge chunk—until it's gone. It will be outrageous and flagrant. Bellagio's part of the MGM/Mirage group, so that should work, shouldn't it?

Elko says that would be trickier but doable. He'll see if he can set it up with casino management. They may be so happy to get their money back, they'll agree. But it's more of a Hail Mary than a slam dunk. He'll see what he can do.

Third: Mark has what he terms a "neat idea" for his Lena reunion. But it will require the cooperation of Lance Burton. He outlines his idea.

Elko agrees. "Once a year, I decide to trust someone," he says. "Whether it makes sense or not. This year: you're the guy."

"Thank you. Really, thank you," Mark says. So now I'm off—returning the money that was swindled...and a little extra." Mark's excited. Enthusiastic. His face is pink and doughy; his grin, wide. "Last twenty-four hours!" he says. It's a glass half filled with glee, half with rue.

Sitting alone now in the Café Bellagio, Elko calls Michael Vincentes at The Mirage. "Hey, good news! Spread the word!" He fills Michael Vincentes in. Elko relates how the diverted whale-money got lost by the careless scammer and then found by an innocent. He says that the innocent's going to reenter all the money into the system in a play that's half-fantasy, half-scheme. Elko assures Michael Vincentes that the innocent is someone to be trusted. "He's a Boy Scout on a night out," Elko says. "He'll buy in at a private table in the Bellagio VIP room for the full amount and then will sit there—having the betting time of his life—until it's gone." Elko assures Michael Vincentes that this time tomorrow, all the money will be back in place. Michael Vincentes seems skeptical, but gives Elko the name of Manny diCorregio at Bellagio.

Elko calls Manny. The whole idea delights Manny and makes him laugh. "Great little drama! Great solution!" Manny says. "I know just how we're gonna do it. Can you come over sometime in the next hour?"

"I'm here," Elko says. "I'm sitting in your coffee shop even as we speak."

"I'll be right down."

Manny arrives shortly and after introductions tells Elko to follow him. A left, a right, another left and they're in the baccarat high-limit room. Manny places a RESERVED sign on one of the baccarat tables.

He grins and points up. "Best cameras," he says. "You need to bring him to this table. There's his seat. I'll clear all of this with surveillance. There won't be any problem unless he causes it. Tell him he can bet any amount he wants. No limit. Tell him there's a hundred-thousand minimum. What time can we expect him?"

"Sometime this afternoon," Elko says. "He's drinking with a friend right now, but he'll be alone when I bring him in. Possibly drunk."

"Guy gets to enter the world of make-believe for a few hours—hey! That's what we're all about!" Manny says. "Should be fun to watch."

And they shake.

Climbing the landing to his office, Elko hears crazed and furious shouting and recognizes the voices. It's Donald Trump and Hillary Clinton with Betina-Betina attempting to mediate. Elko feels his brain lurch and shudder. The two hate each other—even as *look-alikes* they hate each other—but it's not easy to find a Donald and a Hillary in the same town.

When Elko opens the door, Betina-Betina says, "Thank, God!"

Hillary grabs Elko. "Whatever garbage he throws—don't listen!" she says. "He's so full of shit he could fertilize the corn belt!"

"Bitch!" Donald says.

Elko steps between them and pushes in opposite directions. He hears, "She wants to—!" and "He refuses—!"

Elko puts his hands up for them to stop. He takes a breath. "Okay," he says to Betina-Betina. "Fill me in. What's the deal? What's happened?" He points a finger—first at Donald, then Hillary. "You *both*... *both* of you—stow it! And be patient."

Betina-Betina says Sheldon Adelson called. He wanted Donald and Hillary to have an intimate dinner at Bouchon. He likes the idea of them being seen together; calls it *a Major Bipartisan*. He thinks there will be all sorts of rumors that spread out. He'll make sure any autograph hounds are kept at bay.

Donald leans forward, but Elko stops him. "Are you in or out?" he asks. "In or out. Both of you. One word."

There's a quarrelsome silence. They nod. Agree. Grudgingly. Betina-Betina produces their standard contracts, and they leave.

"It's like a fucking debate that never ends," Elko says. He does a quick fill-in with Betina-Betina: "We've got our man! I've got him on the honor-code for 24 hours." Elko hoists a fisted thumb into the air then puts in a call to Lena over at Treasure Island. The house operator rings her room phone four times; then a computerized voice comes on and invites Elko to leave a message. He hangs up and tries again. Then again.

On the third attempt a very groggy Lena answers. "What time is it?" she asks.

"Lunch time."

"Shit," she says.

"My friend, Shaq, describes you as being in rare form last night at a place called *The Bruised Bronco*," Elko says.

"Error in judgment."

Elko says he'll be over within the hour.

"Did you find him?" Lena asks. "I smell something: you've found him."

"I'll be over within the hour," Elko says again.

"I need some fresh air," Lena says. "I'll be down at the pool."

When they meet, Lena looks terrible. "I want my husband," she says.

"We're getting close," Elko says, taking the lounge chair beside hers.

"No. Listen, Elko...I'm feeling played out. And uncertain. And afraid Mark—you've found him, haven't you?—won't take me back."

"Well, that's a question for the audience to consider isn't it? Will he or won't he?"

Lena's drinking a Long Island iced tea; Elko flags the waitress and orders a Tanqueray Ten.

"You fucker! You've found him; you've found Mark!" she says.

"Tone down," Elko suggests.

"I *know* you have. I *know* it."

"Maybe it's your voices."

"Fucking A! It's my voices!"

"Speaking of voices, keep yours down, please."

"It's the iced tea." She lowers her volume. "So, I'm right...right? You've found him."

"*Found*'s a complicated word," Elko says.

"Okay. So, give me a report."

"I've gotten *this* close," Elko says. And he shows her his thumb and index finger pressed together.

"That's not close, that's connected."

"I'm sorry." He separates the two digits by a hair. "I think we need to try an experiment," Elko says.

"Not another comedy club," she says. "I can't do that."

Elko broadly outlines an agenda for the evening. Much of what he says is unspecific. "So, you aboard?" he asks.

She takes a long sip of her drink. "Hey, what are my choices at this point?" she says. "You haven't really said anything. But if we get within fifty feet of a stand-up comic—"

"For me, comedians are an aphrodisiac!" Elko says.

"So, what time?"

"Five thirty? Five forty-five? I'll call up."

"I'll be ready," she says. "You better have him. You better have found him. I can't live without him. I know I told you that already. But now I'm out of money."

Elko decides to save the shaving and showering until all his ducks are in the lagoon and in some semblance of a row. He makes all of the calls he's promised Mark he'd make. Not all of his requests land happily, but he scrambles—inventing assurances, making contingency promises. Finally, he's able to get Lance Burton on the line.

"This is not exactly abundant lead time," Lance says.

"Still, you have to admit, it's great theater."

"Or, possibly, a great fiasco."

"It's the stuff of legends."

"Right. So was the Hindenburg."

Elko calls Faye. "Hey, Baby," she says, her usual sultry self.

He asks: Is she into high theater?

"It depends," she says. "Whose?"

He invites her to join Lena and himself for a command performance by Lance Burton.

With the inclusion of Lena, she resists.

"It'll be good. It'll be good for your soul," Elko says.

"My soul's not what needs your attention," Faye says.

"Hey, I'm wrapping up loose ends."

"Yeah. I've got a few of those for you, too."

♦ ♦ ♦

Elko heads back over to Bellagio and finds Manny diCorregio leaning against a marble pillar at the entry to the high stakes room. Elko can see that Mark's at the RESERVED baccarat table. But Manny looks grim.

"So, how's my man doing with his fantasy?" Elko asks.

Manny doesn't smile. Instead he pivots and nods across the room to where Mark sits with phalanxes of chips stacked in front of him. "I'm sure he's having a ball," Manny says.

"So, how'd he doing?"

"Last count: he was up over ten million."

Elko laughs a nervous laugh and shrugs. "Luck's a bitch—right? Still, we both know it's just time."

"Well, you may know that…but I don't."

Elko saunters to the baccarat table where Mark sees him and grins. "Hey!" Mark says. "How's Lena?"

"She's preparing herself," Elko says.

"It'll be so amazing—our reunion!"

"You don't know the half of it," Elko quips.

Mark is almost a tropical storm of energy. "Hey! Watch this!" he says.

Elko eyeballs his stack after stack of gold chips. He's got roughly a million bet on the present hand. He loses and Elko feels a very pale shade better.

"Watch this!" Mark Goodson repeats.

He doubles his bet, loses, and Elko feels even better.

Mark Goodson winks at Elko, then pushes almost half of what he has left onto the banker bet. The croupier deals the cards, and Mark wins. He opens his palms in a gesture of helplessness. "I can't lose," he says.

Elko stands behind him, puts a cautioning hand on his shoulder. "Lose," he advises. "And fast. Winning is not an option. Lose."

"Elko, I mean it. I'm dipped! I'm anointed!"

"You'll be anointed with cement if you don't do what I'm saying. Listen to me. Here's what you do. Bet everything. Bet everything on Player."

Mark looks up at Elko—all helplessness and innocence. The dealer's waiting. "Everything?"

"Everything."

"It's over ten million!" Mark says.

"Everything," Elko repeats a third time. And Mark does.

Player wins. Mark wins.

"Again," Elko instructs.

"But—!"

"Everything. *Player* again."

Mark bets it. Wins.

"Keep going. Keep doing it," Elko insists. "*Everything.* On *Player.* Bet it all. And don't change."

Two minutes later, the dealer's check rack is empty and he's waiting for a fill.

Elko senses Manny diCorregio, who's stepped in beside him.

"This your ingenious system of pay-back?" Manny asks.

Elko holds his hands up—palms flat, fingers spread—a gesture of surrender. "At some point he's got to lose," Elko says.

"And that point's *where* exactly?" Manny asks. "It would help me to *locate* it. His losing point. What's its latitude and longitude?"

"Look, he's not a gambler," Elko says. "He has no idea what he's doing."

"Well, we've got about a third of a billion dollars out there," Manny says. "We may not have any more chips in the vault. Gaming could take away our license if they walked in here right now."

"But he *knows* he doesn't get to win. He *understands*—"

Manny's hands are huge and meaty. They're the hands of a defensive tackle, and he coils one of them around Elko's upper arm and draws him to one side, where he leans in like a loan shark giving a client just one more hour. "Somebody told me once," he begins. "Somebody who'd put in his time in this business once pointed out to me— we were talking about card counters and whether they're actually dangerous to a casino—that a person could be the smartest player in the world...but if that person had no luck, he'd be down the tubes. And it's true; I've seen that. Often. *Conversely...*" Manny goes on, "*conversely* my friend said, another person could have shit for brains but, if he had luck..."

"For the record, I'm pretty smart," Mark pipes in from ten feet away. He's still waiting for the dealer's cheques tray to be replenished.

"Mr. Goodson, you stay out of this," Elko says, turning back to Manny. "I understand your concern," he says.

"I'm not sure you do."

Elko walks back to the table and lowers one hand on each of Mark Goodson's shoulders. What he feels through Mark's shirt is an almost-electrical current. "This has been fun, right?" Elko says.

Mark grins. He nods.

"The kind of stuff legends are built of," Elko offers.

"Exactly!"

"So, mission accomplished, right?"

Mark's look is more equivocal. He shrugs.

"Okay," Elko says. "Get up."

"Get—?"

"Up," Elko says. "Up."

"And?"

"*And* nothing. That's it. Get up. Leave the chips where they are. Take the moment in, take everything you can in—commit it to memory... And walk away...A deal's a deal."

Mark Goodson squares his shoulders under Elko's hands.

Elko waits. Watches. He can see that the dealer is doing the same thing and knows as well, that they've gotten the attention of Manny diCorregio.

Mark takes a deep breath and stands up. "A deal," he says. "Oh, I gave Darrin Folger a hundred thou. He was happy," he says.

And he walks away.

40 ♦ A Higher Being

When the phone rings in J. Bob Marshall's Mirage suite at four in the afternoon, he's with a fringe porn-star hooker named ZZ Oral. He's made a kind of saddle blanket out of one of his leather vests and is riding her. He's told her, "Every time I go deep—snort like a mustang," and she's doing that. She's doing that when the phone rings.

"Pardon me," J. Bob says.

"Hey, Cowboy, it's your rodeo; no problem," ZZ Oral says.

And J. Bob picks up the phone.

The call's from Michael Vincentes. His voice is animated, like a broker at the height of the bubble with a hot IPO. "Mr. M!" he says.

"Michael."

"All your money's back!" Michael Vincentes announces.

ZZ Oral is cupping her 42F breasts, touching them with her tongue. It's her show for J. Bob, and it distracts him.

"Say what? Excuse me?"

"Your million! Your million-nine is back!"

"Whoa!" J. Bob begins—then feels he needs to signal ZZ that he's not speaking to her. *She* shouldn't stop.

She snorts, giggles.

"How'd that happen?" J. Bob says. "Was it the guy? Was it my double? Did that sonofabitch—"

"I'm not really at liberty to say," Michael Vincentes says. "Point is—"

"I get it. I understand, Michael. And I'm grateful," J. Bob says.

"I'll just say it took some arranging."

"Which, hey, I appreciate. Still, it would be helpful for me to—"

"Mr. M., please. We squeezed here, we squeezed there. But the details...I can't say. And, as *you* know: as soon as we discovered the theft, we did adjust your account appropriately. Even if we hadn't gotten the money back, you would not have suffered one nickel of loss. But I *will* tell you—and...and this is for your stress and the *inconvenience*—I *will* tell you that we've added an extra hundred thousand to your account. With our compliments. How's that?"

"That's good," J. Bob says. He's smiling. "That's good." He's nodding his approval, but it's hard—even for him—to finally know whether he's more pleased about his money or about the show ZZ Oral's putting on.

"So, we're straight, right? Everything's cool?"

"Michael, I just want to know if that-little-prick-of-an-asshole took the initiative...or if you had to...you *know*, force it."

"Mr. M, I can't," Michael Vincentes says. "Money moves. Money moves; it's *here*; it's *there*. "It's all confidential."

"I understand. That's fine. Your call," J. Bob says. "Thank you."

And they hang up.

ZZ Oral is kneeling on J. Bob's king-sized bed, wearing his Stetson. "Good news?" she asks.

"Yeah, excellent. Excellent news," J. Bob says. "News I wasn't expecting—to tell the truth—but excellent."

"I'm glad," ZZ Oral says.

"Likewise," J. Bob says. His mind is still in a bit of a float—loosed both by Michael Vincentes' call and zz's question. "Do you believe in forgiveness?" J. Bob suddenly asks.

"Hon—?"

"Forgiveness. Do you believe in it? Do you have cause in your life to believe in forgiveness? Exoneration...exculpation? If somebody does you wrong, do you try to *forgive* them?"

"Well, I was raised Seventh Day. So—"

"I was raised Baptist."

"I think *they* forgive."

"But do *you?*"

"I try."

"What if someone called you a *slut* and a *whore?*"

"Well, I *am* a slut and a whore."

The phone rings again. It's the Onda Restaurant, inviting J. Bob to be their guest at dinner. *Hey, why not?* he thinks; after all, he's hungry, so J. Bob makes the arrangements, hangs up, seems pensive.

zz studies him. She doesn't like the lack of action in the room. "Do you want to do me again?"

J. Bob sits on the bed, pats zz's knee.

She runs her fingernails down his back. "You have the energy?" she asks.

He shakes his head, laughs. "You know...normally, I'd love to. Normally. Normally, I'd go on for hours. But right now—somehow— all I can think about is forgiveness." He lies back on his bed and stares up at the ceiling. "I think you're on to it; I think you've got it. For- giveness."

Billy Spence spends two hours at Sunrise Emergency, where the staff cauterizes his finger stub and wraps the wound. He feels ashamed and humiliated when the chief resident asks to see the severed finger. "Where is it?" the chief resident asks. "If we had it, we might be able to—"

"Someone took it," Billy says. "Someone took it for his finger collection." And that ends the medical history.

After Sunrise Emergency, Billy goes back to his Vegas Towers apartment. He paces the floor and recites monologue after monologue. "Now is the winter of our...I bring you illusion in the form of... Willy was a salesman, and for a salesman...The dead don't stay inter- ested in us living people for very long"—Shakespeare, Wilde, Ionesco, O'Neill, Miller, Albee. He holds his hand up in a theatrical gesture before the mirror. Even professionally bandaged, it looks more now like a claw or turkey foot than a hand. He practices stage gestures where his hand alone might command attention, compel people. "A horse! A horse!..." Given the right venue, he'll be able to rivet an audience, hold them in the palm of this grotesque three-fingered, half- thumbed hand.

What's he going to do? How's he going to save his other fingers? Any thought that he can repay his debt—find nearly two million dollars somewhere—to return to J. Bob is absurd. Making amends is out of the question; Billy's not an amends-making sort of person. J. Bob has vowed to hound Billy and exact a finger a week, but the threat is bogus. How could anyone—*anyone*—find The Master of a Thousand Faces? *Hey*: Billy doesn't have to *run away*! He can stay right here in town and elude this *stupid redneck fuck*. Forever! If he chooses, he can move to the idiot's own home town—Smallville—and the man will never know!

However...with the Demerol wearing off and his hand starting to throb, simple evasion isn't enough. Billy needs a play. So, okay, consider this: kill J. Bob. Create a brilliant disguise, travel back to The Mirage, find J. Bob, strike up a relationship, get himself invited up to J. Bob's suite...and—what's to stop him? why not?—simply kill him. How much cash would a man like J. Bob carry? Billy could kill him, then *become* him one final time and walk away with at least an initial buy-in of three-hundred thousand. What would be the problem in that?

Billy calls The Mirage. "Mr. Marshall," he says and gives the room number.

There's a pause. The switchboard rings him through.

When J. Bob answers, Billy affects Italian: "Onda would like to invite you to be our guest tonight," Billy says.

There's a back and forth. They settle on eight thirty.

"Will you be bringing a guest?" Billy asks.

"Possibly," J. Bob says. "Possibly."

"As you wish," Billy says, then hangs up. Immediately, he calls The Mirage back and makes dinner reservations at Onda for himself— under the name *Billy Crystal*.

At eight fifteen, Billy sashays up to the maître d' podium at Onda and is immediately recognized. "Mr. Crystal," the hostess says.

Billy feels pleased with his work. "My goodness, I'm recognized!"

"I watch the Academy Awards," the hostess says.

"Well, I guess you can run, but you can't hide," Billy smiles.

"Certainly, in your world."

"Certainly, in my world. Listen, I had a—"

"Yes. We know. We were expecting you."

Billy keeps his bandaged right-hand in a pocket. "You're too good," he smiles. Then he requests a private table—"private as possible," he says.

"We anticipated that," the hostess says and leads him to one. "It must be hard, never really being offstage," she says.

"Well, *let me play the fool,* as the Bard says."

She tells him that it would be Onda's pleasure to have him as their guest and urges him to enjoy his meal.

Billy thanks her and, again, feels smug. He *needs* smug. He *needs* generosity and recognition after the day he's had.

He begins by ordering a Grey Goose martini. "Keep them coming, if you will," he instructs his cocktail waiter.

From Billy's alcove seat, he can study Onda's entry, and he begins watching for J. Bob Marshall's arrival. Eight fifteen. Eight twenty. Eight twenty-five. Billy begins to feel his blood rise. Eight thirty. Eight thirty-five. Eight forty. Billy surmises J. Bob to be a man who keeps to his own schedule—not anyone else's. He could be in a hot game. Billy simply has to be patient. He's cool; he understands: the curtain rises whenever it rises.

At eight forty-five, Billy's on his second martini when an outrageously stacked blonde in a dark business suit enters. Billy watches as she has a brief exchange with the Onda hostess, watches as the hostess checks a piece of paper then escorts the blonde to a table not far away.

The stacked blonde sets the menu in front of her but seems compelled to look around, take the restaurant in. Something about her reads *tourist*, Billy thinks—someone having a Campari, alone, on her first night in Venice, on St. Mark's Square. When the blonde's eyes sweep Billy, her vision stutters. She leans forward, squints, fumbles in her small, sequined purse, takes out some glasses, slips them on. Billy tries to look away, but the stacked blonde has already waved toward him.

Understanding it to be a mistake the minute he does it, he waves back.

The blonde fumbles in her handbag again and withdraws a three-inch block of Post-its. She rises and approaches. "Hey," she says.

"Hey," Billy says.

"You're Billy Crystal, right?"

"Busted," Billy says.

Still fumbling in her purse, she says, "I know I have a pen in here... Can I sit down for a minute?"

"Hey, be my guest." Billy motions to a chair. *Why is he saying these things? Where is J. Bob?*

The blonde sits and tosses her block of Post-its in front of Billy. "Will you write your autograph for me?" she asks, still fumbling.

Billy reaches over, takes the Post-its, finds a pen in his pocket and with his good hand signs the top sheet *Billy Crystal*. He slides the block back to the woman.

She leans into Billy. "Would you like mine?" she asks. "My autograph? I used to be pretty famous. ZZ Oral. I did a lot of fuck-films. Ten, fifteen years ago. You've probably seen me."

"I may not recognize you with—"

"I know: *my clothes on.* I've heard it. Have you eaten the steak here?"

"Actually, this is the first time I've—"

"This was so weird—how this happened? Why I'm here?"

Jesus, get this woman away from me! Billy thinks. *Where is J. Bob?*

"I was doing this client? You know, upstairs? This rich Texas guy— in his suite?"

Suddenly, Billy has a bad feeling. Déjà-vu. He feels he knows what's coming next.

"We'd gone a couple of times. He'd had me ride him—you know— like we're in a rodeo? And his phone rings, and it's this place, this restaurant, inviting him to dinner. And he says *Yes* but then—maybe a half hour later—he decides he's going to take his jet back to Texas, and he calls the restaurant up, says thank you, says but he's not going to make it, says but his friend Miss Oral—that's me, zz—will take his place."

Billy can't help himself: "You're saying he went back to—?"

"Texas—yeah. So, he said, *Why don't you take my place at Onda— have a steak on me?* And I said, *Isn't Onda Italian?* I ate here once before with a client, but I didn't want to say that. And he said, *Italians eat steak—*"

Billy can see waiters hovering...not exactly sure—given the scenario—what their moves should be. He thinks of signaling one of them over and ordering. Still, he can't help himself; he wants to hear the rest of what zz has to say.

"—So, I think *why not?* You know a good steak? It can make me cry! Weird thing this guy...this Texan...For a while—just before he decided that he was going to fly back to his ranch or wherever— I thought *he* was going to cry. He said there'd been a *miracle*, that something that had been *lost* had been *found.* He kept asking me if I believed in *forgiveness.* Is that strange? What do you think that was about?"

"Well—"

"I mean—fuck!—*forgiveness.* So, should I sign the Post-it under your Post-it. Should we swap autographs? You can think of mine as a pornograph."

Billy feels confusion, relief, disappointment.

zz suggests that they dine together, being as they are both alone.

Billy isn't agile enough to refuse.

So, while he measures out his lobster risotto and his salad of endives, beets, and pine nuts, zz scarfs down two rare New York steaks. During the meal, her voice populates Billy's brain like a nest of snakes. Outside, he watches The Mirage volcano erupt and tries to clear his head.

"Hey, Billy Crystal!" Billy hears a nearby male voice call out. "Yo!" Billy waves his one good hand in the voice's general direction. Translation: *thanks for recognizing me, but I'm busy.* Despite, whatever zz has said about his *having gone to Texas,* J. Bob, Billy knows, will sneak into his dreams when he falls asleep and exact finger after finger. It will be a life now of waking suddenly to the shock of severance and a phantom pain in his hands.

Do you believe in a higher being? he remembers J. Bob asking. And, in the moment, he'd thought: *what a strange question from this particular person.* But possibly Billy has been wrong. Possibly it was precisely the right question.

Billy leaves Onda, leaves zz, wanders off. He thinks maybe he'll amble up the Strip to the Flamingo. Usually—between ten and twelve—they have karaoke in the Garden Lounge. Most nights, the tourists taking the microphone are almost unendurable. Maybe tonight he'll take the mic himself, lift it from its cradle with a flair. He imagines a murmur going through the crowd: *It's Billy Crystal! It's Billy Crystal!*

But he'll surprise them. With the mic in his hand, he won't do Billy Crystal. He'll do Anthony Newley. He'll sing, *What Kind of Fool Am I?*

41 ✦ Abracadabra!

At 5:50 Lena meets Elko in the Treasure Island lobby. What she's wearing is expensive, but it's also tight and sequined.

Elko asks her to scoot back up to her room and change, "…into something more appropriate. Less *street rap,* more, *sonnet.*"

"I can be who*m*ever I want," Lena says, humming the *m* of *whom.*

"I think they call that a personality disorder," Elko says.

"End of the day, admit it: you *like* me."

"End of the day: it's a good thing we're not married."

"I'm the girl of your dreams."

"Hey, I'm in therapy for those dreams," he says.

At 6:01, Elko tips a valet named Lincoln, slips into the driver's seat of his z, and he and Lena zip up to Bellagio. She rides in a pensive silence, finally and almost tentatively touching his right elbow.

"You've been very good," she says. "To me, I mean. So, for what it's worth...thank you."

Elko tells her that he tries to be good to *all* his clients. "So don't feel special," he adds.

"You found him. He's okay. He wants me back. I *know* it," Lena says.

"The voices again," Elko quips.

"They never fail," Lena says.

"So, if he's had an accident—falling from a great height—and is paraplegic, you'll take care of him, right? And if he's fallen in love with another woman, no problem; you'll support that."

"You can be an asshole sometimes. You know that?"

"Actually, the *sometimes* is when I'm *not* an asshole."

"So, do I look okay? I want him to cry when he sees me. I mean cry—*happy*."

"Who says he's going to see you?"

"Yeah, yeah, yeah! Seriously, Elko: I have to admit—I am so fucking *nervous*."

"Kid, you're a walking DSM of nervous disorders."

At 6:12, they pull into Bellagio's valet park zone. This time the valet, Chad, compliments Elko on his wheels. "Not his choice of women?" Lena calls over the hood from where she stands at the far side of the car. Chad says: *that was understood; of course; women, too.*

At 6:20, as they're being seated, Elko apologizes to the maître d' at Michael Mina for being twenty minutes late. Elko is reassured that it's a *quiet night* and there's no problem. *Please enjoy your meal,* he's told. Elko recommends the vegetarian sampler with wine pairings, and Lena, smiling, tells him, *that's fine; she's in his hands.*

Their predinner drinks arrive—Lena's strawberry daiquiri and Elko's double Tanqueray. Elko toasts: *To rabbits in hats!* And they drink, Elko slamming his double down and signaling their waiter for another.

"Now *you* seem anxious," Lena says. "Usually *I'm* the one who's drinking that way—like I've just come up from underwater gasping for air."

"You've been gasping for air the whole time I've known you," Elko says.

"So, okay; fine, I gasp. We live in a world that invites gasping."

"True. Still…look on the bright side. It's a nice night. *Magical.* Man compliments me on my car. Headwaiter was totally cool with our being late."

Elko's second drink arrives. He drains it. "I'm doing a guest spot at a comedy club at midnight," he says. "I'm preparing myself."

Lena studies him, studies his eyes with their mix of opal and anthracite. He's brought her to the edge of something, she thinks. She keeps looking around the restaurant for Mark. Elko's planned some sort of weird-ass reunion: she senses it.

Elko tells the waiter that they need to finish their meal by 7:15; they have a commitment.

"We have a…excuse me: a *what?*" Lena says. "What have you cooked up? Where are we going?"

"I'm going to ask that—this one night—you stifle your need to challenge. *Capisce?*"

"So, okay—what are we *committed to?*"

"Satisfaction," Elko says. "Resolution. Dénouement."

"I hope that's French for *you found my husband.*"

At 7:12, bill paid, Elko pulls Lena's chair and she rises. She asks, *So c'mon, what's next?*

He says, *What's next is a walk—a very short one. Two casinos.*

They begin their slow, mute, each-differently-brooding-walk down along the Bellagio lakeside paths, then along the Strip. When Elko moves them into a turn and up the stairs into the Monte Carlo, Lena's breath thins.

"Please, what's happening?" she says. "I'm getting a bad feeling. What are we doing here?"

Elko weighs various options. "Briefly pausing," he says. "There's a new comic at their club here. I want to steal stuff from him."

"Elko, please! I've humored you…so to speak. *Done* comics with you. Enough."

"Well, then—" And Elko grabs her hand and hauls her behind him.

At 7:36, Lena notices that the aisle they're moving along leads directly to the Lance Burton Theatre. "Hey!" she blurts. And then: "I suspected! I knew it!"

"Ah! The usual suspicion!" Elko spots Faye and waves. Faye waves back.

"Elko, seriously, please!"

But now the two are three, and Elko is making introductions:

Lena—Faye, Faye—Lena. He has the tickets out and now they're inside the Lance Burton Theatre where an usher guides them to the aisle of their seats. "Enjoy the show," he says.

Lena says, *Oh, Jesus,* then *Oh, fuck!* then tells Elko, "I'm getting bad vibes here. I'm getting *very, very* bad vibes."

"It's okay. In just a minute the voices will come and clear everything up."

"I smell rats."

Elko nods to Shaq, entering behind them. They high five.

"*OhmyGodJesus!*" Lena, noticing, says.

Elko apologizes to Faye. "I'm sorry. The lady's frequently rude. And ungrateful."

He gestures that the women should precede him into their row. He smiles at Lena and disregards the brush fire in her eyes. Once they're seated, she leans in and says, "These are the *same seats!*"

"You two talk," Elko says. "I have to see a man about a horse." And he slips back out the aisle and disappears.

At 8:02, the lights begin to dim, and Elko edges his way back and takes his seat beside Lena, who is taking megahits on her inhaler. "Please! Elko, please!" she hisses. Her low whispered voice has a thin lacquer of tears. "Even though I know what you're doing, just say it! Being even the tiniest bit uncertainty really scares me," she says.

Elko puts his hand flat against her upper back and presses in a rhythm of breathing. "Relax," he says. "It's just a show."

At 8:07, Lance Burton appears on stage. He's all in black—black dinner jacket, black pants. Norah Jones is singing, "Feelin' the same way all over again..." Lance Burton stretches his right arm into the glowing trunk of a spotlight and, in his luminous palms, a peacock appears. A ripple of wonder breaks and washes across the dark. He lifts the peacock slowly, slowly—a priest making an offering. Now Joni Mitchell is singing "A Case of You," and when Lance Burton's hands reach their full extension, a phosphorus scribble ignites the air, the bird's gone, and where it had fanned its tail, wine glasses appear, which Lance begins to juggle.

And so it goes. Various known things of any of our lives drift into the light, drift out, surprise us. A woman and an ocelot trade places, then trade back again. A carnation boutonniere becomes a small forest of calla lilies becomes a three-minute rain of red rose petals. Lance Burton sweeps the fallen rose petals into a pile, which melts, and transforms into a koala. Lance asks if any woman in the audience is wearing white gloves, and a woman, in the middle of the audience, raises her hand. Lance gestures her toward the stage, and when she's near, he indicates that she should toss her white gloves to him. She does, but just as the gloves are about to reach Lance, they freeze in the air and begin to gesture as though they were the hands of a mime. For a moment, Lance's hands and the gloves have a kind of "conversation," then, underscored by an offstage *whooshing* sound, the white gloves become white doves.

"The eye is quicker than the hand," Elko says.

Lena says nothing,

At 9:27, Lance Burton requests a *male volunteer*. He moves to the footlights and puts his hand up to his brow as though he were Meriwether Lewis or William Clark. He scans. "You!" he says, and points unequivocally at Elko.

"No! Please!" Lena says.

But Elko is up and moving and Faye, on Lena's other side, restrains her.

"Trust him. Really, you have to. Trust him," Faye is saying.

Lena, again, is in her purse, rummaging for her inhaler.

Elko bounds the stairs onto the stage while the audience applauds his clear willingness to submit himself to a world of dark and unpredictable art.

Faye has a tight grip on Lena's wrist.

On the stage, Lance Burton chitchats with Elko. "They're telling secrets," Lena spits. "I know what they're saying."

But then, into the microphone, "Tell us your name," Lance says.

"Elko Wells."

"Elko..." Lance says, "I can change your name...into Winnemucca."

The audience laughs.

"So, did you not need these?" Lance asks. And he holds a pair of black dress socks up in the air in his right hand.

Elko lifts his pant legs and, though his shoes are still there and tied, his ankles are bare and without stockings.

Again, the audience laughs.

"Never trust a magician," Lance Burton says and hands Elko his socks.

Elko slips one of the socks onto his right hand and makes a puppet out of it.

"You want to take over this show?" Lance Burton asks.

A large metal box is wheeled onto the stage.

"This is what we do with puppet masters," Lance Burton says. "Send them away to Hand-Puppet Land!"

Lena covers her eyes. Faye says: "Baby. Baby, hey, come on, it's a show," and pulls her hands down.

Lance flings open the doors on all four sides of the huge box then passes through them—side to side, back to front—to demonstrate that the box is empty. An assistant, with a gold tuxedo draped over her arm, walks on stage. Lance takes the tux, displays it, then hurls the tux onto the stage floor and does a Riverdance number on it.

Lena, slouched down beside Faye, mutters: *I hate this...really hate this! Elko could have made the whole thing simple. Instead he's made it complicated. I hate complicated!*

Lance straightens the rumpled tux on its hanger, hooks the hanger onto a wire, sweeps his hands in a grand and overdramatized gesture, and the tux is hoisted above the stage where it hangs in a small pin of light. "Now!" Lance Burton says, and he summons Elko over to the box. "Are you prepared, Reno?" he asks.

"Elko," Elko says.

"Right. Sorry."

Suddenly, inside the box, there's a five-foot hologram of the casino fronts on North Virginia Street connected with the neon sign reading "Biggest Little City in the World."

"Sure it's not *Reno*?" Lance asks.

The audience applauds. Lance sweeps a hand presenting an imaginary red-carpeted path, and Elko walks along it and into the box. And the four doors of the box swing shut.

Now, there's a drumroll...then a flash of light where the gold tuxedo hung. In a pulse, it's gone! *Thin air!* Only an atmospheric and lightly drifting swirl of motes, under which Lance Burton does a kind of tango then throws open the four doors of the chromium box to reveal...

Nothing!

Lena Goodson inhales a breath almost devouring itself. Again, Faye squeezes her hand.

But "nothing" isn't exactly right. The previously vanished gold tuxedo is now hanging in a transparent garment bag from the roof of the box.

"So! One more time!" Lance Burton announces from the stage, and he flips all the metal box's doors shut.

Once again, for all those leaning forward in the Lance Burton The-

atre, life on Earth seems tentative and twilit. Again, there are flashes
of fire—here, there—shooting stars. Again, Lance does his magician's
tango. Again, he throws open all the silvery box doors to reveal...
     A huge terracotta bull—so imposing and massive that it fills almost
the entire box. Red beams of laser light arrow from its eyes. And
then the bull explodes, bursts open, flies off into pottery shards. And
inside is...
     ...Mark!
     Lena stares. Her heart quickens. *OhmyGod!* she says.
     Faye, beside her, grins. "You see?" she says. "Always trust Elko."
     Center stage, Lance Burton bows. The audience applauds.
     "It's called the *art of misdirection,*" Elko says from where he now
stands at the end of the dark aisle, four seats away.
     Lena is crying, sobbing. "Excuse me, excuse me," she says, moving
along the aisle.
     Mark, wearing the gold tuxedo, has stepped out over the shards of
terracotta and, grinning, moves toward the lights. He bears the pride
and arrogance of the Minoan bull he's just broken from.
     Lena reaches the aisle and attempts to rush the stage, but, in her
too-tight dress, trips and falls.
     The audience gasps. *Is this part of the show?*
     Lena struggles to her feet. Above, Lance Burton's, saying "We
appear! We disappear!" He extends his magician's hands toward
Mark and...*poof!* There's smoke! Mark's again gone.
     Lena spins back, shakes her head, shudders—all spitfire—toward
Elko. She gapes her inhaler almost as though it were cotton candy.
Her hand holding the inhaler shakes. Atomized mist *whooshes* everywhere.
     "Fucker!" she wheezes at Elko just ahead of her.
     "It's called the art of misdirection," Elko repeats. He seems amused.
     Lena's sobbing. "*Fucker!*" she screams. "I *believed* in you! I *trusted*
you!"
     "Never trust a magician or a man who runs a look-alike agency,"
Elko says.
     Now *Shaq's* standing beside Elko, both with their attention on
Lena. In the whole theater, there's an atmosphere of concern.
     "Mrs. Goodson!" Lance Burton calls out from the stage. Then
again: "Mrs. Goodson! Hello? Featured magician here!"
     All turn to the man they paid, that evening, to see.
     "Thank you," Lance Burton says. "Thank you; thank you all. And
Mrs. Goodson, what I'd ask is that you remember: *it's never over 'til*

it's over, never done 'til it's done. The final curtain only *looks like* the final curtain. Most times it's just a veil...And that concludes my show," Lance Burton finishes.

Now there's thunderous applause.

"Abracadabra!" Lance Burton says into his wired microphone.

"Abracadabra!" the assembled echo.

The four exit—Lena needing the support of both Elko and Shaq. "So, what have you done? Where's Mark? Where *is* he? Where did he go? Seriously! Where is he now?" Lena blathers.

"Welcome to overtime," Shaq says.

"*Where's my husband?*" Lena shrieks, stumbling.

"And the impatient shall be made patient," Elko says; then, when Lena looks confused, adds, "Revelations, twelve eighteen."

"*You promised me my husband, you fucker,*" Lena growls.

"And I'm a man of my word," Elko says.

"So—? Where—?"

In the background, Rebecca Windham is singing "That Old Black Magic."

Out of the theater, Elko steers them toward the nearby Brand Lounge. He touches Lena's limp head, lifting it. "Chin up," he says. In effect, he's directing her toward where a very attractive woman sits drinking cognac with a tall, confident-looking man.

Lena freezes.

"Never over 'til it's over," Elko says, and applies encouraging pressure to Lena's back. "The woman with him...is from the other side of the looking glass," Elko quips. And then he encourages, "Mark's ready. It's a new world. He's waiting. Go get 'em, Tiger," he says.

Lena takes one step, then another.

"Good luck, honey," Faye wishes behind.

Lena takes slow step after slow step. There's something hypnotic both in the way she moves and the way Mark—his reaappeared and confident way—compels her.

Lena arrives—slightly adrift, like smoke.

"She looks scared," Faye observes.

"She *is* scared. *Scared's good. Scared's* a kind of antipsychotic for her," Elko says "Better than Seroquel."

"...Unsure. Tentative. What do you think her husband's saying?"

"Maybe something like, *Sit down; we need to talk.* And I'll guess that the lovely lady *with* her husband is doing her best to be assuring—saying something like, *It's all right. I'm just a friend. I'm not who you're worrying that I am. Think of me as your sister.*

On seeming cue, Lena seats herself in the table's third chair. There's a clear sense of triangulation. Mark holds a hand up, signaling a server.

At their distance, Shaq squeezes Elko's shoulder. "Seems I'm done," he says, and grins. And he gives both Faye and Elko a rugged hug, then wanders off.

"Another case to file away." Elko smiles at Faye, who smiles back.

"I was afraid—in there—she might not make it," Faye says. "I wish her well."

"I wish her well...as well," Elko agrees. And then he motions into the uncertain distance ahead. "Time to split," he says. Time for the two of us, I think, to make our own *abracadabra.*"

"So, what's your pleasure? My place or yours," Faye asks, smiling.

"Let's get a room," Elko suggests.

"A room. What an idea! What a notion! A room, indeed. But... why not? There are rooms everywhere."

"Rooms everywhere."

"A whole *cosmos* of rooms. Tens and tens of thousands of ways to disappear."

"I love this town," Elko says.

"Abracadabra," Faye says...and she takes his arm.

About the Author

DAVID KRANES is a writer of seven novels and three volumes of short stories—most recently, the novel, *Making the Ghost Dance* (2006), *Selected Plays* (2010), and the short-story collection, *The Legend's Daughter* (2013). The novel, *Crap Dealer,* is forthcoming. His novel, *The National Tree* (2001), was made into a film of the same name by Hallmark. He has won the Pushcart Prize for fiction, and his short works have appeared in publications such as *Esquire, Ploughshares,* and the *Transatlantic Review.* Over forty of his plays have been performed in New York and across the US, in theaters such as the Actors Theatre of Louisville, The Mark Taper Forum, Manhattan Theatre Club, and the Cincinnati Playhouse in the Park. His *Selected Plays* was published in 2010. His recently contributed to an evening of six short plays by Iraqi and American playwrights on the theme of bravery. His play *A Loss of Appetite* was performed (with an honoring of his body of work) at Salt Lake Acting Company in April, 2014. He has written for radio, film and for dance companies. The opera, *Orpheus Lex,* for which he wrote the libretto, was performed at Symphony Space in New York, February of 2010 and again, in Salt Lake City. For fourteen years, he directed the Playwrights' Lab at Robert Redford's Sundance Institute and has created a successful national version for the Salt Lake Acting Company. Mr. Kranes is an award-winning mentor and continues mentoring whenever and wherever he can (most recently, in Provence, France).